THE RAVELING

AGE OF FAITH: BOOK EIGHT

TAMARA LEIGH

WWW.TAMARALEIGH.COM

Cover Design: Ravven
Stock Photo: Period Images
Male Model Photographer: Sam Harrison
Male Model: Skyler Schmanski

ISBN-10: 1942326327
ISBN-13: 978-1-942326-32-8

ALSO BY TAMARA LEIGH

CLEAN READ HISTORICAL ROMANCE

THE FEUD: A Medieval Romance Series

Baron Of Godsmere: Book One

Baron Of Emberly: Book Two

Baron of Blackwood: Book Three

LADY: A Medieval Romance Series

Lady At Arms: Book One

Lady Of Eve: Book Two

BEYOND TIME: A Medieval Time Travel Romance Series

Dreamspell: Book One

Lady Ever After: Book Two

STAND-ALONE Medieval Romance Novels

Lady Of Fire

Lady Of Conquest

Lady Undaunted

Lady Betrayed

INSPIRATIONAL HISTORICAL ROMANCE

AGE OF FAITH: A Medieval Romance Series

The Unveiling: Book One

The Yielding: Book Two

The Redeeming: Book Three

The Kindling: Book Four

The Longing: Book Five

The Vexing: Book Six

The Awakening: Book Seven

The Raveling: Book Eight

AGE OF CONQUEST: A Medieval Romance Series

Merciless: Book One (Winter 2018/2019)

INSPIRATIONAL CONTEMPORARY ROMANCE

HEAD OVER HEELS: Stand-Alone Romance Collection

Stealing Adda

Perfecting Kate

Splitting Harriet

Faking Grace

SOUTHERN DISCOMFORT: A Contemporary Romance Series

Leaving Carolina: Book One

Nowhere, Carolina: Book Two

Restless in Carolina: Book Three

OUT-OF-PRINT GENERAL MARKET REWRITES

Warrior Bride 1994: Bantam Books (Lady At Arms)

*Virgin Bride 1994: Bantam Books (Lady Of Eve)

Pagan Bride 1995: Bantam Books (Lady Of Fire)

Saxon Bride 1995: Bantam Books (Lady Of Conquest)

Misbegotten 1996: HarperCollins (Lady Undaunted)

Unforgotten 1997: HarperCollins (Lady Ever After)

Blackheart 2001: Dorchester Leisure (Lady Betrayed)

*Virgin Bride is the sequel to *Warrior Bride; Pagan Pride* and *Saxon Bride* are stand-alone novels

For new releases and special promotions, subscribe to Tamara Leigh's mailing list: www.TamaraLeigh.com

TO SKYLER HUNT

~

From front cover to back and all in between, The Raveling is dedicated to our Parisian son. Thank you for coordinating the photo shoot four thousand miles away to honor my wish for you to appear on the eighth book in the Age of Faith series. You, our very own knight and amazing wordsmith, are the perfect Sir Elias De Morville. Je t'aime, mon cher fils.

CHAPTER 1

BY HONOR BOUND

Forkney, England
Fall 1164

*H*e had lost a son he had not known he had—providing the child was his. After all, there was a reason he had not married the mother. More, a reason she had not wished to wed him. And it appeared the reason had not changed.

"Dead," she repeated, then lowered her voice. "'Twas the d-devil took him."

Elias had reached for his purse to put coins in her palm, money he prayed would not be spent on drink, but he stilled over those last words sent past teeth no longer pretty.

He considered her gaunt face lit by a torch outside the alehouse from which she had stumbled minutes earlier, then once more eschewing French for the language of the English people conquered a hundred years past, rasped, "The devil, you say?"

Fear leapt from jittering eyes.

"Why the devil, Lettice?"

She moistened colorless lips, glanced around as though to ensure no others listened. "Marked by evil, he was. I had no choice. Ye must know I did not."

One question answered only to breed more. "How marked, and for what had you no choice?"

She opened her mouth, left it ajar as if reconsidering her next words. Then she raised trembling fingers to the corner of her left eye and swept them down cheek and jaw. "All red and purple he was, as if kissed by...ye know. *Him.*"

Elias dug his short nails into calloused palms. A mark of birth, possessed by many—though rarely so large or visible—did not a devil's child make. But as ever, superstition ran rampant.

"That would alarm, indeed," he said with control lest he frighten her away. "What did you do?"

"I couldna keep him, Elias." She shuddered. "Though lovely one side of him, that other side...that mark..."

Lord, he prayed, *no matter my son or another's, let her not have been so cruel to set the babe out in the wood.*

"What would have been said of me?" she bemoaned.

Would it have been much worse than what was said of her when she took coin for the use of her body? he wondered with resentment he should no longer feel for a woman he had mostly ceased loving years ago.

He unclenched his jaw. "How did the babe die?"

She flinched, drew a shoulder up to her ear. "I did not wish to know. It was taken care of."

It.

Pain. Anger. Disgust. All set their brand upon Elias. It seemed naught remained of the woman he had loved. In looks, speech, spirit, and heart, she was unrecognizable. And just as he had been unable to save her then, he could not save her now. Worse, he could not save the babe who might have been his.

Though he longed to walk away, remembrance of what he had once felt for her bade him open his purse. "Promise me," he said as her gaze shot to the leather pouch, "you will take what I give to better your circumstances, not—"

"How much?" she gasped.

He hesitated, then cinched the strings, and as she whimpered like a child shown a sweet and denied it, removed the purse from his belt. "Much," he said. "If you spend wisely, 'twill last through this season into the next."

He handed it to her, and she snatched it to her chest and ran.

He was tempted to follow, but for what? Just as her life was hers to live, the coin was hers to spend.

"Lord," he groaned, "let it not become a stone upon which to stumble. Let it bless her."

Once darkness stole her from sight, he lowered his head and felt the sting of tears of which he would not be ashamed even had the one who knighted him told he ought to be. But Sir Everard Wulfrith of that family known England to France as the mightiest trainers of knights said only those unworthy of defending king and country were bereft of tears for the hurts and sorrows of their fellow man.

"Lettice," he breathed.

"Milord?"

He jerked, cursed himself. Tears were naught to be ashamed of, but succumbing to them in this place at this time of night—leaving himself open to thievery and gutting—was unworthy. An instant later, the one who had stolen upon him knew better than to quietly approach a warrior.

Back against the alehouse's wall, a Wulfrith dagger at his throat, the man who had gone as still as the dead gaped.

Elias assessed him. He was attractive and fairly well groomed, near his own age, shorter by a hand, more bone than muscle, and of the common class as evidenced by a tunic fashioned of homespun cloth—albeit of good quality and showing little wear.

"What do you want?" Elias growled in the man's language.

"But to earn a few coins." He splayed arms and opened fingers to show empty hands. "No harm intended, milord."

Elias thrust his face near and smelled drink, though not of the sour sort. "I have given the last of my coin."

A loud clearing of the throat. "Surely a lord as fine as you can get more."

He could. His squire awaited him at the inn which lay opposite the direction Lettice had fled, in Theo's possession several purses fatter than the one with which Elias had parted. "Why would I wish to do that?"

"The harlot's babe. I can tell more about him than she."

What else was there to know? Elias wondered, then asked it.

The man moistened his lips. "There is much that none but straight-fingered Arblette can reveal, milord."

Straight-fingered, Elias silently scorned. Could a self-proclaimed honest man truly be that?

"Buy me a tankard of ale, milord?"

Elias released him. "One, and if you think to make a fool of me, every drop I shall spill from your belly."

CHAPTER 2

TO SEEK THE FOUND

*H*ow know you of the babe? And what?"

Straight-fingered Arblette raised one of those fingers, and Elias thought it ironic it had a bend to it, then the man looked to the pretty girl who approached the table chosen for its relative privacy at the back of the inn Elias had insisted on over the dilapidated alehouse.

"There ye be!" She lowered two of four tankards—so hard ale slopped and dripped between the planks onto Elias's boots. "I be back for me coin."

As she turned toward a table occupied by a half dozen men, several of whom seemed overly interested in Elias and his companion, Arblette slapped her rear.

She gasped, teasingly protested, "Naughty!" and swayed away.

Lifting his tankard, Arblette returned his regard to Elias. "Not as naughty as she wishes me to be." His grin would have been all teeth were he not missing several. "But I aim to marry better, so unless she defies her brute of a father, she must needs be content with pats and pinches."

Then given the chance, he would ruin the lass without ruffling his conscience. Disliking him more, Elias searched out the owner of the inn in which he and his squire had taken a room for the night. The man was of good size, his fat bettered by a greater amount of muscle that bunched as he stared at the one overly familiar with his daughter.

Arblette was not the only patron to trespass, a man at a nearby table hooking an arm around the young woman's waist as she delivered his tankard.

Again she protested, though without teasing, then swatted free. And yet it was at Arblette her father continued to stare.

"You have your ale," Elias said. "Now tell how you know of Lettice's babe."

He took a long draught, belched. "I know 'cause my grandsire disposed of that devil-licked thing."

Though rarely moved to violence outside of defending himself and others, Elias curled his fingers into a fist atop the table. "Disposed?"

"Ah, now!" Arblette splayed a hand as if to ward off an attack. "Not that way, milord, though 'twas as my grandsire was paid to do."

Then the child was not dead? Or had he been snuffed out in a supposedly more humane manner than exposure to the elements and beasts of the wood?

"What way?"

"The way of a good Christian." He took another drink, wiggled his eyebrows. "Albeit one in need of funds."

As Elias tensed further in preparation to lunge across the table, the serving girl reappeared. "Give over, milord."

He drew breath between his teeth, opened the purse his squire had delivered him upon his return to the inn, and dropped a coin in her palm that more than covered the ale. "Go."

She gave a squeak of delight and trotted away.

"That there coin buys me three more fills!" Arblette called.

Laughing, she flicked a hand as if to rid herself of a fly.

He dropped his smile. "Tell milord, how much would you pay for a look inside my head?"

Elias shifted his cramped jaw, dug two more coins from his purse, and pushed them across the table.

Arblette grunted. "Since we seem to be talkin' about yer son, surely more is warranted."

Elias raised his eyebrows. "If what you know is useful."

The man blew breath up his face, causing straight black hair to fly upward and settle aslant on his brow. "You are good for it?"

"As told, *if* what you know bears fruit."

Arblette leaned across the table. "Seven, mayhap eight years gone, the mother of your harlot—er, Lettice," he corrected as Elias's face warmed, "sent for my grandsire. It was to him all 'round these parts turned when they could not stomach ridding themselves of undesirables."

Senses warning he and Arblette had become of greater interest, Elias glanced around. Though the voices of those unconcerned with what transpired at this table ensured privacy, he further lowered his own. "Undesirables?"

"Unwanted babes, whether of the lesser sex when 'tis a son a man needs, sickly, deformed, misbegotten, or devil-marked like your boy."

"Continue."

"My grandsire was paid for the disposal of Lettice's newborn son." Hastily, he added, "Though as told, not the usual sort of disposal."

"What sort?"

"Whilst setting out a babe some years before, my grandsire was approached by one who offered to pay him for all those destined to breathe their last in the wood." He raised a hand to keep Elias from speaking. "He agreed, as ever it was with heavy heart he did what needed doing and he was certain whatever their fate it was better than death by abandonment. A decent man he was. Now what she does with those babes..."

A woman then, but for what purpose did she buy *undesirables?*

"I pray..." Arblette's voice caught, and he gripped his hands atop the table as if to address heaven. "I pray the Lord forgives my grandsire and me for whatever part we played in that woman's ungodly schemes."

Chill crept through Elias. He was not superstitious—rather, not foolishly so—but he knew there was evil in the world eager to manifest itself through weak men and women, whether they acted on behalf of the devil or in their own interest.

Arblette looked up from white-knuckled hands. "Though in the beginning my grandsire thought her intentions good, that she provided for the babes as best she could, he began to suspect she was sent by the devil to claim his brood and those whose only sin was of being born of poverty and shame."

He believed she gave the babes to the devil? Through sacrifice?

Now it was Elias who addressed heaven. *Lord, not that.* Heart making its beat felt, he said, "What roused his suspicion?"

"Ever she denied him her name. Ever she kept her face hidden. Ever she appeared within hours of him marking the tree beneath which he was to leave a babe."

"How was the tree marked?"

"As instructed, a rope tied 'round its trunk."

Elias jutted his chin. "What else?"

"Were she not walking hand in hand with the devil, she would have to dwell near to daily pass that portion of the wood to verify the rope was present, and only once a month—more usual every other month—the tree was marked. And yet ever she appeared when summoned, and for all the babes given into her care over the years, there is no evidence of her or them in these parts."

"No others have seen her?"

"Only my grandsire and I."

Elias narrowed his eyes. "Once he suspected her intentions, why did he continue selling her babes?"

Arblette raised his palms apologetically. "Not being of a superstitious nature, I dissuaded him from such thinking. And when I began to believe as he did, I reminded myself—and him— the undesirables were destined for unconsecrated ground. Thus, already their souls were lost." Moisture gathered in his eyes. "It was selfish, but her coin put more food in our bellies, better clothed us, and made the lean winters more bearable."

Elias wondered how much was truth and how much fiction. And hoped the latter was heavily weighted, that this was an act to gain more coin. Not only did the life of the boy who might be his son depend on it, but the lives of other innocents.

"I would speak with your grandsire."

Arblette blinked. "Did I not say? A slow sickness laid him abed two years past, and a year later I put him in the ground. God have mercy on his soul." He touched a hand to his heart. "Hence, the business is mine."

"You call it a business?" Elias struggled with anger so sharp he hardly knew himself—he who preferred to laugh, tease, riddle, and arrange words pleasing to heart and soul.

"What else to call it, milord? A business it was, and a fair good one with coins from the wretched mothers one side and coins from the faceless woman the other side."

"*Was?* It is no longer your business?"

Arblette winced. "Still I perform a much-needed service, but no more do I take coin from the one who paid me better than the mothers."

"Why? Have you now proof of those babes' fate rather than mere suspicion?"

Arblette rubbed his temple as if pained. "The last time I delivered a babe to—well, let us call her what she is—the witch, I prayed for the Lord's protection and followed her, and what I saw…"

"What did you see?"

"I did not stay for all of it. I could not, it grieved and frightened me so, but 'twas an unholy ritual. She danced around a fire in the wood, chanted, and held the babe aloft as if in offering. I vowed then to never again summon her no matter how great my need for coin. And I have not these three months, though my purse is hardly felt upon my belt."

Elias continued to watch him closely, well aware among his own shortcomings was gullibility resulting from the need to believe the best of others. It was the poet in him...the teller of tales...the composer of songs. But as for the actor in him, that side was of little use in determining if this man he hardly knew wore a face not his own.

"You think all the babes dead?" he asked.

"I do not. Though surely a great many have been consigned to the dirt, methinks some rove amongst us in search of good Christians to enlist in service to the devil."

Vile superstition, but therein the possibility the babe, who would now be a boy, lived. A boy in need of a father.

Arblette leaned farther across the table. "Most unusual twins were born in our village a year past. Joined they were—here." He tapped his chest. "Though sickly, I gave them into the care of the witch thinking they would be comforted as life left them. Then, not long ago I heard rumor such babes are exploited by a troupe of performers who charge to look upon the spectacle, and for it King Henry has ordered their company to leave England."

"You believe the woman sold them?" Elias said through his teeth.

"I know not what to believe, but it makes one question if the babe I gave—"

"*Sold!*"

The man lowered his chin, nodded. "Now I wonder if 'tis a business for her as well and what other babes suffer that fate. If your son..." He fell silent, providing time in which to imagine Lettice's babe exploited for his marked face.

Elias wished the man would look up so his emotions could be read, but when finally he did, he went behind his tankard and drained its contents.

"I must know more about the woman," Elias said.

Arblette tapped the table. "As told, my business is not as lucrative as it was."

Elias removed two more coins and pushed them to the man who swept them into his palm.

"I know not her face."

"As already told."

"I know not her name."

Elias glowered.

"I know not whence she hails."

"But you know how to summon her to *dispose* of babes," Elias growled.

"True, but do you recall, I vowed never again to do so no matter how much she offers."

"What of *my* coin?"

Arblette raised his eyebrows, motioned to the serving girl. "All this talk makes me dry."

Grudgingly, Elias waited as the knave's vessel was refilled. This time Arblette pinched the girl, eliciting a squeal.

Seemingly unconcerned by the anger leveled at him by the innkeeper, Arblette said, "What do you propose, milord?"

Elias set before him a purse of a size slightly larger than the one given Lettice, this one holding a quarter of his remaining coin. "Half now, half when you deliver the woman to me."

Arblette stared at the offering. "May I?"

Elias loosened the strings and spread the leather to reveal the contents against a silken red lining.

Arblette whistled low.

"Agreed?" Elias said.

"I can but summon the witch under pretense I have another babe to dispose of." He raised his eyebrows. "'Tis for you to capture her ere she disappears in a sudden fog—which she does sometimes. I would not have the wrath of one such as that fall on me, especially as I am no mighty warrior as your blade proclaims you to be."

The Wulfrith dagger on his hip, worn not only as a matter of pride but to warn any who thought to set upon its bearer.

"When I have her in hand," Elias said, "you shall have the second half of your coin—though no clearer conscience if you continue to believe the Lord approves of leaving his loveliest creation in the wood to die."

"Loveliest..." Arblette snorted. "You may say that of babes merely unwanted for poverty's sake, the lack of food taking them a bit later than were they left to the wood, but you cannot say that of those sinful creatures born out of wedlock and abominations come forth with misshapen heads and bodies and marked faces." He nodded. "I do the Lord a service."

Who crawls beneath my skin? Elias wondered. Not even when foul trickery caused him to yield Lady Beata Fauvel—now Marshal—to an unwanted marriage had he so longed to harm another. Prayer was what he needed. And assurance the boy he may have fathered was not in need of rescue.

He cinched the purse, shoved it at the man. "Summon her."

CHAPTER 3

HERE BEGINS A TALE

*S*ix months. They felt like years.

Honore of no surname lowered her forehead to the floor. Gripping her beads, she prayed, "Almighty, You are all. You see all, hear all, feel all." She drew a shaky breath. "You can do all. I beseech Thee, wherever Hart is, turn him back. Deliver him to these walls unharmed and smiling his sweetly crooked smile. Bring him home."

To give the Lord time to consider her request in the hope He would finally act on it, she waited some minutes before setting before Him others in need of grace and healing.

When the bells called the sisters to prayer an hour later, she pressed upright. Soon the chapel would fill with holy women, one of whom Honore was not and would never be. She engaged in work of a different sort—of equal import, possibly greater.

She stepped out the side door and paused to allow the sun's heat burning away the clouds to warm places grown cold whilst she prostrated herself. It felt wonderful, tempting her to delay her duties, but she was too long gone and Lady Wilma had been generous enough with her time.

Honore bounded down the steps and headed around the rear of the chapel to sooner reach the dormitory. And halted a step short of colliding with a squat nun.

"Forgive my recklessness, Sister Sarah." She nodded deferentially. "I am late to—"

The nun raised a staying hand, and when Honore seamed her mouth, tapped her own lips.

"Dear me!" Honore gasped, belatedly realizing how loudly she had spoken, in the habit as she was of compensating for a muffled voice whilst moving about the abbey grounds. She drew up the thick linen cloth draped against her neck which respect for the Lord—and the abbess's assurance He thought her beautiful—made her lower before addressing Him in His house.

"I was at prayer," she said as she arranged the gorget not over chin as most often done by those of the abbey but over mouth. "In my haste to relieve Lady Wilma, I neglected to set myself aright." She reached beneath her head veil and adjusted the gorget's ties at the back of her crown to ensure the covering did not slip. "I thank you, Sister."

It was not cruelty that bade the nun remind the younger woman of what was best kept concealed. It was kindness, Sister Sarah well-acquainted with the superstitious at Bairnwood, especially those who resided within the convent due to advanced age, a babe whose birth must be concealed, or to escape an unwanted marriage. The most disapproving of these nobles was the elderly Lady Yolande whose generous gifts to the abbey bent Abbess Abigail to her will—that will being to keep from sight as much as possible those unfortunates she believed born beneath a moon across which the devil cast his shadow.

"Tell, Honore," Sister Sarah said, "how fares your good work?"

"Well, Sister." It was true, though it felt otherwise these six months.

The nun inclined her head. "I pray thee a good day." She sidestepped and continued to the chapel.

Resuming her course to the dormitory, Honore muttered, "You must cease this grieving. It does him no good. It does you none. Hart is gone. Pray for him and leave him to the Lord who can protect him far better than you."

Easy to say. Difficult to do. The loss of the boy hurt deeply, and worry over him nibbled at her every edge. If she did not gain control of her emotions, she might find herself eaten all the way through.

Honore jumped out of the path of a cluster of nuns also destined for the chapel. As they passed, she fell beneath the regard of a middle-aged woman bringing up the rear, one not yet garbed as a bride of Christ. But soon, the novice's family having supplied funds to make a place for her at Bairnwood.

Honore held the woman's keen gaze, refusing to be cowed by one who was her equal—or nearly so. Had Honore wished to become a nun, for a dozen years now she would have worn a habit. Instead, she had been permitted to use the monies paid for her keeping in a way surely as pleasing to the Lord.

As the novice neared, she shifted her eyes to the gorget concealing the bottom half of Honore's face, then lowered her gaze further.

Honore closed a hand around the short string of prayer beads usually tucked into her bodice. As noted months past, it was similar to the ones hung from the girdle of the novice who moved past her.

Slipping the beads beneath the neck of her gown, Honore continued to the farthest dormitory which housed the abbey's female lay servants.

As soon as she entered the building whose northern end had been converted from a dozen individual cells into one great room a decade past, Lady Wilma hastened forward. "Settle yourselves, children," she called over her shoulder, "else no honey milk with your dinner."

As groans and mutterings answered her, Honore noted the woman's anxious eyes. "What is amiss, my lady?" she asked as she lowered the gorget beneath her chin, it being unnecessary in this blessed place where all were accepted regardless of what the world deemed imperfection.

The woman halted. "That raggedy lad was here."

Honore drew a sharp breath. She had hoped not to see Cynuit again, that the abbey's plans to render the boy's master useless would be completed before she was called upon to once more leave the safety of these walls.

"His master bids you meet him two hours ere matins," Lady Wilma continued.

Midnight, then—a perilous hour, especially if the dense mist of these past nights returned.

"He told you are to bring twice the amount of coin."

"Twice?" Honore exclaimed.

"For two."

"Twins?" Honore's thoughts flew to two such babes born in the village of Forkney a year past—rather, the rumor of them.

"I asked the same. The boy said he did not know."

"Is he still here?"

"He is not. I fed him a good meal, gave him a coin, and sent him away. Poor lad. That master of his near starves him."

How many times had Honore offered Cynuit a home here? As many times as he had declined. And now he was too old to be granted sanctuary.

She nipped her lower lip. She did not want to go to the wood, especially after what had happened the last time, but she must.

Lady Wilma touched her shoulder. "Methinks you ought to take big Jeannette with you."

She wished she could. But dared not.

CHAPTER 4

OF RAVELING

Though no slight thing, increasingly Honore felt dainty alongside the young woman who accompanied her. Lady Wilma had argued it was time to give Jeannette more knowledge of the world beyond the abbey so she was better informed in deciding her future. Still, Honore had resisted—until the lady suggested Jeannette clothe herself as a man and remain visibly distant during the exchange. The young woman's accompaniment would make it appear Honore had a protector whilst ensuring Jeannette had space in which to flee if necessary.

Now beneath a three-quarter moon and amid mist so thick they could hardly see their feet, Honore looked sidelong at her charge and felt a flush of pride for all she had become. When she could not have been more than one, she was set out in the wood, either due to illegitimacy, poverty, a drifting eye that frightened the superstitious, or all.

No longer the babe in fouled swaddling clothes whom Honore had hastened to Bairnwood fourteen years past, she stood a half foot taller than her savior's five and a half feet, was as broad-shouldered as many a man, had a figure surprisingly feminine for one of such proportion, and possessed a fairly pretty face made prettier when she smiled. Not that she smiled often, of such a serious nature was she.

Of further surprise to those who judged her by appearance was her intellect. Her size, wandering eye, and tongue of few words lulled many into believing her simple-minded. She was not. And Abbess Abigail knew it, encouraging Jeannette's studies beyond writing and reading to include numbers and Latin. The abbess did not say it, but she implied a way could be found for the young woman to become a bride of Christ.

As the two negotiated the wood, Honore wondered if Jeannette would wish to take holy vows were one of common birth given that rare opportunity.

She hoped not and immediately repented for being selfish, then silently explained to the Lord the rescue of foundlings would be much furthered once Jeannette's studies were completed and she came fully alongside the one who had begun the work ten and four years past.

Honore had help from a few lay servants and kind convent residents, but more could be done. And once alterations to the abbey's outer wall were completed, as they should have been weeks past, more would need to be done to accommodate a greater number of foundlings. But that was not to ponder at the middling of night in a dark wood and soon to be in close proximity with Finwyn.

Though Honore assured herself the exchange would be over soon, she shuddered.

"Are you afeared, my Honore?"

My Honore, as Jeannette had called her since first she could speak. It was the same as the others coming up after the young woman named the one whose questionable birth denied her the title of *lady.* But far Honore preferred it over the loftiest title. Ever it reminded her she belonged to someone—many someones.

"A little frightened. The one I meet, hopefully for the last time, is not to be trusted. Thus, do not forget you are to remain distant enough he will not know you for a woman."

Jeannette's white teeth flashed in the dim. "I could become accustomed to such garments." She plucked at tunic and chausses borrowed from a male servant who dwelt outside the abbey. "I feel all held together."

"Are they truly comfortable?"

"Ever so. I have naught flapping about my legs and feet, naught to hinder my stride."

A very long stride, though Jeannette patiently kept pace with Honore's shorter reach.

"Do not tell Abbess Abigail," Honore said. "She will think it unnatural you are clothed as a man."

"And sinful?" the girl said wryly.

Were Honore not so tense, she would laugh. "An abbot might name it sinful, but not our abbess, especially considering your mission."

"Mission," Jeannette repeated. "I like that."

Honore wondered, as sometimes she did, why the Lord had not made Jeannette a Jean. Not that she wished it. Had her first foundling been a boy, he would no longer dwell at Bairnwood. As required, males left the community of women upon attainment of their tenth year. Blessedly, thus far all had been placed in good homes before that age.

Fewer females were as fortunate, but as yet there was no great need. As long as Bairnwood—and Honore—could support their numbers, they were welcome to remain. However, that would not always be so, and all the sooner those numbers would become unsupportable once the man who summoned Honore became dispensable. She would have to work harder, but she had naught else to fill her days—and heart.

Returning to the present, Honore instructed Jeannette that if she must converse henceforth, she ought to whisper.

19

The two crossed a stream, keeping shoes and hems dry by traversing the immense rotten tree that had toppled from one bank to the other long before Honore took her first forbidden walk outside the abbey and found Jeannette. It had been two years before she dared approach the one she had seen set out the little one, but her task had become easier thereafter—until the old man took ill and his grandson determined to make the *business* more profitable.

However, though Finwyn required greater compensation than had his grandsire, Honore had not been summoned as often since the old man's passing. Until recently, she had thought it was because the grandson was not as trusted to discreetly dispose of unwanted babes, but the rumor of twins born to a newly widowed villager a year past made her think it could be something else. Were it—

"My Honore?" Jeannette forgot to whisper.

"Quiet now," Honore rasped. "We are nearly there."

They continued across the wood until the ground rose before them, then Honore veered to the right. "Remain here. Once I am over the top, follow and place yourself between those trees so the moon is full at your back." She pointed to the rise where two ancient oaks stood like royals before their lessers. "You have only to stand there," she repeated what had been told ere they departed the abbey, then tapped the tapered stick tucked beneath Jeannette's belt. "Hold this to the side, its point down like a sword."

"I will look a fierce warrior."

And all the more threatening amid moonlit mist, Honore imagined and hoped it would prevent Finwyn from trespassing as he had done the last time when he wrenched her gorget down.

"No more is required of you," Honore said. "Now I would have your word that if anything goes afoul, you will run straight to the abbey."

"Already I gave my word."

"I would hear it again."

The young woman sighed. "If anything goes afoul, I shall return to the abbey forthwith. My word I give."

Honore leaned up and kissed Jeannette's cheek. "God willing, this night we shall each have a babe to sing to sleep." She stepped back and lowered her chin. "Almighty," she prayed, "bless us this eve as we seek to do Your good work. Amen."

After securing the gorget beneath her nose, Honore lifted her skirts and ascended the rise. Upon reaching the crest, she set her shoulders back and increased her stride.

There was no disguising herself as anything other than a woman, but she refused to appear meek. If Finwyn drew too near again, she would do more than slap him. She touched the stick beneath her belt that was half as long but twice as thick as Jeannette's. In addition to coin, the knave would depart the wood with lumps and bruises. Or so she told herself, Finwyn being the first and last person she had struck.

I shall do so again if I must, she assured herself and set her eyes on the distant tree, a portion of whose aboveground roots served as a cradle. As the mist rose thicker there, she would have to draw near to confirm the exchange was possible. On occasion it was not, the cradle empty due to a babe's death.

"Lord, let the wee ones be hale," she whispered and sent her gaze around the wood in search of movement whilst straining to catch the sound of fitful babes. Were they in the cradle, Finwyn would be watching.

She glanced over her shoulder and saw Jeannette had placed herself as directed. The young woman did present as a warrior—the moon's glow at her back outlining her hulking figure and what appeared to be a drawn sword. She would not go unnoticed, and Finwyn would know exactly why Honore had not come alone. Hopefully, once more he would honor the agreement made when he assumed his grandsire's role of one who disposed of unwanted babes. Following her departure, he would collect his coin.

When she was near enough to see the humped roots near the tree's base, she silently thanked the Lord. Amid the mist, two bundles lay side by side, unmoving as if both babes slept.

Though careful to pick her way amongst the roots extending a dozen feet from the tree, twice she nearly twisted an ankle, causing the coins to clatter.

Once she stood before the bundles, she raised the pouch to show the one watching she paid the price required to save two innocents, then set it in a patch of moss. Hopefully, it would be the last payment she made.

As she straightened, she noticed a rope around the tree. Did Finwyn seek to tell her something? Might this be a threat? Assuring herself the rope was not fashioned into a noose, she nearly laughed at allowing her mind to move in that direction. She did not like the man, but he had never given her cause to fear for her life.

She positioned the sling worn over her short cloak so it draped one shoulder and rested on the opposite hip, then reached for the first bundle.

"There is naught for you there, Woman."

She stilled. Someone showed himself, and it was not Finwyn who, amid the ring of chain mail, spoke in English more heavily accented than the French of England's nobility. Heart thinking itself a drum, Honore turned.

CHAPTER 5

AND TRAVELING

Sweeping her gaze over the wood, Honore saw Jeannette on the hill, then the one whose shadow across the mist glided up her own figure to cover her head.

Though less than twenty feet distant, she could make little sense of the one who appeared to radiate moonlight the same as Jeannette. What she knew was here came a warrior. And from his accent, he who spoke the language of England's commoners—though surely not with as much fluency as she who easily moved between French and English—was born of France.

Fifteen feet.

Grateful his shadow masked the fear in her eyes nearly as well as the cloth hid her trembling mouth, she pulled the stick from beneath her belt.

Ten feet.

She thrust her weapon forward, in English warned, "Come no nearer!"

He halted, causing the short mantle pushed back off his chest to slide forward over one shoulder. Still, the sword and dagger hung from his waist were visible, further testament to his ability to make a quick end of her.

Honore shifted her gaze past his shoulder, saw Jeannette had yet to run. But then, nothing ill had happened. At least, not that the young woman could know with certainty.

Wishing she had better prepared her for what constituted *afoul*, Honore demanded, "What do you want?"

When he finally answered, he punctuated each word as if it needed no other to be understood. "My son."

Honore nearly looked to the babes behind, but she dared not move her gaze from this man. Besides, she would wager the quiet bundles were merely lures. Doubtless, Finwyn had learned of the installment of a foundling door in the abbey's outer wall and thought to gain every coin possible ere being rendered obsolete.

What she did not understand was this warrior. Surely he was not meant to kill her. Unless...

Might this be Finwyn's attempt to preserve his business, proving her a fool for believing she had no cause to fear for her life? If so, it would be for naught. Abbess Abigail would see the plan through. However, Honore's death would serve another purpose were Finwyn less worthy of his grandsire's name than believed—revenge. And yet in light of this warrior's words, that made little sense.

"I know naught of your son, Sir Knight," she afforded him a title he might not be owed since he could be a mercenary of the lower ranks. "I fear Finwyn has misled you for his own profit."

"Finwyn?"

"Finwyn Arblette."

"Ah. Certes, I do not like the man, but thus far all has come to pass as told."

Perhaps he was as fluent in English as she. "All?" she asked.

"Are you not here to buy unwanted babes?"

She could not see his eyes move to the pouch she had deposited, but she sensed it there. Wishing Jeannette would run, she said, "I am here for an exchange—the coin Finwyn requires for the children whose parents dispose of them."

"How kind of you. Tell, how do *you* dispose of them?"

Though she longed to vehemently protest the insinuation, she said, "Not as Finwyn would have you believe."

"Then you will have no difficulty delivering the child unto me."

That all depended on the boy's identity. "'Tis possible. Tell me how your son became lost to a warrior when those for whom I give coin are most often of the common class."

For some reason, his hesitation lessened her fear. She had no experience with men of the sword, but they had a reputation for being forceful, brutally decisive, and short on shame. And in this man's silence she sensed none of those things. She felt emotion, sorrow, regret.

"Only recently did I become aware of his existence," he said. "And I am not certain he is mine."

"Then like many a man, you made a promise to a maiden to persuade her to lie with you and the next morn left her with child. I suppose I am to think it honorable now you wish to take responsibility. Or is it something else? Mayhap *you* seek to dispose of the boy to ensure your sin remains hidden?"

"If he is mine, I wish to claim him."

"How do you think to prove he is yours? You believe he will have your eyes? Your nose? Not that it is impossible, but it may be too soon to tell. Nay, Sir Knight, it is best for all you tell yourself you tried and pay a priest to put finish to your troubled conscience." She raised her chin, causing the gorget to strain against her mouth. "Now step aside so I may gain what sleep remains to me."

He tilted his head, and she felt the intense gaze of one seeking to see beyond her eyes. No chance of that, cloaked as she was in his shadow.

But then he moved, and moonlight poured over her.

She did not know how it was possible to be sure-footed

amongst mist-ladened roots, but of a sudden he was before her, his shadow once more covering her as he grasped her forearm to render the stick impotent—had it ever been of use against such a man.

Fearing for Jeannette, Honore strained to the side and saw the young woman ran forward as if to give aid with a sword that would prove another stick.

"Run, Jean!" she cried, surprised by clarity that caused her to speak the male form of the young woman's name. Immediately, a figure emerged from behind a tree to the right and, sword drawn, lunged after Jeannette.

"Run!" Honore screamed.

The young woman swerved and reached her legs opposite.

"I thought him here to protect you," the warrior said as he looked across his shoulder. "Not as he appears, hmm?"

Honore did not struggle against his hold, certain it would drain her of strength better saved should she be presented with an opportunity to escape. "You have me," she panted. "Pray, let him go."

He did not respond, and a moment later his companion disappeared over the rise.

"Jean is but a boy," she protested. "He cannot defend himself—"

"That was no boy."

Then he guessed her protector a woman? More likely, he thought Jeannette the man she was made to appear. "Regardless, Jean is no warrior."

He shrugged. "Providing he does not seek to harm my squire, he is in no danger. Theo will bring him back, and whatever you will not tell, I will learn from your man."

She swallowed loudly. "You wish to know of your son."

He turned her with him into moonlight, and she was surprised he was almost boyishly handsome, the hair brushing his shoulders thick with wave and framing a face fit with dark eyebrows, long-lashed eyes, a well-shaped nose, and a mouth whose compression could not hide how full-lipped it was. Doubtless, his years fell short of her thirty and two.

"You are young," he said, and she caught her breath at the realization he studied her as intently. Though she spent no time in front of a mirror, lacking access to that which only noblewomen could afford, on occasion she caught her reflection in water or on the silver platter with which Abbess Abigail and she were served light fare when they met to discuss the foundlings. She did appear younger than her years and might even be lovely—providing one viewed only that visible above the gorget. Blessedly, this man made no attempt to divest her of the covering.

"Not the crone I expected," he murmured, and she was struck by the resonance of a voice deprived of accusation. Though deep, it was almost gentle and held a note of wonder, causing warmth to sweep her neck and face.

Honore's reaction was uncomfortably foreign, though it had not always been. In her younger years she had felt something akin to this in the presence of a handsome young monk who accompanied his bishop to Bairnwood once and twice a year. Time and again she had repented for imagining how it would feel to stand near him, clasp his hand, tuck her head beneath his chin, feel his arms around her. She had even wondered at his mouth upon hers. And ever that imagining returned her to reality—a reality all the more painful when he had discovered the reason the gorget was worn beneath her nose.

The warrior before her raised his eyebrows.

Realizing she stared, she recalled his words and said, "Nor are you the miscreant I expected, though I suppose you will do as well as Finwyn."

His lids narrowed, though not so much she could not see where his eyes moved when they left hers. Her masked lower face roused his curiosity. Though modesty bade widows and nuns avail themselves of the wimple and greater modesty the gorget, the latter was worn either across the chin or beneath

27

it. Were the weather chill, the gorget might be drawn over mouth and nose for warmth, but it was too temperate this eve.

When the warrior spoke again, once more accusation sounded from him. "Where is the boy?"

Were he amongst those Finwyn and his grandsire had delivered to her, there were three places he could be, one readily accessible, one barely accessible, and one impossibly accessible—the abbey, the home of adoptive parents, and the grave. She prayed it was not the latter, though it could be for the best if this man meant the boy ill.

Honore raised her chin. "Regardless of what Finwyn told—"

"He says you are a witch."

A chill rushed through her and slammed against her spine with such force she nearly bent to it. His words surprised as they ought not. And frightened as they certainly ought. It was not mere cruelty to be named one who consorted with the devil. It was deadly.

She moistened her lips. "Do *you* think me a witch?"

"I do not believe you possess ungodly powers, but that has little bearing on whether you believe yourself so equipped and commit foul deeds in the hope of strengthening those powers."

"You do me ill to suggest such!"

"Then for what do you buy babes?"

"To save them. Their parents hire Finwyn—as they did his grandsire before him—to set them out in the wood. For a dozen years I have given coin to deliver those innocents from cruel deaths."

"*You*, who look to be fortunate to clothe and feed yourself, have a brood of children?"

Honore resisted the temptation to peer down herself. Though simply dressed, her gown and cloak were in good repair. But she supposed one who could afford to leave pouches of coin for abandoned babes ought to possess the resources of a noble. And she did—or had, there being little remaining of the wealth that had accompanied her to the abbey as an infant.

"Appearances can deceive," she said, "especially when the one in possession of a good fortune pleases the Lord by committing it to His good work rather than indulging her vanity."

"Twelve years," he said as if she had not spoken. "How many babes is that?"

She glanced at the motionless bundles. "Were this not trickery, those two would have grown the number to sixty and six, including the few I was able to save ere striking a bargain with Finwyn's grandsire."

He snorted. "Unbeknownst to those of the village of Forkney, you reside nearby with that many children?"

"I do not."

"Then where are they? Where can I find the boy?"

He would not like this. "As some are sickly and tragically ill-formed when I receive them, many have passed." Ignoring his harshly-drawn breath, she continued, "Of the thirty-seven who survived infancy, they have been placed in good homes or yet reside with me."

"Where?"

She hesitated, but as he was one warrior and the abbey's walls were secure, there seemed little risk in telling all—and perhaps it would prove Finwyn was the one not to be trusted. "I am of Bairnwood Abbey."

His eyebrows scissored. "You claim to be a nun?"

"Nay, a lay servant who answers to the Lord and her abbess."

"Your name?"

"Honore."

"Only Honore?"

She inclined her head. "Of no surname."

He moved so swiftly she had no time to tighten her grip on the stick, but he released her after tossing her weapon aside.

Honore stepped back and her lower calf struck a humped root.

Determined to gain more ground to better assure her escape, she said, "I would know your name."

"Sir Elias de Morville come from France to learn the fate of the boy born to Lettice of Forkney. You know her?"

Denial sprang to her lips, but she hesitated. The name was familiar, but distantly so. "I do not. The agreement is the parents remain nameless, not only to ensure their privacy but protect the one who breaks with them to give their babes into my care. Too, as Bairnwood is fairly isolated, I leave its walls only when summoned."

Not true, she reminded herself of those first years she had ventured forth on her own, but before she could correct the lie, he said, "Summoned by way of the rope."

She glanced at that which had never before adorned the tree. "You think that is how I know when a babe is to be abandoned? That I haunt the wood nightly? Is that how Finwyn convinced you I am a witch?"

"He told the rope alerts you to leave coin for a babe."

More and more Honore feared what unfolded. "He lied."

"If not the rope, what?"

"Who," she corrected. "Finwyn sends a boy to the abbey, and that same night I bring coin and pray it is not too late for the babe."

"Was it too late for Lettice's son?"

"As told, I know not whence the babes come. But if you tell how old he would be, mayhap I can reveal his fate."

"Seven years."

She startled, having expected the one he sought to be much younger. Were he seven, that would be the year she paid Finwyn's grandsire for three male infants spaced several months apart. And among them was one she could no longer account for.

"What else can you tell me about him?" She winced at the desperation in her voice. Hoping his delayed response was not born of suspicion, she held her breath.

"On the day past, I spoke to Lettice. She said the babe was given to the wood for the stain on his face she feared to be a mark of the devil."

Honore was grateful she was prepared for his answer. Had she not been, her knees might have buckled.

"After her departure," the knight continued, "Finwyn Arblette revealed he had overheard our conversation. He said his grandsire did not leave Lettice's babe in the wood but sold him to you."

Hence, the ruse. Doubtless, Finwyn had been paid to deliver the one who had last seen the babe alive. Mere coincidence he overheard this knight and Lettice? Or did he yet earn coin as his grandsire had rued—arranging the intimate favors of women? Might this Lettice be among those whose sin he promoted?

"Have you this boy?" the knight pressed. "Does he yet live?"

Why could it not be the boy adopted by a childless husband and wife in the village of Dunwidden? she silently bemoaned. Or the babe laid in consecrated ground after a four-month struggle to survive?

"You are too silent," the knight said.

She considered telling him his son was the one who had passed, but said, "I know the one you seek."

"Where is he?"

Glad she was not short, wishing she were taller, she said, "He ran away six months past."

A shifting of chain mail, then he had her left arm again, and moonlight revealed anger about his eyes and mouth. "I am to believe you?"

"'Tis the truth." As she tried to free herself, she caught a flash of red on his hip and saw it was a jeweled dagger a moment before he dragged her close.

"Why would he run? Did you mistreat him?"

"Of course not! I am very fond of him."

"Fond, and yet he did not want to be with you."

It was wrong, but Honore wished she had told him his son had died. "He did not like his discipline for inappropriate behavior. We argued, and the following morn he could not be found inside the abbey nor outside, though many went in search of him."

As he considered what she revealed, she cast back to the argument with Hart. Eschewing chores that included helping with the youngest foundlings, the boy had stolen out of the abbey, endangering himself and the friend who accompanied him.

"Methinks you lie," said the warrior. "Did you sell him?"

"Sell?"

"Sacrifice him?"

"Neither! Never would I harm my charges. It is the Lord in heaven I worship, not the evil one."

"You have three options," he said. "Give me the boy—"

"I do not have him."

"Take me to the one to whom you sold him."

"I did not sell him."

"Or deny me, and I will hand you up to be tried for a witch."

Fear and outrage were terrible playmates, Honore thought as the two careened toward each other. When they collided, leaving in the wake of scattered reason the primitive need to survive, she thrust her free hand between them and closed it around his dagger's hilt. Having no experience with weapons, she was grateful he wrenched backward as she dragged the dagger from its scabbard. Otherwise, her attempt to put the blade between them might have opened his throat.

He captured her wrist, and she had only a moment to note his ominous expression and a whistle across the wood before he fell on her.

"Almighty!" he erupted as he carried her down toward roots that could snap a back or neck. But of a sudden he released her. Had he not, she would have struck the roots, and all the harder beneath his weight. Instead, she had just enough time to twist around and thrust her arms out before her.

Her hands landed on moss-covered ground, but her hip struck

a root. Though it hurt, it surprised the pain was not ten-fold worse considering how loud the crack of bone on wood.

Was this shock? If so, De Morville would have no difficulty subduing her, especially as she was no longer in possession of his dagger.

She thrust onto her side. Further astonished the movement did not more greatly pain, she searched beyond the drape of her veil for the blade amid misted roots. And before her was the reason she merely ached.

The knight lay face down on roots that formed the near rim of the cradle. The crack had not been her hip but his head striking a root. But what sense to be made of the shaft protruding at an angle from his upper back? How had that come to be? And was he dead?

Dear Lord, she silently despaired, *what evil is about?*

The rustle and squelch of fallen leaves brought her chin up, and she followed the sound to one who approached from far to the left of where De Morville's squire had earlier concealed himself.

He carried a bow, and as he advanced, hooked it over his head and an arm and let it fall across his torso like the sling Honore had brought to carry the foundlings.

Recalling the whistle heard before the knight fell on her, she understood. De Morville had not attacked her. The force of Finwyn's arrow burying itself in the knight had driven him against her. And in saving herself, the man who sought his son was the one victimized by the roots—were he not already dead by way of the arrow.

"Heavenly Father," she whispered, "preserve him."

CHAPTER 6

BEYOND THE MOONLIT VEIL

*N*ever had she seen a dagger as mean as the one Finwyn drew, its blade long and curved. Fearing it was meant for her, she thrust to her feet.

"I would not!" he shouted. "My throwing arm is better than my bow arm."

The moment she saw him she ought to have fled. Now, as he had traversed much of the distance, it was unlikely his throw would miss even were his boast without merit.

Near where De Morville had earlier halted, he did the same. Despite moonlight at his back, she saw the grin favoring one side of his mouth. "'Tis a pity it must be this way, Honore of Bairnwood, but you give me no choice."

Her tongue clicked off her palate, and in like English she demanded, "What say you?"

"You think to ruin my business. Unfortunately for De Morville, he set my plan in motion earlier than intended. Fortunately for me, his interference shall make the tale of the unholy one who steals babes all the more believable when 'tis discovered she and her kind murdered a nobleman who sought to claim his misbegotten son."

Honore shifted her gaze to the fallen knight, searched for proof of breath, but detected no movement beyond that of the milling mist. Were he no longer of this world, was it due to a cracked skull?

Guilt gripped her. Had she not wrenched free, she would have struck the roots and the knight would be putting an end to Finwyn.

"If he is not yet dead, he shall be," the murderer said, and her insides churned more forcefully knowing their thoughts were traveling companions. "As for you, I am thinking after your man shot Sir Elias, I rushed to the knight's defense and you and I struggled over the dagger you took from him. I gained it, but not before you cut out your tongue—with aid from me, though those who have begun to question the fate of undesirables need not know that."

She stared. Though what he told was horribly fantastic, it must be the truth, the same as the rumor about joined twins which made some question if Finwyn did leave babes to the wood or further profit from them. Thus, another must be blamed, not he who would claim that after he did as paid to do, a witch stole the little ones.

He raised his eyebrows. "A good tale, eh?"

"Hardly believable," she hissed. "Why would I cut out my own tongue?"

"So you could not be made to reveal the devil's schemes."

Those schemes being Finwyn's, she thought, hopelessness moving through her.

He whistled low. "You will burn all the brighter for that. And when 'tis seen what you hide 'neath your covering..."

Beginning to tremble, she tried to convince herself this was not happening, that it was imagination terrorizing her until the bells of morn or a fitful foundling awakened her.

Keeping his dagger pointed at her, Finwyn stepped alongside De Morville, further stirring the mist in which the knight was partially shrouded. "There is the second half of what is due me." He toed something, and she heard the jangle of coins. "He paid far better than expected for an introduction to one who might lead him to his son."

Stalked by the horror of witnessing the evil worked on the knight and the creep of apathy telling her she could do naught to prevent the same from befalling her, Honore reminded herself how much she was needed by those in her care and those to come. "Do not do this, Finwyn. You know it is wrong."

"You forced me to it."

She opened empty hands. "I near the end of my coin. By next summer I would have no more to give."

He scoffed. "Bairnwood is rich. More coin can be had."

"Perhaps, but of greater import is saving those whose parents cannot afford to pay to set out unwanted babes and do so themselves. Once they can leave them at the abbey, none need know they have abandoned a child and their hearts will be less weighted by desperation that otherwise condemns their babes to death."

"But those who can pay no longer shall, will they? And have you not considered that do you not pain their purses, they have no reason to be more cautious in breeding undesirables?"

Honore nearly choked. He thought only of the coin to be had from others' suffering.

"In the cradle." He jerked his chin at the depression amidst the roots.

She nearly asked the reason, but he had given one. There he meant to remove her tongue. "With or without me, the abbey will receive foundlings," she said.

"I think not. Though the sisters may continue your work for a time, they did not commit their lives to the Lord to tend needy children. Nay, they are happiest on their knees glorying in the great peace promised them, and that is where they shall return."

"You are wrong."

"We shall see." He drew his arm back as if to send the dagger flying. "Get in."

"Consider your grandsire, Finwyn. What would he say?"

"What he cannot. 'Tis good he is dead, hmm?"

That hurt. Though he had earned his living in a heinous manner ere the bargain struck with her, she had seen enough good in the old man to become fond of him.

His grandson sighed. "Ever I rued disappointing him, especially when he had drink in him. You know he beat me, aye?"

She did. He had owned to it years past, asking her to seek the abbess's prayers for the defiant and unruly boy whom he feared would become a deceptive and violent man. His wife's fault, he had claimed. Ever the boy's grandmother was soft on him. After her passing, it had fallen to her husband to take Finwyn in hand—and that old Arblette had done. But when he came to the end of his patience, he resorted to slaps and punches to control the boy's wayward leanings.

"But we have no time for the past," Finwyn said. "Though I expected I would have to put through the squire ere doing the same to his lord—and a great risk that would be had he cried out—it was a boon he chased your man who is not a man."

Honore caught her breath. How did he know of Jeannette?

Before she could ask, he continued, "Providing the squire does not soon return, and does so without your long-legged *Jean*, he shall make a good witness to your murder of his lord. As for who shot the arrow that killed this unfortunate warrior, it seems reasonable a third witch got away whilst I fought you for the dagger."

Honore's head lightened with imaginings she stood before the devil.

"Now get in the cradle." He jerked the hand alongside his ear, once more threatening to throw the dagger.

As if she ought to fear it over that other death planned for her, she mused. But a moment later, something leapt in her—something akin to humor, though of a sort she hardly knew. Not unlike that with which she *was* acquainted, it roused bitter laughter.

"What?" Finwyn demanded.

She pushed a hand back through her hair, causing veil and gorget to slide down around her shoulders. Not planned, and the loss made her catch her breath, but she laughed again. She had naught to hide from this miscreant who already knew her affliction. And of further benefit, the more unsettled he was, the more likely his aim would suffer.

Wondering if moonlight made her more unsightly, she raised her chin higher, causing him to wince. "You think one who is to lose her tongue, be lashed to a stake, and set afire fears the quick death of a dagger? As your grandsire bemoaned, you are too boastful of past and future successes that oft fail."

Certain it was hurt slackening his face, she felt a stab of guilt over wielding such against him, but the grandson old Arblette had prayed would not become a deceptive and violent man stood before her. And was more to be feared than ever imagined.

Baring his teeth, he jabbed his dagger toward the cradle. "Move!"

With his blade no longer ready to fly, she nearly took the opportunity to flee, but what she glimpsed when she looked where he indicated presented another opportunity.

A flash of red and silver alongside the bundle on the left revealed De Morville's dagger had landed there. She did not know if it was a better opportunity, but the blade was a means of defense, and though she doubted she could turn it on another person, the threat of doing so would give the squire time in which to return before her tongue could no longer defend her.

No stretch to appear defeated, she slumped her shoulders as she picked her way among the roots. She walked wide around Finwyn, then drew so near the knight her gown brushed his shoulder. Once past him, she hitched up her skirts and stepped into the cradle.

"On your knees," Finwyn ordered.

All the better, she thought as she lowered before the bundles and ran her hands over the lures.

Finwyn chuckled. "The babes are not real, fool!"

But the dagger she had earlier pulled from the knight's scabbard was, its iron hilt cold in her grasp. Slowly drawing it across the cradle's floor under cover of mist and straw-stuffed bundles, she sat back on her heels.

"We shall make quick work of this," Finwyn said, having turned alongside the knight to face her, "but first…" He bent and swept his dagger low.

She nearly cried out for fear he meant to cut the knight's throat to ensure his death, but a heartbeat later, he held the purse cut from De Morville's belt.

As ever, boastful, Honore reflected as he thrust the stolen coin inside his tunic.

"Now for that tongue of yours." He began to move around the cradle's rim to where she sat with her back against it. She did not know why she had not guessed he would come at her from behind, but her expectation she could hold him off by brandishing the dagger was for naught.

Panic tightening her throat, she struggled against the impulse to spring from the cradle, which would likely see her stuck.

But what else to do? she silently demanded of Honore of no surname.

When Finwyn's hand was in her hair, fear-driven instinct provided an answer. As his blade came around the side of her face, she used the knight's dagger to part her mantle and swept it upward. The ring of metal on metal told the two daggers met, and the sting above her ear that she had not entirely escaped a keen edge. Then a clatter sounded that made her fear she had once more lost the knight's dagger, but her hand remained upon it.

Realizing the sound was Finwyn's blade, she surged forward. Though her scalp protested the strain on her hair, she wrenched free. With his hands scrabbling at her back and shoulders, she sprang from the cradle and, ignoring the ache of a bruised hip, clambered over the roots.

Finwyn's curses resounded around the wood, and more loudly when she reached less treacherous ground. Now she had only to outdistance him.

Or so she thought until halfway between cradle and rise something pierced the air alongside her. Certain it was an arrow, she continued to run toward moonlight. A fool thing for the target it made of her, but this way was Bairnwood—and De Morville's squire who could prove an ally if she could reach him first.

PAIN. Above his eyes.

Throbbing. At his shoulder.

Voices. Scornful. Threatening. Angry.

A woman's laughter. Triumphant. And yet not.

A lightening about his waist. The loss of his purse.

A clatter. Metal on wood.

Snarling and cursing. Finwyn Arblette.

As Elias struggled to regain senses so staggered he felt as if he had imbibed much, he suppressed the impulse to thrust upright by dragging forth a lesson taught by Sir Everard. He could not think where it numbered among those learned to gain a coveted Wulfrith dagger, but its import was not forgotten.

Should you find yourself beneath your enemy's boot, let not pride tempt you to show your hand ere reason and strategy are given their due.

In this moment of increasing clarity, both urged him to remain still whilst his vulnerable back was exposed to the one who had landed him among tree roots. And that was surely Arblette.

The huff of a loosed arrow made him tense. Was that what had knocked him into the woman? It was. He had heard it before his head struck the root.

More curses. Then boots scrambling, accompanied by the jangle of coin.

Tensing in readiness to gain his feet, Elias silently commanded, *Hold!*

With his left eye unhindered by the obstruction to which his right was blinded, that side of his forehead intimate with the humped root, he peered through the mist at the ground and listened.

The footsteps grew distant, and no matter how hard he strained, he heard no movement or drawing of breath to indicate any remained near.

Slowly, he raised his head. Grinding his teeth against pain shooting to the back of his skull and down his spine, he turned in the direction of those who left him for dead.

He glimpsed a figure wearing a gown before she disappeared over the rise but gained an eyeful of the one who followed with bow in hand.

Elias sat up. Blinking against blood trickling in his right eye, he dragged the back of a hand across it and assessed his surroundings. He was alone but would be keeping company with Arblette and Honore soon.

It was difficult to stand, his head reeling and shoulder aching.

That last a reminder of what had knocked his feet out from under him, he reached around and found the shaft stuck through his mantle. He pulled it free, not from flesh but material and the links of chain mail that had not failed, though they might have at the close range with which the arrow was loosed had he not swung to the side when the woman turned his dagger on him.

41

Regardless, all he must suffer beyond questioning if he was worthy of a Wulfrith dagger was an aching head and shoulder.

He turned to negotiate the roots, then continued toward the mounts his squire and he had brought to the wood.

It was slow going, his stride uncertain and vision partially obscured by blood he wiped away several times, but at last he was atop his destrier. He took the reins of Theo's mount, guided both horses out of the trees, then becoming predator to the one who had made him prey, put heels to his destrier.

CHAPTER 7

THE ARROW FLIES

$\mathcal{T}$wo more arrows, but her jagged run kept her to the left and right of the deadly shafts. Unfortunately, her less than straight flight allowed Finwyn to quickly close the distance between them.

There. The log across the stream. Once over it, she would be aided by cover of the trees before the abbey. God willing, soon she would be inside the walls where she prayed Jeannette awaited her.

She veered again, heard the hum of another arrow, saw it impale the stream's bank.

"Witch!" Finwyn cried, and she was shaken by how near he was. She glanced over her shoulder at where he gave chase a dozen paces behind and saw him cast aside his bow. He had fired his final arrow, then. Providing he had not retrieved his dagger before setting after her, she would have the advantage of being armed should he overtake her.

Gripping the knight's dagger tighter, she drove herself toward the fallen tree and found purchase on it. Unlike Finwyn, she knew its every soft, rotten, and broken place, but he did not need to know she realized when she heard him splash into the water. There having been little rainfall of recent, the stream ran shallow, the only reason to go by way of the log to prevent slippers and hems from becoming sodden.

Creature of habit! she silently rebuked, but before she could avail herself of the faster means of fording the stream, she was snatched off the tree.

She landed on her side in water no deeper than the span of her palm. Whimpering over the burn in her hip, she maintained her hold on the dagger and pressed her free hand to the stream's gravel bed. But as she levered up, Finwyn thrust her onto her back, straddled her, and caught the arm sweeping the dagger toward him.

"Nay!" he shouted, flecking her with saliva as he forced that arm down, then the other that reached to rake his face.

Water trickling into her ears, Honore cried out, "Lord!"

Moments later, she was in greater peril when Finwyn repositioned himself, settling his weight just beneath her collarbone and pinning her upper arms with bent knees. It rendered her unable to slash, slap, and scratch while allowing him the use of both hands to try to take the dagger from her.

She had not known she possessed the strength necessary to thwart his prying and gouging, but eventually her grip would fail. And it nearly did when his fist struck her nose and knocked her head sideways.

Hold! she commanded quaking fingers as the stream's water slid over her tongue. *Else all ends with silence and blood filling your mouth, a stake against your spine, fire devouring your flesh.*

His grip on her thumb threatening to break it, she pressed its length harder against the nails of her fingers, turned her face up, and coughed past the blood running from her nose into her mouth—spraying him with crimson.

He released her hand and reared back, though not enough to

free her arms. "I will have that dagger," he snarled and reached to her throat.

Honore gulped air lest he determined he did not need her alive after all and it proved her final breath, but it was the prayer beads to which he turned his attention.

"Would not want any to know you for a Christian," he said and wrenched them off with such force she was surprised the string did not snap.

"Worth little. Indeed, so plain as to be ugly." He dropped the necklace over his head.

It sickened her to see upon him the beads she had not been without since the abbess gifted them to her at the age of nine. *Never think you do not belong,* the older woman had said. *By these prayer beads know you have family.*

So she did—the abbess who was as near a mother as possible, several nuns, a few ladies of the convent, and her foundlings. Family, though sometimes she ached for something deeper. Something forever.

Certes, something you shall never know if this eve you die, she returned herself to Finwyn.

"Poor Honore," he said. "See what comes of doing good?" He sighed so heavily his breath nearly made her gag. "But soon all will come right."

"What did you do with the joined twins?" Though it would be further torture to die this night informed of what ill had befallen them, she had to know. Too, the longer she delayed the taking of her tongue, the greater the chance of being rescued by whomever the Lord sent—quite possibly De Morville's squire. Hopefully, Finwyn had forgotten about him and that it was in this direction the young man had chased Jeannette.

A snort. "Such atrocities, their chests sewn together by the devil himself. But of value to those who like the peculiar." He shrugged. "Sick of head such men and women may be, but of good profit to me."

"Then the rumor of the traveling troupe is true. They exploit children—put them on display." Realizing all of her shook, she wondered how only now she felt the chill water soaking her and the rough gravel into which her back was pressed.

She swallowed bloody saliva, tasted iron.

"The rumor is no rumor." Finwyn shifted his weight farther forward, grinding his knees into her arms. "Is that the only one you have heard?"

"You sold others?"

"Indeed, a babe born with webbed fingers and toes. She did not bring as much as the twins, but more than you would have paid me."

"How many have you sold?"

"Since my grandsire's demise, four."

"What other babes? What were their afflictions?"

His eyebrows rose. "One was not a babe."

One year aged? Like Jeannette when Honore first delivered her to the abbey? "How old?"

"Seven years."

Orphaned, then? Or had the parents done their best to raise the child and determined it was too difficult? "Its affliction?" she asked again. "Why was the child not wanted?"

He reached forward, and she feared he had sufficiently recovered to once more wrestle her for the dagger, but he patted her cheek. "Devil-licked. Here."

Honore was so stunned she had to remind herself to hold tight to the dagger.

"Hart!" she choked. "*You* took him." It had to be how he had known Jeannette was no Jean. Though she knew not how he had gained entrance to Bairnwood, he must have been inside and seen the young woman whose size made it impossible to overlook her.

"Hart," he drawled. "You speak of the babe born to Lettice of Forkney, the same that knight came looking for, he whom my grandsire told had upon his face as near a map of Britain as can be had."

"You stole him!"

"Not possible."

"I am to believe there are"—her teeth clicked so hard she had to clench them and speak between them—"two boys with the same mark?"

He laughed. "I did not say the one I sold to the troupe was a boy, but were he this Hart who no longer wished to make his home at the abbey, I could not be said to have stolen what belongs to me."

"He does not belong—"

"You think not?" He leaned nearer. "Would you not say he resembles me—well, one side of him? That other side was surely given by his mother to mark the sin of conception."

Honore could hardly believe what he told. This eve, De Morville had sought to claim Hart. Now Finwyn, whom she had never looked so near upon, claimed him.

Though she did not see a resemblance, she said, "It was you who made a babe on Lettice of Forkney?" In the next instant, she gasped at the realization of how she knew the name Lettice beyond Sir Elias's naming of the mother of the boy he sought. Was it ten years past old Arblette told his grandson was enamored of a girl by that name and said she would do better to look elsewhere for a husband? Had she, it seemed she had done so after making it possible Finwyn fathered Hart.

Dear Lord, Honore silently appealed, *let not Hart suffer more for her sins.* She swallowed, said, "You tell you are Hart's father? And your grandsire knew?"

"Of course he knew. Of all the babes sold to you, was it not Hart he most often asked after?"

It was. With the old man, the exchange of coins for babes was most often done face to face, and she could not remember a time he had not asked after Hart. But even if he believed the boy was his great grandson, it did not mean he was. Hart could as easily be De Morville's. Would sunlight upon the knight's face reveal resemblance moonlight had not? Not that she would look upon De Morville again. Just as there was little chance she would escape Finwyn's plans, there seemed none the knight had.

"So you and Lettice of Forkney are Hart's parents," she stalled.

"We are—well, *I* am. She *was.*"

Wondering if the chill she had taken was responsible for the confusion pressing in on all sides, she said, "Was? But yestereve De Morville spoke with her and gave her coin."

"And a most generous purse it was."

She drew a sharp breath. "What did you do to her?"

"Not I—you. The sins of the one who steals innocent babes for her own devices are great."

She did not wish to believe he had killed Hart's mother, but it sounded what he owned to. "If he is your son, I cannot believe you would sell him. Where is he?"

"Mayhap the troupe. Mayhap my home. Mayhap the grave. Mayhap I know not at all. But God can tell better than I, and this night you may ask Him."

Though that was all the warning she had before he once more set upon the dagger, she had enough time to strengthen her hold. But the struggle nearly ended when Finwyn slapped her hard across the face.

"It seems I must gain it by other means," he said and rose slightly, flipped her onto her belly, and resettled atop her.

Water rushing into her mouth, she whipped her head to the side. But he gripped the back of it and, nails gouging her scalp, pressed her face into gravel-pocked silt.

"Loose it!" he yelled.

She writhed and kicked, but for naught, just as she would gain only temporary reprieve if she exchanged the dagger for air. And just as a blade to the back was preferable to being burned at the stake, so was drowning, though in that moment the latter was so terrible she was tempted to pay the price for a single breath.

"Release it!" he commanded again, and she realized her struggles would soon be little more than muscle spasms.

No harm in yielding the dagger, apathy assured her. *You will not rise again. It is over.*

Not so long as I have thought in my head, countered the fear of being shorn of tongue and set afire. Were that to happen, better first she was dead.

Dear Hart, she silently called to wherever he was, *be safe. I would rather be long without you in heaven than too soon meet you there.*

CHAPTER 8

THE DAGGER PLIES

A shout heard above the pound of hooves drew Elias's regard. Amid moonlight, someone crouched in the stream near a fallen tree. Then that one's head came around, he thrust upright, kicked at something, and splashed through the water toward the opposite bank.

Pained head increasing its efforts to dim his consciousness, Elias bellowed, "I come for you, Arblette!"

The man made for the trees. If he reached them ahead of his pursuer, he would be fortunate. Regardless, the wick of that good fortune would soon be trimmed past all hope of flame.

That belief proved false when the figure face down in the stream took form, skirts and mantle splayed in the shallow water.

Elias was tempted to leave the woman to a fate likely decided, but he could not were there a chance of reviving her. He reined in the horses, sprang from the saddle, and nearly dropped to his knees as ache rimmed his skull.

With his world tilting side to side, he strode into the water, thrust an arm between the woman's abdomen and the stream's bed, and dragged her upright.

Honore of no surname was soaked through and limp as the dead where she hung over his arm, but before he could regret not pursuing Arblette, she convulsed and began spitting up water.

He maintained his balance and support of her, but nearly lost both when her heaving and spluttering ceased and she began to struggle.

"Miscreant! Devil! Knave!" she cried, doubtless thinking him Arblette.

He braced a leg behind, turned her to face him, and pulled her against him.

She snapped her head back. Though moonlight revealed hair too wet to know its color and a gravel-bitten face and blood running from nose to chin, he could see she was as lovely as her upper face foretold. Though perhaps ten years beyond the age at which most maidens plighted their troth, she was not as old as his twenty and eight.

"You will not take my tongue," she gasped, then her eyes widened. "You!"

Head beginning to come right, he said, "Me."

"I-I feared you dead." The stiff went out of her, her chin dropped, and her forehead fell against his shoulder. "Where is...?" She coughed. "...Finwyn?"

"You speak of your accomplice who set upon you?" Elias scorned as he carried her from the stream.

"Put me down!"

He obliged, and her knees buckled and she landed on her rear. Shaking and coughing, she drew up her legs, positioned the gorget beneath her nose, and secured the ties. Then she dragged the wet wimple up from her shoulders and over her head.

"I am not his accomplice," she said, muffled voice and chattering teeth forcing him to strain to catch her words. "I am as much a victim as you."

"I am to believe you were not party to relieving me of my coin —and my life?"

Wrapping her arms around her knees, she gathered them close. Only eyes and nose visible, she said, "You pulled me from the w-water. You must know he put me there."

"It would not be the first time one partner in crime turned against the other to avoid sharing ill-gotten gain. I am sure drowning you presented the most expedient means."

"That was to subdue me. Had you not come, he would have c-cut out my tongue and given me to the villagers to be burned as a witch—a thief of babes the same as he tried to convince you."

"Why would he cut out your tongue?"

Her head bobbed against her knees. "He intended to say I did it myself so I could not be made to reveal the devil's schemes. But it was so I could not reveal *he* is the devil." She coughed harshly as if to clear water from her lungs. "For that, I would not yield your dagger."

He examined her words, asked, "Where is it?"

"He must have..." She shook her head. "Nay, had he gained it, he would have spared the seconds required to cut my throat lest you revive me. Search where you drew me from the water."

He did so, and something in his soul settled when he pulled his prized possession from the stream's bed.

Moonlight shot through the ruby set in the hilt—a gem that had adorned Everard Wulfrith's own dagger years ere he ordered it set in the dagger of the one who had helped make possible the life he now shared with Lady Susanna.

Having angled his body so he would not lose sight of Honore of no surname, Elias heard before he saw the one moving out of the trees into which Arblette had fled.

"My lord!" Theo called, sword in hand as he ran forward.

Elias glanced at the woman. Shaking harder, she buried her veiled head between shoulders and knees. The weather was mild for an autumn eve, but it would not seem so were one drenched.

His squire, of somewhat slighter build than his lord and nearly of an age and skill to receive knighthood, halted on the stream's opposite bank. "The man was fast, my lord, but I could have overtaken him had I a bit more space in which to do so."

He spoke of the one this woman claimed was a girl.

"He made it to the abbey and—" Theo's words slammed to a halt, then he exclaimed, "My lord, what was done you?"

That which no longer bled profusely, though the gash throbbed. "What shall be avenged," Elias slid back into his native French to match Theo's, which would likely elude the woman's understanding. "Now finish the tale."

"The man slipped into the abbey ere I was upon him, my lord."

Here evidence of some truth to what this woman told.

Elias slid the dagger in its scabbard, and denying Theo an explanation of how he came to be here with the one believed to know the fate of the boy he might have fathered, asked, "Upon your return here, did you happen across others?"

"None, my lord." He glanced over his shoulder. "Would you have me scout the wood?"

Might he find Arblette? Or was the knave long gone?

Elias strode from the stream and sank to his haunches before the woman. "Honore of no surname," he reverted to English, speaking loud enough to be heard by his squire, "tell me where to find Arblette."

Teeth clicking, she said, "F-Forkney."

"Where?"

"The outskirts. To the east."

"My lord, should I scout the wood?" Theo asked again.

Elias looked around. "Non, Arblette is surely gone, and I have what I want."

A hand touched his arm, and he returned his regard to the woman.

Still she clasped herself close, still only her eyes were seen above her knees. "If I do not flatter myself in believing I am what you want, Sir Elias, you bear correcting," she said in French, evidencing she was as adept with his language as he was with English. Further proof she was as claimed despite the absence of a surname? Might she be a nobleman's misbegotten daughter made on a commoner, well enough regarded she had been educated?

Casting off pondering for which he had no time, he said, "You shall take me to Arblette's home, the sooner to be done with this farce. And I shall know the truth of the boy who may be my son."

"Your son," she said low, then louder, "I will give aid, but deliver me to Bairnwood first. Jeannette will be afeared for my safety, and I must change clothes. I am so cold."

"Jeannette?"

"As told, not a man. Sh-she just appears to be."

"I do not care how she appears. All that concerns me is bringing Arblette to ground ere he flees Forkney."

She was silent, but just when he determined to scoop her up no matter what fight she gave, she said, "You are right. He knows where Hart is." She shuddered. "We must find him."

"Hart?"

"He who m-may be your son."

Elias paused over the peculiar name, wondered if it referred to the life-giver beating in one's breast or a male deer, then he called, "Mount up, Theo!"

Drawing the woman to her feet, reflexively he wrapped his arms around her when she fell against him. As much as she shook, he did not think she feigned the need for support. Too, she was not without her own injuries.

Elias swept her into his arms, regained his precarious balance, and crossed to his destrier. It was impossible to secure her on the fore of his saddle, not because her weight was burdensome but due to lack of cooperation. She did not fight him, but she was more concerned with ensuring the blood-dappled gorget remain slung across her lower face than stabilizing her seat.

"Your modesty is noted and unnecessary where I am

concerned." He pulled her hand from beneath the veil and pressed her palm to the pommel. "Hold to it!"

Her fingers splayed as if she meant to defy him, but she turned her head away and gripped the pommel.

As Theo gained his saddle, Elias swung up behind Honore. When he put an arm around her to draw her back, she strained opposite.

Though tempted to anger, he leaned forward and said, "Hear me. If you have spoken true, you have no cause to fear me. All I want is your aid in finding Hart."

Her head jerked as if in agreement, then she coughed and muffled, "I have never been so c-cold."

"Then turn into me. Hold to me. I shall warm you."

She held herself separate a moment longer, then came around, gripped his waist, and tucked her head beneath his chin.

Feeling the wet of her garments seep through his, he called to Theo. "Ride!"

CHAPTER 9

BEWARE THE MISTS OF DREAM

*T*he cottage on the outskirts of Forkney was so distant from others one might think it outside the village's borders. Old Arblette had said it was not and those who engaged his services were more comfortable doing so were he not daily in their midst. Thus, he had lived apart from and rarely went amongst those of Forkney and neighboring villages who might one day need him to set out a babe.

Though following his grandsire's passing Finwyn continued to inhabit the cottage, Honore doubted he was as scarce or discreet, especially if he did sell women's favors.

"You are certain he lives here?" Elias De Morville asked, having halted his destrier just in sight of the wattle and daub structure whose softly glowing windows evidenced the fire at its center waned as night moved toward day.

Missing the warmth of the knight whose beats of the heart she had counted throughout the ride, and in doing so nearly lulled herself to sleep, again she matched his French. "I was here only once, but I know it to be the one." Though she longed to return to his broad chest and subdue the cold creeping across her skin, she reminded herself Hart might be inside. Not likely, but it tempted her to abandon the saddle.

"Theo," De Morville said, "remain here with the woman. If Arblette is within, I shall bring him out." He passed his reins to the squire, caught up one of Honore's hands, and set it on the pommel.

"May I go with you?" she asked.

"You may not." He curled his fingers over hers to ensure her grip, dismounted, and with drawn sword set out across tall grass toward the cottage at the wood's edge.

Honore fought the urge to follow. And lost. She slid from the horse opposite the side on which Squire Theo sat his mount, heard his low curse as her knees struck moist ground.

"Woman!" he rasped.

Confident he would not raise his voice or noisily pursue her astride lest Finwyn was alerted he was no longer alone, she surged upright, snatched up her skirts, and followed De Morville.

Moments later, she caught the sound of the squire's boots and saw his lord swing around. But the knight was too near the cottage for him to voice his anger. Thus, he snatched hold of her as she tried to run wide around him and clapped a hand over her gorget-covered mouth. "Not his accomplice, hmm?"

Then he believed she meant to sound a warning.

She tried to speak into his hand, but his palm and fingers were so hard against her lips it almost hurt.

"Hold her," he said and passed her to the squire, then it was the younger man's hand suppressing what he also believed were screams.

Overcome with fatigue and cold, grateful for the support despite Theo's hand over her mouth, she stilled and watched De Morville take the last strides to the cottage and kick in the door. Sword going before him, he lunged inside.

She prayed to hear Finwyn's protest or a struggle, but the only sound was of one set of feet searching the narrow confines.

Was Finwyn long gone? Did he hide nearby? Did he watch? Might Hart be with him?

The knight reappeared and took hold of Honore. "Keep watch," he instructed his squire and pulled her into the cottage.

The remains of the fire in the central pit barely lit the single room in which old Arblette and his grandson had lived.

"Regardless of whether he paused here," the knight said, "I do not believe he will return soon."

Neither did she. They were too late. And Hart...

She shivered, coughed.

De Morville released her and pushed her toward the fire pit. "Warm yourself."

It was a kindness, and it made her want to explain why she had dismounted. As she lowered and thrust her hands toward the glowing logs, she said, "I spoke true. I am not in league with him. I just hoped..." Hearing a clatter, she looked around and saw the knight searched the items atop a rough-hewn table, doubtless for evidence of where Finwyn had gone.

"I thought Hart might be here."

His head came up, lids narrowed. "You said the boy ran away."

"As believed, but this eve Finwyn revealed he sold babes to a troupe of performers who display them. And among them is one no longer a babe, one with a mark of birth upon his face."

After a long moment, he said, "Then why did you think the boy was here?"

She nearly revealed Finwyn's belief he fathered Hart and hers that were it true he could not be so cruel to one of his blood. However, she had sense enough to withhold that information—alongside hope of bringing Hart home which she doubted could be done without the aid of a warrior, a nobleman, a father seeking to do right by one he suspected born of his sin. If she revealed Finwyn's certainty he was Hart's sire, it would be all the excuse De Morville needed to turn his back on one in need of rescue.

"Why did you think him here?" he repeated.

"Finwyn likes his games. I thought mayhap this was one, that he took Hart to taunt me. Hence, I but hoped he was here."

He grunted and moved his search to the corners of the cottage into which shelves and crates were tucked.

Honore scooted nearer the pit, breathed in blessedly warm air, and startled when the knight shouted, "Lord!"

She looked to the small chest over which he stood gripping a limp pouch. "What have you found?"

"The coin purse I gave Lettice, one smaller than that which Arblette took from me this eve, both fashioned of dark leather lined with red." His head came around. "She lives here? With him?"

"I do not know. I..." She gasped in remembrance of what Finwyn had revealed of Lettice.

The knight strode to her. "Tell me!"

"I fear Finwyn may have harmed Lettice." Peering up at him, she moistened her lips and tasted the blood tainting her gorget. "He boasted of the generosity of the purse you gave her. When I asked what he had done to gain it, he said it was I who did her ill, as if..."

As if Honore of no surname had killed Lettice, Elias silently finished. Emotion clamping around his heart, he pulled the woman upright and hastened her from the cottage.

"I did not harm her!" she exclaimed.

His mind whirled, tumbled over the need to ensure the loss of coin did not bode ill for the woman he had once loved. He did not believe it—not truly—but he dared hope. Years ago, he had accepted Lettice was so broken he could not put her back together, and yestereve he had seen it was even less possible—that she was so shattered pieces of her were destroyed. But he had to reach her, save whatever was left of her.

The horses were outside the cottage, Theo having summoned them with a low whistle.

Ignoring Honore's protests, Elias ordered his squire into the saddle, but as he started to swing the woman atop his own mount, a voice called in English, "Do not hurt her!"

Holding her with one arm, Elias turned his hand around his sword hilt and set his gaze on the figure emerging from a low shack of the sort used for the keeping of chickens. A tall bony lad, aged ten or more years.

"Boy!" Elias called in English, "Where is Finwyn Arblette?"

"Gone! My master departed on his horse not long ere your arrival."

"His destination?"

"I know not. He was in such a rage, I..." He halted a stride distant. "After he walloped me upside the head, I hid, milord."

Elias's heart pounded harder. Had Arblette not already harmed Lettice, he might do so now.

"These past six months," Honore said, "was there a boy of about seven years at your master's home, Cynuit?"

"Not that I seen."

Feeling her body moved by what seemed a sob, Elias said, "We must ride." Then he lifted her onto the saddle and swung up behind her.

"Take me with ye," the boy beseeched. "Does he return—"

"He will not," Elias bit, but as he started to turn his mount toward the village, the lad gripped his leg.

"He will kill me, milord. If not this day, another."

Though Elias meant to shake him off the sooner to spur away, he paused over the lad's desperation.

"Pray, have pity," Honore beseeched.

Silently cursing being moved to kindness he had no time to spare, Elias said, "Theo, take the lad up behind you."

"I thank you," the woman before him said as Elias urged his destrier in the direction of the cottage where once he had courted

Lettice. There he had delivered her tokens of love purchased with coin he earned as one of a dozen performers whose travels were delayed when the lord of a nearby castle engaged the troupe for a full season. Here upon this barony, the life Elias had chosen over that of a noble had unraveled. Now, even ere he bounded from the saddle outside the dim cottage, he sensed the life to which he had returned was also about to come undone.

He heard the approach of his squire's mount but wasted no time instructing him to keep watch over the woman.

Hoping to find Lettice with her mother and siblings for whom she had sacrificed all, he thrust open the door. But though the occupants of other cottages upon this road stirred, whether due to the pound of hooves or the bark of dogs, the only thing stirring inside—albeit slightly—was an exceedingly tall figure in the farthest corner. Not truly tall, though he assured himself it was so even as he lunged toward one possibly capable of putting a blade through him.

CHAPTER 10

A SWING OF ROPE

*E*lias wrapped his arms around the thighs of Lettice who only appeared to be seven feet in height where she hung from a rafter. "Lord, not this!" he shouted and, taking tension off the rope, lifted her so high the back of her head bumped the ceiling.

"Theo!"

He need not have called, the squire immediately appearing beside him with a stool.

"Cut her down!"

He need not have spoken. As he continued to fling prayer to the heavens, the cool body of Lettice gently jerked as the rope around her neck gave to Theo's blade. Then she slumped over Elias's shoulder.

He slid her down his body. "Lettice," he choked as he settled her to the earthen floor.

Theo lowered on the opposite side. "I fear she is long dead, my lord."

Refusing to look too near upon her death mask, trying not to breathe the dark scent of her, Elias slid a hand over her abraded neck in search of a pulse that had probably coursed its last on the night past after Arblette took her coin.

A gasp sounded from the doorway, and Elias knew it was Honore who claimed to be as much a victim as he. True or not, neither was as unfortunate as Lettice. It may have been made to appear she had taken her life, but he did not believe it—especially with so much coin to her name.

On his knees alongside her, he lowered his head into his hands and beneath his fingers felt the open flesh of his brow. His search for a boy who might be his son had set this in motion. Had he let it be, Lettice would be alive. And were Honore of no surname innocent, there would have been no cause for her to be summoned and suffer Arblette's attack.

He dropped his hands, looked around. The veiled woman was on her knees just inside the doorway, the boy who served Arblette standing over her as if his measly collection of bones, muscle, and sinew could protect her. Were he six feet tall, armored and hung with the keenest sword, he could not protect her were she, indeed, Arblette's accomplice.

Was she? Surely she would not have entered the cottage were it lies she spilled. She would have fled the instant Theo followed his lord inside. The lad had to be the means by which Arblette summoned her.

Though Elias wanted to absolve her of wrongdoing, his desire to believe the best of others could see a warrior dead. Thus, he would cease with the accusations but keep close watch on her.

Feeling twice his weight, he forced himself upright and crossed to the woman. "It does not end here, Honore of no surname."

She lowered the hands clasped against her chest, raised her face.

"There will be some gain amid so great a loss," he continued. "Regardless of whether you truly have a care for her son, regardless of whether I am his father, you will aid me in finding him. For her."

"I shall," she said so softly he barely caught the words above the sound of villagers come to investigate what was of such import their sleep should be disturbed.

Elias turned on his heel, started back toward Lettice, halted as Everard's lesson to give reason and strategy their due once more returned to him. It mattered not what number it was, only that never had he greater cause to heed it.

He was certain he could prove his innocence if accused of Lettice's murder, but soon the sheriff would be summoned and the inquiry could last days, easily putting a hundred leagues between Arblette and justice.

As the shadow of someone approaching the doorway lumbered across the moonlit floor, Elias strode to the body laid on the scant rushes, dropped to a knee, and rasped in the English of the woman he had loved, "Whither thou goest my heart's first love, I go not until your son is safe and justice done. My vow I give." He kissed her chill brow. "At long last, be at peace, sweet Lettice."

And now to the inn to retrieve his belongings. Then the hunt.

CHAPTER 11

THE SNAP OF HOPE

*H*ow long since pieced-together heart yielded to flayed-wide pain? How long since diamond-pricked night yielded to fire-torn day?

Once more rejecting the first of the questions shaped into verse by the poet seeking to distract him from reality, Elias narrowed his eyes to gauge the sun's position. Mid-morning, meaning they had been astride for...

It mattered not, only that Theo was right. It was time to water and rest the mounts pushed hard whilst bearing more weight than usual.

Elias reined in near the stream his squire had scouted and looked to the woman turned into him. "Honore?"

She did not stir, not even to shiver as she had done often while dark yet shone upon the earth, but just as he accepted she slept, she said with no note of drowsiness, "Sir Elias?"

"We rest now. And talk."

"I am glad. Do I not soon relieve myself, you shall like me even less."

He understood her urgency, though not how she could speak as if informing him of the need to fill her belly. Little modesty which, in his experience, even women of common birth at least feigned had they occasion to address that bodily function. Because she was more accustomed to the company of children than adults?

Elias turned her forward, swung a leg over, and dropped to the ground. Ache shot behind his right eye, reminding him of the injury to his head and making him aware of how taut the skin where blood had dried brow to jaw.

He glanced at Theo and the lad hunkered upstream quenching their thirst, then raised his arms to the woman. "Come unto me, Honore."

She peered at him across her shoulder, and he was struck by eyes lovelier than seen by moonlight. They were as blue as blue could be. Not merely a pretty shade of gray, but neither an unearthly shade of purple. That same shade glimpsed when day first kissed night.

She shifted around, and when she reached to him, he saw the red in the weave of the gorget had darkened, above it a nose lightly bruised on one side up to the inner corner of her eye.

I shall kill you, Arblette, he silently vowed and was surprised by how great the longing that should be reserved for avenging Lettice's murder.

"Do you not lift me down soon, Sir Elias, truly I may give you good cause to hate me."

Rebuking himself for staring, he gripped her beneath the arms and lowered her.

"Go," he said and called to her back, "Do not make me come looking for you."

Evidencing a slight limp from her encounter with Arblette, she slipped behind a tree.

He held his gaze to it, and though she soon reappeared, he did not seek his own relief until his squire's private business was concluded and he took watch over the woman.

When Elias returned to the stream, Honore knelt on the bank a fair distance from Theo and the lad. The gorget in the grass alongside her, she scooped water over her face under cover of the hair veil.

Though pricked by curiosity over the whole of her visage, which the blood running from her nose had afforded only a glimpse last eve, he rebuked himself. He ought not care what loveliness was hidden—certes, not whilst he walked in the long shadow thrown by Lettice's murder.

Allowing Honore the distance she had put between them, he knelt and swept water over his face, grimaced when careless fingers grazed the lightly-scabbed gash. Had there been time, he would have had the flesh sewn to ensure the scar was less unsightly, but better it would serve as a reminder of when he had come looking for a son and set in motion the taking of Lettice's life.

He closed his eyes, and when he opened them, saw Honore sink the gorget in the water to cleanse the blood from its weave.

As his squire and the lad began filling their bellies with viands purchased from the innkeeper in the dark hours of early morn, Elias bent farther forward and stuck his head in the chill water to cool his scalp and dissolve the blood crusting it. He scrubbed fingers over it, then tossed his head back and sent water flying.

He stood, turned to Honore where she wrung the moisture from the gorget. After shaking it out, she gave her back to Elias and lowered the veil to her shoulders. She positioned the gorget, secured its ties, and draped the veil over it.

If truly a lay servant, why so modest? he wondered, then told himself he did not care and strode to where Theo and the lad sat chewing bread and dried fish and passing an ale-skin between them.

The boy looked up, and Elias saw from the swelling and

purpling at his temple he had been struck hard. Though Finwyn Arblette's suffering would be great, even then his debt would not be paid in full.

"You are called Cynuit?" Elias asked in English.

The lad gulped down a mouthful. "Aye, milord."

"How long have you served your master?"

"Near on two years."

"He pays you?"

"Food and shelter, milord, for which I try to be grateful." He winced. "A mean fist he has."

"In what capacity do you serve him?"

"Cleaning, cooking, errands—whatever he requires, though sometimes I fail."

Elias jutted his chin toward Honore. "You feared I sought to harm her. You know her well?"

"Not well, but ever she is kind, feeding me and giving me coin."

"Ever?"

"When my master sends me to the abbey to arrange meetings."

As she had told.

"You have attended these meetings?"

"Nay, milord. I but tell her when, not even where."

Further proof she *was* as much a victim as he? "You know how Arblette earned his living?"

Cynuit lowered his gaze. "By way of sin. He arranges for women to sell their bodies."

Was that how Lettice knew him? Thrusting aside the question, Elias asked, "What of the babes set out?"

"Aye, another means of earning coin."

"On the nights he takes an infant to the wood, they are the same he meets with that woman?"

"Sometimes, milord."

Meaning when Arblette did not send the lad to her, he sold

undesirables to the troupe whose rumor the miscreant had himself passed along?

"Why did he wish to meet with her?" Elias asked and, hearing a cough, looked to where she moved toward them.

"I did ask, milord. Only once." The boy drew a shoulder up to his ear in what seemed more defense against being struck than a shrug. "It angered my master, and he gave no answer."

Honore halted to the right of Elias and set a hand on Cynuit's shoulder. "I am sorry he hurt you again and grateful you came away." There was a rasp to the muffled words she spoke in English, and he guessed it a result of her cough. "You are done serving him. Like it or nay, I shall find a home for you."

"I thank ye, but I am all hope this knight will give me work." He shifted his gaze to Elias. "I am young and not very strong, but I will grow older and stronger."

Elias had no need of him, his squire serving him well, but he said, "We will speak later. Now Honore and I must talk."

"Aye, milord."

Elias accepted the bread and fish Theo passed to him, then took hold of the woman's arm but released it when she tensed. He gestured to a slab of rock, and as she walked beside him, asked, "How did you injure your leg?"

"Not my leg. When you fell on me at the tree—an attack, I thought—I turned aside." She raised an arm, coughed into its crook.

Might she be seriously ailing? He prayed not, for her sake as well as that of finding Hart.

"Rather than break my back on the roots beneath your weight, I struck my hip. I believe it only bruised like my nose, but it is of some discomfort." She looked sidelong at him. "I thought he put an arrow through you, and when I saw no evidence of breath, feared you dead."

"The blow to the head rendered me unconscious. My chain mail saved me—and, methinks, you."

She halted. "Me?"

He turned back. "At close range, the arrow could have penetrated my mail had it struck straight on, but when you drew my dagger against me, I swung to the side and the arrowhead proved of more detriment to my mantle."

"Then I ought not feel guilty I let you take the brunt of the fall?"

"Indeed not. And had you suffered greater ill, I would be more shamed at being knocked senseless by a root."

She lowered to the rock and, as he seated himself a suitable distance away, turned her partially-covered face to him. "As it seems you are well enough satisfied I spoke true, let us turn our attention to recovering Hart."

He met her gaze. Not as blue as earlier, but yet a shock of color in her pale face. And now he noticed age at the corners of her eyes. They were fine lines of the sort indicating she smiled often. Could he look beneath the gorget, he imagined their cousins would reside alongside her mouth. If, as seemed likely, she had given her life to saving unwanted children, had the little ones written those lines in a face he very much wished to see in its entirety?

Cease! he silently admonished. *There is naught for you here, troubadour. If ever you are to prove worthy of your training, stay the warrior who requires but one thing from her—aid in finding Hart.*

Slamming himself back into the armor of Elias De Morville, he broke off a chunk of bread and passed it and a piece of fish to Honore.

She hesitated, and he wondered if she did so over concern for how to satisfy her hunger without removing the gorget in his presence. She took both, cupped them in her lap.

"Tell me about Hart," Elias said.

Wariness glinted in her eyes. "What more need be told?"

"I know only he was born to Lettice, was to have been abandoned to the wood because of the mark, you bought him from Arblette's grandsire, and he is aged seven and of a disposition that requires discipline."

Her eyes widened. "All children require discipline, as did I and, assuredly, you."

"I would not argue that. Now tell, what offense did the boy commit that led to the belief he ran away?"

She looked down, picked at the bread's crust. "He stole out of the abbey, endangering himself and a friend who joined him. They wished to fish at the stream, but they are too young to protect themselves from the beasts of the wood whether those creatures are of human or animal form."

Adventurous, restless, daring, Elias mused. *As was I at that age.* That last reminded him of another thing he wished to know that might prove whether he was the boy's sire. The answer would not keep him from searching out Lettice's son, but it would prepare him for how great his role in Hart's life.

"In what month was he born?"

Her fingers crumbling the crust stilled, then she pinched off a soft portion and carried it halfway to her mouth before lowering her hand as if remembering the gorget. "It was long ago. Late winter? Early spring?" She shrugged. "You would know better than I."

He would not, though only because Lettice had not been faithful. He knew the one time he had been intimate with her but not when others had been. "What makes the mark on his face so special he should be sold to the troupe?" he asked. "There are others born with such stains."

Her eyes flew to his. "To many who have gazed upon it, it is very special."

"How?"

"It is interesting, even beautiful. Though less obvious when he was an infant, as he has grown, its shape has emerged fully to depict Britain—England, Wales, Scotland—much like a map."

Then for that, Hart was exploited, a mark that resembled a

country whose shape and boundaries were less certain than the dried ink which time and again sought to render an accurate representation of this island kingdom.

"Even the bishop who visits Bairnwood once and twice a year never departs without looking upon Hart. Unlike other foundlings, whether they are hale of body and face or present deformities of birth or accident, Hart intrigues him, so much I have had to entreat the abbess not to allow him to take Hart into his service."

Of that Elias approved lest the man's interest was no more pure than men and women who paid coin to look upon those displayed by the troupe.

"At least, not until he attains his tenth year," Honore added, "and only then if I cannot place him in a good home."

"Why ten?"

"That is the age at which boys must leave, the abbey being a refuge for women, whether they have given themselves as brides of Christ or committed to have no relations with men."

Elias nodded. "What else can you tell me?"

Fine, dark eyebrows arched. "I have told much. Now the question is what you can tell of the information gained when we paused at the inn. I am guessing it was that which sent us in this direction."

The innkeeper had been eager to discover what stirred the village past middle night and aghast when he learned of Arblette's attack on Elias and a lay servant of Bairnwood. Elias would not have spent so much time relating the events had he not sought information in kind. Information he prayed was accurate.

The innkeeper had spilled much in the hope a man he disliked would be brought to ground. It was he who had questioned Arblette's meetings at the inn with a member of the troupe which often passed near the village, he who put together the two rumors —the first of joined twins born to a local woman who had them set out in the wood, the second of such twins secretly on display for those who wished to ogle evidence of the devil walking the earth.

"Oui," Elias said, "the innkeeper sent us in this direction."

"Which is?"

"Toward the coast. As Arblette dare not return to Forkney, there is a good chance he followed the troupe King Henry ejected from England, the same the innkeeper told named its secret sideshow of what they call *peculiars,* Théâtre des Abominations."

"Abominations?" she gasped as if dealt a blow, then lowered her head and leaned forward. "Oh, dear Hart." When finally she sat back, the soft had gone out of her eyes. In its place determination, she said, "Think you the troupe remains in England?"

"As it passed through Forkney a fortnight gone, not likely." Meaning, he did not say, it had probably been on French soil before Elias departed for England. He might even have crossed the channel on the same ship from which the troupe disembarked. "Still," he continued, "methinks Arblette will be fast on their heels."

"What if we cannot overtake him ere he crosses the narrow sea?"

"Regardless of whether we run him to ground, regardless of whether he follows the troupe, we go to France. Though I will see that knave punished, of greatest import is finding Hart. If the boy was never at Arblette's home as Cynuit tells, it seems our greatest chance of recovering him is to locate the troupe. And there we may also find Arblette."

"I understand, but...I have never been more than ten leagues distant from the abbey, and only then to visit the children placed with families so I may ensure they are treated well. Do I not soon return to Bairnwood, my abbess will fear—"

"I paid the innkeeper to send word to her that you aid Elias De Morville whose family holds French lands from her king and is kindly regarded by Henry."

What he did not tell was that when Elias asked after Lettice's family, the innkeeper revealed her mother and all but one of her siblings had died from a sweating sickness. The one surviving brother blamed their deaths on the sins of his sister and left Forkney. All those for whom Lettice had rejected Elias were gone.

"And the sheriff?" Honore asked. "He must be told what happened."

"When he arrives to investigate Lettice's death, the innkeeper will inform him Arblette attacked us and of his motive for Lettice's murder as evidenced by the coin purse found at his home."

He had thought of all, Honore reflected as another itch in her throat ached to be scratched by a cough. She swallowed, whispered, "I see," then coughed into the crook of an arm.

A hand settled on her back. "Methinks you sicken, Honore."

She did. Usually quite healthy, it was obvious when illness crept into her. She glanced at the viands of which she would not partake until alone, then returned her gaze to the man whose resemblance to Hart she could not find. And sensed a struggle in him.

Finally, he said, "Though I covet your aid so greatly I have risked your reputation and health, if you wish to turn back I shall have Squire Theo escort you to Bairnwood."

She heard his words with nearly the same intensity she felt the warmth of his large hand between her shoulders.

I am depraved, she thought. *After the horror of what happened not even a day gone, I am moved by his touch.*

Feeling weaker yet, she longed for the strength it seemed to offer—so much it frightened her, not only for the sin of falling prey to the carnal but because the love and comfort of a man was forbidden her. Never would she make a marriage. Thus, no comfort. Certes, no love.

"Honore?"

Further she ached at the concern in his voice that made music of something as plain as her name. It tempted her to move nearer, turn into him, press herself close as done throughout the ride. But it would be wanton, just as her mother may have been in conceiving Honore of no surname. Too, more forbidden it would be were this knight wed.

Alarmed by how warm she had become, she closed her eyes and silently prayed, *Lord, what mire is this? Do you test me? Or is it the devil who tempts me?*

"Honore?"

Though her lids were lowered, all of her knew he leaned nearer. All of her felt his hand on her back move to her shoulder.

She brought her head up sharply, glimpsed surprise on his face. "You trespass, Sir Knight. I am not one such as that with whom you made a child. Pray, remove your hand from my person."

Her request was honored so quickly, she was ashamed by what she implied, especially since he was in the midst of mourning the woman from whom he had parted with such beautiful words Honore had wept.

He stood, and when she looked up, his eyes were dark, nostrils flared, mouth flat. "Her name was Lettice. Unlike you, she had no one to care for her, no one to aid in providing for her mother and siblings. And ere you say it, not even me who professed to love her and yet let her go. Dare not judge her, Honore of *no* surname."

She felt as if struck, but it was not undeserved. She did not know this knight's tale, nor that of Lettice of Forkney. All she knew of either was Hart whom *she* loved, that desperate Lettice had paid to have her marked babe set out in the wood, and whether or not Elias De Morville was the boy's father, he had come to England to accept responsibility for him.

And there was another thing she knew. It was she who trespassed. This man had shown concern for her ailing, and she had made far more of it. He was not attracted to her. His mind and emotions had not ventured anywhere near where hers had gone.

"Forgive me," she muffled, then louder, "Pray, forgive me. I—"

"Eat," he spoke over her. "We shall allow the horses another half hour's rest, then Squire Theo will return you to Bairnwood."

Holding to the bread and fish, she thrust upright, stumbled, and saw his hand shoot out to aid her—and just as quickly return to his side. Thankfully, she kept her feet beneath her though the effort placed her nearer him.

"I would accompany you, Sir Elias."

"You will slow me, thus further endangering the boy," he said, then Hart's greatest hope of rescue started back toward those who might not have heard all spoken between the two but understood enough to warrant the offense on Squire Theo's face and wariness on Cynuit's.

Resisting the impulse to snatch at the knight's sleeve, Honore hastened past him and turned into his path, forcing him to halt. "I will not slow you. I vow I will not. I will do as told—"

"You are not needed nor wanted."

And less she would be had she not lacked tolerance for superstition in her weakened state which caused her to retain the gorget's cover. If he knew of her defect, like many who believed it rendered ill luck to keep company with those of malformed and marked bodies, he would have greater cause to reject her accompaniment.

"And as there can be no doubt you are ailing," he continued, "all the more reason we part ways."

That she could not argue, but she could beg. God willing, he would recover Hart, but if he claimed Lettice's son as his own, it was unlikely she would see the boy again. France would become his home.

She stepped nearer. "If I cannot keep pace, *then* your squire can return me to the abbey." A greater inconvenience than if they began the journey now, but she prayed he would be moved enough to grant her request.

His eyes told he was not, and desperation once more sent offensive words across her tongue. "I ail because of you—the foolery worked on me to deliver me to the wood!"

The steel in his eyes flickered, hardened, flickered again, then he loosed a harsh breath. "The moment the baggage of you becomes too weighty, you shall go your way and I shall go mine."

She momentarily closed her eyes. "I thank you, Sir Knight. I will not disappoint you."

"Too late for that," he muttered and stepped around her.

CHAPTER 12

THE BROKEN UNREDEEMED

Barony of Cheverel
England

*T*he minor barony of Cheverel did not appear as minor as when he, then known as Elias Cant, sold his sword arm to its lord—a less than admirable man now years beneath the soil.

Its new lord, Sir Everard Wulfrith, had embraced his duty to administer the lands until the heir earned his spurs at Wulfen Castle. Wed to the boy's aunt, Everard was not only uncle to Judas but had become the father long denied him.

Were not the loss of Lettice so recent, Elias would have smiled as he recalled the role he had played in securing Cheverel for Judas, which had not been an entirely selfless act.

The light of dusk darkened by an approaching storm, Elias glanced over his shoulder at Cynuit who had held to him a half dozen hours, then hastened his mount toward the manor house of which a glimpse was barely afforded now the wooden walls enclosing it had been replaced with stone and raised several feet higher.

Elias would not be surprised if the wooden house was also stone and boasted the powerful presence of a castle when Everard passed the keeping of Cheverel to Judas.

Defense, Everard had once said to Elias. *Master it ahead of the sword come unto you, and less often must you defend what others think to take.*

Cheverel was now more difficult to conquer, even under siege. One day it might be nearly impossible.

"There are friends here," Elias said when Theo drew alongside. "Though I prefer to continue on, soon that storm comes to earth."

For that, an hour past he had adjusted their course to see them sheltered by those he trusted would not only provide the best care for Honore but ensure her safe return to the abbey.

He glanced at the woman who clung to the squire's back, head resting against it, face turned opposite. She was surely less comfortable than when she had ridden before Elias, but her only complaint was the cough that continued to sound from her.

When his anger had eased after they departed the stream, he had offered to return her to the fore of his saddle, but she had refused as if truly fearing for her virtue. He was a fool to have been so familiar with her.

He cleared his throat. "Soon you will be abed and well cared for, Honore. Lady Susanna Wulfrith is a kind soul."

She turned her veiled face to him. "I shall be grateful for being all the more ready to resume our journey once the storm passes."

That last was said firmly as if to assure him he need not leave her. But it was decided. He had one woman's death on his conscience. He would not have another's.

It had been a long hope Everard was in residence with his wife and young son, rather than at Wulfen Castle training up England's worthiest warriors. Now all three brothers were wed, that responsibility was divided between them, but the seasons of spring and autumn were Everard's. Either responsibilities had been reapportioned or consideration given him for his wife's advanced pregnancy.

"Elias Cant!" Everard greeted as he ducked beneath the rising portcullis and strode onto the drawbridge, both of which were new additions, as was the still water moat that would rise and churn with the coming rain.

"Stay the saddle, Cynuit," Elias ordered in English, then dropped to the wood planks and passed the reins to the boy.

A moment later, Elias was embraced by his friend who had once believed him a rival for the affections of the lady watching them from the outer bailey. Alongside her stood a husky boy of very blond hair. Three and a half years aged, his hand was held by his mother, rather than her hand held by his as when last Elias had been in their company.

Over Everard's shoulder, Elias gave Susanna what he hoped passed for a genuine smile, then sent up a prayer this pregnancy, unlike her last two, gave her another babe in arms. How he loved her and her husband. Surely, no better brother and sister could be had.

Everard drew back and grasped Elias's upper arms. "Other than a blow to the head, of which I expect to hear tale," he said in French that carried less of an accent than Elias's, "you appear in good health. What brings you to our shores?"

Doubtless, the warrior had assessed Elias's traveling companions when summoned to the wall to receive visitors. Was he remembering the night Elias had ridden on Wulfen Castle with Lady Susanna and Judas in the desperate hope of gaining Everard's aid and shelter from those whose pursuit could have ended in murder? As then, now again Elias brought a faceless woman to the man's walls. And a boy.

"You also appear in good health," Elias said and noted Everard's hair was as blond as his young son's and just above shoulder length the same as Elias's. Now the warrior had the love of Susanna, no longer had he reason to shave his head.

"In very good health," Everard said.

"I am glad. As for my tale, I come to England for a boy I recently learned I may have fathered years past."

Everard released him and looked to Cynuit. Doubtless, he questioned the boy's bruised temple—as he would Honore's injuries once she showed herself—but Elias guessed the warrior also sought to determine if the lad was worthy of Wulfen training.

"Here your son?" Everard finally said.

Noting disturbance on the boy's brow, Elias said, "Non, but a lad in need of aid."

Everard shifted his gaze. "And the woman who shares your squire's saddle?"

"A servant of Bairnwood Abbey, Honore assists me in recovering the boy who may be mine. Unfortunately, she is taken with a cough. For that, I would see her abed ere we speak further of what transpired."

"Of course." Everard turned and led the way beneath the portcullis into the outer bailey.

Elias retrieved the reins from Cynuit and urged his destrier forward, then paused to receive Lady Susanna's greeting as her husband swung their son onto his shoulders.

"I am gladdened to see you, Elias!" She drew back from their embrace and, peering up, winced over the injury to his forehead. But it was his mouth that longest held her regard. She tapped its corner. "I am much concerned over this."

He frowned. "What?"

"I know well your smile, and it has gone missing."

"With good cause, but I shall share the reason once the woman who accompanies me is attended. As told your lord husband, she ails."

Susanna looked to Honore where she rested against Theo's

back. "Fear not, I shall tend her and, if necessary, summon the physician."

"He is not here?"

She hooked an arm through his and turned to follow her husband and son to the manor house. "He departed yestermorn to treat a woman in the village who continues to bleed after losing a babe born well ere its time."

Once more reminded of the two Susanna had lost early in the pregnancies, Elias said, "You are well?"

She touched the bulge pressing against her skirts. "The seventh month, and we have much movement from this little one. I hardly cease praying for another healthy child, and though I know not how the Lord shall answer me, I have great hope Everard and I will grow our family to five."

Elias did not question that number, knowing their nephew, Judas, was as a son to them. "As ever, I shall keep you in my prayers, my lady."

Upon reaching the manor house, Elias disengaged from her, and as Cynuit dismounted, stepped to his squire's horse. "Come down, Honore."

She straightened, and again he noted the bloodstain on her gorget was not entirely washed away. When he raised his arms, she slid into them.

As he set her to her feet, her hands on his forearms tightened and her blue eyes, now shot with red, widened. "Truly, I am sorry for my mean, thoughtless words, Sir Elias. Do not leave me here."

He had hoped not to discuss the matter further, that he would simply arise early on the morrow and be gone ere she awakened. But she guessed his intent. "If you are sufficiently recovered, you may accompany me. Otherwise, I shall concentrate my efforts on Hart. Do you truly care for him, you will agree he is of utmost importance."

Her lids momentarily lowered, then she released him. "I agree."

Though she had earlier accused him of impropriety, he would

have scooped her into his arms were she not fairly steady on her feet. Still, he gently gripped her elbow as they crossed to where Everard and his wife awaited them before the manor.

"Sir Everard, Lady Susanna, I beg you make the acquaintance of Honore of Bairnwood Abbey. Honore, here are my friends, the Lord and Lady of Cheverel."

"Honor," said the little boy perched high, his dimpled chin resting atop his sire's head. "Knight's honor, Papa. Knight's honor!"

Everard smiled. "That is one kind of honor, Ambrose. This is another." Eyes upon what could be seen of the veiled woman, Everard said, "I am pleased to welcome you to Cheverel, Honore."

"As am I," Susanna said and drew the woman out of Elias's hold. "I know you must be weary. Allow me to show you to your chamber."

Honore did not resist but looked around as she was led forward, first at the darkening sky then Elias, and her eyes voiced what her mouth did not—pleadings he not abandon her.

Remorse gripped him, but not so hard he revised the morrow. He would leave her to speed her recovery so she might sooner return to Bairnwood.

Elias instructed his squire and Cynuit to ensure the horses were properly stabled, then followed Everard into a modest-sized hall. When the two women ascended the stairs, the Lord of Cheverel said, "Worry not, I shall see her safely returned to the abbey."

As thought, he had heard the hushed exchange with Honore. And understood Elias's search for Hart was more easily accomplished without her. "I thank you, my friend."

Everard gestured toward the hearth, called for wine, then lifted his son from his shoulders and lowered into the chair opposite the one Elias took. As he settled the boy on his thighs, the heavens began to rumble.

"A storm, Papa," his son said excitedly.

"Indeed. We may have to kindle the fire, especially now Sir Elias is here, he who ever has a good tale to weave."

Ambrose considered Elias without the wariness of the young, whether because he recalled other visits by his father's friend or was as bold as a Wulfrith ought to be. "Does your tale have a sword, Sir Knight?" he asked in a voice smaller than his presence.

"It does."

His breath caught. "A dagger?"

Elias winked. "Oui, and no simple one this—a Wulfrith dagger."

The boy's eyes shot to Elias's belt, and after appreciatively eyeing the jeweled hilt, he said, "Ten and seven years, then I have one." He peered over his shoulder. "Oui, Papa?"

"Do you train hard," Everard said, "and I believe you shall."

Ambrose gave a decisive nod and returned his attention to Elias. "What else your tale have?"

Elias's thoughts shifted to last eve. "A wood tucked up in blankets of middle night mist, a woman who conceals her fair face behind veil and gorget, a villain armed with bow and arrow, ropes and lies." Once more he drew a smile from his depths. "Some of which I will tell now, some of which must wait until you are nearer being awarded a Wulfrith dagger."

The boy bobbed his head. "I am ready."

Thus, Elias wove a tale just a little frightening but well enough true that Everard knew the questions to pose once his wife's maid retrieved his son to see him fed and put to bed.

CHAPTER 13

LOOK NOT BEHIND

*M*ay I aid in removing your wimple and gorget?"

"Non!" Refusal shot from Honore, and more she regretted it at the widening of Lady Susanna's eyes. "What I mean is you are kind to offer but...it is a matter of modesty." And that was true, though it was more something else.

Summoning a smile, the lady stepped around Honore. "I did not know there existed an order of sisters who cover so much of their faces." She turned the coverlet back from a plump pillow, the sight of which made Honore's lids heavier.

"There is not, my lady. At least not at Bairnwood, and as Sir Elias told, I am..." She cleared her throat to avoid coughing. "...a lay servant."

Honore knew the explanation was lacking, but there was naught else she could tell without revealing the reason her modesty surpassed that of a nun, the truth of which could do worse than expose her to heartless words and behavior to which she was no stranger. It could provide a superstitious Sir Elias further cause to leave her behind. And much she longed to be at his side when he recovered Hart.

"Selfish," she whispered.

"What is?" Lady Susanna asked.

Lifting her chin, Honore saw the woman had turned back. "I am. I should not waste your time that is better spent with your husband and Sir Elias."

"It is no waste. Now let us see you beneath the covers ere my maid returns with your drink."

Hot and of honey and mint she had instructed the woman who met them on the landing abovestairs. Imagining that sweet, fragrant warmth sliding down her throat the same as it did her ill foundlings when she eased spoonfuls between their lips, she said, "I would like that," and reached to her cloak's clasp. But it was the sling her fingers found. Since realizing she had been fooled into believing she was to deliver two more infants to the abbey, she had forgotten that which had served many babes over the years.

She lifted the worn, limp carrier over her head and set it on the mattress.

"I thought that for an injured arm," Lady Susanna said, "but it is for a babe, oui?"

Honore began to work her cloak's clasp. "It is, but methinks it best Sir Elias explain the absence of an infant."

The woman did not press, simply watched as Honore struggled with the clasp that should not be difficult to release. Honore sighed. "With this I would appreciate your aid."

Lady Susanna stepped nearer, and as she unhinged the clasp, Honore guessed she was several years younger than herself.

"There." The lady lifted the cloak from Honore's shoulders. "Do you reside with us a while, I shall see it laundered."

"I thank you, but I depart with Sir Elias on the morrow."

Thunder clapped, and the lady said, "Perhaps." Before Honore could assert she would leave with the knight, the woman added, "If this storm settles in, it may be some days ere any journey far."

Moments later, the wind began to whip at the manor and hard rain sounded on the roof. "It has arrived," Lady Susanna said and hastened to the window and closed the shutters.

Honore removed her girdle, but as she gathered up her skirt, the realization the veil and gorget must first be removed made her abandon the longing to shed the garment that was as much in need of laundering as her cloak.

"I pray you will forgive me should my gown sully your bedding," she said as the lady returned to her, "but I prefer to remain clothed."

"You are chilled?"

That too. "Oui, my lady."

Though the woman's smile reached her eyes, Honore saw it kept close company with suspicion. "Then you must retain your gown. Now beneath the covers you go."

Sheet, blanket, and coverlet were drawn up to Honore's shoulders. Though gloriously warm, it had no effect on her spasming throat and aching chest that once more set her to coughing of such strength she did not realize the lady had settled on the mattress edge.

"Pray, tell," Lady Susanna said as Honore lowered the hand she had pressed over gorget and mouth, "how long have you been ill?"

Honore moistened her lips. Tasting the stained weave of the gorget, she longed to tear it off so she might breathe easier. "I took water into my lungs on the night past." She cleared her throat to stave off another cough. "I am certain once I expel the last of it I shall be well."

"You near drowned?" the lady exclaimed, then shook her head. "Speak no more. Rest is what you require, and methinks that best achieved on your side to more easily clear your lungs."

Honore knew that but had not applied the good sense with which she believed herself gifted. It was as if only half her mind were present. A sign she was more ill than thought? Too fatigued to ponder it, she turned onto her side away from the lady and closed her eyes.

When a hand touched her shoulder and a soft voice said her drink had arrived, she nosed just enough above sleep to shake her head.

"It will be on the bedside table," Lady Susanna said. "I shall return shortly."

When thirst awakened Honore, it was still day. Or so she thought until her eyes adjusted and she saw light was thrown by candles and brazier coals. Sir Elias was yet in this place where his friend had given him a surname different from the one by which Honore knew him. Once more, curiosity plucked at her—until she was struck by the possibility the knight had departed, which was possible had she slept one night into the next.

Counseling calm though her heart vied to outrun the wind and rain besieging the shutters, she pushed to sitting and saw the cup on the table. Leaning back against the headboard, she retrieved it and was surprised it was warm, as was the liquid she gulped after snatching down the gorget. She understood, and it made her heart ache knowing just as she cared for her foundlings, someone cared for her. Lady Susanna had ensured the drink did not go cold. How many times had she replaced it?

Honore forced herself to sip and savor the honey- and mint-flavored water. When its last drop slid down her throat, she clasped the cup to her chest. For however long she had slept, it had done her good. Her chest ached, but not sharply.

"Thank you, Lord," she whispered and dropped her head back and stared at the ceiling over which flame flickered. She would depart Cheverel with Sir Elias and join him in rescuing the children whom those without a conscience named *peculiars* and *abominations*.

"Dear Hart," she whispered and hoped the strong, determined boy persevered and his faith sent its roots deeper and sprouted taller no matter what he endured.

"You shall see him again," a voice preceded the one who rose from a chair to the right.

Honore gasped, looked to the Lady of Cheverel. Of less surprise than her presence was her choice of words that evidenced Sir Elias had revealed how Honore came to be in his company.

"I pray you are right. He is dear to me." She set the cup on the table. "I thank you for keeping the drink warm. It soothed."

Lady Susanna lowered to the mattress edge. "You feel better?"

"Oui, though still tired. Was I coughing much?"

"Several times I have come and gone these hours, and for a time you did, but less so of recent. Methinks you have cleared your lungs." She put her head to the side, considered Honore's face. "Your color is better."

Honore touched her cheek, in the next instant clapped a hand over her mouth and reached for the gorget.

"Honore." The lady touched the fingers tugging the material up from beneath her chin.

Honore turned her head opposite. "Pray, do not look!"

"Already I have looked, and methinks you make much of little."

"Much?" Honore shrilled, then gave a cry of frustration when her attempt to reposition the gorget's ties caused the veil to drop to her shoulders.

"I am sorry," the lady said as Honore jerked the knotted ties into place. "I suppose it is not for me to say what is of no consequence, but I think it a small thing."

The gorget once more taut beneath her nose, Honore closed her eyes. She was ashamed, not over how God had fashioned her and how another of his creation had tried to correct the deformity, but her reaction to the lady gazing upon that which many believed ought to remain out of sight.

"Forgive me." Honore drew the veil over her head, saw understanding in the lady's eyes. "I can never know who will look upon me with superstition and distaste and who will see..." She touched the gorget. "...only me."

Lady Susanna inclined her head. "I am guessing Sir Elias does not know."

"He does not, and I beseech you not to speak of it."

"You misjudge him, Honore. Just as he is unconcerned the son he seeks bears a mark on his face, neither would he look ill upon you were he entrusted with knowledge of your injury."

"It is no injury. It is as I was born—or was. Whilst yet a babe, an attempt was made to correct it."

Was it distress passing over Lady Susanna's face? Confusion?

Honore moistened her lips, wished for more drink. "I could hardly suckle. Had my lip not been repaired, I might not have survived."

The lady nodded. "I have heard of children born with defects, but this one is unknown to me. My nephew was himself born with an affliction, though it is one rarely visible to the eye."

As ever, Honore took interest in such talk that could aid with current or future abandoned children. Angling her body toward the woman, she said, "With what does he suffer, my lady?"

"A loss of breath. When Judas was young—"

"Judas?" Honore was certain she must have heard wrong.

"That is his name. And that is another tale."

"Forgive me. It is just that only in the Bible have I heard the name given." Thinking she made matters worse, she repeated, "Forgive me."

"Worry not. It is a name little known in England."

Who would be so cruel to strap the name of Jesus's betrayer to the back of an innocent boy? Honore wondered. As much as she longed to know the answer, she said, "Tell me about his breathing difficulty."

"When young, so often did he lose his breath I feared he would suffocate and not grow to manhood."

Honore had experienced such with one foundling. It had been frightening but of little threat to the child's life. "And now?"

"The more years he gains, the less severe the attacks, and when they strike he knows what is required to quickly recover."

"I am glad. Life is difficult enough without providing the heartless another means of making themselves feel superior."

"You speak true."

After an awkward silence, during which curiosity over Elias's name returned, Honore said, "My lady, your husband called Sir Elias by the surname Cant. Is it not De Morville?"

Her mouth curved. "It is, but for a time he was known by Cant —a darker time than this best told by him."

Then likely she would never hear it, but there was another curiosity to which the lady might give answer. "Is Sir Elias wed?"

A question sparkled in the lady's eyes. "Though much his father wishes it for the sake of the family name, he is not. But methinks he must yield soon." She stood. "I shall go for viands."

"I thank you, but I am not so hungry I would rather fill my belly than sleep." Honore frowned. "Know you what hour it is?"

"I would say two until middle night."

"You ought to be abed yourself."

"As I am assured you are recovering, there I shall go—after I deliver a tray for when you are ready to eat."

Hating she further delayed the lady's rest, Honore wanted to decline but said, "I would like that though the drink need not be warmed."

"Already it is. A large pot was made for all and left over a warming fire."

Honore caught her breath. "Have others taken ill? Cynuit? Squire Theo? Sir Elias? Your son?"

"Worry not, all are well." With a rustle of skirts, the lady crossed to the door.

"Lady Susanna, you will not tell Sir Elias of my mouth, will you?"

The woman looked across her shoulder. "I will not, but may I ask what you fear?"

"It may be true I misjudge him, but there are others I did not believe would turn from me when they saw the Lord shaped me differently, yet they did. As for Sir Elias, I fear he would desire my company even less since some believe ill luck befalls those who travel with ones whose bodies appear formed by the devil."

"You speak of superstition, Honore. Sir Elias—"

"Still," Honore gently interrupted, "I would not risk it. Pray, grant me this."

The lady inclined her head. "I shall leave the matter be and pray Sir Elias is not long in proving worthy of your confidence."

"I am grateful, and if you will bear with me, one more thing I would ask. If Sir Elias determines I am not sufficiently recovered to accompany him on the morrow, do not let me sleep though his departure. I would speak with him before he leaves."

"The boy means much to you."

"He does. I love all those with whom the Lord entrusts me, but methinks Hart is as near a son as ever I shall have. I would see him one last time and be assured as much as possible his life will be good."

"Then if the storm passes, I shall awaken you."

"I am grateful, my lady."

A lovely smile, then the woman was gone. Though Honore tried to wait for her to return with drink and viands, sleep was too persuasive.

CHAPTER 14

THOU WILL NOT FIND

I do not argue the necessity of rescuing the boy," Everard said where he stood alongside Elias inside the hall, the manor doors open before them. "I would do the same, but do you continue your pursuit in weather like this"—he jutted his chin at the rain-soaked sky—"your chance of success is seriously jeopardized. Stay and be comforted knowing Arblette must also shelter until the storm passes."

No rising sun to be seen across early morn, Elias shifted his jaw. "Already he has many leagues on me, mayhap enough he is beyond this foul weather."

"I think not, Elias. That storm smells of conception on the sea and birth upon the coast. Were I my brother, Abel, I would wager all travel along the eastern coast crawls."

As would Elias, but despite hours of prayer on the night past that made his eyes gritty, teeth throb, and throat ache, little peace had he found amidst the interruptions to which he subjected himself.

Whilst kneeling before the Lord, memories of what had

transpired in the wood jostled him—flashes of Honore face down in the water, Lettice hung from a rope, inappropriate familiarity with one he had no cause or right to be attracted to. Then there were imaginings of the children being exploited by the troupe. And revenge.

When he ought to have prostrated himself, his arms had quaked with the force of bunched fists. He knew he should not make decisions with such emotions coursing his blood, but the peace required to temper his feelings remained elusive.

"Stay," Everard said.

Elias shifted his regard to the warrior. "If France is Arblette's destination and he hunkers down to wait out the storm, once it passes he will take the first boat across the narrow sea. Thus, I need these hours to gain on him lest he reaches the troupe first and takes Hart, leaving me no trace to follow."

"I understand, but I also know you will be of little use to the boy if this weather proves your undoing."

"It will not. Do I leave the woman and boy, this day Theo and I can cover many leagues."

Everard's brow lowered. "Providing you do not lose your way whilst rain falls so thick you can hardly see the land before you. Providing your horse does not stumble and break a leg—and your neck. Providing you do not turn ill from a drenched body. Providing you choose the same port by which Arblette departs England. *If* he departs."

Argument shot through Elias, but a voice within made itself heard over the churn of blood. *Until you can submit heart and mind to the Lord, let this warrior—your friend—be your peace.*

He exhaled sharply, nodded. "I wish you were wrong."

"As do I. Now let us talk of other things." Everard closed the doors and returned to the hearth where they had broken their fast with sweet white bread and goat cheese.

"How goes the training at Wulfen?" Elias asked as he dropped into a chair.

"Intense as ever." Everard stretched his legs out before him. "And more work it is now all three brothers are rarely in residence at the same time."

Elias raised an eyebrow. "Is that regret?"

"Some." Everard smiled. "But for naught would I exchange my life with Susanna for life before. She is what it means to be complete—to be alive beyond the draw of breath and the trudge of days."

Elias was surprised he could laugh without reminding himself to do so as done whilst giving tale of the events at Forkney to Everard and his son. Amid this current darkness, it seemed Elias Cant could still be found. "You sound a poet, my friend," he mused.

"Susanna again. That two become one in marriage are not merely pretty vows. She composes words of love for me and our son—in ink, wax, dust, and upon the air. As for my effect on her, she may not be sword-wielding Lady Annyn, but the greater our days together, the more fierce she becomes. Woe to any who think to make sport of those she holds dear."

Elias had seen it himself. The desperate, emotionally abused lady whom he had aided in fleeing Cheverel with her nephew no longer existed, the sorrow of her slain by love. The thought lightened Elias as he mused only love ought to have the power to slay.

"You are smiling," Everard said.

So he was, and it seemed wrong so near Lettice's death. Easing the curve of his mouth, he asked, "How fare Garr and Abel? Their wives and children?"

"As blessed as I. I think there will be no shortage of Wulfriths for years to come."

"Let us pray never. Certes, it is as your king and queen do."

Everard inclined his head. "Now they have our family's support."

As once they had not, Elias reflected. "Who lords Wulfen Castle now?"

"Abel that I shall be at my lady's side when she gives another son or daughter into my arms."

Elias quaffed the remains of his ale, asked, "How goes Baron Soames's training? Has he proven Wulfen worthy?"

"More and more. Though Abel was averse to instructing him and displeased when I determined that were the offer made—no matter it was but a taunt—it must be honored, methinks he has taken a liking to the baron. Not that he would admit it."

That surprised. Soames had been a party to drugging Elias so the baron could wed Lady Beata against the queen's wishes. Thus, Elias had no great liking for Soames, even though that marriage had been annulled and Queen Eleanor had arranged for him to wed another. Hoping his wife was not miserable—that Soames was Wulfen worthy—Elias thanked the Lord that King Henry's wife had yet to seek a match for him as Elias's father would be pleased for her to do. But if Elias did not soon wed one of his own choosing...

He closed his eyes. Of such things he should not ponder following the loss of one he had loved and would have wed had she been faithful. He nearly spoke her name, but the sense of being watched returned his regard to Everard.

"Truly," his friend said, "I am sorry for your loss. It is one kind of ache to lose a woman to another man, a more terrible one to lose her to death."

Elias could not be offended. Everard had experience with the same, though his first love had not suffered the violence to which Lettice had been subjected. Everard had shared that tale some time ago, honoring Elias with friendship of a strength he could be entrusted with something so private.

Susanna had said that, providing Elias was judicious, only occasionally dipping beneath the surface of the Wulfriths, the troubadour knight could serve as the family's tale bearer. And so he did when he had occasion to entertain their family and others in need of lighter hearts. Much remained beneath the surface, but when he dipped he was careful to change certain names and places. Perhaps with the Wulfrith's permission, one day he would write what could be called The Book of Wulfrith. Though hard to believe such a family would fade across the centuries, parchment and ink would ensure they were not forgotten.

"Where have you gone, Elias?"

Everard's question made him sit forward. "Respite only, and refreshing it was."

"Doubtless, you slept poorly on the night past."

Could it be called sleep, Elias thought. "So I did, but I am not so tired I could not further entertain were I called upon."

"Another tale would do us good."

Sensing tension about Everard that had hovered just out of reach until that moment, Elias said, "Something is amiss?"

Silence.

"I would not presume to be your confidant, Everard, but do you wish to speak, you have my ear and my aid."

Just when Elias determined the private Everard would tell no more, the man said, "The Wulfrith siblings may number beyond five."

"What?"

Everard nodded. "It could be false, but Garr fears not."

"Then your sire..."

"Our parents' marriage was a poor one. No love, no friendship, little forgiveness. Thus, it is possible we have one or more misbegotten siblings."

"I am sorry. If there is anything I can do, you will let me know?"

"I shall." His gaze flicked past Elias, and he said low, "Hopefully, the matter will soon be put to rest and our mother saved further heartache."

"Papa!" called the one who had come to his father's notice.

Everard leaned to the side and beckoned to Ambrose who tugged free of Susanna as the two came off the stairs. The boy flung himself across the distance, slapped hands to Everard's knees. "I want to play with my wooden sword."

"What does your mother say?"

The boy groaned. "Eat first, sword later. She not a warrior."

Susanna halted alongside Everard and set a hand on her husband's shoulder, over which the knight placed his own hand.

"Not a warrior?" Everard said. "Are you certain? I think your mother most formidable."

Ambrose looked to her. "She has not a sword. And there a baby in her. If bad man comes, I would have to 'tect her."

"Possibly, but methinks she would prove fierce, especially with the babe to protect."

The boy blew breath up his face. "I wish her not a girl."

Everard chuckled. "Then she would not be your mother."

"A boy can fight with a sword."

"A woman can learn the long blade. Is not your Aunt Annyn proficient with such?"

A grunt. "You say, but I not see her wear one."

"Once she did."

Ambrose leaned in. "When?"

"Elias," Everard said, "Mayhap you would tell the tale of Lady Annyn Bretanne and our son's uncle, Baron Wulfrith?"

His wide-eyed son swung around. "Another tale, Sir Knight!"

Something lit up inside Elias, and he did not doubt Everard knew what was required to unburden—even if only temporarily—his friend. "I would be happy to weave another tale."

"Whilst you eat, Ambrose," Susanna said.

He hopped to the platter of viands on the table beside his father, grabbed bread and cheese, and seated himself at Elias's feet.

"Think now, young Wulfrith," Elias began. "What if a woman were to disguise herself as a man so she might train at Wulfen

Castle? Preposterous? Non, it happened. What might cause one lovely of face and slight of figure to do so bold a thing? Vengeance? Oui, that which seeks to twist the soul. What terrible wrong was done her that could only be set aright by the edge of a blade? Think, Ambrose Wulfrith. Think. Now...listen."

CHAPTER 15

PLUCKED PETALS WITHOUT BRUISE

*I*s the tale true?" Honore whispered.

"He embellishes here, unembellishes there—if that is a word." Lady Susanna smiled. "But it is mostly as told me by Lady Annyn. And her husband did not gainsay her. He but gazed upon her much the same as Everard gazes upon me, as if only half present, the other half praising God for the one he beholds."

Honore savored the lady's words that were as nourishing to the imagination, heart, and soul as those penned in the depths of Sir Elias and sent across tongue and past lips for nearly an hour. Upon hearing his voice, she had started to return to her chamber, but the tale of a woman garbed as a man and in possession of a sword had made her lower out of sight on the stairs.

The story had intrigued, and more so knowing there was truth to it, but what entranced was the means by which it was delivered. Sir Elias was no ordinary warrior. He was that of which she had only heard tale—a troubadour knight. And as he had woven his words under and over and in and out of her imagination, she had longed for her foundlings of an age not easily given to fright to sit at his feet. They knew happiness at Bairnwood, but—oh!—to lose big and small hurts in this man's company.

"Certes, a gift he has," Honore said low, though the conclusion of the tale had caused those gathered around him—including Squire Theo and Cynuit—to chatter and their feet to creak the floorboards.

"Indeed," Lady Susanna said where she had lowered alongside Honore upon discovering her on the stairs.

"Were he not noble," Honore continued, "methinks a good living could be made traveling village to village and castle to castle with such tales."

The lady laughed softly. "Who says he has not?

Honore stared. "Has he?"

"That is best heard from him though…" Her shrug was apologetic. "…I would wait. Methinks the story of Lady Annyn and Baron Wulfrith has lightened him, but his loss will surely be eager to return to his shoulders. And with one who possesses a heart like his, that loss may be weightier beneath guilt over this brief escape."

Honore understood, in that moment jagged by guilt at the realization she had escaped fear and worry over Hart. She had gasped, smiled, suppressed laughter, and at times felt so light she was happy.

"Mama! You missed Sir Elias's tale!"

Both women startled to find the little boy before the stairs, and Honore held her breath as she looked up the man whose hand Lady Susanna's son held.

"I did not miss it." The lady gripped the railing and raised her bulk. "Not a single word, did we Honore?" She looked across her shoulder.

Honore hastened to her feet. Unfortunately, the added height made it more obvious she avoided Sir Elias's gaze, having ventured no higher than his tanned neck.

Less grateful for the gorget's cover that provided no distraction for the eyes above, the blue of which surely reflected guilt as if she had eavesdropped, Honore set her eyes upon his. "No word did we miss," she said and wished it were the troubadour knight before her, certain the excitement and joy in his voice had shown upon his face. Once more there was no lightness about it. Once more, she was the woman who accused him of her own wrongdoing.

"A well-told tale, Sir Elias," she said as Lady Susanna descended the steps. "Many a time I was near breathless."

His eyebrows rose, then as if she paid him no compliment, he said, "Your cough is resolved?"

As evidenced by its absence that had concealed her presence on the stairs. "I feel better. Lady Susanna tended me well. When you are ready to depart, so shall I be."

"You are leaving, Sir Knight?" the boy exclaimed.

Sir Elias looked down. "Regrettably, not this day. But God willing, on the morrow."

"Then you can speak me another tale!"

"Perhaps this eve."

"About papa and mama?"

"Possibly, or your Uncle Abel and Aunt Helene. Too, I have tales of your aunts Beatrix and Gaenor, and one of my friends Sir Durand and Lady Beata that began upon a storm-tossed sea."

"And Judas?" The boy's eyes widened further, and there was no doubt he admired his older cousin.

Sir Elias ruffled his hair, and once more Honore heard lightness in his voice when he said, "Judas as well, though his tale is best told alongside your parents' tale."

"That is the tale I want!"

"I make no promise, but I shall do my best to reveal it ere Squire Theo and I depart."

Honore stiffened. Oversight only? Or did he plan to leave her behind regardless of her health? She descended a step. "May I speak with you, Sir Elias?"

He looked to her, and she wished he retained some of the smile he had gifted the boy. "Of?"

Before she could answer, Lady Susanna said, "We shall leave you to it," and turned her son back into the hall.

Displeasure flickered across the knight's face, and she guessed it due to the accusation she had made at the stream.

"Of what do you wish to speak, Honore?"

"As told, I am sufficiently recovered to continue our search for Hart. I seek assurance you will allow me to accompany you."

He set a forearm on the wall alongside its turning up the stairway. "I fear you and the boy will slow me. Were you able to ride a horse—"

"I am able. If Sir Everard will lend me a mount, I can keep pace."

"Just because you have been astride a work horse and tugged the reins and tapped it forward does not mean you know how to ride."

"Certes, not as you do, but as told, I have visited the children placed in homes outside Bairnwood."

"As also told, never have you been more than ten leagues distant from the abbey. That does not make you able."

"But I am." She moistened her lips, and once more tasting the fouled gorget, wished there were time to launder it. "I did not walk my horse all those leagues. I gave it full rein. It was dangerous, but only until Brother Will gave me lessons. And that he did because I sat a horse well. A natural, he said."

He did not look pleased at being denied an excuse to break their agreement. But that did not mean he would honor it.

Keeping her feet firm on the one step up that allowed her to look directly into his eyes, she pressed, "Provide me with a horse of my own, and I will not fall behind."

"I believe you will."

"Do I, I shall not begrudge you for leaving me."

He glowered. "You think me so dishonorable I would abandon you, a woman, that you find your own way back to Bairnwood?"

The prospect was daunting, but she had a solution. "Methinks I could if necessary, but it will not be. Many are the abbeys across England. You could deliver me to one, and I would be returned to Bairnwood."

From the pinch of eyebrows and flare of nostrils, he was frustrated, but if it meant she was winning the argument…

He pivoted, but before he could stride opposite, she snatched his sleeve. "Sir Elias!"

The momentum carrying him forward yanked her off the step, and she stumbled against him and might have gone to her knees had he not steadied her.

They were almost as near as when she had sat the saddle before him, but she felt the narrow space between them more than the absence of space when she had rested against him.

She released him at the same moment he released her. Ashamed he so affected her, praying he did not know it, she said, "I am sorry for accusing you of impropriety. My only excuse is you were not alone in suffering Finwyn's ill. I was not myself. I know one such as me does not…"

She halted her explanation that would not entirely make sense whilst she hid behind the gorget. But before she could correct her course, he said, "One such as you?"

"A…servant."

The narrowing of his lids told her explanation fell short, and she guessed he was thinking of another servant—Lettice with whom he believed he may have made a child. But had she truly fallen short? After all, he had not wed the woman. In the absence of a ring, he had relations with her.

Wishing she could work a smile on him as some women did to move a man in a direction he did not care to go, she said, "Pray, Sir Elias, keep the word of a Wulfen-trained knight. Until I prove a burden, do not leave me behind."

He closed his eyes, opened them. "Weather permitting, we depart at dawn. Be ready."

CHAPTER 16

MOMENTS IN TIME

*T*he word of a Wulfen-trained knight. A powerful thing. All the more reason not to speak it unless certain of what one promised.

Elias looked over his shoulder, first at his squire who kept pace though the boy holding to him further burdened his mount and the wet ground from which great clods of earth flew sought to slow horse and rider.

Next, he looked to Honore where she rode several lengths behind. The palfrey Everard had given her was swift and of good temperament, but pushed to its limits by the woman whose dark blond hair whipped out behind her like the turbulent waters of the English Channel toward which they rode. Given no choice but to remove the veil to avoid losing it, Honore had retained the gorget draped beneath her nose.

Elias hated acknowledging it, but though she could no longer be named a young woman, it appeared she was cut from a cloth similar to Queen Eleanor who was ten years older than her husband, Henry.

Excepting Honore's eyes, he did not think she possessed the great beauty for which the queen was lauded, though that could not be truly known without seeing the entirety of a face glimpsed when he dragged Honore from the stream. Regardless, likely she would still be lovely a dozen years hence upon attaining Eleanor's forty years.

He sighed, once more regretted keeping his word. Though four hours into the ride with one stop to take water, thus far she slowed them only enough to tempt him to deliver her to an abbey.

Think Lettice, he reminded himself as he returned his attention to the land. But he ached over memories of their love before her desperation caused him to believe her too broken to make a life together.

Combating hurt, he turned his thoughts to one he prayed had not been broken by Arblette's ill. *Think Hart, find Hart, save Hart.*

～

Port of Sandwich
England

SHE HURT. Her muscles spasmed, bones knew not their places, neck burned and cramped, head felt as if cracked. But she had not fallen far enough behind to satisfy Sir Elias's desire to be rid of her.

Now as he strode forward to aid in her dismount, it took much that remained of her strength to drag a leg over her horse and set her feet on the ground before he reached her. And there she remained, clinging to the strap of leather from which the stirrup hung, longing to drop her head against the palfrey's side, legs so bereft of feeling she feared her next bed might be upon the ground.

"Honore?"

She opened her eyes, mused it was nearly as dark before the

inn at which they would pass the night as it was behind her lids. "I am well. I just need a moment—"

He did not give her one, swinging her up into his arms. "You proved yourself," he said with grudging. "Now hold to me."

She was too tired to resist, but not so much she could not tug up the gorget slipping from beneath her nose. To this she pressed a hand, then slid the other up around the knight's neck. "I am going across the channel with you?"

"It would seem," he said, then instructed his squire and the boy to stable the horses and afterward deliver their packs to the inn.

When he shouldered open the door, Honore was not surprised there were few guests at the scattered tables. It was late, their entrance into the port town of Sandwich delayed while soldiers inspected all who came and went. For whom or what they had not revealed though Sir Elias inquired. Suffice it was well over an hour after all those ahead of their party were searched—most thoroughly carts and wagons—before they were let in.

The knight carried Honore to a table against a wall and set her on a bench. "Remain here whilst I arrange for lodging and a meal."

Telling herself she did not miss his arms around her, she nodded.

Past the glare thrown by the puddling candle at the center of the table, she watched him cross to the bar where a woman of middle years bent her ear to him. Whatever his first request, it turned down her smile. Her smile returned moments later and she nodded.

Guessing there were no rooms available, though drink and food would soon appear, Honore fought the temptation to lower her head to the table and set to tightening the gorget. Once done, she unknotted the veil she had tied around her neck for the ride and draped its wrinkled folds over her hair. Then clasping her hands before her, she studied the other occupants of the inn— four men cast in shadows at a corner table, a man and woman on bar stools, and a bearded fellow at a distant table, his nodding head telling soon he would sleep.

Sir Elias returned to her with two tankards, set one in front of her, and lowered alongside. "No rooms, and the innkeeper tells we are not likely to find any elsewhere, the storm having delayed all travel these past days. But as offered these others, she will provide blankets and accommodate us here for a quarter the cost."

Abandoning the hope of a straw-filled pallet, Honore said, "I can find my rest on a bench. But what of a ship to deliver us across the channel? Does she think they will sail on the morrow?"

"That is the hope, but she says not to expect to depart for several days since many ahead of us have secured passage."

Might Finwyn be among them? she wondered, then asked, "What are we to do?"

He took a long drink. "I shall buy my way aboard ship, but I do not think it possible to find space for three more and our mounts."

Then he meant to leave her. "But—"

He leaned near. "I asked the innkeeper if she knew of a troupe that recently set sail. She said none sought drink or rooms here, but she heard of one making the crossing to Boulogne ten days past. Regardless of whether Arblette has set after them or yet seeks to, the troupe is of utmost importance—even if I must leave you and the others to sooner reach Hart."

"I understand, but we will follow, will we not?"

His hesitation was a barb beneath her skin. "Be assured, Theo and I shall look well over those who board the ships lest Arblette has secured passage."

Hoping the miscreant had chosen the small port of Sandwich and had yet to depart so one threat to Hart could be removed, Honore watched the innkeeper approach with viands and two more tankards for Theo and Cynuit once they finished with the horses.

More keenly feeling her thirst, she was glad there were so few people within. She had but to turn aside and none would see her lower the gorget.

The woman set the tray on the table. "Eat hearty, rest well," she said.

Bread, cheese, slices of ripe fruit, and thin cuts of an unidentifiable meat made Honore long to set herself at them. Not since departing Bairnwood had she eaten well. Except in easing the worst of her hunger at Cheverel in the privacy of her chamber, she had mostly nibbled.

Her stomach groaned, and as heat climbed up her neck, Sir Elias reached forward and pinched the candle's wick, inviting shadows to close around the pungent gray smoke ribboning upward.

"Allay your hunger, Honore."

She could only make out the shape of his face and sparkle of eyes drinking in what light remained in the room. "I thank you," she said, but still she turned her shoulder to him as she tucked the gorget beneath her chin. She drank half the ale before joining him in picking viands from the platter.

"Forgive me," she choked when their fingers brushed, causing sensation to spring up her arm. *Fool,* she silently berated, *he does not warrant nor want such feeling. Beware lest your heart turns in a direction that leads nowhere but ache.*

A short while later, he said near her ear, "We are watched. And closely."

Keeping her chin down lest his eyes had adjusted well enough to see what she would not have him see, she turned her face toward his. "Are we in danger?"

"Methinks more than those four do they move upon us ere our numbers match theirs."

Hoping the squire and boy would soon appear, dissuading the men at the corner table from acting against a knight and the woman with whom he kept company, Honore said, "What should I do?"

"Eat." He reached to the viands. "But be prepared to act as I order should they approach."

She chose a piece of cheese that went down so dry she had to follow it with ale.

As she lowered the tankard, one of the men rose.

"Another bite," Elias said low and, as his left hand moved to his dagger angled in the space between them, she chose a slice of meat.

The tall man said naught until he reached them, and when he spoke it was out of the depths of a hood that, in the absence of candlelight, revealed little of his face. "Sir Knight, I understand you seek passage across the channel," he spoke in the French of the noble.

Elias stared at the one who had either overheard the conversation with the innkeeper or been informed of it when the woman served him and his companions.

Wishing he had not snuffed the candle to provide Honore privacy, Elias said, "You are?"

In the strained voice of one who either much abused it or sought to render it unrecognizable, he said, "One upon whom you need not draw a Wulfrith dagger, my son."

Just because he addressed Elias as would one of the Church did not mean he was of the brotherhood. "Your name?" Elias asked again.

"Brother Christian of the Gilbertine Order. And you?"

Elias suppressed a startle when Honore's hand gripped his thigh, and once more he regretted her accompaniment. Her fear was a distraction, and of greater detriment was the need to safeguard her. He glanced at the table whence this man came and, confirming the others remained seated, said, "Sir Elias De Morville."

"I know the name. Your family holds French lands from our sovereign, and your sire is..." He paused as if to search his memory. "...Otto?"

If his knowledge was meant to put Elias at ease, it did, but not enough to lighten his grip on the dagger.

"May I sit?" Brother Christian nodded at the bench opposite Elias and Honore.

"You may."

He lowered and folded his hands atop the table. "I am also in need of reaching France. Unlike you, I have the means to do so."

"For what do you tell me this?"

"I require the services of a knight possessing the honor and skills of one trained at Wulfen."

Though grateful for the reputation bestowed by Everard, Elias needed none to tell him he was less worthy than many who received that training. Thus, he availed himself of further training at Wulfen Castle each time he visited England in the hope one day he would prove capable of all expected of him by those who noted the dagger on his belt.

"Continue, Brother Christian."

"I have business with the pope some would thwart by denying me and my brethren the right to depart England. Thus, in exchange for passage across the narrow sea, I would buy your protection. Do you agree and does the weather hold, we shall leave well ere first light ahead of the ships and boats whose numbers are too few to accommodate all who seek to reach France."

His proposition appealed, but there was much he did not tell. "I guess it is not a ship you have secured, Brother Christian."

The man grunted. "They are too well watched by those who wish to keep me from the pope."

Here the reason for the search of those entering and exiting the town. "My party numbers four, including my squire and a boy," Elias said. "Our horses number three."

The man nodded. "The skiff that shall carry us across the channel can accommodate four more, but your horses will have to follow later, the arrangements for which I am sure the innkeeper will make for a few coins." He reached beneath the table, set a purse on the wooden planks. "More than enough coin to hire worthy mounts in Boulogne."

That place where the troupe had landed and might now perform. Tempted by the guarantee of passage for all even if he must collect their horses later, Elias asked, "Who thwarts you, Brother Christian?"

"One I loved as a brother who so loved me in return he entrusted me with the care of his son. One I would not have believed a tyrant until he revealed his love was contingent on the death of my conscience and betrayal of the Church."

"Who?"

"It matters not. What matters is I reach France quickly." He turned his head toward the woman beside Elias. "I know not the reason you are with this knight," he said, "but methinks you must agree with what I offer, Honore."

She gasped, voicing Elias's own surprise, and her hand that had eased on his leg dug into it. "Do I know you?"

"We met at Bairnwood. Recognition of Abbess Abigail's beloved servant and that your traveling companion is Wulfen-trained persuaded me to risk much in approaching you."

Elias did not doubt the man's revelation was meant to further assure the one whose service he hoped to engage that, as presented, he was a man of the Church. It did, though Elias hesitated as he recalled words so forcefully spoken past crossed quarterstaffs Everard's saliva had wet his opponent's face.

Here is a lesson, Elias Cant who can if he will but heed the instructor. Given time to plot and maneuver, engage the mind ere the muscles.

Then Everard had hooked a leg around Elias's and sent him crashing to the ground.

"I think we must aid him," Honore cut across the silence.

"I thank you," Brother Christian said, and when still Elias did not respond, added, "I vow, Sir Knight, I am about God's business."

Which would sooner see Elias about the business of Hart. "Very well, my sword arm and that of my squire for passage across the channel ere first light."

The man's sigh was so long he hunched over it. "God is on my side," he said, then more softly, "though I must needs tend my sheep from afar." He lowered his head further, and Elias guessed he prayed. When he rose, he said, "Let us beseech the Lord for kind seas and gain whatever sleep can be had."

As he started to turn away, Elias said. "I do not require your coin, Brother Christian. Passage only."

Though it remained too dark beneath the man's hood to make sense of his visage, what sounded like tears were in his voice when he said, "God bless you, my son."

After he returned to his companions, Elias looked to Honore and saw the gorget once more covered her lower face. "You do not know him?"

Her shrug was tense. "I do not recognize his voice and name, but that does not mean we have not met. I have been at Bairnwood all my life and oft I join the abbess and her visitors to speak of our work with foundlings."

All her life... That which he did not seek of her distracting him from what he sought, he guessed her a foundling. Whether conceived by a noblewoman sent to secretly birth her misbegotten babe at the abbey or born to a commoner who set her out in the wood, it must account for her devotion to abandoned babes.

He moved his thoughts back a space. Had her mother been a commoner, for what had she put out her infant? Poverty? Illegitimacy? A defect of birth?

That last drew his gaze to the gorget he had been told was worn for the sake of modesty. A lie? He had seen Honore without it but not clearly. The only thing of note in the dark of night had been blood running from nose to chin. Had it hidden something of which she was ashamed? A mark of birth like that which caused Lettice to reject her son? For this was Honore so fond of Hart?

Her hand came up, touched the covering as if to ensure it had not slipped.

Rebuking himself for making her uncomfortable over something that did not matter, he reminded himself of what mattered and said, "Then we have only the man's word and his recognition of you to establish he is as he claims."

She averted her gaze, lowered her hand and cupped it over the other at her waist. "Likely a Brother Christian visited Bairnwood. Perhaps in daylight I shall recognize him."

Once more her response bothered. Had it a false note? Or was it but weighted by undue attention shown her? Or fatigue over the long ride that put her claim to horsemanship to a test she had struggled to pass?

Before he could probe further, two entered the inn. Packs slung over their shoulders, they stamped mud from their boots and crossed to their lord. And learned what the darkest of morn held for all.

CHAPTER 17

LOSS FEEDING RHYME

She slept as Theo's lord had done until awakened to take the last watch.

Leaning against a wall alongside a shuttered window, hand resting on dagger's hilt, Elias considered Honore where she stretched atop a bench.

Over the past half hour, the blanket given her by the innkeeper had slipped to her waist as restless sleep moved her on her narrow bed. Before turning her back to him this last time, she had murmured something from which he picked Finwyn's name, then shaken her head.

Guessing her dreams were disturbed by remembrance of the attack at the stream, Elias had been tempted to awaken her, but she had resettled and spoken no more.

Until now.

She drew a sharp breath, dropped onto her back so near the edge of the bench she might soon find herself on the floor, and sent one rasping word through the gorget's weave.

Bishop?

Elias strode to the bench, bent to turn her, and stilled when the single torch the innkeeper had left lit cast a glow across one side of a face wrapped all around in cloth. The veil had shifted upward, exposing golden hair, the gorget downward, though not so far her entire mouth was revealed. One side of the upper bow was beautifully arched, the other distorted by the table's shadow.

Something moved so stealthily through Elias it nearly slipped past him—attraction, that which he ought not feel and certainly not so near the tragedy in Forkney.

Before he could distance himself, she moaned, and this time he heard clearly, "I need him. For Hart."

Guessing he figured into what she dreamt, Elias waited. But once more she rolled away, exposing to light the bruise on the side of her nose dealt by Arblette. It had faded enough that one almost had to look for it to see it.

He drew the blanket up over her shoulder, but as he turned away, he sensed a change about her. And stilled.

Honore sprang open her eyes. Had Elias's presence awakened her? Was it him she felt almost as strongly as if he hunkered on this side of her? Reminding herself to breathe, she narrowed her lids and, past the dim beneath the table, saw the corner where two of the brethren slept upright, the other two on benches.

Leave me be, she silently entreated the knight who stood over her, but he remained unmoving as if aware she had awakened.

Feeling the gorget's edge across the seam of her lips, she thanked the Lord she faced opposite. Otherwise, Elias might satisfy his curiosity over one of those things hidden from him. Though her lower face was the least of these, she was increasingly self-conscious as she had been made to feel years past when trust in one she believed would overlook her imperfection proved a painful mistake. Afterward, she had rebelled against hiding how God had touched her in a way He had not touched them and cast off the gorget. But not for long.

At the apologetic request of the abbess who relied on the funds provided by Lady Yolande, once more Honore had covered her face outside her dormitory so noble ladies and others easily given to superstition and distaste must not so often cross themselves or hasten opposite.

Yanking herself back to the present, Honore silently bemoaned that Elias had yet to retreat. What did he want? To allay suspicions over what else she hid?

Once more, her conscience berated her for naming those things merely hidden. Whether by word or omission, they were lies. She could not be certain of Brother Christian's identity, but she suspected the truth as strongly as she believed Finwyn was likely Hart's father. But the same thing that made false of her over the boy's parentage made false of her over the tallest of the brethren. She needed Elias's aid, and were she to reveal her suspicion, he might turn from her as quickly as if given greater cause to question he had fathered a foundling.

Discomfited by the softening gorget absorbing the moisture of her inner lip, Honore hoped what she did next would move Elias away.

She sighed long, slid a hand up her face to shift the gorget higher, scratched her temple. Then she let her hand drop alongside her face.

"Honore?"

It was not her name that made her gasp. It was the speaking of it so near.

"Oui, you are awake," he said low where he bent over her.

"I would return to my rest," she whispered.

"I apologize for awakening you. You were restless and talking in your sleep. I only meant to ensure you did not fall from the bench or lose your blanket."

One moment she was touched by his kindness, the next jolted. Her back had not always been turned to him? The blanket now over her had slipped? Might he have seen what she did not wish seen?

"You are kind," she rasped.

"Turn to me, Honore."

She stiffened.

"So our words may stay between us."

She longed to retort their voices would not carry at all did he allow her to sleep, but she doubted it would send him away.

Hoping he did not wish to discuss Brother Christian, as avoided when Cynuit and the squire entered the inn, she ensured the gorget was in place and shifted around.

As he eased back on his haunches to give her space, she pushed onto an elbow. "Of what would you speak that cannot await morn?"

Lowering his voice further now they were face to face, he said, "The brethren trouble me. The urgency prompting their leader to enlist my aid so none thwart their departure makes me certain they are the reason all are searched at the town gates."

"As I am also certain." She hoped her agreement would make him more receptive to the answer she must give.

"You are sure you do not recall a Brother Christian at Bairnwood?"

A man by that name she did not, but there was another whose visit was unforgettable—he who, not then of the Church, was accompanied by a boy of greater consequence than himself. But that man and the one sleeping in the corner might not be the same.

Still you deceive, her conscience stabbed.

"I do not recall a Brother Christian," she clung to her determination to aid in finding Hart. The boy needed her, did he not? Just as he had been nearly a son to her, she had been nearly a mother to him. And even if this man was his father, he would present as a stranger, all the more frightening after whatever Hart endured. Hers would be the familiar face and arms the boy needed to put him back together, and that was only possible if Finwyn did not reach him first and ensure he was never found.

Honore tried to look nearer on the knight to read his expression, but though his features were more intimate with torchlight than hers where she remained in the table's shadow, all she knew for certain was they appealed as much in the night as they did in the day. And if she did not uproot her growing attraction she might once more be pained by something dangled so far above her heart she could never reach it.

"Methinks I ought to reconsider the bargain with Brother Christian," Sir Elias rent the silence.

She sat up, dropped her feet to the floor. "If we do not depart with him, there is no guarantee even you alone will make the crossing on the morrow, and if already Finwyn is in France..." She drew a shuddering breath. "I am afeared it will be too late to recover Hart. But if it is not and we chance more days in which he can be further exploited—"

Elias moved from his haunches to his knees, leaned in, and set a hand over her gorget-covered mouth. "Quiet."

Realizing her voice had risen and tears rimmed her eyes, she stared into his face and felt the knuckle of his thumb beneath her nose and the warmth of her breath on it. Though once more tugged toward him, more she was moved to despair over the numbering of her fears. Fear for Hart's fate. Fear she would greatly regret what she withheld from Elias. Fear of defying those who sought to prevent the brethren from leaving England. Fear of what would become of her foundlings if ill befell her.

She had told herself she knew enough of the world inhabited by this knight that she could move through it, but it was so thick with danger, intrigue, and uncertainty that the weak of her longed to be inside Bairnwood's walls.

"Whisper," he instructed and eased his hand from her mouth.

"Forgive me, Elias, but I..." She winced over denying him his title. "There is much to lose." That last came out on a sob, at the end of which she found herself drawn forward. Though she kept her seat on the bench, he pressed her head beneath his chin and her face against his throat.

She knew she should resist being embraced by one she had accused of trespass, but she softened as the scent and feel of him carved forbidden paths through her. Thus, her only struggle was of keeping her hands from sliding around his neck.

"You are right," he rasped. "Too much to lose."

Then he would keep the bargain made with Brother Christian? Would see them aboard the skiff and across the channel?

"Tell me," he spoke into her hair, "how came Hart by his name?"

Her heart lurched, not with alarm but gratitude for what she perceived an attempt to move her mind from the ill of his world to the good.

"I am guessing it refers to a male deer," he prompted.

"Oui. Returning to the abbey with the babe delivered unto me, I happened upon a red hart at the stream…" She caught her breath as new ugly memories flung themselves across old beautiful ones.

"You prevailed," said the one who had pulled her from that stream. "Think on that."

That which made possible she was here with him. She nodded. "Though I had to pass near the hart to cross by way of the fallen tree, it did not bound away. It watched us, and when I reached the opposite side and the babe began to coo, the deer stamped and snorted. Thus, I determined to name the babe Hart."

"A good tale. Hold to it, Honore."

She did, whilst he held her so long that imaginings of forever having his arms to run into warmed her as much as it worried her to want something she could not have.

Ending the embrace, he said, "Sleep," then left her to her bench.

CHAPTER 18

SEE WHAT THE LORD NOW STREWS

"There, Sir Elias. The signal."

Beneath a near full moon dimmed by clouds, Elias saw the same as Brother Christian—a vertical slash of light followed by a horizontal. The sign of the cross.

He looked behind at the figures patrolling the docks past which he and his squire had escorted their charges undetected— thus far. The day was so new, more it could be said the night was in labor than it had given birth. As they continued along the shore toward the point, on the other side of which the skiff awaited them, the darkest shadows to which the party of eight kept could prove kept by others. Much depended on the determination of the one pursuing Brother Christian.

Once more, Elias questioned the bargain struck with the faceless man. What great lord had he offended? What price would Elias and his companions pay were they intercepted?

"They await us," Brother Christian prompted, the shifting of his shoulders causing the pack strapped to his back to rustle.

The packs of the others were secured as tightly and effort

made to quiet the chain mail of Elias and Theo. A long-sleeved tunic was worn not only beneath the armor but over it, the fit of the outermost one so snug it compressed the links and muffled their ring in the absence of great movement. But were greater movement required, whether to run or meet at swords, the extra tunic would be restrictive—until the seams gave.

Elias returned his regard to Brother Christian, and moonlight revealed just enough of his features beneath the hood to confirm he was beyond two score aged. "Patience," he said. "Do we hurry this, all we have gained will be lost."

He felt argument rise between them, but the man sighed. "You are right. For this I engaged you."

Hoping he would not once more prove unworthy of his Wulfen training, Elias said only loud enough for all seven to hear, "I shall advance ahead to uproot sentries patrolling the shore. After a count of one hundred, Theo shall lead you, keeping to the sand and shadows, speaking no word, and listening for my warning should I happen on any who might detain us."

"Oui, my lord," his squire said. "Your warning?"

"Two trills as of a gull, you halt and do not proceed until you hear one. Do I sound three, we are pursued and you are to make all haste for the point. If the patrol are ahead, you shall join me in subduing them, Theo. If they come from behind, you are to fall back to protect the rear, and I will aid you there."

Lord, should they come for us, he silently prayed, *not from both sides.*

He turned to Brother Christian. "If my squire and I must draw swords, continue to the boat and see Honore and Cynuit aboard. God willing, we will be close behind, but delay your departure only as long as you have time to put out to sea. Should it prove necessary to leave Theo and me, all I ask is you deliver the woman and boy to the nearest abbey when you reach France and provide enough coin for all they require lest I am unable to join them."

"As God is my witness, it will be done, Sir Elias."

"Non," Honore rasped where she stood on the other side of his squire. "I will not leave without you."

He stepped near. "Of no benefit are we to Hart if Theo and I must not only defend our persons but yours. Await me in Boulogne, and if I do not appear within a sennight, you will have funds enough to buy passage back to England."

"But Hart—"

"Seek Everard Wulfrith's aid. He knows the tale and will do all he can to restore the lad to you."

After a long moment, she set a hand atop his on her shoulder. "God be with you, Sir Knight."

He did not think. He felt, just as he should not have done past the middling of night when her anguish moved him to pull her against him. Though that with which he was beset was impending loss of a depth he should not feel for her, he turned his hand up into hers. "God be with you, Lady," he afforded her a title that in that moment seemed as good a fit for her as many a noblewoman.

Hearing the sharp breath she drew behind the gorget, he released her and returned to Theo. "A hundred count," he said and began moving across the sand.

Calling on every sense sharpened in the darkened cellar of Wulfen Castle during his training, Elias looked, listened, smelled, touched, tasted—and sought to engage the sense he believed were it not of the Lord speaking into one's soul was of His angels drawing near to give warning.

He was halfway to the point when a shift among the shadows surrounding a cluster of boulders made him pause.

He glanced behind, confirmed those who followed remained unseen and unheard, then narrowed his eyes at where he had caught movement. All was still, but there was a scent on the air not of the sea or its affect on sand, rocks, and vegetation struggling to thrive along the coast. This was of a very unclean body, and as he breathed deeper, he tasted it.

Hoping it was no more than two bodies wafting so great an

odor, Elias turned his face across his shoulder, cupped a hand over a side of his mouth, and trilled twice.

There was no evidence he was heard, but he assured himself the seven did as instructed and awaited the single trill to resume their advance.

Elias strained his senses beyond the tumble of the sea and the foul odor evidencing danger. At last, another shift among the shadows, then a low grunt and the barely perceptible sound of one relieving himself. One of those at the boulders was more vulnerable than moments before.

Staying low, Elias ran and veered to the left to come around the backside. And there before him were two he must render incapable of rousing others, one adjusting his chausses, the other leaning against a boulder.

The first snapped his head up, a moment later went down with a soft grunt. It was the crack of the dagger's hilt against his brow that brought his companion around.

Determined he would not mortally wound one who but did his duty, Elias lunged and drove himself into the man's right side to disable his sword arm. But the soldier was of the minority whose left hand dominated, as revealed when moonlight streaked a long blade destined for Elias's back.

There was only time in which to act on instincts whose raw edges had been trimmed and smoothed as much as possible at Wulfen Castle. Elias sprang to the side, heard the tearing of a shoulder seam, and as momentum and shifting sand caused his opponent to stumble, aimed his hilt at the back of the man's skull. It relieved him of consciousness, but not before the man shouted, "To arms!"

CHAPTER 19

SO FAIR IS SHE

Unworthy! Elias silently rebuked as he leapt from cover of the boulders. Would a Wulfrith have spared a man's life at the risk of others held far more dear?

Determinedly casting out the troubadour, Elias sounded three trills to bring Theo and his charges running had the soldier's hue and cry not already done so, and watched for movement of those he was to deliver to the skiff as well as the men patrolling the docks.

Naught of the former, but as he entertained the possibility the soldier's shout had not carried far, from out of the shadows coming straight for him were two robed figures who should be preceded by his squire.

Theo had fallen back, meaning his charges were pursued, likely by patrol they had slipped past ere the call to arms. As Elias ran forward, exchanging dagger for sword as he felt the giving of more seams, he identified two more robed figures. Behind them came Cynuit and Honore, the lad gripping the woman's arm in an attempt to add his speed to hers. Unfortunately, his aid could see them both brought to ground.

With the sword-wielding Theo bringing up the rear, they numbered seven as they ought to, but moments later an eighth and ninth figure came into sight also armed with swords.

"Almighty!" Elias called on the Lord as he neared the front ranks of the brethren, the height of the one on the left identifying him as Brother Christian. But then that figure looked behind and swept around. Trained up in faith and hindered by a priestly frock the same as Honore in a gown, did he truly believe he could defend the woman and boy?

"To the boat, Brother Christian!" Elias shouted, and the holy man's brethren added their voices to his, urging their fellow to resume his course. But the plan further unraveled when they also turned back to retrieve their leader and drag him toward their only hope of crossing the channel.

"I have not a sword, but I have fists!" Brother Christian shouted.

Elias ran past three of the brethren, snatched hold of the tallest one's cowl, and yanked hard. He did not pause to confirm whether or not the man stayed his feet but shouted over his shoulder, "We have them! Get to the boat!" Moments later, he commanded Honore and Cynuit, "To the boat!"

He heard Honore call his name, then he was alongside Theo who spun around to face the soldiers coming hard and fast.

"Brace yourself!" Elias said what he hoped need not be spoken though this would be Theo's first true test of whether he could save himself and others. Then choosing the largest, swiftest, and most heavily armored of the patrol, Elias lunged.

Their swords clashed. Had those at the docks remained oblivious of what transpired near the point, they were no longer. Though Elias could spare no glance in that direction, more of those who sought to prevent them from crossing the channel were coming.

Hearing the ring of his squire's blade against his opponent's, Elias sent up a prayer Theo would be spared a much-shortened life, then parried a swing meant to open his middle and countered with an upward stroke that caught the rim of the soldier's helm and sent it flying.

"You are welcome," Elias said. "Now you can see, your defeat should be less humiliating."

The taunt was intentional. Were he to aid Theo, increasing the chance they reached the skiff before it sailed, he must make quick work of his opponent. And often the best way to accomplish that was to rend the man's concentration by making the encounter overly personal.

The soldier cursed and surged forward. His blade struck Elias's upper arm and skittered down tunic-covered mail. However, its point momentarily found blood in crossing the back of Elias's left hand.

It would pain later, but now he felt little more than warmth slicking his fingers—and the need to be the one to next draw blood. Thunder in his ears, he knocked the man's blade aside with a backhanded slice and a loud tearing of seams.

His opponent recovered, and his wildly swinging sword cleaved the air where Elias's head would have been had he not ducked. That move and the one to follow had been taught him not by Everard but his friend, Durand, whilst they were yet wary acquaintances.

Elias came up directly in front of the soldier whose sword arm had yet to unwind from where it had completed its swing across his chest, rocked his head back, and slammed his brow into the man's nose. For Elias, it was a relatively soft landing, sending tolerable pain through his skull, but not for his opponent who howled over a broken nose, lost his footing, and went down.

Elias delivered another blow to ensure he did not soon rise and glanced at the docks. Three of those who had patrolled it were absent. Certain they advanced amid shadows, he ran to assist Theo whose battle with a short but spry soldier had moved them toward moonlight come through a break in the clouds near the shore. But Elias's aid was not needed, his squire bringing his sword down with such strength his opponent's blade snapped. Then Theo delivered a kick to the chest that dropped the man to his back.

"To the boat!" Elias shouted.

The squire's hesitation told he longed to ensure his foe did not regain his feet, but then he was running ahead of his lord. As Elias followed, above the sea's song he heard the ring of mail, grunts, and curses of the dock patrol giving chase.

Reaching the point behind Theo, Elias saw the skiff had taken to the water, a half dozen oars on the right side rising and dipping. It was not so far off shore it could not be reached, but if the oarsmen applied themselves, soon the boat would be in water too deep to be negotiated beneath the weight of armor. And they would find themselves outfitted in chains of a different sort.

Theo requiring no prompting to continue forward, Elias drew breath with which to bellow the name of the tall Gilbertine lest those aboard could not determine whether the two pounding the surf-hardened shore were friend or foe.

"They come!" Honore's cry shot from sea to sand. "Pray, turn back!"

"Brother Christian!" Elias shouted.

Once more the oars rose and fell, and not in a direction of benefit to the warriors who made it possible for six of their party to depart England. Because Elias and Theo were too closely pursued?

A glance behind told they were not—yet.

Did Brother Christian betray them? Or had the one captaining the skiff determined the risk was too great? Regardless, were Elias and Theo to be captured, the patrol would have to get wet to wreak vengeance on those who aided the brethren's escape.

Raised voices ahead as Elias followed Theo into the tide,

amongst them Brother Christian's and Honore's. Raised voices behind, unfamiliar and portending great ill.

"Sheathe your sword!" Elias called and thrust his own into its scabbard.

Theo complied, and as their pursuers neared, those ahead raised their oars and left them angled heavenward. They would not row back, but neither would they row away until given no choice.

Hoping the seabed gently inclined, providing purchase for their boots all the way to the boat, Elias and his squire forged onward.

They were less than twenty feet from salvation when the sand below fell away and they dropped, the water swirling about their hips suddenly at their throats.

Struggling to keep feet firm to the rock below as the sea wavered between pushing them back toward the patrol and pulling them into depths that could drown them ere they shed their mail—were it even possible encased in tunics—Elias beseeched the Lord to deliver them.

As did Honore, calling, "Your Grace, save them!"

"Row for them!" Brother Christian bellowed.

The oars dropped, and the skiff shot toward Elias and Theo. It took two strokes to bring the bow alongside the warriors and a sharp backward stroke to arrest its progress. With the patrol shouting as they leapt through the tide, Elias and Theo raised their arms and were gripped and hauled aboard.

Hardly were they loosed than the boat surged opposite.

As Elias sat up, Honore dropped to her knees beside him.

"Elias!" She threw her arms around his neck and clasped him close as if all her world had nearly gone wrong. And he supposed it might have. It being possible he was Hart's father, he was her best hope of rescuing the boy.

He set a hand on her back. "All is well."

Brow pressed to his shoulder, she jerked her head as if in agreement but did not release him.

Beside them, Theo rose and dropped onto a bench upon which sat the tallest of the brethren with his back to moonlight. There was little to glimpse beneath the hood he held closed at the neck to prevent the air stirred by the speed with which the oarsmen began their journey from dropping the covering down around his shoulders.

"We thank you, Brother Christian," Elias said. "I know it was a great risk to return for us."

In a voice less graveled than before, the man said, "As was the aid you gave me." He sighed. "A greater risk on both sides than you yet know, my son."

Those words sent a chill through Elias that had naught to do with soaked garments—words that portended his quest to find Hart would prove more dangerous.

Releasing Elias, Honore sat back on her heels. "I feared you lost to us."

Wondering why he missed her embrace, he said, "Far from it." He stood and reached to her.

As he pulled her upright, she exclaimed, "You bleed!"

As was becoming habit in her company. "A cut to the back of the hand that ought not require the needle."

"Allow me—"

He pulled free. "My squire will tend it."

She nodded and settled on a bench distant from Brother Christian.

Elias turned toward shore. The patrol there could only stare after their lost quarry as the skiff's captain ordered his men to row faster.

Out to sea they swept. Out of reach of whoever did not wish a man on a low rung of the Church to carry tale to the pope.

CHAPTER 20

HUMBLE BEAUTY

$\mathcal{B}$ecket.

Though an hour had passed since he who called himself Brother Christian picked his way past the oarsmen to the bow and dropped his hood to watch the sun rise, only now did he turn and reveal the lie.

It was many years since Elias had performed for nobles that included one who had been King Henry's chancellor before being further raised from modest beginnings to the office of Archbishop of Canterbury, but Elias knew the long, albeit somewhat fuller face. Yet handsome, it boasted a broad brow, large eyes no longer bright with good humor, aquiline nose, and firm mouth whose spread on this first day of self-imposed exile flashed no teeth.

A greater risk on both sides than you yet know, my son, he had said.

Elias De Morville, his family vassals of the Duke of Normandy —a man yet more powerful for also being England's king—had aided in snatching from Henry who ought not be crossed a man who stood far above the lowest rungs of the Church. So far that

132

Thomas Becket would have the pope's ear providing the sea churned by the wind billowing the sails did not turn deadly.

"Dear Lord," Elias rasped, "what have I done?"

The holy man raised the hand he had pressed to his belly, beckoned to the one who had not felt less worthy since Sir Everard bestowed knighthood with a slap to the face made all the more memorable for leaving Elias bruised.

"Sir Elias!"

The shout roused several, including Theo and two brethren, but it was the lifting of Honore's head where Cynuit and she huddled on one side of the boat that captured his regard. Her gaze flew to the archbishop, and when next it flew to Elias, her eyes widened further.

Alarm because only now she realized who had secured the services of one whose fealty belonged to Duke Henry? Or because she had known the identity of Brother Christian and feared Elias's anger? Hoping the former, ignorance far easier to forgive than deception, Elias crossed to her.

That she did not avoid his gaze breeding more hope she was innocent, he said, "You know who that is?"

Her nod was wary.

"When did you first know?"

Movement behind the gorget told she moistened her lips. "With certainty...now."

Though the qualifier condemned her, he was loath for it to do so. "Last eve you suspected he was more than a Gilbertine? That he is the one with whom your king quarrels?"

Her throat bobbed. "I am sorry, but the sooner we reach France—"

"The sooner *you* reach France!" Feeling the sharpening of eyes upon them, he bent near. "*You* who I told was not needed. *You* whose guile and recklessness further endangers the boy. *You* whose thoughtlessness could see me and mine stripped of our lands. *You* who for all your modesty know well how to move a man beyond his purpose."

Tears wetting eyes whose beauty he refused to acknowledge, she offered no further defense.

"I would speak with you, Sir Knight!" Thomas called.

Elias straightened, considered the man in the bow, then slashed his gaze to the betrayer. "You and I are done, Honore of Bairnwood. When we reach France, I shall leave you at the nearest abbey."

"What of Hart?"

"He is my responsibility. You did your part in saving him from the beasts of the wood, now I shall save him from the beasts of mankind." Salty air whipping hair across his brow, he strode to the archbishop who stood several inches taller than he. Elias bowed, took the hand offered, and noting the absence of an extravagant ring that would have revealed he was no mere priest, kissed Thomas's knuckles.

"Your Grace," he said, the honorific returning him to the struggle to reach the skiff. It was as Honore had named the man, though Elias thought it God she called upon to save him and his squire. She may not have been certain of Brother Christian's identity, but certain enough she should have alerted Elias.

Thomas the archbishop resettled his hand on his belly. Grimacing as if pained by the boat's movement across water he surely prayed did not turn more turbulent, he considered the knight, during which Elias wondered if he was recognized as one who had years past woven for the chancellor and other nobles a tale of the Norman Conquest of England. Not likely. Elias had been considerably younger and painted his face in the manner for which his troupe was known.

"I hope you will forgive me the deception, my son. As feared, it was necessary to gain your aid, and methinks we both know you would have been loath to give it had you known whom you acted against."

"Henry."

Thomas inclined his head. "A man who thinks naught of gaining something against one's honor and, upon attaining it, regards the corrupted as contemptibly weak. He whom I so happily took to heart I did not see my folly, too late realizing one such as he ought to be approached with the greatest restraint and fewest words."

"I do not question your analysis nor your regret, Your Grace, but it does not change that I answer to one who is owed the fealty of me and mine."

"I understand, but surely you know there is another to whom you answer first." He looked heavenward. "If you believe God appointed Henry Plantagenet King of England, you must accept our heavenly father as Henry's sovereign—*our* sovereign above all no matter how magnificent the earthly crowns His appointed wear."

"I do not argue that. I argue against answering to you. You claim to be God's representative on Earth, but so do those who oppose you in standing Henry's side. You believe you know God's mind, and perhaps you do, but until I am blessed with greater discernment, I know not who speaks true. Now, rather than stay the side of the one I serve here on Earth, your deception renders me a traitor."

The archbishop laid a hand on Elias's shoulder. "*My* deception. To that I shall attest should the king learn you aided me."

As if Henry would heed a man now his enemy...

Dear Lord, Elias silently bemoaned, *mayhap I should have remained a commoner, a performer, a poet.* Had the spare heir not returned home to be groomed to take Otto De Morville's place, Elias's uncle could have been heir. And surely his actions would not have threatened to ruin the family.

Elias berated himself for not staying current on England's politics that would have put meat on the bone of suspicion that made him reconsider his bargain with Brother Christian.

Tidings of the growing rift between Henry and his archbishop had crossed the channel, and much had been made of the disagreement unraveling the friendship that had once roused nearly as much talk as when Henry wed Eleanor of Aquitaine. As Otto's heir and vassal to Henry, Elias had attended to the tidings as seriously as he was able. But upon learning he might be a father, he had become nearly deaf to them as he put his affairs in order the sooner to sail for England.

Knowing he had violated one or more Wulfrith lessons, he said, "I do not mean to be disrespectful, Your Grace, but if your disagreement with King Henry has so widened you must flee England, I see no worth in you defending me."

Pain shot across the man's face, but not from Elias's words as told by the hand on his belly that curled into a fist and the groan suppressed behind colorless lips.

Elias gripped his arm. "Your Grace?"

"I suffer from disturbed digestion, but the sea..." He shook his head. "All the more it makes havoc of my infirmity."

"You ought to sit."

"Not until I set eyes on France." He glanced over his shoulder, sighed. "You are right, my son. My defense would be of no benefit, but be assured never will I or my brethren speak of what you did for us."

Of little consolation. The clash with the patrol and the skiff's escape would lead to an investigation to discover who had fled England. And were the innkeeper questioned and did she reveal she accepted coin to arrange for the transport of horses, those who sought the archbishop might find De Morville. Though Elias had not provided his surname, that which he had called himself while performing with the troupe—Cant—could lead to him, even if he did not reclaim those worthy mounts.

"As I would not further impose on you," Thomas said, "I will understand if you wish to part ways as soon as we are ashore."

Ashore where Elias would make arrangements for Honore's

return to England. "May I ask if you plan to pause at an abbey, Your Grace?"

The archbishop hesitated as if questioning whether to trust Elias with his plans, said, "My man, Herbert of Bosham, traveled to France ahead of me. We shall reunite at the abbey of Clairmarais."

That holy place of both monks and nuns, Elias reflected.

As if guessing the reason behind the inquiry, Thomas said, "You are angry with Honore of Bairnwood." When Elias did not respond, the archbishop sighed. "A risk I took in revealing she and I had met, but as it seemed the greatest obstacle to securing your aid was doubt I was of the Church, I chanced it. I but hoped in keeping my face hidden and disguising my voice she would not guess my identity—and did she suspect, she would say naught." He nodded. "For this a great division grows between you."

He made it sound as wide as that between Henry and him. Was it? Resenting memories of the night past when he held Honore and thought...

What had he thought? Or had he thought? Certes, he had felt. But what?

Naught, he told himself. "Against my better judgment," he said, "I allowed the woman to accompany me to search for a boy I may have fathered. Now her silence could cost me and mine all."

Thomas frowned. "You speak of one of her foundlings?"

"I do. When I learned of his existence, I journeyed to England to claim him if he is mine and discovered he was stolen from the abbey six months past."

The archbishop's gaze sharpened. "For what was he stolen?"

"A large mark of birth on his face resembling—"

"Britain," Thomas said, that knowledge surely gained when he visited Bairnwood and met Honore. And, it seemed, Hart.

Thomas nodded. "Remarkable it is, though I did not look as near and long upon it as did Prince Henry."

The King of England's heir, Elias realized, having forgotten

Thomas had once fostered the boy. As told whilst under cover of the name Brother Christian, once he was greatly esteemed by a man now his foe.

"For that you believe he was taken?" Thomas asked.

"I do."

"By whom? And what makes you think he is in France?"

"You have heard of Théâtre des Abominations?"

The archbishop's eyes widened. "I petitioned King Henry to eject that foul troupe from England when we met at Clarendon Palace ere..." He rubbed his head. "Ere I realized the slope upon which I found myself was so steep I might lose my footing and yield up my life." He looked past Elias. "I fear I shall not see England again."

Might he know something of the troupe that would aid in locating Hart? Elias wondered as he waited for him to resume their conversation. When he did, it was in no way welcome.

"Honore approaches, De Morville. Doubtless, you will not like my expression of gratitude, but it is her due as the Lord would agree."

CHAPTER 21

THE HEART SHE DOTH PROVOKE

*H*e was done with her. As he should be, Honore supposed. She could only pray she did not prove the ruin of his family. Regardless, all the greater her offense if Hart was not his son—and greater yet did he learn she had known of Finwyn's claim on the boy.

As she moved her gaze from the knight's back to the archbishop, a rogue wave struck. Struggling to keep her feet from slipping, she slapped a hand to the nearest bench, gasped as spray wet her face and gorget.

Though she felt the gaze of the oarsmen whose labor had eased with the raising of the sails a half hour into the journey, she feigned ignorance and silently beseeched, *Lord, deliver us to France.*

Though a storm had yet to set down, the weather so stirred it was possible the ships seeking to depart Sandwich later this morn would not. That was her hope, though only if Finwyn meant to board one.

When the skiff resumed its relatively sedate course, Honore caught the sound of retching and looked behind. Once more,

Cynuit leaned over the side emptying his stomach. Though her own insides roiled, thus far she had not heaved. Hoping she would not now, she looked to those at the bow whose mantles were more heavily flecked with water, then resumed her negotiation of the narrow aisle between the benches.

As she neared, Thomas stepped to the side to receive her, and she felt a pang of sympathy for the gray cast to his face and the arm against his midriff. Though she knew not if his cause was just, his discomfort further disposed her toward him. She summoned a smile to her eyes, and when he managed the same, more clearly she recalled his visit to Bairnwood accompanied by King Henry's eldest son, a boy whose adoration of his guardian had been evident.

The invitation for Honore to join the abbess and her visitors to discuss the foundlings had included Hart. Wary lest the chancellor show interest in him the same as the bishop who believed the mark a sign from God Britain would be united under one king, she had been glad Hart was then of too few years to understand the reason for scrutiny of his face.

Honore had sensed arrogance and indulgence about Thomas, but he had seemed of a different bent from the bishop. He had said she need not wear her covering in his presence and only a slight frown had appeared when she lowered it. Of greater consolation, he had been kind to Hart and made so little of the mark one might think he looked upon a freckle.

Still, she had been surprised when the king later ensured his friend and chancellor was elected archbishop despite the protests of many of the Church who believed Thomas would put the interests of Henry ahead of God. And further surprised when, thereafter, their friendship deteriorated.

Was his argument with the king a clash for power? Or done out of love for God to protect the rights and privileges of the Church as Thomas claimed? Unfortunately, that she could not know since who but the Lord could separate the dark from the light within a man's heart? Still, on the night past she had trusted Thomas enough to deliver them to France and keep his word to Elias that if ill befell him, she and Cynuit would be safe.

When she reached the bow, Elias turned. Though she longed to avert her gaze, she set it to his. She hated deceiving him, but not enough she would do differently were she able to relive this day that would see them in France by nightfall if the sea remained tolerant of their small craft. True, soon he would abandon her, but he would be nearer to rescuing Hart.

It might be only one life at risk—to many a small, inconsequential life—but not to her. Nor God. Never would any convince her Hart was less loved by the Creator than those who wore crowns fashioned not of thorns but gold, silver, and gems. Even were this knight not the boy's father, Hart was worthy of the same sacrifice King Henry's vassals would make to recover an abducted prince.

Halting alongside Elias, she widened her stance to counter the boat's movement, bent and kissed the archbishop's hand. "Your Grace."

"I am in your debt, Honore of Bairnwood. As methinks you know, it is unlikely my brethren and I would be aboard without Sir Elias's aid."

She straightened. Deeply feeling the presence of the man at her side, she said, "For that I fear I have made as great an enemy of Sir Elias as you have made of the king."

Thomas gave a grunt between disbelief and discomfort, the latter drawing her eyes to where he gripped his middle. "I would not have thought you given to exaggeration, Honore. I am quite certain that, after time and reflection, the honorable Sir Elias will forgive us both our transgressions."

She looked sidelong at the knight and glimpsed beneath a wave of hair upon his brow the scabbed gash evidencing the ill Finwyn had dealt him. His eyes met hers, and in his she saw as much condemnation as when he had stood over her.

"Until you called upon *Your Grace* to save the knight," the archbishop said, "I believed you no more than suspected my identity. Tell what revealed me."

"Your claim to have met me, your height, and something in your voice recalled Thomas the chancellor come unto the abbey with Prince Henry. Too, having heard your disagreement with the king had grown, I considered those differences had become so great you must flee Henry's wrath the same as Brother Christian and his brethren fled one who sought to root them out from those entering and departing Sandwich. Even when—"

The boat listed heavily, and as she snatched hold of the railing, Elias gripped her arm. When she found her balance, he released her so swiftly, she wondered if she had imagined the aid given her.

She swallowed. "Even when I bestowed your title to remind you of your duty to protect your flock and not allow the captain to leave behind men who would be severely punished for aiding you, I could not have said with certainty it was the Archbishop of Canterbury beneath the hood. Only when you lowered it."

A smile moved his mouth. "Thus, I am in greater need of Sir Elias's forgiveness than you."

Was he? More, did it matter? She smoothed the covering across her mouth, braved another look at Elias.

"You know you need not wear the gorget in my presence, Honore," the archbishop said.

She flew her gaze back to his.

"Just as I am sure you need not wear it in Sir—"

As if understanding what spasmed across her face, he quieted, then cleared his throat. "Sir Elias, I would speak with Honore alone. As I am sure you slept poorly, you ought to gain your rest. And do spend time with the Lord that He may aid you in forgiving the deceivers."

As if Elias wished to be anywhere but at Honore's side, he pivoted.

"He does not know," the archbishop said as the knight distanced himself.

She raised her eyebrows. "For what does he need to know?"

"I would not have thought it of consequence but..." He lowered to a bench, patted the stretch beside him. "After what I witnessed on the night past, perhaps it *is* of consequence."

Not until she accepted his invitation to join him did she make sense of his words. Face warming, she rasped, "You were...?"

He dipped his chin. "Awake with prayers for the safety of all and a good crossing."

Discomfited more by what he had seen than might have heard, fairly certain Elias's voice and hers had not carried enough to make sense of them, she said, "It seems God listens to you."

"He listens to all. Where one's faith is most greatly tested is waiting on and accepting His answer to questions and beseechings. Blessedly, thus far my most fervent prayers of the night past are well answered. And yours?"

Did he seek to move her back to what he had witnessed between Elias and her? Uncertain of what he had seen though it made her betrayal of the knight tenfold worse, she asked, "Did Sir Elias reveal the reason we wished to make the crossing?"

"Hart's abduction, and that he may be the boy's father. But I need not verify you pray for the child's return. What I question is what you, a woman of virtue committed to saving and bettering the lives of foundlings, pray for yourself—if you seek more than an embrace from a handsome knight of noble birth."

She gasped. "You make it sound as if I might sacrifice my virtue to him."

"I do not think that of you, and I believe Sir Elias honorable enough not to seek such, but I would be remiss did I not add my voice to that of your conscience in warning nothing good can come of moving beyond an embrace. I do not think he is wed, but even were he not..." He sighed. "I would not hurt you, but not only do you lack the noble and legitimate breeding to move him to marriage, you are no young woman with years ahead in which to birth enough babes to ensure at least one survives to continue his father's line."

Neither was she an old woman, Honore nearly retorted. However, had she years enough to birth a sizable brood, it would not change that not only was she likely born on the wrong side of the sheets, but had she noble blood it was diluted by common. Nor would it change that she had betrayed Elias.

"Your concern is appreciated, Your Grace, but just as I have no illusions I could be raised above my station as were you through friendship with our king, neither do I wish to live life for any but my foundlings. What you witnessed last eve was no more than compassion shown by a man who could not know he would regret it. Thus, Sir Elias has no need to be apprised of the reason I cover my face, and certainly no further cause to reject me." She stood. "That we may reach France whole, I shall leave you to your prayers."

He touched her arm. "I did not mean to offend."

"Fear not. I know my place in the world, and as I am certain it pleases God, I am content." She inclined her head, turned aside.

As she made her way past the oarsmen to Cynuit, she located Elias where he and his squire stood in the stern with their backs to her.

"I am content," she whispered into the wind. But the stirred air tossed the words into her face.

No more, she silently conceded. *But once Hart is safe, I shall seek to be content.*

CHAPTER 22

HER EYES, HER EYES

Boulogne
France

*A*ll was falling dark when the skiff gently slid onto the shore of Oye in Boulogne as if eased out of God's palm.

After offloading the passengers a league distant from the port of Gravelines, the captain took payment from one of the brethren and he and his crew put out to sea again.

When it became evident Thomas was so sick of stomach and weakened by exhaustion he was unable to complete the journey to Gravelines without assistance, Elias sent Theo with one of the archbishop's companions to secure mounts though it was unlikely any of worth would be found in the small community near the sea.

They returned with a single packhorse less worthy than expected. However, the animal sufficed to carry Thomas, allowing their party of eight to reach the town two hours after nightfall.

Just as throughout the remainder of the channel crossing

following the audience with the archbishop, no further word passed between Elias and Honore as they walked to Gravelines with Elias at the fore and his squire bringing up the rear.

At last they reached a wayside inn. The aid given Thomas having already greatly endangered the De Morvilles, Elias determined it best the two parties enter separately. But though tempted to consign Honore to the brethren, a single woman amongst men of God would draw more notice. Too, as he had not considered in Sandwich, it would be better if she appeared to be his wife. He did not like it, but as wroth as he was with her and the archbishop, he would protect both.

After the brethren aided in Thomas's dismount in the alley between inn and stables, Elias said, "Have any a small ring that can be set upon Honore's hand?"

"For what?" she asked.

"This eve you play a knight's wife. Granted, a humble, modest one."

Her eyes widened, and he thought she might protest, but Thomas said, "I have one." He raised hands above the cuffs of wide, hanging sleeves and tugged a ring from his smallest finger. "It may be too large, but do you keep your fingers together, none need know it was not given by Sir Elias." He extended it.

When she remained unmoving, Elias took it. "Given by Sir Elias, indeed," he said and lifted her hand, "though I do not know it will make the part easier to play." He slid the ring on. It was loose, but not noticeably so.

Her eyes rose from the simply elegant band, and he thought he glimpsed hurt there.

"Done," he said and looked to Thomas. "We go in first. If all appears safe, I will send Theo to you. When you enter, note where we sit and choose a table in back of us and well within sight so I can protect you should it be necessary."

The archbishop inclined his head. "We thank you, Sir Knight."

Elias looked to those he claimed as his own though Honore

would not much longer be among their ranks. "Speak little, listen much," he said, then took her arm and led her forward with the other two on their heels.

The inn was fairly crowded, forcing Elias to claim a central table not easily defensible should any think to increase their fortunes by setting on a nobleman surely in possession of far more coin than they.

After seating Honore to his right, he took the chair facing the entrance and motioned Theo into the one across from him so the squire could watch those at the rear. Cynuit dropped into the chair to Elias's left, lowered his head to the table, and sighed.

Elias could not deny the lad reprieve due one his age who had not complained despite being ill throughout the crossing and weak of knees as they made their way to Gravelines.

Once the other occupants of the inn were assessed and Elias determined who should be watched, he nodded for his squire to signal the brethren.

As Theo strode to the door, Honore set a hand on Elias's arm. "We are safe?"

Hating so simple a touch could make him overly aware of the space between them, he said, "We are not." When fear surfaced the beautiful blue, he added, "But the risk is acceptable."

She withdrew her hand.

As Elias ordered drinks and viands, Theo returned. Minutes later, the four men of God entered and garnered more interest than had Elias's party though all kept their heads covered as they strode amongst the tables. They passed, and he heard them take the table behind and to the left.

The din increased as others joined or began conversations, but there was a low hum about the inn, calling to mind wisdom imparted by the greatest trainer of knights, Baron Wulfrith.

Listen for the small voices, whether your own or others'. Oft they are small only because they carry such depth of meaning they have either come out of hiding or seek to hide.

Elias hoped he was wrong about those voices but doubted it. Aboard the skiff he had heard talk between the oarsmen of Thomas's flight from Northampton a fortnight past, the many days it had taken to reach Sandwich evidencing his route had been circuitous to evade capture. Likely, word of it had spread to France.

Though it could not be known he had reached these shores, his arrival must be expected. It was confirmed when Elias heard a man to his left rasp, "Do you think it him?"

Lord, Elias silently appealed, *if any move beyond speculation, I may have to offer further protection. Pray, let Thomas and his brethren be discreet.*

After the serving woman delivered drink and food, the furrowing of Theo's brow as he looked past Elias made his lord raise an eyebrow.

The young man leaned forward on the pretense of gaining a handful of nuts on the far side of the platter. "They have lowered their hoods, my lord."

Elias tensed, though greater suspicion over the holy men could be roused if they kept their faces concealed. Reaching to Theo's side of the platter, he pinched a piece of rye bread. "Are there shadows enough to conceal him?"

"Oui. He seated himself well, but…"

Theo glanced up at the serving woman who bustled past their table. "He is notable—his height, bearing, air of authority. If he speaks, I fear—"

The archbishop did speak, ordering for him and his companions in a voice that, though not loud, impressed upon listeners his refined diction and fluency of speech.

Silently naming him a fool, Elias wondered how Thomas had risen so far in station.

"He is going to reveal himself," Honore said low, and Elias saw her look sidelong at Thomas.

"Whatever happens," he said to her and Cynuit who lifted his head to partake of the meal, "you are to stay clear and await my command or Theo's."

Both nodded, and lest their table draw too much attention, Elias took a draught of ale and set about decimating the food—no difficult thing as hungry as he was.

Naught untoward happened as the newest arrivals at the inn availed themselves of drink and food. However, after the serving woman retrieved the empty platters, one whose orders to those attending the patrons told he was the innkeeper, approached the brethren's table.

Though the man's smile seemed genuine, Elias set a hand on his sword hilt and discreetly placed his feet and angled his body to launch himself from the chair.

"A fine establishment you have here," Thomas greeted the man.

"Lord, I thank God I am deemed worthy for you to grace my home."

Above Elias's inward groan, he heard Honore's sound of distress, but he did not spring to Thomas's defense. From the innkeeper's manner, it was not he who could prove a danger to the archbishop beyond the prideful words that could rouse those sympathetic to King Henry.

"Who am I, then?" Thomas asked with what seemed genuine confusion. "Am I not but Brother Christian?"

When the innkeeper spoke again, his voice was so low Elias barely heard. "I know you are a great man, though your king spreads tidings far and wide that Thomas, formerly Archbishop of Canterbury, fled the realm like a traitor."

As if pained by the denouncement, Thomas was slow to respond. "You do me great honor." Acquiescence carried upon his words. "I am in your debt, and more greatly shall I be if you have even the smallest, barest room in which my brethren and I may pass the night."

"The inn is full, Your Grace, but you shall have my quarters."

Elias did not catch Thomas's response but knew it was of

acceptance when he heard chairs scape as they parted ways with the table. Sidelong, he watched the brethren cross the room and ascend the stairs behind the innkeeper.

"What will you do?" Honore asked.

Elias glanced at Theo, noted Cynuit's head was down again. "It seems the holy man with no place to lay his head has found a room at the inn. It is we who shall bed down in the stables."

"And come the morrow?" Theo asked.

"Much depends on whether I am able to learn anything of the troupe, and that I shall seek to do whilst you, Honore, and Cynuit gain your rest." He glanced at the bar. "If there is anything to be known, there is where I shall find it." And he knew how to extract information that aroused the least amount of suspicion. He would turn performer, donning the behavior of a nobleman so eager to gain respite from a nagging wife he appeared to consume great quantities of drink whilst playing on the advances of any woman who saw him as easy coin. Though particularly averse to the latter that made ruin of Sisters of Mary by men who then named them Daughters of Eve, his attentions would not progress beyond a public embrace.

"Regardless," Elias said, "on the morrow we shall see the brethren set upon the road to Clairmarais so Thomas may rendezvous with his man."

Clairmarais, Honore mused, a Cistercian abbey inhabited by monks as well as nuns. "You intend to set me upon that same road," she said.

"The archbishop will arrange for your return to England. If Cynuit wishes to enter my service he may. If not, he shall accompany you."

She stood, looked to the squire. "I am tired. Will you escort Cynuit and me to the stables?"

You have no right to be angry with Elias, she told herself as Theo pushed upright. But she was and not only because he readied to leave her behind. He should not be so considerate and accommodating ere she gave him cause to be otherwise. Had he continued to treat her like the witch he first thought her, she might not have known how much more loss she must contain beyond that of Hart.

It was silly to feel this way about a man she hardly knew, especially one as far out of reach as was heaven for Lettice's murderer. The archbishop having seen she moved in a hopeless direction, she could not deny she had arrived—and wearing Elias's ring that was not truly his. Nor hers.

I do not love him, she told herself.

But you could, she dissented.

She turned, not for the first time noted the regard of the servant who attended tables on the other side of the room. The woman's eyes were all for Elias. Though she possessed a fairly plain face, were it as flawless as it appeared, she would be more appealing than the woman believed to be the knight's wife.

Shortly, Theo, Cynuit, and Honore made their beds in a large, vacant stall strewn with fresh straw by the stable boy given a coin to make it as comfortable as possible.

Too much aware of the loose ring on her hand, Honore did not expect to sleep, but she did. For a while.

THEO BREATHED DEEPLY. Cynuit snored softly. And Elias...

He yet sought information inside the inn. Or slept elsewhere.

Leaning against the stable wall to which she had put her back upon awakening, slowly rolling the ring on her finger, Honore peered through darkness at the bit of light between the stalls on this side of the building and the other side.

Feeling far from rested, she guessed the day she had crossed the channel had yielded to the day she would be abandoned here. And just as she would not likely remain long in France, quite possibly she would not see Hart—or Elias—again.

Throat tightening, she told herself to return to sleep. But she did not move off the wall even when she caught the grumblings of another also come to bed down in the stables.

"We were of an understanding, she and I, then he—"

"Hush on you, lad," a gruff voice rebuked. "There is nothing to be done."

"But he—"

"Is a nobleman. Always the greater coin and stronger, cleaner body take the prize."

"And the greater sin," the younger one snarled as the two briefly appeared in the aisle between the stalls. "Was that not the knight's wife with him?"

Honore ceased turning the ring at the realization it was Elias who offended.

"It would seem, lad. But pity the man wed to one either so frigid with modesty she can be no fiery brick in the marital bed or so unsightly she must cover near all her face."

"Then he should not have wed her!"

He had not—and would not—Honore thought and became aware of a weight on her chest. It was not all imagined, she realized when she looked to her ringed hand pressed between her breasts.

She closed her eyes, wished the pain there had naught to do with her heart, that Elias's tryst but made her question the character she had deemed honorable enough to safely travel with him unchaperoned. She believed it was the seeking of information that made him remain in the bar, but to learn it had become more for one whose final words to Lettice so touched her...

Regardless, all the more reason not to enlighten him about the possibility Finwyn had fathered Hart. And all the more reason to keep hidden what Elias would think unsightly at best, poor luck at worst.

The quieting of footsteps told the men must have found a stall to accommodate them, the only sound above that of disturbed horses being groans of relief.

Honore removed her hand from her chest, hooked fingers in the gorget, and dragged it down. She touched the imperfect bow on the right side, slid a finger up the unnatural ridge.

Unsightly, as Lady Yolande and others at Bairnwood named it though the abbess scorned such. Like Abbess Abigail, Lady Susanna had called it a small thing, and that it would be were it upon one's arm. It was altogether different on one's face, especially that of a woman. Were Honore a man, it could be esteemed as a scar won in battle, and were the one who bore it other than a fighting man, facial hair could cover it. However, among other less than desirable circumstances of birth, Honore had been born a woman, though not even such a woman as the one with whom Elias now kept company.

She cringed over that last regret. Though that woman might be in the arms of a man for whom Honore felt, she could not envy one who gave body, dignity, and faith for coin, whether out of desperation, desire, or both.

This defect of birth could be tenfold worse, and still she would be blessed not to be the one upon whom Elias might now father another Hart.

She eased down the wall. And did not cry.

CHAPTER 23

HER LIPS DENY

*N*o sleep, but much had come of the night.

Elias's vigil on a stool at the bar yielded up tidings of a troupe recently arrived from England that had passed through Gravelines a sennight gone as they journeyed to Saint-Omer, a fort northeast of Thomas's destination of Clairmarais Abbey. Though the troupe may have moved on, it was there Elias would journey even if only to learn their next destination. God willing, it was the same troupe that made perversion of those born different from others.

Elias had also learned more about that which caused the Archbishop of Canterbury to flee England. Having refused to give way on the rights of the Church which King Henry wished bent to his will, Thomas found himself accused of embezzling royal funds whilst he held the office of chancellor.

Elias could not know if there was truth to the charge, but the heart with which he ought not think was moved to believe it was an attempt to control a man determined to answer to his heavenly sovereign ahead of his earthly one.

That hard stool had been of further benefit, allowing Elias to ensure a measure of safety for the brethren sleeping overhead. Had a commotion ensued, in moments he could have been abovestairs with sword in hand.

The serving woman who had often sought his gaze across the room whilst he was at meal had furthered his purpose, aiding his performance so none would question it. She had hung on his shoulder, shared his drink, and several times scooted onto his lap. Once the tables were mostly vacated he had made it appear he so succumbed to drink he could not move from the bar.

Clumsily, he had removed coins from his purse, pressed them into her hand, then dropped his head atop the leather bag—a seemingly drunken move that ensured none cut his purse from his belt.

The woman had departed, and during the hours remaining of night, Elias made it appear he slept off his stupor. It gave him time in which to think on all that had transpired these past days. And the woman he must pardon for the greater role in the part she had unwittingly played when he conspired with Finwyn to summon her. Before he left her at the abbey, he would forgive her.

Now once more leading the brethren, this time along a fairly well-traveled road to Clairmarais and Saint-Omer beyond, Elias's head throbbed from lack of sleep and disquiet over an encounter with a mounted knight an hour past.

The young man and his companions had indulged in falconry, as evidenced by a prize bird on the knight's wrist.

Thomas's hood had been down. Had that not raised suspicion amongst those who surely knew the Archbishop of Canterbury sought sanctuary in France, his great interest in the gyrfalcon would have. Of the exploits abandoned upon his resignation of the chancellorship to devote himself to his new position with the Church, probably best known was his passion for falconry.

Thus, shortly after the young knight bestowed on Elias a scornful lift of the eyebrows, doubtless over his fellow nobleman's foul and mountless state, he had called out, "Is this not the errant Archbishop of Canterbury?"

Though enough distance was maintained between Elias's party and the brethren to make it appear they but traveled the same road and lessen further exposing Elias to association with his liege's enemy, he had readied mind and body to defend Thomas.

It had not been necessary, the guffawing of one of the brethren and scorn of another who said the pompous, extravagant archbishop would never lower himself to travel so humbly causing the hunting party to pass by without further comment.

Now a rumble raised Elias's gaze to the darkening heavens no longer in a mood to delay the storm gathered to its bosom. Still, he would push their party to slog through it. He wanted to believe the young knight would forget the encounter, but danger lurked in the possibility he would revisit it, even if only to tell a good tale that could alert others the archbishop headed in the direction of Saint-Omer.

A quarter hour later, the rain added hail to its assault on the travelers, turning the road muddy and slippery.

It was the one who had avoided him all day—speaking few words and averting her gaze—who caused them to seek shelter when pelting ice knocked her slippered feet out from under her as it only threatened those who wore boots.

Cynuit reached her first, but Elias scooped her up.

Muddied chest pressed to his, she hooked an arm around his neck and set her face against his shoulder as he commanded all to follow him into the wood.

Shelter was not easily found, but finally Theo called from where he scouted ahead and led them to an outcropping of rock whose chiseled center was deep enough to offer protection from the onslaught and high enough for all to enter without bending.

"I thank you," Honore murmured when set to her feet, then turned from Elias to adjust veil and gorget.

She was a mess and had made him one, but that was not the

reason he begrudged aiding her. Despite her deception, too much he liked the feel of her.

While they waited out the weather, they partook of provisions provided by the innkeeper with whom Thomas had spent time in prayer before departing the inn.

Elias left Honore to herself while she ate apart from the others, but when it was clear she had finished, he decided to settle things between them as much as possible.

He crossed to where she sat with her back him. "I do it for Hart," he said. "More easily I can aid him with you safely tucked away."

Her head turned slightly toward him. "I understand." There was no muffle to her voice, evidencing the gorget remained beneath her chin. "Is that all?"

It should be. "I also understand, Honore."

"What?"

"The archbishop's deception. Perhaps even yours."

She secured the gorget, stood and turned. "I wish I had not deceived you, but I feared if you thought it the archbishop who would sooner deliver us to France, you would not give aid and it could be long ere a crossing was possible—days that could matter to Hart."

Though it was dim and the storm beyond made it difficult for others to hear their exchange, Elias stepped nearer. "Days which would have been of no benefit to him had the guard at Sandwich intercepted us. Though we escaped, now the threat of disposal hangs over all that is not yet mine to dispose of."

"I am sorry, but I believe the life of the boy who may be your son is more important. Too, you made a promise."

He raised his eyebrows.

"I heard the words you spoke to Lettice. They were so heartfelt I believed you worthy of the trust required for me to travel with you."

He did not want to return to that dark hovel and the one who had not been of great height but of a length of rope, but there he was again. *Whither thou goest my heart's first love,* he had said to one long gone, *I go not until your son is safe and justice done. My vow I give.*

"If you meant it," Honore said, "then I am justified in denying you the temptation of showing more concern for your lands than Lettice's son."

"I meant it," he said sharply. "I will find Hart, but even to keep such a promise I would not become thief nor executioner."

"Thief? Executioner?"

"Thoughtlessly endangering my family as it appears I have done. I would have given time to considering other means of retrieving the boy who may be—"

He closed his mouth. Though the miscreant with whom he had found the woman he loved could as easily be Hart's father, in that moment he determined that no matter his sire's disapproval and anger over a half-common boy bearing the family name, henceforth Hart of no surname had one. "I would have sought another means of more quickly retrieving Hart De Morville."

Honore gasped at hearing him claimed. It warmed one side of her that found much to admire in Elias, chilled the other lest it prove a false claim that gave him naught to admire in her. Though she longed to seek confirmation he would stay true to his word even if he knew with certainty Hart was not his, she could not risk it—especially if it led him to consider the foul Finwyn had fathered the boy. If anything caused him to abandon his vow to Lettice, it would be that, whether out of distaste for the boy or Hart's abduction being of less concern committed by a parent.

Elias sighed. "As difficult as you have made this for me and mine, I know you did what you believed was right. Now tell, what else do you keep from me?"

She dropped back a step.

His eyes momentarily closed. "There *is* something."

Glad he gave her no opportunity to lie, she said, "Though later I may bear your wrath, it cannot be revealed."

"When?"

"I do not know it will be necessary, but my word I give you will know it should you need to."

His nostrils flared. "So just as I resolve to forgive your deception, I learn once more you would have me venture forth half blind."

She gripped his arm. "What I do not tell has little bearing on what we do in France." Providing, she did not say, he stayed true to his promise.

He glanced at her hand on him, and she saw what he saw—that which she had worked around and around since first it was placed there to proclaim her the wife she could never be.

"If what you withhold further harms my family, I do not know I will be able to forgive you, Honore."

"I am aware."

He pulled free and, as he started to turn away, said, "As soon as the weather lifts, we resume our journey."

Clasping her right hand over the left, feeling the ring temporarily binding them, she said, "Elias?"

He looked around.

"I understand why you shall leave me at Clairmarais, but rather than arrange for my return to England, allow me to remain there until Hart is found so I may see him one last time and be assured he is well."

Refusing her answer, he returned to the others.

CHAPTER 24

WHAT TRUTH THE BLUE HATH SPOKE

Clairmarais Abbey
France

*H*erbert of Bosham was shocked and made no pretense of it, even when Thomas chastised him for clucking over a grown man. But no further word did he speak on how wretched the archbishop appeared.

Jaw clenched, a tic at his mouth, the man who had preceded Thomas in fleeing France accepted introductions to Elias's party, then said low, though not so much others could not hear, "You are certain they can be trusted, Your Grace?"

Thomas's faint smile showed in the light of torches set on either side of the abbey's gate. "I do not believe I would be here without their aid. At much cost they have done as the Lord would have them do."

Elias's patience approaching a length beyond which it could stretch no further, it being dark and all damp, chilled, and exhausted, he said, "What news have you from England?"

Herbert flashed him a look between annoyance and resentment, said, "Come, Your Grace, there is much to discuss and little time."

Having dismounted, Thomas raised his hunched shoulders and stepped through the narrow doorway at the center of the large gate. And halted so abruptly his brethren jostled each other to avoid trampling him. "Little time?" he said before Elias could ask the same.

"After I have arranged accommodations for this knight and his party, I shall take you to the abbot. He is eager to welcome Your Grace."

"Sir Elias and the others shall join us."

"But—"

"Do not argue, Herbert. As your urgency bodes ill, whatever news you have of England will likely affect those who aided me."

The man grunted, then led them not through the great courtyard but into a dim alley that barely allowed two to walk abreast—acceptable only if one did not require room in which to wield a sword.

Not given to letting down his guard in unfamiliar confines, Elias gently pushed Honore in back of him, looked past her to ensure Theo took up the rear behind Cynuit, and set a hand on his sword hilt.

"By what way do we go, Herbert?" the archbishop asked.

"All will be explained, Your Grace. Suffice to say, it is best we discreetly gain the abbot's quarters."

Elias liked this even less. Were the brethren not between him and Thomas's man, he would demand an explanation.

Shortly, light swept into the passage. "Make haste," Herbert rasped, and when he closed and bolted the door behind Theo, his sigh of relief was so great the scent of onions swept over all.

He led the procession down a short corridor and up wooden steps whose creak and groan would announce their arrival well in advance. Though it appeared to be a back way to the abbot's quarters, Elias thought it might be more discreet to use the main stairway.

Herbert's three quick raps on the door granted them entrance, and all filed into a room more sumptuous than would be expected had Elias not known the purpose of the stairway they ascended.

Beautiful tapestries warmed the walls, thick rugs covered the floor, an oaken table set around with upholstered chairs was at the center, two standing desks were in opposite corners, a stone fireplace radiated heat, and a sideboard boasted food and drink.

The abbot, shorter than Thomas and a score of years older, was less kind with his shock over the archbishop's appearance, but there could be no doubt he was concerned for the well-being of the man whose hand he bent over. A hand to which had been returned the ostentatious ring of Thomas's office that in no way resembled the one loaned Honore.

"Your Grace, it is an honor to welcome you to Clairmarais."

"I thank you for your hospitality, Abbot." When Thomas's hand was released, it dropped so heavily it swung.

"Methinks you ought to offer the archbishop a seat, Abbot," Elias said. "The journey has been arduous."

The holy man looked to the knight whose damp, muddied garments must be an offense, and a question rose in his eyes, likely over the reason for Elias's presence. Then he said, "Forgive me, Your Grace. I must seem foolish to be so distracted by your presence." He motioned to two monks on the far side of the room where they stood alongside arched doors beyond which would be a stairway worthier than the one ascended.

The monks hurried forward, pulled out chairs on either end of the table, then those between.

Thomas started to lower into the nearest, but the abbot entreated him to take a high-backed chair so broad it looked almost a throne.

Soon all were seated and a blessing spoken over the meal. As the monks carried platters and pitchers to the table, once more introductions were made, this time by Herbert.

"I know of the De Morvilles," the abbot said as he considered Elias. "Is not the second son now heir?"

"I am, Abbot. My brother passed."

The man arched an eyebrow. "You were thought to have passed before him."

Beside Elias, Honore stirred despite fatigue that surely made her long for bed. And now she would know even more about Elias than he knew of her, and there was shame in that.

The tale the abbot probed was of a son so discontented and selfish he had pained his father. Following the eldest son's death and unaware the youngest yet lived, Otto De Morville had sought to make more male heirs on an exceedingly young wife whose body had given what it could—daughters only—before ruination that would see no more children born to her aged husband.

"With much regret, I was thought to have died," Elias allowed.

The abbot nodded. "Was it to England you went with your poems, songs, and dance?"

More stirring beside Elias.

"Abbot, we understand there is much to discuss and little time to do so," he said.

The holy man waved a hand. "Now you are here, we have time. Let us first satisfy your hunger and thirst."

Longing to shake the man, Elias watched curiosity rise on his face as he moved his attention to the woman in their midst. "Honore of Bairnwood," he said. "How do I know the name?"

Elias felt her glance. "I work with foundlings."

"With what?"

"Foundlings."

He leaned forward. "As my hearing has begun to fail, pray do not exercise such modesty in the company of godly men, my lady. Lower your gorget so I may hear you better."

She eased back in her chair as if he were near enough to divest her of the covering, said more loudly, "You are kind to think me a lady, especially as fouled as I am by travel, but I am not. I am but Honore, and it is my habit to wear a gorget in this manner."

"But you cannot eat or drink."

"Thus, perhaps you will allow me to take my meal where I shall rest this eve."

He sighed, and as if forgetting the answer her muffled voice had denied him, began picking at the viands on his plate.

Elias leaned toward Honore. "Certes, you hunger and thirst. I will arrange for you to be shown to your lodgings."

"Non, I shall remain."

Frustrated she denied herself sustenance, he kept his hand nearest her firm on his thigh lest he yank down the gorget to allow her to eat. "As you will," he said and set about curtailing his own hunger.

The archbishop was also eager to make quick work of the meal, his long, elegant fingers popping morsel after morsel into his mouth. With minimal chewing, he swallowed and, shortly, pushed away his plate. Motioning the others to continue eating, he looked to Herbert. "Begin at Canterbury. What did you gain there, my friend?"

Herbert's mouth flattened. "Not as much as hoped—one hundred marks and some silver cups."

Thomas's breath shuddered from him. "Disappointing, but that is the least of my concerns, is it not?"

"Permit me," the abbot said and cleared his throat. "On the day past, Your Grace, Henry sent envoys to France by way of Dover— two groups, one to ride to Sens to meet with the pope and seek your deposition, the other to meet with King Louis at Compiègne to gain his assurance he will deny you refuge."

Thomas's hand atop the table curled into a fist. "I am guessing Gilbert Foliot and the Earl of Arundel are among the envoy."

"They are. Also there is Hilary of Chichester and Roger of Pont l'Evêque. But they are of no immediate concern. That to

which you must attend is Saint-Omer since it is where you mean
to go next, is it not?"

"It is."

"Either delay, Your Grace, or bypass. Henry's envoys lodge
there this eve."

Where Elias hoped to find the troupe.

"God help me," the archbishop murmured. "You can
accommodate us a day or two until they set off?"

"We can, Your Grace, but circumstances dictate you leave us
this eve."

"My presence endangers you?"

"Non, you are the one in danger and, quite possibly, Sir Elias.
This day, three soldiers from Sandwich arrived at our gate."

Heart beating hard, Elias heard Honore swallow, felt Thomas's
eyes shoot to him.

"They enquired if three—mayhap four—brethren in the
company of a knight and his companions paused at Clairmarais,"
the abbot continued. "When I said we had no such visitors, they
requested several nights lodging whilst they search the vicinity.
Lest you arrived this night, I had them placed in rooms at the rear
of the guest house to lessen the possibility they noted your
entrance. As further precaution, Herbert delivered you to my
apartment by way of the rear stairs."

"Then I cannot remain even one night."

Truth, Elias silently agreed. If those from Sandwich laid
hands on the ones responsible for the fallen on the beach,
capture by King Henry could prove of less detriment. And here
was another truth—whilst the soldiers lodged here, Honore
could not.

But an excuse, his conscience elbowed him. *The abbot can keep
her hidden until his guests depart. Think better on it, Elias De Morville.*

He would. Later.

"I believe it safe providing you depart ere first light, Your
Grace," the abbot said. "You and the brethren may take my

sleeping chamber, and there are two rooms at the back of the chapel where pallets can be laid for the others."

Thomas shook his head. "I fear it best we leave this eve."

"I can arrange for a rowboat to take us across the marshes to Oldminster," Herbert said.

Elias frowned. "Oldminster?"

"A hermitage not far from here," the abbot supplied. "Oui, it seems the best course. There you shall have days aplenty in which to recover, giving Sandwich's soldiers and the king's men time to distance themselves."

Though Elias balked at the troupe gaining a greater lead and further exposing his family to Henry's wrath, he said to Herbert, "Is the crossing to Oldminster safe?"

"It is. Your services are no longer required, Sir Knight."

Elias looked to Thomas who inclined head. "Here we part ways, De Morville. But know this, regardless of what becomes of Thomas the archbishop, formerly Thomas the chancellor, never shall our tales cross. Does history remember my name, it shall not do so alongside yours. Never will it tell of the great service rendered me."

Elias felt Honore's relief nearly as much as his own. Even if the troupe he followed to Saint-Omer was not the one they sought, he would be days nearer to finding Hart. "Then we shall avail ourselves of the rooms, Abbot."

"And horses," Thomas said. "I am sure Clairmarais can provide worthy mounts to speed your journey."

With reluctance, the abbot agreed, then directed the monks to lay three pallets in one room, one pallet in the other.

Honore rose with the others and made it to Thomas's side ahead of Elias. "Your Grace?"

He motioned his brethren to continue. "Honore?"

She removed the ring. "No longer do I need this."

He glanced at Elias where he halted beside her. "You are certain?"

"I am."

He took it, mused, "A gift from Henry during our younger, better years." He touched one of the small sapphires, then sighed so long his chest sunk. "As it no longer holds meaning for either of us, I give it to you, Honore." He extended it, and when she stared, caught up her hand and returned the ring to her finger.

"Your Grace—"

"If not in remembrance of me and gratitude owed you, accept it that you may sell it to aid your foundlings."

"But—"

"It will bring a pretty sum," he spoke over her again, then made the sign of the cross. "May God bless and speed your journey, my friends."

They gave back his words, but the parting with the Archbishop of Canterbury was delayed a moment longer when he drew Honore aside. For her ears alone, he said, "I pray Sir Elias and you find your son, Honore."

Then he was gone as if their tales had never crossed.

CHAPTER 25

PRAY DO NOT HIDE

*H*eart heavy over the parting with Thomas, once more Honore tried to distract herself from his choice of words.

Your son, he had said with more than singular meaning, as if she would parent Hart alongside Elias. He erred. And in another thing—that she would further participate in the search for Hart. When she arose in the morn, Cynuit and she would be under the abbot's protection, Elias and Theo gone.

Having satisfied thirst and hunger, she rose from the wool-stuffed pallet in the room given her separate from the others.

Were they abed? She guessed they must be, having heard no sound from the other side of the wall for a quarter hour.

Though she had raked snarls from her hair and washed her face and hands in a basin of water, still she was unclean, the mud in which she had slipped having soaked through her garments.

Having earlier secured her door, she unclothed and washed the dried dirt from her body, then opened her pack and removed the change of clothes wrapped in linen and bound with twine.

The bundle was so thick she was certain Lady Susanna had provided two changes of clothing, but it was one, the thickness due to quality Honore had only seen worn by ladies of the convent.

She held her breath as she unfolded a lustrous dark red overgown Lady Susanna had said belonged to her mother who had been taller and of a more sizable bosom than herself. Next, an undergown of the same color but of a lighter fabric, then a thin chemise and hose.

These were hardly the garments of a servant. Upon her person she would appear the lady she had played at Gravelines and look far more the impossible—Elias's wife.

She considered returning them to the pack, but it was either look and feel what she was not or look and feel less than she was. She lifted the chemise above her head. It was so soft and light drifting down over her that it seemed little more than a cool breeze come through a window.

She slid her hands down the fabric. Though Lady Susanna had said she need not return the garments, she would send them to Cheverel when her journey with Elias was done. Once she was back at Bairnwood, there would be no occasion to clothe herself in finery. All this would be memory and, providing Hart was recovered, one secretly cherished. Though not as cherished as...

"Child," she named herself what one thirty and two years ought to be ashamed to affix to her person. Elias had been within reach only as long as he played the part that made it acceptable for a woman not of ill repute to travel with men.

Fingering the embroidered neckline, she recalled what she had learned of him at Cheverel when Lady Susanna and she attended to his tale, then what the abbot had added in revealing that before the young man became a knight he had been of poems, songs, and dance. And for that had deserted his family and country.

She doubted she would ever know the tale of when the name Cant replaced De Morville, but she longed for it. And him.

Ashamed her heart and mind had drifted so far from where they belonged—with the boy Finwyn had stolen who had likely suffered much humiliation, perhaps even abuse, she considered the comfort of the chapel beyond the door.

More than sleep, she needed prayer.

Refusing to allow herself to linger over the fit and feel of her garments, she donned hose, undergown, and overgown. And paused over damp slippers she had wiped as clean as possible, the insides having been nearly as muddied as the outsides. Since the altar could not be more than twenty paces from her room, she could do without footwear.

Though tempted to leave the gorget ever she removed whilst at prayer, until certain she was alone in the chapel she would wear it. But not the veil.

Quietly, she unbolted her door so she would not rouse those sleeping in the next room, and opened it only wide enough to slip through. Leaving the door ajar, she traversed the short corridor amid the whisper of skirts rather than the rustle to which she was accustomed.

She did not realize her hands had caught up material as soft as a babe's skin until shivers coursed her sensitive palms.

She splayed her fingers, clasped her hands at her waist, and surveyed the chapel lit by a dozen candles on the altar. She had it to herself.

Continuing forward, she tugged down the gorget, then prostrated herself behind a wide kneeler where she would finish her prayers after the chill floor ensured it was her beseechings rather than the breath of sleep in God's ears.

As she settled in, she felt a presence and nearly looked around lest she was watched by one of flesh.

It is our Lord in this Holy place, she assured herself. *He who sees me. He who hears me. He who will save Hart.*

~

THE DARK RED OF A ROSE. And nearly the shape, as if that flower in full bloom, cupped in the hand of God, had loosed the first of many petals and that single one drifted from on high to the floor before the altar.

Kind Susanna. Before Elias could ask her to provide Honore a change of clothes, she had informed him she had done so, but he had not thought to ensure she chose ones that would not draw attention. The color of the gown was extravagant, the quality and style befitting a most noble lady.

For an hour of the first watch Elias had taken, he had stood at corridor's end observing the woman who sought to slip from her room without awakening others. But he had heard her restlessness on the other side of the wall, then the slow slide of the bolt and opening door.

He had let her go, guessing she wished to pray. And so she did, though as fatigued as she was, he had expected she would not long prostrate herself. If not for occasional whispers that revealed she had lowered the gorget, he might have thought she slept.

Having exited the room shared with Theo and Cynuit only after he could do so without alerting her to the watch he kept over her, he had come too late to glimpse the face now exposed to the floor, but when she rose he should be able to see all of it—providing she completed her prayers before the candles snuffed their charred wicks in pools of hot wax.

He shifted his shoulders where he leaned against a wall, rolled his head side to side, stilled when Honore sat back on her heels.

Chin lowered, hair curtaining her face, she remained unmoving as if she yet prayed, then stood.

Elias straightened in anticipation of returning her to her room, but she kept her head down. Yet denying him the whole of her face, she stepped to the altar, settled on the kneeler, and clasped her hands atop the shelf. Doubtless, more prayer for Hart.

That thought led to another that had not found its end. Did he or did he not allow Honore and Cynuit to accompany him to Saint-Omer? Garbed in such vibrant clothes Honore would draw attention, but not the unwelcome sort for any searching for the party that included a woman simply clothed—providing she could be persuaded to eschew the gorget whose unusual placement made her appear to be from middle eastern lands.

That would decide it. If she agreed, she would depart with him ere dawn.

So he would not startle her, he strode forward absent stealth. But she remained at prayer, even when he halted alongside her.

He considered the kneeler and was moved to join her, it being weeks since he had humbled himself in prayer.

"Elias," she whispered.

Surprised by her acknowledgment, he lowered beside her. And there was the reaction expected, which made him feel the fool for not realizing it was in prayer she spoke his name—head snapping around, candle-lit eyes springing wide, lips...

Her imperfectly bowed mouth opened to take in breath she expelled on a cry that she tried to shove back inside by clapping a hand over what the gorget had hidden.

"Honore!" Elias turned a hand around her arm, rose with her, and lost hold of her when she wrenched away. He could have caught her back, but lest she think he aggressed, he engaged his longer stride, passed her, and turned into her path.

With a flurry of red skirts and tumble of golden hair, she halted. Above the hand gripping her lower face, she looked from him to the corridor beyond.

"Forgive me." He raised a hand. "I did not—"

She sprang to the side.

He followed. "Honore, hear me."

"Non!" Her muffled protest became a whimper when her flight ended in a corner to the right of the altar. Back to him, she said, "Leave me!"

Not wishing to incur accusation of trespass as dealt at the stream, he left ten feet between them. "Do not fear me."

"Pray, go!"

"Honore—"

"Go!"

He sighed. "I am coming to you."

She swept around. Hand over her mouth, she looked right and left, then as if accepting she could not slip past him, thrust her back into the corner.

He halted, leaving a reach between them.

Honore turned her face to the side, as best she could distancing him from what he now knew was scarred though in Sandwich he had thought the distortion a shadow.

"Do not look at me!" With her free hand, she snatched at the material gathered beneath her chin.

"Why?"

Her eyes flicked to his, flicked away. "You have seen why."

"So I have, and for that I ask what you do not answer."

"It needs no further answer! Cease playing with me."

He stepped nearer. When he caught the fingers seeking to position the gorget, her chin came up. As she strained to free herself, he saw her other hand clasped her lower face so tightly its nails would leave marks.

"Honore, I do not play—"

She snatched her fingers free, but also the gorget. Its ties having come undone, her arm's forward motion pulled it from her shoulders and loosed it from her hold. As she grabbed for it, she came up against Elias.

Cupping her shoulder, he eased her back. "I do not mean to distress you."

Her lashes swept up.

"My word I give, I play no game." He smiled encouragingly, then lifted his other hand and set his fingers on the backs of hers that marked her face. "Let me look closer upon you." Lightly, he drew his thumb across the side of hers pressed beneath her nose.

She shook her head, between her fingers said, "I am no monster, nor devil-touched. I am the way God made me."

Then what he had seen was no injury. This the reason for her passion for foundlings? Once she had been one? "This I know. Do you think it makes me feel differently toward you?"

"Of course it does."

She was right, the attraction he battled for feeling what he should not so soon after Lettice's murder had grown. The bowed mouth he had imagined as perfectly shaped was not, one of two gentle ridges between nose and lips far from gentle. But not unsightly, though from her reaction someone had named it that. It marred her loveliness but was naught against the whole of her—like a small bruise on a sweetly crisp apple fallen from its branch whilst its sisters clung to their places among the leaves in the hope someone thought them perfect enough to climb up after them. Many there, especially amongst the topmost branches, would go to rot whilst the fortunate passerby delighted over what he nearly trod upon.

"You do feel differently," she said.

He pulled himself out of his imaginings. "You are right, but what I feel is opposite what you fear."

She gasped. "You think to dangle me from a string!"

"I do not." He dipped his thumb against the base of hers, gently pried at her hand. "Show me, and do you watch me, you will see what I see."

Her gaze wavered. "Elias," she protested but ceased resisting.

He eased her hand down, and as he shifted to allow candlelight to more clearly illuminate her face, felt the intensity of her moist gaze. He did not fear it, since he need not engage the actor to hide revulsion over a scar that began just shy of her nostril and coursed a fairly straight line down the right bow to the indented under curve of her lip that hitched slightly above even teeth. What he feared was the longing to know her mouth better by way of his own.

"Words forsake you," she whispered. "I do not know it is better than speaking as you find."

Raising his gaze in which she would have to imagine revulsion to find any, he said, "I think you more lovely."

Anger leaping from her, she raised her chin higher. "You are more adept at playing a part than thought. Though this is no longer monstrous as it must have been upon a babe ere it was sewn closed, there is naught lovely about it."

"Honore—"

"Unless your sight is exceedingly poor, you can see how wrong my lip is."

"I see the scar, and it is a small thing."

She laughed derisively. "You speak the same as Lady Susanna."

"She looked upon you?"

"I did not mean her to, but she did—and said the same as you, though I know not how either of you can expect me to believe it."

"We speak in truth. It *is* a small thing."

"It is not! It drags up one side, making me appear to sneer. Not even a young, beautiful woman appeals when disgust contorts her mouth."

"You are wrong. For this ever you hide half your face?"

"I do not. I refuse to be ashamed. I…" She seamed her lips.

"Continue." He bent his head so near he felt the warmth between their brows. "I want to understand."

Honore peered up at the man who set himself over her, his breath mingling with hers that stole past lips he would have her believe did not disfigure her face. Only once before had she found herself like this, a slight lean and tilt of the head away from her first kiss.

"Tell me," Elias said.

Here in God's house was not the place to do so with their bodies touching, but she said, "His name was Uther, a young monk who accompanied his bishop to Bairnwood. He was handsome and kind. When I was ten and six, he happened on me in the courtyard. We walked and talked, and he asked the reason I wore the gorget as I do." She swallowed. "I told him a lady of the convent insisted I cover my lower face when I moved amongst her and others. He said he did not know why that was necessary, as pretty as I was, and surely she was jealous. We were very near, and when he said it was impossible to kiss a girl with her mouth hidden, I could not think what to say or do. Then he lowered the gorget and..." She swallowed. "He did not like what he found and crossed himself all the way out of the courtyard and never again did he accompany the bishop."

"Then he was more a fool and even less a man of God," Elias growled.

Her throat tightened. "I did not give him sufficient warning and, unlike you, he was not adept at bending his feelings out of their natural shape."

"You think that is what I do? That is why I do not fumble for words and distance myself?"

She raised her eyebrows. "Does not Elias Cant know well his audience?"

"It is not the troubadour before you, Honore. It is Elias De Morville whom you wrongly judge. Hence, no reason to hide your face and no cause to fear my wrath."

His wrath? Why did he think she—?

She nearly caught her breath at the realization he thought this the other thing she had kept from him besides Thomas's identity. But then, as she had said it had little bearing on what they did in France, the covering of her lower face was a better fit than the reality of Finwyn's claim on Hart.

"Believe me," he prompted.

"If 'tis true my sneer does not trouble you, Elias, it is only because candlelight is far kinder than Uther's light of day."

"I would not have you judge me by another man's feeble,

childish behavior, Honore. But if you must, I think there a remedy for that which you name a sneer."

"You think wrong. My defect was remedied as much as possible, for which I am grateful since it allows me to work with foundlings without cover that would otherwise make them fearful of me."

"What I speak of is a smile, Honore. Surely you know how to do that, even if only for your little ones."

She gasped. "*That* is your remedy? Simply smile and my scar will disappear?"

"As long I have known how beautiful your eyes"—

Long? She snatched hold of the word that made it sound as if years had passed since they met.

—"and now how pretty your teeth, methinks if you add a slightly imperfect smile even Bairnwood's foul noblewoman would find naught amiss. So oui, simply smile."

Feeling more heat than her new garments could impart, Honore said, "If you are right, and I do not think it, what am I to do when there is naught to smile about?" It was a silly, argumentative question, but more and more she feared what he did to her. If she frustrated or angered him, perhaps he would give her space to distance herself.

"There is almost always something to smile about," Elias said, "even if but for the moment, even if that moment can be had only by casting into the past—or future."

"If only for a moment, why bother?" she furthered the argument.

"The sweetest of life is made of moments—"

"As are the vilest."

Were candlelight on him as much as her, she was certain she would see frustration. "Hence," he said gruffly, "seek the moments you would have number themselves into years. If you are blessed, they will."

Here the poet, seemingly without effort sliding words onto her emotions like beads on a string. And Elias was the clasp toward which her heart aspired—one that would never be strong enough to allow moments over which to smile and dream to number into years.

Infatuation, she told herself. *From it you can recover, but do you not cease, ever you may carry the hurt of what cannot be.*

For this she was grateful he would leave her at Clairmarais. For however long it took him to deliver tidings of his search for Hart, alongside prayer for the boy's recovery she would pray away what she ought not feel for this man.

She moistened her upper lip, winced over the dip. "I require my gorget, Sir Elias."

"You do not."

"While I am out in your world, I do. Pray, step away so I may retrieve it."

"You have naught to hide. As told, you are lovely. As not yet told, henceforth it is of benefit you not—"

"Lovely enough to kiss?" Scorn leapt from her even as regret over the impulsive response landed like a stone in her belly. If not an invitation, it sounded a challenge. If not a challenge, pleading.

"I-I did not mean that."

His eyes lowered to her mouth, and she realized no air moved between them. Then he angled his head.

When she jerked back and her head struck the wall, Elias slid a hand into her hair and gently probed her scalp. More than ache there, she felt the warmth of his touch like embers that slowly, languorously drifted up through her. "Forgive me," he said, "I did not mean to startle you. I believed you ready to be kissed."

Then he had thought it an invitation.

The servant of Bairnwood wishing he would remove his person from her, the never-before-kissed woman hoping he would not, she said, "I know it sounded that, but they were only angry, thoughtless words."

"Then you do not wish to be kissed?"

"Not by one who does not truly wish to kiss me." More words she regretted.

"What of one who more than wishes to kiss you?"

The shake of her head was nearer a shudder. "I would be a fool to believe you so inclined."

"And I would be a fool not to kiss you, Honore."

CHAPTER 26

BE BY HIS SIDE

The hand cupping the back of Honore's head drew her forward, and when their mouths met, she surely knew what so many before her knew—the lips were wonderfully sensitive, and what happened above affected all below, weakening her head to toe. But when she slid her hands around Elias's neck, he groaned and lifted his head.

She felt his gaze but did not open her eyes, instead savored something she had thought never to experience that would not likely happen again.

Finally, Elias said, "Is this not something about which to smile?"

That too. And she did as she raised her lids.

His eyes moved from hers to her mouth. As the self-consciousness she deplored slunk back, he said, "A pretty smile. Still..."

She tensed.

"...it is more. It is beautiful."

"Beautiful?" she exclaimed.

"Have you never looked in a mirror, Honore?"

"I have no access to such, but it is enough to catch my reflection in water, glass, upon a silver platter—and in eyes ere they scuttle away. Be assured, I know it well."

"You do not. All those distort. Thus, if you will not take my word for how lovely your smile, I shall have to secure a mirror, else in the light of day you must dwell longer on your reflection in my eyes."

She knew she should resist such talk, but he seemed so sincere she could not fight a bowing of lips and show of teeth only ever achieved when the weather was temperate enough to allow her foundlings to venture to the walled enclosure that had once been a neglected garden. The abbess having granted Honore's request to transform a portion into a play area, there the children crawled, ran, jumped, sang, and laughed distant from those who might approve of Bairnwood's commitment to saving unwanted children but did not wish to hear or see the fruits of those labors.

"Beautiful, indeed." Elias returned her to this abbey where it was not her arms holding a contented child but his holding a woman who longed for contentment. "Granted, your smile has a mischievous slant, but it is all the more entrancing. Hence, do you unnecessarily concern yourself over this small scar..." His thumb brushed it. "...as told, you have but to smile, dear Honore."

Dear. Might she be that to him? Or was he only being kind? Worse, what if he but sought to seduce her? Had she not overheard the young man at Gravelines complain Elias had stolen from him the favors of a serving woman she would not have considered such, but as he so soon sought intimacy following the loss of Lettice, perhaps he was even better at playing a part than believed.

Seeing he frowned, she realized she had lowered her smile. "For pity's sake do you kiss me, Elias?"

"Had pity moved me to try your sweet lips, I would have

resisted for both our sakes. Non, Honore, I wanted to kiss you—so much I put from my mind where we are and why we are here."

Though she longed to believe him, she said, "Did you also put from your mind who we are?"

"Who?"

She drew a breath that caused her chest to brush his, quickly exhaled the excess. "You are fairly young. You are noble. You are legitimate. You are of the world. I am not young. If I am noble, likely I am just as common *and* illegitimate. Regardless, ever I shall remain unacknowledged because of this defect of birth. And I am of this world only insofar as I venture into it to pluck unwanted babes from dark places."

What seemed discomfort passed over his face, and she knew he understood that whereas it had been but a kiss to him, it had moved her to expectations to which such intimacy ought not give rise to one such as she.

"Thus," she said, "as we have no godly future and never would I be to you the same as the woman in Gravelines, I shall be glad for your one kiss and naught else."

He released her. "The woman in Gravelines?"

She leaned back, let the wall become the support he had been. "I speak of the grumblings of a young man who, also seeking a bed in the stables, resented losing the favors of a woman to a knight. And there was only one knight in that inn, Elias."

"You think..." A curt laugh bounded from him. "Though I told I remained behind to gain information—and I did—you believe I lay with a woman."

"It is that over which the man complained."

"Upon my honor, I was with her at the bar and only there. And when I gleaned from her all I could, she became cover to learn more from others. Afterward, I gave her coin, sent her away, and feigned sleeping off drunkenness so I could aid the archbishop did any disturb his sleep."

Though she feared believing him, she was moved to do so.

Determining she would, she said, "Forgive me. It was difficult to conceive you could be intimate with a woman so soon after what happened to Lettice, but..."

His face tightened.

Wishing she had not reminded him of his lost love, she said, "My only excuse is I know so little of you."

Now eyes that had looked so kindly upon her pierced. "Do you? Then you ought not allow me to kiss you, especially as you yourself tell only forbidden intimacy is possible between us. In yielding, you risk making lie of your claim to never become that which drops coin into the palm of women like the one who kept company with me at Gravelines."

"I would never—"

"You think she knew what desperation would make of her ere it ruined her?" His voice having risen, he snapped his teeth and momentarily closed his eyes. "I am more at fault. Though as told it was not pity or kindness that made me kiss you, nor the hope of seducing you, I know better than to yield to desire that ruins women and makes fatherless children."

Only desire. But better that than mere pity or kindness, since it was as near she would come to what went between married men and women.

She pushed off the wall, and as she smoothed her skirts was reminded of the finery that had surely aided in tempting Elias. Come morn, she would seek the laundering of her soiled garments the sooner to return her to a semblance of one whose life was devoted to foundlings.

Remembering the lost gorget, she moved her gaze over the floor, a moment later swept it up. "As I know you must rise early to be away from Clairmarais ere those from Sandwich resume their search, I wish you Godspeed, Sir Elias."

"For that," he said as she turned aside, "I approached you this eve."

She came back around. "Plans have changed?"

"Perhaps, though now..." Emotions shifted across his face, and she guessed what had led to their kiss was being reconsidered.

Hope leapt through her, and she sounded almost a girl when she said, "You will take me with you?"

"I had thought to, but only were you willing to forego the gorget and clothe yourself as I find you now."

"Why?"

"The manner in which you wear the gorget is too memorable, as well as the simple clothes worn by one whose pretense of being a knight's wife was made believable only by the presence of a ring. If you accompany me, you must further transform lest we are unable to avoid those from Sandwich or others who could connect our party with Thomas's at Gravelines or on the road to Clairmarais. A fine, unwed lady you will look—"

"Unwed?"

He inclined his head. "We shall be traversing lands in which my family and I are known. Thus, better you play my English cousin whom I escort to my home to take up residence for a time."

It made sense, but she hesitated. Mostly she believed Elias viewed the scar as of little consequence, but not all would. Many would stare and talk out the sides of their mouths. Some would cross themselves and hasten away—though perhaps not as many were she clothed in the finery of a lady. Such offense was more easily dealt a commoner than a noble.

"I know it is a fearful thing, Honore." Elias stepped near again. "But do you eschew your cover, I believe you will be safer with me."

Once anger had moved her to refuse to conceal her lower face, and it had been freeing. Thus, when it had been required to ensure Lady Yolande remained generous with her donations, she had resented it. She ought to be glad to accommodate Elias, especially as it would allow her to be with him when he recovered Hart, but the thought of baring her face was almost as disturbing as she imagined it would be were she to bare her body.

Ridiculous, she scorned. She was thinking not much different from wild animals of which she had heard tale that, following years of captivity, might be inclined to slay their captor given the opportunity but when provided a chance to escape their cages did not take it—either so in the habit of living inside the bars or grown fearful of what lay on the other side. She had thought it exaggeration, but here she was longing to remain behind the gorget.

She did not know how she came by a smile, but she felt it when she looked up. "I shall forego the gorget."

Keeping his gaze from a mouth whose smile moved him, Elias stared into her blue eyes. But they were more devastating. "You are certain?"

"Gladly I shall abandon it."

He admired her determination. "Then you shall require rest as much as I." He strode toward the corridor, traversed it, and halted alongside her door.

She paused on the threshold and tilted up her face—one that, though not of a young woman, was far from aged as she made herself sound in listing the reasons there could be no future for them.

How old was she? He would guess one or two years younger than he, meaning at least ten years older than his father would have him wed to ensure plenty of childbearing years, but to Elias a more acceptable age than a woman hardly out of girlhood.

"You need not reconsider permitting me to remain with you, Sir Elias. Be assured, I will not seek further kisses. And henceforth, I shall not forget ours is a relationship of necessity."

Brave words, but he sensed the hurt behind them. And hated he was responsible. "Fear not, I shall awaken you well ere dawn."

She stepped inside.

"Honore, how many years have you?"

She slowly turned, gripped the door's edge. "Thirty and two."

Unable to keep surprise from his face, he said, "I believed you less than my twenty and eight."

A small smile. "You are kind, but as told, that is a mark against me—too few years in which to give a man many children. Quite impossible, Sir Elias." She stepped back, closed the door, and bolted it.

He eased out his breath. A mess he had made of the night. He had chosen the wrong means by which to assure her she need not hide behind the gorget. He had fallen to temptation as if unaware of the attraction between them. And when she reminded him of the impossibility of pursuing a relationship beyond forbidden intimacy, he had been offended by her assumption he had sinned with the woman at the inn. And guilt over kissing Honore so soon after Lettice's passing had turned him cruel in placing blame on her for their kiss, warning she risked becoming a harlot and confirming they could have no future beyond sin.

His only defense—a poor one—was his response ought to discourage her from gifting him more of her heart than already she did.

And what of your heart, Elias De Morville?

He shook his head. Given more time and too little consideration, he might have been in danger of losing it, but it remained his. A good thing. Once the boy was found, Elias had amends to make and promises to keep.

The obligation owed his sire was coming due.

CHAPTER 27

AND BREATHE THE AIR HE BREATHES

Saint-Omer
France

*G*one. And no great feat to learn it. Though two days had passed since the troupe's departure, many were the tales of performances that for five days and nights enthralled the castle folk and inhabitants of the town outside the fortress. But it was not enough to return Elias's party to the road.

He needed to discover the troupe's destination, if possible confirm it was the same expelled from England for its sideshow, and seek the name of Finwyn amidst their ranks. Thus, he sent Theo and Cynuit among the town folk and mounted Honore on their horse as much for show when they entered the castle walls as to ease his discomfort over the morning's ride, throughout which her curves fit against him.

As agreed, she did not wear the gorget, and Elias was pleased with both his squire and the lad when their greatest show of surprise was the boy's exclamation over how pretty she was.

Elias had seen her tension ease and the beginning of a smile, then she had undone the bow of her lips and said low, "You were kind to prepare them."

He could not naysay her without coloring it a lie. He had told the two the only way she might accompany them was to drastically change her appearance, then said to prepare themselves for the whole of a pretty face from which not even a small scar could detract. But he was not certain he had done her a disservice. So offended had she been she had raised her chin higher and, excepting when the road was theirs alone, kept it up as if daring any who gazed on her to unman himself with a show of fear.

Upon closer inspection of one believed to be a noblewoman, a few smiles had fallen, some had wavered, and surprise and question had shifted the light in appreciative eyes.

When they had neared the town gates, Elias had said, "Chin up and a glare in those blues of yours. I do not believe it as good as a smile, but if you insist on being self conscious, it serves."

"Under the circumstances, it comes naturally," she had replied.

Elias had thought her trial past, but when they entered the town, he had nearly rebuked women who were less discreet. They had stared, mumbled prayers, crossed themselves, and scurried away. Fortunately, they numbered only a handful and most were of advanced years. And Honore's chin had not moved from on high.

Now as Elias guided his horse alongside hers toward the donjon, he looked sidelong at her.

Catching the flutter of her lashes, he was certain she felt his gaze, but she kept hers upon the gathering of knights before the steps.

Elias wished they did not have to enter the hall, but there he might learn what Theo and Cynuit could be unable to discover. Too, having passed no noblemen of obvious import on the road, he would confirm King Henry's envoys had departed Saint-Omer rather than dally with Thomas on the loose.

Honore did not go unnoticed by the nearby knights, but their reactions were much the same as other men encountered. They might lose interest because of her imperfection, but they could appreciate her loveliness enough to rise to her challenge not to show fear for a woman.

Elias dismounted, straightened fine garments donned this morn, passed his reins to the groom who appeared, and crossed to Honore. The show of courage had worn her weary, and more was needed for what awaited them.

He raised his arms to her, and she came into them with what seemed relief. Since they were watched and she could not play the wife here, he knew he should set her back, but he clasped her close and put his mouth to her ear. "My brave Honore."

He felt her sink against him, but then she stepped back and whispered, "Brave perhaps, but not yours. Pray, do not speak thus. Though I know you mean no harm, memories are made of such."

Memories he ought not want, he told himself and released her.

"Now, Cousin," she said, "offer me your arm and escort me into this den of wolves."

Hating it was that to her, Elias cupped her elbow, led her past the knights, and up the steps into a den that included one with a fondness for falconry.

THE YOUNG KNIGHT WAS OBSERVANT. Elias had hoped him too concerned with one mistaken for the Archbishop of Canterbury to recall those who preceded the brethren on the road to Clairmarais, but often his eyes moved between Otto De Morville's heir and the one who played his cousin. Where he sat at a lower table across from the one at which Elias and Honore also partook of the meal, he put his head near that of an older nobleman and spoke words that caused the other to glance at the two come late to the hall.

Had Elias noticed the young knight sooner, he would not have accepted the lord of the castle's invitation to join him for the nooning meal.

Another lesson violated, he silently chastised. *You shame Everard Wulfrith who entrusted you with his family's reputation.*

Once more wishing he had been gifted with Wulfen training from an age at which he was first able to heft a sword, Elias determined he would not further fail his friend. As he carried a spoonful of stew to his mouth, he evaluated his circumstances.

There was naught he could do about the attention paid Honore, but providing the young knight did not consider she had earlier concealed her scarred lip beneath a gorget, she was convincing as a noblewoman accustomed to finery. Though uncomfortable eating in sight of others, she comported herself well.

Like her, Elias looked the prosperous nobleman in garments far distant from the foul, muddy ones worn en route to Clairmarais. Other than his face the young knight had glanced over, he ought to be unrecognizable. However, of note was the Wulfrith dagger he had worn then and now—a greater rarity in France, most of those who received their training from the Wulfriths being of England. Likely, the dagger had been previously noted, especially as it was worn by one absent a horse who had looked a common soldier rather than a knight.

But it was too late to remove it. Had he come to the attention of the young knight when Honore and he first entered the hall, the dagger could be responsible for the interest shown Honore and him. Thus, its removal might confirm the man's suspicion.

"Elias?"

He looked around.

Honore smiled—wide-eyed and false. "You feel it too?" she asked.

He was glad she was not oblivious to the attention paid them, and though he had not alerted her to the one passed on the road to Clairmarais, she surely recognized him. "I feel it."

"What are we to do?"

Though Henry's men were no longer in residence, he had gained no word of the troupe's destination from those with whom he conversed before the meal. Hopefully, Theo and Cynuit would fare better.

"At meal's end," he said, "we depart without delay."

She returned to the trencher they shared and pulled off a piece of broth-soaked bread.

A half hour longer they played at having no care for those who observed them, and when the meal ended, Elias raised Honore to her feet. Leisurely, he guided her past the others, many of whom also sought the out of doors. And he did not need to look around to confirm the young knight was among those who followed.

Elias paused behind others gathered before the lord to thank him for his hospitality. Though he prayed the one with whom he wished to avoid a confrontation would continue to the doors, he did not.

Elias urged Honore forward, dipped his head. "My lord, my cousin and I thank you for the fine meal and good company. We hope one day our family can repay the hospitality."

The man smiled. "It will not be the first meal owed me by the De Morvilles. Godspeed your journey, Sir Elias."

They stepped past. And were followed.

Upon reaching the base of the donjon steps Elias acted on the lesson that in the face of battle one's best defense was offense, a show of aggression more likely to put finish to a threat ere the shedding of blood.

He released Honore and turned in front of her. Setting a hand on his dagger's hilt, he widened his stance as the two coming off the lowermost step faltered. "Either you insult my lady cousin with lascivious imaginings"—he met the young knight's gaze

—"else you have issue with me." He shifted his regard to the other man. "Better the latter as I have little tolerance for offenses dealt women, especially those of my blood, so consider carefully ere enlightening me as to your interest at meal."

The young knight's self assurance having fallen down around his ankles, he opened his mouth but formed no words.

"Pardon, Sir Elias," his companion said. "Our interest is not meant to offend."

Elias raised his eyebrows. "You are?"

"Richard De Lucy of recent pilgrimage to Santiago de Compostela now returning home to England. Or so I hoped."

"An admirable undertaking, but that does not inform me of your interest in me and mine."

"The Archbishop of Canterbury," the young knight answered.

Elias had not expected such honesty, but he fit confusion on his face. "What has that rebel priest to do with me?"

"You and the lady were traveling with him on the day past on the road to Clairmarais and Saint-Omer." His eyes flicked to the dagger. "Certes, it was you."

"We traveled that road," Elias allowed, honesty amid dishonesty making the latter more believable, the same as tales spun to entertain, "but we did not keep company with men of God."

"They followed behind, among them Thomas Becket."

Elias nearly startled when Honore stepped alongside him and set a hand on his arm. "Brethren did share the road with us, Cousin. You must have been so distraught over the theft of our mounts you did not notice. And I remember when this knight and his companions passed us." He heard the smile in her voice when she directed her next words to the young man. "Was it good hunting, Sir...? Oh, I know not your name."

She played it so well Elias longed to place himself beside the one she addressed so he might watch her.

The knave's gaze too low to be upon hers, fascinated as he was by a near view of her mouth, she repeated, "Your name, Sir Knight?"

He looked up. "Sir Neville of the family Sorrel, trained into knighthood by Count Philip of Flanders."

Elias tensed further. Even if this one no longer served the count, he had ties with the King of England's cousin.

"I am certain," Sir Neville continued, "among those brethren was the archbishop all know to have fled England."

Honore put her head to the side. "If so, we were unaware. But then, I would not know him by sight. Would you, Cousin Elias?"

"I would have no occasion. Now as we have long delayed our departure, we bid you good day."

"De Morville!" De Lucy said as Elias took Honore's arm.

"Sir Richard?"

The man stepped near. "It is imperative I discover the archbishop's whereabouts."

Elias shot his eyebrows high. "Then I wish you well."

"Sir Elias, know you who passed the night here?"

"Not until two hours ago did we arrive at Saint-Omer. As we but sought our rest and a meal, I have no care for who lodged here."

"It was King Henry's envoys, men tasked with leashing Becket."

Elias shrugged. "Your king—my duke—may be my liege, but his squabbles with the archbishop have only to do with me insofar as you are determined to make them my problem."

"Early this morn they departed," De Lucy said as if Elias had not spoken. "One group rides to Sens to meet with the pope over the matter of deposing Thomas, the other toward Paris to meet with King Louis to persuade him to deny the archbishop refuge and use his influence with the pope to support Henry's actions against Thomas. Hence, I must find him."

Elias sighed. "I say again, I know naught of the man. But I am curious. Why do you concern yourself over that froward priest?"

"I am his vassal and friend, and this break with Henry..." He raised his hands in a gesture of helplessness. "I fear it will ruin him, perhaps even our king."

He seemed sincere, but another Wulfen lesson growled through Elias—*Beware the wolf. Oft he wears the fleece of the slain lamb. Do you not see the long nose, then seek the eyes. No cunning will you find in a lamb's.*

On the pretense of sympathy, Elias stepped near, set a hand on De Lucy's shoulder. "I understand your distress." He studied the dark eyes. "And much I admire your loyalty to your liege." Was that a glint of cunning? "But I cannot tell what I do not know. I wish you well, Sir Richard. And you, Sir Neville." He moved his hand to Honore's arm. "Come, Cousin."

Elias felt their gaze until Honore and he went from sight in the outer bailey.

"Do you think you were believed?" she asked after he paid the stable lad.

"We played our parts well, but there is too much at stake and so many clambering for a piece that, in the hope of marrow, the dogs will gnaw on a seemingly barren bone."

"We are the bone."

"Unless another with meat upon it can be found. Though our parting with Thomas ensures we are of no danger to him, we shall have to be vigilant."

She lifted a hand to a string tied around her neck and fingered her way down it. Elias had not noticed it before, but now he saw the ring threaded on it. It was not sizable or elaborate, but if any of the four sapphires set in the band at intervals like the directional points on a map caught light, it would draw the eye—especially for the disparity between it and the crude string from which it hung.

"You ought to keep that hidden," he said.

She followed his gaze, tucked the tip of a finger in the ring. "Surely you do not think any would recognize it?"

Had someone? The man who claimed to be Thomas's vassal

and friend? "Was it inside your bodice whilst we conversed with those knaves?"

"I...believe so."

"Let us pray so."

Flushing, she dropped the ring down the neck of her gown.

Once mounted, they rode into the town to reunite with Theo and Cynuit. And God willing, confirm the troupe that had performed at Saint-Omer was the one they sought and learn their destination.

CHAPTER 28

AND LET HIM KISS

*T*he tidings were unsatisfactory. No confirmation it was the troupe they sought since no amount of discreet inquiry revealed they offered a secret sideshow. And of the names of its members none recalled *Finwyn.*

But Cynuit had discovered their destination was a castle known to Elias—Château de Sevier whose heir had attended the troupe's first performance at Saint-Omer and engaged them to travel south to his home. That castle was held by one who also owed allegiance to Duke Henry and, of further note, abutted De Morville lands.

Unfortunately, Elias would not be well received by that family. The Costains and De Morvilles were not enemies, but Elias had offended last year when Otto sought to betroth his heir to the eldest daughter—barely the eldest, having all of ten and four years to her sister's ten and three.

Elias was not his father. When he wed, it would be to a woman not a girl half his age.

Gaze bridging the fire, he settled it on Honore where she sat on a blanket Cynuit had spread for her. Another blanket clasped around shoulders draped with golden hair, knees drawn to chest, eyes peering over them into the flames, she seemed not of his world. And she was not, her stay here temporary.

Here was a woman, he mused, but she was far older than would be acceptable to Otto De Morville.

Elias growled low over his mind's wanderings. More and more he felt for Honore, but even were she ten and five, they could never be. He had given his father his word, and he would keep it no matter the sacrifice.

"My lord, what say you to a tale?" Theo said.

Once more Elias was jolted, though more by Honore's blue gaze shooting to his than his squire's words. Her eyes… Dear Lord, her eyes…

"Aye, a tale, milord," Cynuit prompted. "Pray, in English that I may better understand."

It felt like snapping chains to break from the blue, and he felt strangely weakened when the links gave. "Methinks a good night's sleep better sought," he said.

Cynuit glanced at the slowly darkening sky. "'Tis not even an hour past twilight."

"We rise early to make Sevier Castle ere the nooning hour," Elias reminded.

"A short tale, then, milord."

Touched by the boy's pleading, Elias said, "What sort? One woven of adventure? Laughter? Loss? Darkness?"

"Love."

That single word, which he had not intended to speak himself, returned his gaze to the one who spoke it.

Chin on her knees, Honore said, "And adventure, laughter, mayhap even loss."

Though something warned it was at his peril he acceded, he said, "That would be quite the tale. I do not think I know one capable of fulfilling your requirements."

"Oh but there is one, Sir Elias. I have not heard it—only of it—whilst we paused at Cheverel. The hero's name... Was it Cant?"

Blessedly, he was prepared to engage the actor, covering an outward show of surprise with confusion. "Cant?" he said, though he knew how she had come by it. It was what Everard had called out upon the arrival of his friend's party. Had Honore asked Susanna about it? Had its origins been revealed?

"I am certain you must know it," she prompted. "I believe it tells of a young man who cast off his nobility to travel England with a troupe of performers." Her smile was slight.

Still, Elias meant to refuse her, but Cynuit said, "That is a tale I would like to hear, milord."

The lack of guile in the boy's eyes told the name that had not escaped Honore had escaped him.

"It sounds too unbelievable," Theo said.

Elias looked to his squire who knew enough of the story to understand how personal it was. Thus, he sought to aid his lord.

"I know some of the tale," Elias acceded, "but Theo is right. It is unbelievable, and I would not disappoint you, Cynuit. Nor you, Honore."

"You forget I heard the tale poured into the imagination of Sir Everard and Lady Susanna's son," she said. "I am sure you can make it passably believable."

She would have him bare his soul, make sense of all that had delivered them to this time and place. But he would not. That was in the past and there it must—

He reined in his thoughts. His quest to retrieve his son had made the past his present. And he had made it hers.

Bare away, Elias, he told himself. *It is the least owed her. Something to remember you by when once more her life is spent in service to the Lord whilst yours is spent in service to the De Morvilles. A sea between you.*

He cleared his throat. "I shall aspire to do the tale justice."

Her eyes widened, evidencing she did not expect him to yield.

He raised his wineskin, took a draught. Then snatching on the person of Elias Cant, he tossed high his hands. "Hearken to my tale. Hearken well! This one be of adventure, laughter, longing and"—he pointed to Honore—"love." He turned his mouth down. "But not of a love that lasts. One of loss most tragic. Are you prepared? Have you heart for it?"

Honore blinked at the open-faced man beyond the fire, one she hardly recognized for what seemed joy on a face that, heretofore, had little cause to reflect anything other than momentary pleasure—except when his attempt to coax a smile from her led to a kiss. That had been more than a moment, though it was gone and ought nevermore be felt.

"My lady!" Elias surged to his feet, the garments and weapons of a warrior a stunning contrast to what he was becoming. "I must know. Have you heart for my tale?" He raised a finger. "But ere you answer, 'tis only fair I warn this one is sure to make you ache near as great were it your tale and most true." He raised his eyebrows, and she realized he sought a response as if she were also a player.

She sat straighter. "My heart is strong enough to weather your tale."

He smiled as she had not seen him do, moved his smile to Cynuit. "You bear witness, lad. Does the lady's heart fall from her breast, I am not to blame."

Cynuit laughed. "If you will not aid the lady in retrieving her heart, I shall."

The heart of which they so lightly spoke made more space for this boy, further crowding her foundlings, Hart, the abbess, and...Elias.

"Then we continue." He winked. "The setting... Let us place the tale here in France, specifically Normandy held by that wild, flame-headed king of England, duke this side of the narrow sea. The hero... Simply Cant, the second son of a nobleman and spare heir to one determined to see the boy trained for knighthood though his interests lie in poetry, song, dance, and storytelling."

Though Honore had guessed it must be so, she felt for the boy into whose hands weapons had been placed rather than quill and parchment.

Elias groaned. "Forbid he should defy his sire. And truly impossible for one so young and dependent. Until..."

A single stride carried him to Cynuit, and he dropped to his haunches. As the boy stared at him, the teller of tales said, "At the age of ten and six, Cant rebelled. Have you ever rebelled, lad?"

The boy jerked his chin. "Against my master."

"Good. No matter how heavy the boot on one's back, the Almighty would not have men or women suffer servitude, do you not agree?"

Cynuit looked uncertain but murmured, "Aye, milord."

Elias rose. "But—caution here!—that does not grant one permission to harm others with their rebellion. One must think and pray ere acting. *That* Cant did not do. He wished another life, one he thought possible only if he"—Elias shot arms high, splayed fingers, danced them downward—"disappeared."

Honore startled when his eyes sprang to hers.

"With hardly a thought for those left behind who would think ill befell him, he fled the lord with whom he fostered and crossed to England." Elias returned to his place before the fire and dropped to sitting. Legs crossed, hands loose on his knees, he lowered his head. "Selfish, cruel, immature."

She stared. Though he played a role, it was *his*. And she did not doubt his remorse required little acting.

He was silent so long she thought he would end his tale there, then he surged to his feet.

"Four years!" He held up that many fingers. "Four years Cant traveled town to town, castle to castle playing the troubadour. Much he loved the living. Much he did not." He rounded on Theo.

"Not? you ask. Had he not what he longed for? Days and nights of laughter, song, and dance? Aye, and an audience who inhaled his every word whether he snatched them from the air"—he closed fingers around a handful above his head—"or spilled forth those practiced for hours and days on end. And the ladies! Oh, the ladies!"

He winked, came around the fire, bowed before Honore. Then he captured one of her hands clasped around her knees and pulled her to standing.

"Elias!" she cried as the blanket fell from her shoulders. "You cannot!"

"The name is Cant. And I *can*—do you allow me, my lady."

Distant from him by half the length of his arm, she looked up. "Allow you what?"

"To lead you in the dance."

"I know not how to dance."

He laughed. "For that, I shall lead, my lady."

"I do not..."

"I will take that as agreement." He retrieved her other hand, pulled her away from the fire. "Step as I step, as if you are my mirror."

"Elias—"

"Cant," he corrected again and looked across his shoulder. "Encouragement, lads! If the lady is to forget propriety and see the fun in life, even if only this night, you must encourage her. Clap, whistle, snap your fingers."

And so they did, uncertainly at first, then enthusiastically when Elias demonstrated between their bodies the steps and movements of the tune sounding from his throat.

"Now you, my lady." He met her gaze.

"I was not watching closely."

"Not watching closely, she says! Mayhap she is too rapt over joining hands with the charming Cant, eh lads?" Another wink.

She *was* rapt, but she said, "You flatter yourself!"

"So I do. And often." He chortled. "It seems I shall have to give the lady what she truly wishes—a dance of the common folk."

He reeled her in. When she stumbled against him, he slid one arm around her waist to anchor her to him, raised her left hand, and pushed his fingers through hers. "Dear lady, either stand on my boots or I shall have to lift you higher against me."

Against him... "Methinks the tale well enough told," she said.

"Hardly." He lifted her off her feet, resumed humming his tune, and turned her so swiftly cool air swept up her billowing skirts.

Honore knew she ought to further protest, but...

This is warmth for cold nights when all that shares your bed are memories made of Elias, whether of De Morville or Cant, spoke the voice with which Elias was making her familiar. *Embrace it, Honore. It is but a dance. Longing in it, true, but no sin.*

"He turns her 'round again," Elias announced. "And dips her."

Finding herself bent back over his forearm, loosed hair swinging, she looked up and saw his body followed the bend of hers, firelight in eyes and rimming his smile.

"Dips her lower."

So he did.

"She thinks he may steal a kiss. And he would but, alas, he dare not offend her betrothed." He straightened. Once Honore's feet settled atop his boots, he looked past her to Theo and Cynuit whose encouraging din had abated.

They were entranced, though not as much as she who ought not be.

"Betrothed? you ask." Elias's wink was more exaggerated than the others. "There must be one, for who would not claim so lovely a maiden?"

He went too far in reminding her of what could not be. Just as he would wed another, she would remain wed to her work at Bairnwood.

"Elias," she whispered, and when he continued to bestow a

smile upon his audience, pulled her hand from his and set it on his shoulder. "Elias!"

His face came around, and their noses brushed.

She eased back. "I am not part of Cant's tale, and that is the tale we seek." She hated the tears the fire would bring to light. "Not the tale of Elias De Morville, a Wulfen-trained knight whose quest is to find his son. Cant's tale. Only that."

As he peered into her, on the other side of Cant who held her she saw Elias who should not hold her. That one pushed through and said low, "Forgive me." Gently he set her back, loosed one of her hands, and as he turned to face Theo and Cynuit, smiled so broadly she knew that expression more false than any she had seen him wear.

"End of act one," he announced. Then raising her hand with his, he bowed low.

Honore knew she ought to fold over as well, but like the steps of the dance, performance was foreign to her.

Belatedly, Theo and Cynuit clapped.

"Much appreciated," Elias trumpeted and led her back to her place before the fire. As he released her hand, he said, "I thank you for your assistance in demonstrating how well the women liked Cant, my lady."

Not knowing how to respond, she was grateful when Cynuit said, "What happened next, milord?"

As Honore lowered and drew her blanket around her, Elias turned to the boy. "Much, lad. But do you know, some of the best tales are those not told in full, giving the audience time to mull and imagine the road next traveled. For that, methinks we ought to take up the remainder another night."

"Ah nay, milord! Though you gave much time to the dance, it is early. Tell, why did Cant not love the living? Something bad happened to him?"

Despite the dance, Honore also wished him to continue, certain Hart was at the end of Cant's tale. Still, she felt for Elias who surely longed to take first watch and slip away among the trees.

"Please, milord."

He returned to his side of the fire, but rather than seat himself on the ground, further distanced himself by perching on a large rock. "The living was not as Cant imagined. But though at times he regretted rejecting his life of privilege, mostly he was content."

"You no longer show, milord." Cynuit looked to Elias's squire. "Aye, Theo?"

At the young man's shrug, the lad said, "You just tell, milord."

So he did, Elias silently acknowledged. A tale merely told was not worth the breath expended. But it had been too easy to become Cant and push boundaries he should not, especially with Honore. It was long since he had so greatly missed being one other than Elias De Morville. Becoming the performer again, he could do and be, think and say, and want and choose as he pleased. Thus, he had wanted, as Honore guessed, to make her part of the carefree troubadour's tale.

"You are right, Cynuit. I am better than that." He sat straighter and, determining it best to look only to the left and right of Honore, returned volume and life to his voice.

"Mostly Cant was content. But then he learned that which he played at was no game. He discovered the power of the nobility, the helplessness of the common man. Ah!" He leaned forward. "I have your interest again, Cynuit. Have I yours, Theo? Aye, I see the devilry in your eyes, the lust for story."

"Take the devilry from our eyes, milord!" Cynuit cried.

Elias slid a bit of devilry into his laugher, then once more set his face in serious lines. "Cant's troupe was engaged to pass the winter at a barony in Northern England." Upon which the village of Forkney lay, he did not say. "There the young man fell in love with a serving girl who hung on his every tale. And what of she?" He grinned, winked. "Of course she returned his love. Madly. Deeply. Wondrously. But"—he held up a hand—"too soon, too soon, dear listeners. Pray, curb your enthusiasm. Hold not thy breath, for a lengthy detour we must take."

The boy groaned.

Honore, out of sight but not mind, tempted his regard. And Theo, who was to know more of the tale than before, ineffectually suppressed a sigh.

"I vow 'tis essential," Elias said and, knowing Theo and Honore would substitute the name Lettice said, "Her name was Violet, and a violet she was—fair, soft, fragrant. And sweet, though her burdens were many for one so young."

It was no act to express sorrow. The act would have been in suppressing how great that sorrow were Elias not many years removed from Cant. "Violet's father had died, and so deeply her mother mourned she neglected her little ones, leaving Violet to care for them with the coin earned as a servant—so little she had to seek other work."

Feeling his hands move toward fists, Elias opened them and, attempting to incorporate his reaction into the tale, turned them palms up. "The work of..." He hesitated, not for effect but to question if he should relate this to a boy of ten. Cynuit was from Forkney where such work was mostly shrugged off. Too, his master had been Arblette.

"The work of a joy woman," Elias said, and Cynuit's slow nod told he knew that was the name preferred by women whom men were more likely to name harlots. "Cant tried to save her by sharing his food and earnings so she need only serve at the castle, but she persisted until he vowed to leave the troupe, remain with her, and make her his wife."

Elias did not mean to look to Honore, but his eyes played him false and once more he saw she peered at him over her knees.

"Did she stay true?" Cynuit asked, further evidence he was exposed to those moved by desperation to barter their bodies.

"Cant believed so." Elias stood, looked to the heavens. "The Lord sees all. He knew Violet's sins. He knew Cant's. He knew what had been, what was, and what was to be. Thus, he knew never would Cant speak vows with Violet."

"Because she did not stay true?" Cynuit pressed.

Elias forced lightness about a face whose muscles sought to express pain. "Accursed desperation, lad. It makes sinners of men and women alike."

"How did he discover her lie? And Sir Elias, again you tell rather than show."

Elias hung a smile whose curve was so weighted it might snap. "Alas, I am fatigued, Cynuit, much of the blame for which belongs to Honore. We shall have to teach her to dance on her own feet, hmm?"

The boy glanced at her. "Pray, finish the tale, milord."

"If you wish the show of it, you shall have to wait."

A long-drawn sigh. "I cannot."

Best I am done with it, Elias determined. *Then no more need be told Honore.*

"Ere Violet and Cant were to wed, he happened on her. He was certain the knight with her had not her permission since her word she had given she would be Cant's alone."

Elias made a show of drawing breath as memories of Lettice in the arms of another man swept him—of her angry protest not directed at the one with whom she was intimate.

Lungs unable to contain more air, he continued in a strained voice, "And so the troubadour set himself upon one whose rank would have been inferior to his had he completed his knighthood training—had he not donned the person, mind, and heart of a commoner. And that knight beat Cant and dragged him before the lord of the castle who had him beat again for being a commoner who struck a nobleman."

Outrage gathered on Cynuit's face. "He should have revealed his noble blood, milord! That would have put end to it."

"Ah, but not only was Cant unworthy of his name for forsaking it, but do you not think it would have sounded a lie?

One so offensive it warranted further beating, perhaps unto death?"

Trying to stay in front of memories of what he would next tell, allowing them only near enough to bring the story to its conclusion, Elias continued, "The wretch sought out Violet, and she whose sweet petals were more bruised than he had known hardly saw her love's bruises, cuts, and swellings. She said his jealousy ruined all, that never would her lord allow them to wed. Though Cant ought to have left her then, he had to know for what she betrayed him."

Elias narrowed his eyes at Cynuit. "Coin to buy shoes for her sister. But still he lingered, assuring her he would have given her coin out of his next earnings." Lettice's face rose before him, and he saw the glint in her eyes and curl of her upper lip. "Then she delivered the blow that snuffed the slightest hope of a life together. Violet said it was only her body and there was no easier way to see her palm filled with coin."

"Desperation," Cynuit breathed.

Elias inclined his head. "At last Cant accepted she was broken —that in times of need the easier way would prevail over love for him."

"So he left her," the lad said with what sounded approval.

"He did, but do you think it best?"

"Of course. Her lord would not allow them to wed, she would not be faithful, and how was Cant to earn a living under the rule of one who ordered him beaten a second time?"

It had been Elias's reasoning, and until Lettice's murder only on occasion had he questioned if it was sound. But guilt over her death argued that had he truly loved her, he would not have given up, would have found a way to make a life with her in which never again must she sell her body.

Impossible, he silently argued. *As a commoner and under those circumstances, no matter your effort you could not have supported her,*

her siblings, and her mother. And Lettice knew it. It was surely among the reasons she hardened herself against you.

Guilt once more shouldered its way in, suggesting had he thrown himself on his father's mercy and reclaimed his nobility, he would have had the resources to pull her out of that life.

Fool, he countered. *Otto De Morville would not have accepted Lettice and her family. Rather than name you his heir, he would have consigned his ruined young wife to a convent and wed another to make more sons.*

It was so, and yet—

"Do you think it best he left her, Sir Elias?" Honore asked, awakening him to the present and its own troubles.

No longer did she clasp her knees, and he guessed beneath her blanket her legs were crossed. And those blues of hers seemed to peer into his soul.

"It matters not what I think. I am but the teller of a tale devised to entertain and encourage its audience not to simply receive words but think on them."

"I have thought on them," she said.

He did not want to prompt her lest her answer further fuel his guilt, but the hole would be too noticeable since he had prompted Cynuit. "Your conclusion, my lady?"

She glanced at the lad. "Though God can do all things, I know free will is a great gift. But what we make of what we find inside the wrappings is not entirely up to us. Much is dependent on what others do with their free will, which can render ours trampled. Thus, I may not be as certain as Cynuit it was best your hero leave Violet, but I do not see he had much choice."

Did she seek to absolve Elias De Morville of a wrong? Certes, she knew it was guilt with which he was stricken.

Elias looked to Theo. "What say you, Squire?"

He was quick to answer though not because he did so thoughtlessly. "It seems all present are in agreement Cant took the only road wide enough to set his feet upon."

Elias longed to believe that.

"Will you not tell what became of Cant, milord?" Cynuit asked.

"It will be a much-shortened tale, lad, but it unfolds like this…"
He picked up the branch with which he had earlier stirred the fire,
lowered to his haunches, and poked at the glowing logs, causing
orange and yellow embers to fly up like rain turned upside down.
"Recompense," he said. "Retribution. Revenge."

The blood of the performer once more flowing through him,
he looked face to face, most quickly past the one whose blue eyes
closely watched him. "The beaten, heartbroken troubadour
determined never again to suffer the helplessness of a commoner
and departed the village to recover in the next. Two days later, a
nobleman came to notice whose boasting became louder and
more vile the greater he imbibed."

"Who?" Cynuit asked.

Elias shot to his feet. "Fortuitous this! Can you guess?"

The lad shook his head.

"It was the foul knight who beat Cant and saw him beat again."

Cynuit gasped. "Did Cant kill him?"

"He wished to, but he controlled that demon, watching and
waiting for the right opportunity to repay him."

"How?"

"Oh lad, it was wondrous! Once that knave was sated near
senseless, he stumbled out of the inn. And our Cant…" He
widened his eyes. "From somewhere beneath the terrible injuries
that left him unrecognizable and barely able to put one foot in
front of the other arose anger so great he felt none of his aches.
And delivered a beating whose marks that knight carries to
this day."

And that, Elias reflected, was as much truth as the rest of it, as
he had recent occasion to look upon that knight.

"Then what happened?" Cynuit's eyes were so alight, Elias
knew despite the lapse in delivering a tale well when he had
spoken of Lettice, he had recaptured his audience's imagination

and made it seem as real as life itself. In the case of Cant, no difficult thing.

"Cant bestowed the great favor of relieving so unworthy a knight of much extra weight."

Cynuit beamed. "He took his armor!"

"And sword. After all, a man without such does not a knight errant make."

"Knight errant," the boy ran his tongue over words he surely found delicious then frowned. "But Cant had not completed his knight's training."

"And he would not for some years. Blessedly, once he left the troubadour behind, he proved well enough versed in all the years given to his training that few questioned or challenged one who knew how to play a part. And eventually, he sold his services to a baron."

An unworthy lord, Elias recalled Lady Susanna's heartless brother who was better in the ground than above it.

"That cannot be all there is to the tale," Cynuit said.

Elias smiled large. "You wish a grand finale?"

The lad bobbed his head. "Did he return to his father? Did he find another love, one as faithful to him as he to her?"

Those last words dragged Elias's eyes where they ought not go, and only with great effort was he able to keep them from traveling beyond the golden hair draped over a shoulder. "Cant returned to his father, but only after the mighty Wulfriths deemed him worthy to be numbered amongst England's greatest defenders."

Cynuit's hands convulsed into fists, and Elias guessed he fought the temptation to clap like a child. Then once more his brow rumpled. "But he was of France."

"King Henry's side of France. Thus, though not truly King Henry's man, he was Duke Henry's."

"Ah." The boy scratched his head. "Was he ever better loved?"

"Alas, the tale ends with the selfish young man's reunion with his father who, having lost his first son, forgave Cant and made him his heir." And now, Elias determined, further explanation for Honore. "However, were I to fashion of my own imagination what came after, I would say our hero kept his word to his father and did his duty to wed well. Eventually, fondness grew between him and his lady and they had...two sons, two daughters." Elias stretched his arms out to his sides. "And here we end our tale." He turned his palms up, bowed.

No applause and none expected since Cynuit did not wish to appear a child and Honore and Theo knew it was no work of fiction.

He straightened. "Now rest. On the morrow, Château de Sevier. I shall take first watch, Theo." He snatched up a blanket, draped it over his shoulders, and ventured only far enough amid the trees to conceal himself from those he protected and any beyond the firelight who might think to steal upon them. As he patrolled the perimeter, every few minutes trading one cover for the next, time and again he looked to the woman who had lain down. So thoroughly encased in blankets was she that had he not felt her gaze searching the dark through which he moved, he would not know her back was to the fire Theo had banked low to provide only enough warmth to see them through till morn.

Though her curiosity over Elias De Morville who had turned Elias Cant and the origin of Hart ought to be satisfied, that was not the end of it. As neither was it the end for him. Better he had left her at Forkney so never again a woman he could not have cause him to return to that place.

I will not sin with her as I sinned with Lettice, he assured himself. *I will not dishonor her nor myself.*

Even so, said a small voice, *Honore of Bairnwood gives you good cause to want to return to that place.*

"Even so," he growled and settled his senses on the land surrounding their encampment.

It was an hour before the sense honed in the darkened cellar at Wulfen felt what could not be seen, heard, or smelled.

Regardless of whether they were followed, there were others out there, near enough they surely knew the wood was not theirs alone.

~

DE MORVILLE. A name only distantly known to him ere this day when he learned of the family behind the face of the knight who made false about the aid given the godforsaken Becket.

But what a wondrous mystery! Neville of the family Sorrel loved each piece that moved him nearer finding favor with that grand duke upon whose brow rested a crown on the other side of the channel. Hopefully, he would be able to give Henry the slippery archbishop, but if De Morville and Becket had parted ways, the vassal who betrayed could be delivered unto him.

Providing Henry was in a vengeful mood—and after listening in on his envoys on the night past he was—England's king would be indebted.

Lands of my own, Neville mused. *Mayhap De Morville's.*

He wanted to laugh, but on so cool and clear a night the sound would carry across the faint scent of smoke to that barely perceptible glow.

He drew back, glanced at the men on either side of him. "Here we pass the night. You take first watch, Desmond…Raoul, second. If there is a third, it is mine."

Desmond, the burly man-at-arms grumbled as he did when reminded he enjoyed a life of leisure only as long as he held favor with the knight whose mother gave Neville much by way of apology for birthing her beloved last of three sons—among her greatest gifts fostering with Count Philip of Flanders though her husband had wished Neville dedicated to the Church. Unfortunately, the count had not offered a position in his household to the one he had knighted.

His loss, as would be felt when Neville proved worthy in the eyes of one mightier than the count—Philip's cousin, the King of England.

"I say we set upon them now," hissed Raoul, also a man-at-arms. Fortunately, what he lacked in intelligence he made up for in sword skill and the throw of a fist.

"Patience," Neville rasped. "First we see if they will lead us to Becket."

"I tell you, the archbishop has gone to ground," Raoul said. "Better we had searched the abbeys between Gravelines and Saint-Omer than—"

"You think those holy men would hand up one of their own?" Neville scorned. "Non, Becket or no, we have De Morville."

"What proof of his duplicity, my lord? Pray, not merely the proof of gut."

There was that, but more there was yestermorn. Having persuaded Saint-Omer's lord to loan a falcon for a few hours of sport, Neville and his companions had departed the castle. It was on the road near Clairmarais he encountered soldiers come from Sandwich who told they were on the trail of seven or eight men who had taken a skiff and stolen away from the port King Henry had placed under watch to prevent the archbishop from seeking refuge in France. The only aid Neville had been able to give was to inform them the king's envoys had arrived at Saint-Omer.

Now for the dozenth time, Neville cursed himself for not heeding the proof of gut when, a half hour later, he happened on Sir Elias's party. It had caused him to submit the tallest of the brethren was Thomas Becket, but he had been dissuaded when made to feel a fool for believing a man so humbly clothed could be the extravagant chancellor who had become an archbishop.

Then this day, four of those encountered on the road who were no longer horseless appeared at Saint-Omer. Recognizing them despite clothes far more fitting a party led by De Morville's heir, Neville had assured his seat at meal alongside De Lucy who had spent much of the evening past with King Henry's envoys.

Previous to Neville confiding his suspicion, the man had been barely tolerant of the attempt to engage him. Afterward, he had shown greater respect. And of benefit to Neville and his quest was the ring around the neck of De Morville's *cousin* who was more likely a mistress. De Lucy had known it for the hand upon whom it no longer sat.

That Neville had not shared with Desmond and Raoul. They would do as told no matter their scorn of his proof of gut—and learn to respect it.

Having kept Raoul waiting on an answer, Neville said, "Proof of gut, knave. Now take first watch."

"But you said second, my lord."

"And you are disrespectful." Neville motioned to Desmond to follow, strode to his mount, and removed his pack.

One of them would sleep well this night.

CHAPTER 29

WHAT HE SHALL MISS

For love he would have wed a commoner, and one hardly pure—a stretch near breaking point to believe of a noble.

Of course, now that Elias was heir, that breaking point had been reached. It was the way of the world. Would there ever come a day when it was not? When any who loved could join their life with any they loved without punishment, condemnation, loss?

One day, she thought and glanced at Elias's arm around her waist. *But not within memory of your days outside of heaven, Honore of Bairnwood.*

She looked up, silently entreated, *Lord, whomever Elias must wed to do his duty, let him grow to love her and her to love him.*

Minutes later, he slowed his mount and Theo came alongside, Cynuit holding to his back. "Château de Sevier is over that rise." Elias jutted his chin at a hill half a league distant, its edges blurred by rain so light it appeared more a mist. "Fortunately, we have good cause to keep our heads covered, and that we shall do lest

Arblette has joined the troupe likely to make camp outside the walls. Understood?"

All agreed, then Elias said, "Providing we are granted admittance, Theo will see to the horses and Cynuit will accompany Lady Honore and me to the donjon. Once the horses are stabled, Theo will wander the troupe's camp, keeping his head down and listening well."

The squire nodded.

"Honore, you shall continue to play my cousin come from England, and methinks you ought to feign illness."

She shifted around. "For?"

"To discover if Hart is with the troupe, we may require more than a night's lodging, and that is more likely granted if you are unwell."

And out of the way, Honore considered. Because of worry she would be unable to sustain playing the lady? Because her scar would draw attention? Because it would embarrass him?

She rejected that last, said, "For what other reasons would you hide me away?"

Though his face was shadowed by the hood, there was no mistaking his frown. "One only—Arblette. If he is at Sevier, it will be difficult enough for Theo and me to avoid alerting him we have come for Hart, and if you are confined abovestairs, there is good cause for Cynuit to remain near to ensure your needs are met."

She nodded.

"Theo, fall back," Elias said. "I must speak with Honore alone." When there was distance between the horses, he said, "My word I give."

"I believe you."

"Honore—"

"I do!" she said more sharply than intended, then sighed. "I do, Elias."

"I am glad."

She started to turn forward.

"I would think it easiest to pretend malady of the..." His voice lowered. "...womanly sort. Can you do it?"

Rather than match his unease over talk of menses, she gave a short laugh. "I am not so old my experience with such is in the past. Indeed, this day I am not long from its reality that could make pretense unnecessary."

As she felt his unease surge, she considered that if her monthly did arrive soon, the pretense would see her supplied with cloths for wherever next they journeyed.

"I did not mean to imply you are too old," he said. "Simply, much has been asked of you thus far, and—"

"I know not your experience with such things," she said, "but to be convincing I need not moan and bend over, though some women do suffer so much they are unable to put a stoic face upon their pain. I have but to express my need and discomfort to the lady of the castle. Unless she has no sympathy about her, she will see me provided for."

His smile was wry. "My experience with such is limited, though there is no doubt as to the monthly suffering of my stepmother who is years younger than I."

"I am sorry to hear that. There are some at Bairnwood who would agree with men it is the curse of Eve visited on them."

"It is good you do not think it that, Honore."

She did not, though like the sisters who would never gain the blessing of a child born of their bodies she might be justified in naming it a curse for having no reason to bleed.

They settled into silence, and she would have been content to remain thus if not for memories of the night past. "I thank you for the tale of Cant. I am glad to know it."

"How much of it did Lady Susanna reveal?"

"Very little beyond it being a much darker time best told by you."

He nodded.

"Methinks you loved Lettice very much."

"I did."

"Many a song you must have written her."

After a long silence, he said, "Ever I meant to, and a few I began, but none I completed or committed to memory. Mayhap I did not love her as much as thought, hmm?"

"Of course you did." Lest he recall his final parting with Lettice, Honore searched for something to move his thoughts elsewhere and landed on a curiosity. "There is something I would know."

"Ask it."

Moistening her lips, she felt the dip in the upper. "How did you learn of Hart so many years after his birth?"

His tension did not abate. "From the man who is as likely the boy's father as I."

She caught her breath. Then he knew Finwyn—?

Recalling what she had pondered on the night past as she watched for Elias moving among the trees, she realized it was more likely he spoke of the knight with whom he had found Lettice.

"The one who beat Elias Cant," he said. "He whose sword and armor I took."

"You saw him again?"

"Not long ago, I was in Rouen on business and paused at a tavern. As I finished my meal, several knights entered. It being dim, I did not recognize any, knew only from their accented French they were English. But ere they reached the bar, the boasting began, and I knew one of their numbers. Though I told myself to leave, it was as if Lettice entered with him, and I had to know what I had long denied myself—how she fared."

A muscle at his jaw jerked. "When a stool became available beside him, I took it. Engaging him in talk, I watched to see if I was recognized. I was not, though I knew well his face, not only for the arrogance scored into it but the bend of the nose I had broken in rending him unconscious ere relieving him of his knight's finery. I bought him a drink, asked after his stay in France, and was told his sword arm was so coveted he had recently left the service of a baron of northern England to serve a greater baron of the south who entrusted him with business in Normandy. Between expressions of great admiration, I probed, and when he revealed the name of the barony upon which he had previously served, I made much of having passed through one of its villages."

"Forkney," Honore said.

He smiled tautly. "I ordered more ale, and we talked of the village we both agreed had little to recommend it—except the women, I made great show of clarifying. He agreed and boasted of a buxom red-headed beauty. Obliged to boast of my own favored beauty, I described Lettice. He said she sounded familiar and had likely been amongst his conquests. When he asked her name, I struggled for it, submitting variations until he supplied it and said he had her many times until she lost her position at the castle and devoted herself to harlotry."

Feeling his ache, Honore regretting asking him to satisfy her curiosity. It was cruel.

"I asked what caused her to lose her position," he continued, "and he said the lady of the castle had her removed when she could no longer hide her pregnancy. The knight laughed, mused it could have been his babe she carried, then said perhaps it was mine." Elias momentarily closed his eyes. "There was naught over which to smile or laugh, but I managed both and said the only way the child could be mine was if Lettice became pregnant eight years ago. He slapped me on the back and said the fathering of her *bastard* fit me as well as him."

Longing to reach to him, Honore gripped the pommel tighter.

"The temptation to beat him again was great, and greater yet when I asked what became of her child. He said he did not know nor care, but when last he glimpsed her six months past she was not as lovely, that such it was with whores."

"Elias," Honore whispered.

He gave a shake of the head. "Knowing I must leave ere I did something I would regret, I concluded my business, collected my squire, and set sail for England."

More silence, during which her mulling returned her to a question whose answer yet eluded. She hated using the opportunity to discover if he could as easily be Hart's father as Finwyn or the knight he had beaten, but guilt over endangering him and his family for something not of his doing pushed her forward.

But if what he tells eliminates him, her conscience rebutted, *will you reveal the truth? Risk losing his aid?*

From what she now knew of Elias, and she hoped she did not fool herself in believing it was more than she did, he would keep his word to Lettice. And Honore would be the ungodly one who had said she could not recall the month in which the babe had become her responsibility.

I know not what I will do, she told her conscience, then said, "Did the knight reveal when last he was with Lettice so you might set it against when last you were with her?"

"I did not ask. He did not say."

So either she rouse his suspicion as to exactly how much she knew by asking him when last *he* had been with Lettice or once more she let it be.

"What is it, Honore?"

In that moment she wished for her gorget, certain she was more easily read in its absence. Though she could think of nothing over which to turn her lips, she smiled. "I am grateful Hart has you for a champion and hope you are his sire. Methinks I would rather lose him to you than have him return with me to Bairnwood."

"You honor me."

She looked forward, silently bemoaned, *All whilst further deceiving you.*

CHAPTER 30

IF HEART HE SEEKS TO SHEATHE

Château de Sevier
France

*T*hey were here, camped outside the walls. As Elias's party had ridden past, few of the troupe's members had shown themselves, though not because it rained with any more enthusiasm. Either they rested or rehearsed the evening's performance.

It had taken all that was in Elias not to begin searching the covered wagons and gaily-colored tents. However, it had surely required more of Honore to remain in the saddle. Had she needed to look miserable over the onset of her flux, a more convincing performance she could not give.

Her hands trembled, breath came fast, color was high, and a sheen of perspiration moistened strands of hair on her brow. Thus, more acceptable it was for him to keep hold of her elbow now they stood before the Costains.

"Sir Elias," a honeyed voice said.

He shifted his gaze from the Lord of Château de Sevier to the daughter handed forward.

Lady Vera was young, flawlessly lovely, and of a kindly disposition. Though she had been more a girl last year, now the fifteen-year-old presented as one firmly on the rungs of womanhood.

All poise and gentle purpose, she curtsied. "I am pleased once more you grace our home. It has been too long."

It had not, especially beneath the weight of ill feeling her parents had dropped around his shoulders the moment they greeted him in the great hall. But it was long enough Elias had not been turned away when he gave his name to gain entrance.

"So it has, my lady." He inclined his head and, ere raising it, slid into Elias Cant for the good will that would make it easier for him to discover if Hart was here. "Though not so long I do not recognize the beautifully blooming flower that was the loveliest bud when last we met."

Her lashes fluttered, and her smile showed fairly even teeth. "I blush, Sir Elias. Is that your intent?"

She was more bold than the ten and four girl she had been, of which neither parent approved, as told by Lord Costain's grunt and his wife's gasp.

Elias eased admiration from his eyes. "Forgive me, Lady Vera. I ought not speak as I find."

His words made her color deepen and mouth bow wider, while beside him Honore's stiff went stiffer.

He was flirting, though with motive rather than feeling which had moved him at Clairmarais. If only he could tell Honore it was Elias De Morville who had spoken pretty words to her in the chapel, not Elias Cant angling to give this young lady and her parents their due and see himself restored to their good graces. But perhaps it was best she thought him easily swayed by beauty wherever he happened upon it. Too much she cared for him.

"Indeed, you ought not speak so, Sir Elias," Lord Costain said.

"We would have no more brawling amongst our daughter's suitors than already we endure."

There was less chill in his voice than when he welcomed Elias to Sevier, doubtless due to the smug belief the knight before him deeply regretted what he could no longer have that had been offered so humbly that Elias's refusal had humiliated the man who longed to join his house with that of the De Morvilles.

Elias summoned a smile of apology. "Forgive me, my lord. It has been much too long, and of further regret is the circumstance under which we meet again."

He looked to Honore who curved an arm around her waist and held her chin high as she weathered the interest of their hosts the same as done those encountered between drawbridge and donjon. "As told the captain of the guard, my cousin who is to reside a time at Château des Trois Doigts is afflicted with abdominal discomfort and in need of rest ere we complete our journey."

Introductions were made between Honore and the five Costains, which included the younger daughter, Lady Gwen, and the recently knighted son, Sir Damien.

"I did not know Otto had family in England," Lord Costain said.

"So we do, albeit of distant relation." Elias did not care to think how he would explain Honore to his sire who would surely be apprised of this English cousin when next the two lords kept company.

Lady Vera stepped near Honore. "Dear lady, I understand your discomfort. Be assured you shall have all the rest and care you require. Though many are our guests come to enjoy performances by a troupe recently crossed from your shores to ours, you shall share a chamber with my sister and me."

"I thank you."

The lady dipped her head. "Come, Lady Gwen and I shall see you abovestairs."

Feeling Honore's hesitation, knowing her mind was on the troupe, Elias released her arm and motioned forward the lad who shouldered her pack. In English, he said, "Cynuit, deliver Lady Honore's belongings abovestairs and remain outside her door." He turned back to Honore, resumed speaking in French. "Do you require anything, Cousin, send him to me."

She inclined her head.

Elias knew he should not watch her progress across the hall behind the two young ladies lest it show too much interest, but she carried herself so beautifully she gave none cause to think her other than a lady.

"Distant cousin, eh?" Lord Costain muttered as she went from sight. "The way you look at her, Sir Elias, there had best be many degrees of separation between the lady and you."

Elias returned his gaze to the man. "You mistake my interest. I am but concerned for Lady Honore's well-being."

Costain chuckled. "For your sake let us hope so. I am well enough acquainted with your sire to know whereas he desired a union between his heir and my Vera, he would not approve of your Lady Honore."

Elias bristled in anticipation of what was to come.

"Not only is there the problem of her age, surely ten years beyond my daughter's"—

Seventeen, Elias silently corrected.

—"but that..." The man grimaced. "Dear Lord, did someone take a knife to her lip?" He shook his head. "Do you not stay clear of that one, Otto may rethink his need to make another heir."

Forgetting he required this man's forbearance, Elias set himself over him. "Your daughter is a lady above reproach, Lord Costain. Or nearly so."

"What say you?" the man's wife clipped.

Holding her husband's gaze, Elias continued, "Unfortunately, she had no choice in her sire, a man of such character he thinks naught of insulting the relation of one with whom he claims friendship."

Anger flared in Costain's eyes but quickly dimmed. "You are right. Lady Honore is an innocent and ought not pay for the offense you dealt my family."

Elias breathed deep. "I apologize again. No injury was intended, and as I am sure you would wish your daughter cherished, I am certain eventually you will be glad I declined to take her to wife."

"I am glad. A pity your father yet hopes for a match."

A hand landed on Elias's shoulder, at the end of which was Sir Damien. "If you and my sire are finished posturing, join me for a drink."

Posturing, Elias mused. It was a good label to affix to their encounter, giving them both a way out. He looked between husband and wife. "I am welcome at your table?"

Stiffly, Lord Costain said, "You *are* Otto's son."

And only for that was he welcome.

Whilst filling his belly with sliced beef, wine pudding, and warm bread, Elias reacquainted himself with the good-natured knight who could have been his brother-in-law. He made no mention of missing him at Saint-Omer and his knowledge the troupe Sir Damien had brought to Sevier had last performed at that castle where the king's envoys had passed a night. Thus, the young knight confirmed all. And added little to Elias's knowledge.

Hopefully, Theo's wanderings amongst the camp would bear proof Théâtre des Abominations was here.

MUCH TALK OF THE ARCHBISHOP, most erroneous, and none of it adding to what Elias knew of Thomas's flight from England nor his whereabouts. And in that moment, he did not care. What Theo had to tell was of greater import.

"It is the one, my lord."

Elias started to praise God their search neared its end, but did it? There was no guarantee Hart remained with the troupe—had he ever been amongst them. No guarantee that in the six months since his abduction he had not lost his life by natural or unnatural means.

Moved from praise to pleading, silently he entreated the Lord to deliver the boy back into Honore's arms.

"How can you be certain, Theo?"

"I heard talk—rather, argument—and the name Fin."

All of Elias that had not set to thundering over the light in his squire's eyes when he entered the great hall thundered. He breathed deep to calm a heart in agreement with legs that urged him to run to the camp, rasped, "Tell."

"The look of the woman who rode upon Sevier drew my regard, her urgency made me suspect. Her hair was an unnatural color of red and body better fit for a young woman than one of wizened face, and her garments—could they be called that—every color I have and have not seen and like a hundred veils from shoulders to calves."

It seemed more than Elias needed to know, but if he had to search her out, he would not mistake another for her. "What of her urgency?"

"I did not know a woman could so quickly dismount without breaking her neck. Hardly had I time to slip behind the tent before she was out of the saddle and through the flap. I positioned myself out of sight of the other tents and did not have to strain to hear her complaints against this Fin, accusing him of undoing all her good with his threat to beat one she called *The Map*."

Theo let that last unfold its meaning, and as Elias once more struggled for control, continued, "She said the boy set himself at Fin and the fool snatched up *Poseidon's Child* and denied the babe breath. His threat ended *The Map's* rebellion but affected the boy such she feared he would be unfit for display this eve."

So dark were the imaginings flooding Elias, he was grateful Honore was not present. But as it was nearly three hours since they parted, he did not think she would wait on him much longer.

"From which direction did the woman come?"

"South by west, my lord."

Then the sideshow did not keep close company with the rest of the troupe, having continued beyond Sevier—likely kept out of sight lest it meet with disapproval as it had in Henry's England. Wise, since King Louis's piety could make France even less tolerant of the mistreatment of children.

Now the question was how distant the sideshow was from Sevier. It could not be far since few would risk allowing strangers to lead them away from the safety of town and castle walls. To earn enough coin to make the sideshow profitable, it would have to be offered in close proximity to the troupe's performance. Thus, under cover of night, Théâtre des Abominations would surely appear outside Sevier's walls.

"What else did you learn?"

"The man with whom the woman conversed cursed Fin, said unless the miscreant once more found a means of stocking their sideshow, they must be done with him."

Stocking. Elias's teeth ached.

"He told her to return and behave as if naught were amiss lest Fin absconded with what their coin had bought," Theo continued. "She said she would try not to slit his throat and departed."

"Riding in the same direction whence she came?"

"Oui, my lord."

Elias thought on how best to ensure Hart did not slip through their fingers, which could happen if Arblette did as the unseen man within the tent feared, then considered his squire who was as near a knight as one could come ere receiving the accolade.

"Pray, ask it of me, my lord," Theo surprised. "I shall prove worthy of the spurs you shall soon fasten to my boots."

Elias longed to remind him of how dangerous—and

murderous—Arblette was, but it could sound an insult to one ready for the ceremony that proclaimed to all he was a warrior.

"My lord?"

Elias gripped his shoulder. "Scout out Arblette. When you find him, do not let him out of your sight."

Though Theo's smile was boyish, his eyes shone with the resolve of a man. "I will not, my lord. Anything else?"

"As soon as we return to Château des Trois Doigts, you are to meet with the smithy and make known the style of spurs that shall adorn your boots."

Theo squeezed a bit more from his smile. "Oui, my lord," he said then dropped the curve from his mouth so any curiosity roused by their meeting would not be furthered, and strode opposite.

Elias moved his gaze around the gathering in the hall that had grown from a dozen nobles when first he had entered to three dozen, all of whom Sir Damien had invited from neighboring lands to enjoy this night's performance.

Elias did not expect his father to attend, Otto's dislike of such entertainment more closely resembling hatred since having learned it was that which seduced his son into forsaking his family. Still, Elias had casually asked of Costain's son if he would be reunited with his father sooner than expected. Damien had said Otto had not responded.

Response enough, Elias assured himself. When this business with the troupe was done and Honore's return to England secured, it would be soon enough to tell his sire where he had been these weeks and how he had come by a son.

As supper would be served within the hour, after which the troupe would delight their audience, Elias decided to ease Honore's anxiety over what was to come and explain his flirtation with Lady Vera. Though he had told himself it was better he did not so she could more easily reclaim the feelings gifted him, he could not bear her to believe he had spoken false in the chapel...

that he had as little regard for her as had the young monk...that her smile was not a beautiful thing.

He strode from the alcove toward the stairs and halted when Cynuit bounded off them.

"Milord, I told her best not, but she comes."

And so she did, pinching up her skirts as she descended the steps.

Glad his back was turned to the milling guests who would not spare Honore their curiosity and, in some cases, disdain, he smiled when her eyes found him.

Though worry lined her brow, she had not spent all these hours draped across a bed or pacing herself into disarray beyond that of their ride. She had put herself in order.

Her garments were straight, brushed clean, and well-laced. Her hair was combed into a golden cape that draped her from crown to shoulders to hips and held in place by a circlet fashioned of tresses braided back off her temples. The simplicity was so becoming he did not doubt when Lord Costain caught sight of her he would reassess her age and think it further removed from the thirty and two he thought twenty and five.

Knowing she was as aware of the interest sweeping the hall as he, Elias said as she neared, "You look rested, Cousin."

She halted alongside Cynuit, found something to smile about. "I am much recovered."

He inclined his head, said, "Cynuit, take yourself to the kitchen and tell Cook you are my servant and require feeding."

The lad's eyes widened. "Am I truly your servant, milord?"

"If you wish to be."

"I do."

"'Tis done. Now go."

His first steps were at a run, but as if remembering he reflected on his new lord, he slowed and continued to the corridor at a brisk walk.

"You have made him happy," Honore said. "I thank you."

He nodded, leaned near. "You tell you are much recovered, but I would guess your state better described as restless."

She raised eyebrows above blue that asked of him questions better answered abovestairs.

"I was coming to you," he said.

"I wish I had known that."

So did he. It was one thing to ascend stairs on his own to what other guests would think his chamber, another to do so in Honore's company, especially since many of Costain's guests were acquainted with him and did not yet know he delivered his English cousin to Château des Trois Doigts.

"We will have to talk here," Honore said.

"Oui, but afterward you ought to return abovestairs."

Neither agreeing nor disagreeing, she glanced beyond him. "Will you not offer your arm and lead me to the left of the hearth? No one is there."

As he guided her across the hall, she asked, "Have you learned anything?"

"Theo did well. The troupe outside is the one we seek."

She stumbled.

Elias steadied her and hoped any watching would believe the tale of her poor health that had surely begun circulating with her appearance, one or more of the Costains having been called upon to explain who she was.

"Then Hart is in one of the tents we passed."

"Non." Wishing this could have been told in her chamber, he handed her onto a bench and lowered beside her. "The sideshow continued on, though not far, methinks."

Her lips pursed over a question, then she said, "Why?"

Moving his gaze from her mouth that he ought not linger over for remembrance of what he should forget, he leaned forward and clasped his hands. "Doubtless they wish to avoid being ejected from France the same as Henry ejected them." He met her gaze. "Arblette has joined the troupe. He is with the sideshow."

Her eyes widened and hand rose toward her mouth.

Resisting the temptation to draw more attention by capturing her hand, hoping she would understand what he commanded of her, he said, "You are my cousin, Honore. Not distressed, merely unwell."

She stayed her hand at the level of her chest, lined her face with discomfort, and settled her arm across her midriff. "Continue, Elias. I shall not forget who you are to me."

In time he hoped she would. He told her all Theo had learned, excepting Arblette's threat to beat Hart and steal the babe's breath. And from a distance she played well the cousin, only Elias able to read the face of Honore of Bairnwood, champion of foundlings.

"I fear for Theo," she whispered. "If Finwyn recognizes him as your squire—"

"He excels at tracking and concealment. Unless Arblette gives him cause to show himself, he will not."

"Cause?" her voice rose slightly, distress once more jeopardizing the part she played.

"*Cousin* Honore, should it prove necessary, Squire Theo—soon to be Sir Theo—will protect the children with his life."

She summoned a smile, and once more he looked too close on her perfectly imperfect mouth.

"I want my Hart back," she said softly.

Momentarily mistaking the boy's name for that which beat in her breast, he forgot the part *he* played and leaned toward her.

"Cousin!" she gasped low.

He stilled, saw the space between them was barely respectable. But as he began to pull back, he heard and saw what he should have sooner—fine leather boots whose cuffs were brushed by the hem of a pale blue tunic.

"I understand we have acquired an English cousin," a graveled voice spoke only loud enough to be heard by the two before him.

Elias set his teeth, looked up into eyes the color of his own though smaller amid folds set in a face whose brow, cheeks, and neck were grooved, as clearly revealing the man's three score years as the silvered hair brushing broad, slightly bent shoulders.

Be Elias Cant, he told himself and stood. With enthusiasm drawn from a deep well, he said, "Father!" and embraced Otto De Morville.

CHAPTER 31

FORGIVE THE FOOL

Someone came for them. Not Honore as he had assured himself for months until awakening to find the floor beneath him rolling and the coast of his country growing distant. But she would send someone to get him out of the mess he had made of disobedience, and just as the others were awakened each morn by her kiss on their brows, once again he would be awakened. If she lived...

She lives, he told himself as done every day since glimpsing proof she might not, then he whispered against hands clasped to his mouth, "She will send someone."

"Quiet, boy!"

He startled where he huddled in a corner of the covered wagon alongside the blue and white painted wooden crate where little Alice had cried herself to sleep.

Suppressing the impulse to defy the man who had lured him from Bairnwood with the promise of sweets the last day in which he had not known how happy he was, Hart met the gaze of the one Inès called Fin.

Though Hart's existence had been one of fear and anger since becoming the property of Jake the Jack whose troupe offered a sideshow of six *peculiars*—now four—he had settled into it as best he could while waiting for Honore. But when Fin had followed them out of England, all had gone from tolerably bad to very bad.

No sympathy had Fin for the tiny babes gone so utterly still that six had become four on the day he appeared as they traveled to Saint-Omer, the man's only concern the sideshow's loss of its greatest draw. And when Hart had seen what he wore around his neck, whatever held him together throughout the twins' passing had snapped.

Though his fists were useless against the devil, his frenzy so upset the little ones the sideshow could not be offered at that castle. Inès had been angry, blessedly more with Fin than Hart.

Now the evil one rose from a stool before the wagon's rear door that had been tossed opened to let in fresh air and the last of day's light. "What you looking at, boy?" He stepped forward. "Do you challenge me?"

It was as Hart longed to do, but now that Fin had discovered how best to control the oldest member of Théâtre des Abominations beyond pinches, slaps, and punches to places below a face that perverse men and women paid to look upon, Hart would behave. He must protect his little ones as Honore protected hers, be to them what she was to them—as much as his seven years would allow.

Fin's fine boots made the floorboards creak and Jamie on his cot draw his blanket up over his head. Rayne was also awake, fearfully peering at Hart through fingers covering her face.

"Do you, boy?" Arblette halted over Hart.

"Leave him be, Fin," whipped Inès's mean voice that could also be softly coaxing. "If ye upset The Map so's he canna stand to be looked upon without wetting himself, Jake gonna look to ye for lost coin."

Hart had been ashamed the first time his bladder let loose as hands tilted his face this way and that to determine the accuracy of what they believed was the island kingdom imprinted on his face, but the few times after that had been intentional when, following hours of being treated like objects, the little ones and he could tolerate no more.

Jake and Inès had cursed him. To no avail. Cajoled him. To some avail. Better food, warmer clothing, and a few toys for the six—now four—had done wonders to control Hart's bladder whilst he waited for Honore. And now whomever she would send to them.

"Someone," he said again.

"What say you?" Fin demanded.

Hart tried to swallow the words rising up his throat, but they burned like vomit that needed spewing to settle one's belly. Hoping Inès would not allow Fin to carry out his threat of a beating, Hart said, "Someone is coming for us. And you. Soon you will be dead like..." He could not speak the names he had given them, had not been able to since the tiny hands clutching his fingers went lax. "...the girls."

"We must start for Sevier soon," Inès warned as she moved toward them.

Ignoring her, Fin scorned, "Dead, you say?"

Hart tilted his face higher. Noting what was no longer around the man's neck, once more he was stirred by sorrow and hatred, with which he had not been familiar until six months past. Had Fin killed Honore to take what Hart had secured beneath his sleeve after all had bathed at the pond yesterday—the loss of which had wonderfully flustered Fin?

Nay, Honore had lost it. Fin had found it. Or perhaps it was not even hers. At Bairnwood he had glimpsed upon an older novice one that looked identical to Honore's. There could be hundreds.

Fin kicked Hart's leg. "Say again, boy. Soon I will be dead like those devil spawns?"

Hating him more, Hart said, "Dead like a worm wishing for wings to fly to heaven when he has only a slimy wiggle to dig his way to hell."

Hart did not see Inès was upon them until he flung himself to the side to avoid the fist aimed at his face.

"Fin!" the fiery-headed crone barked as she thrust forward, landing the two hard against the wall above Hart.

Hearing the little ones whimper, Hart rebuked himself for not cramming the words down. Close to tears, he peered up at the two overhead, only became aware of their shoes against his ribs and legs as they began to wrestle.

He scrambled from beneath them, but as he moved toward the little ones to offer comfort as Honore would do, the two slammed into him. Stumbling sideways, he saw Inès clung to Fin, slapping and punching him.

Alice was wailing now, but before he could reach her, a blow to his chest sent him sliding on his back toward the rear of the wagon. Despite blurred vision, he saw who strode toward him—and the rage that warned of fists that would bloody and bruise.

Regaining his feet, Hart backed away. As terror urged him to run, the flurry of color that was Inès sprang onto Fin's back.

Hart looked to the little ones. They were out of reach, the grappling Inès and Fin between them and Hart.

Run, run! clanged fear, and he launched himself out the doorway and over the steps, bending his knees to lessen the impact, tucking his head to roll out of the fall.

Panting, he peered up at the lantern-lit wagon. No one was visible in the doorway, but above the little ones' cries he heard Inès curse.

If he knew she would prevail, he would stay, but if Fin triumphed, Hart might very well die and be of no use to his charges.

He gathered himself up and retreated far enough to hide amid the shadows of descending night. From there he would watch, returning only if Inès called to him. If Fin sought him, he would go for help. And pray someone gave it.

Crouching in bushes whose thorns pricked, hand gripping the prayer beads through his sleeve, he watched the wagon. And nearly called to Inès when she appeared in the doorway. But she was not alone.

She yanked Fin forward, and there was enough light to see triumph on her face, defeat on his. "Find him!" She shoved him onto the narrow landing, and as he descended the three elevated steps, said, "And do you forget to whom he belongs, Jake *will* make a worm of you."

Hart started to stand and show himself, but Inès slammed the door closed behind her. Shivering, he sent his gaze around the clearing to map a way past Fin that would allow him to gain the wagon without being seen by one he did not trust to take the woman's threat seriously.

Light burst from the front of the wagon, amid it Inès, then the slam of that other door and her shadowed figure lowering to the bench behind the horses. Reins snapped, and the wagon trundled toward the castle where the troupe performed this eve.

Realizing she was leaving him alone with Fin who would mount his horse to bring *The Map* to ground if his efforts to find him on foot failed, Hart ran. Providing he stayed to the shadows, he would not be seen before he overtook the wagon. *If* he could overtake it. A sob escaped him as it picked up speed, trailing behind it the cries of those who needed him.

"Someone!" Hart gasped. "Someone!"

Not *someone*. Fin. As the devil took his prey to ground, he clapped a hand over Hart's mouth, capturing death cries he would not have reach Inès.

"I DID NOT THINK you so inclined, Son." Elias's father drew out of their embrace and set hands on his heir's shoulders as if to look upon him with pride.

An act. Not that he was not proud of the man Elias had become over the years it was believed him a victim of foul play— especially that rare achievement evidenced by the Wulfrith dagger. But in that moment he was less proud than reproachful.

A hastily written missive of little detail had informed him his son was called to England. Though there had been no time to waste dealing with the argument sure to ensue, Elias could have revealed more. He did not fear his father's wrath nor disinheritance. It was Otto's disappointment he strove to avoid and that others in the path of their lord not suffer for it, especially his father's young wife who was more familiar with her husband's disregard than his kind regard and their daughters who were of little consequence for not being born of the sex by which a man kept alive his name.

Returning to the one before him, Elias said, "You did not think me inclined to what, Father?"

Flicking his gaze to the woman who kept her seat, Otto said low, "I am grateful you at least had the foresight to lie to save your family the humiliation of bringing into the home of our neighbor and ally a woman such as that, she who wears her hair down around her shoulders as if yet a maiden."

No surprise Otto did not accept this English cousin. Thus, he guessed her his son's lover—all the more believable when the respectable distance between the two had became nearly intimate.

Before Elias could correct him, Otto said, "What I do not understand is what female problem could be so pressing you could not continue on to Château des Trois Doigts. Our paths having crossed, you would be there now, this charade unnecessary."

Elias pushed up a smile. "Now is not the time to explain. Suffice that—"

"I am Honore," said the woman who rose beside Elias. "If you wish to continue the pretense to avoid casting shame upon your house, Lord De Morville, may I suggest you kiss my hand?" She extended it.

He stiffened, stared, and Elias could see his eyes were too low to be upon Honore's.

Though Costain had informed him of the cousin brought to Sevier, he had not mentioned her mouth, either to avoid offending as he had done Elias or because he thought Otto knew of it. Now the older man was certainly aware—as was Honore.

She reached her hand nearer. "I can see you are unsettled, Lord De Morville, but it will have to be explained later. Now pray, save your family the humiliation you so fear."

It taking great effort to remain light of face, Elias said, "Allow me to introduce our cousin, the fair Lady Honore recently of the convent of Bairnwood Abbey."

His father recovered so quickly Elias would have laughed were the situation not dire. And the way in which Otto returned to life was believable, not for the first time causing Elias to acknowledge it must be from him he had learned to slip into another mind and attitude.

"Little Honore!" Otto exclaimed for all and stepped to the side and caught up her hand. "Forgive my surprise, but who would guess the duckling would become so lovely a bird?" He kissed her fingers, shook his head wonderingly. "Now I see your mother in you. Praise the Lord you outgrew the look of your father. Not that he was unsightly, but..." He jumped his shoulders. "He had not the look of a De Morville."

She curtsied, withdrew her hand. "Certes, he did not."

"Will you do me the honor of sitting with me at meal, Cousin?"

Elias opened his mouth to inform his father she was to return abovestairs, but she said, "As I am nearly recovered from my pains, I shall."

Otto looked to his son. What was in his eyes in no way

reflecting the show he put on for others, he gripped Elias's arm and drew him aside. "You had best have a believable explanation."

"I do, though you will not like it."

Otto's lids narrowed. "Do not forget I can yet set you aside, if not to wed to get another heir, then to pass my lands to my brother."

Whom all knew he disliked, Elias reflected, then said as ever he did, "That is your decision. I trust you will do what is best for your family and people."

"What is best may not be you."

"I am well with whatever you decide."

A long silence, then, "Within the year, you will either make good your word to ensure the family name or I am done with you."

Though Elias's eyes were drawn to Honore, he held them to his sire. "If you wish me to keep my word, I shall."

His father's lids lifted, and the hard line of his mouth eased. "Grandsons worthy of that dagger of yours. That is all I require."

Elias had not thought it asking much, providing he did not have to wed a girl, but in that moment the burden took on weight. "As already told, I shall do my duty."

"Then I will do my best to suffer this imposter until you set her aside."

It tempting further argument to assert Honore and he were not lovers, Elias said, "Soon the meal will be served. Let us gain our seats." He started toward Honore, but Otto reached her first.

"Permit me, my lady." He took her elbow.

Honore peered at Elias who gave her a look of assurance and followed. As they neared those previously denied a clear view of her, he noted her stiffening. But she did not falter, and when they reached the high table and Elias lowered on the side of her opposite his sire, she smiled at him.

It did make her more lovely, the scar less noticeable, but there was strain in it. And he wished Otto De Morville had rejected the invitation to attend this night's performance. Why had he not?

Though Elias had nearly a year to gain a suitable bride, did his father seek to once more place Lady Vera on the altar of marriage? Did he hope the offense dealt the Costains had eased sufficiently they would offer her again?

With a low growl, Elias set his mind to gaining an invitation to see the sights of Théâtre des Abominations.

Observation, he determined. Watch what drew the performers to secretively approach their audience. Failing that, he would search out the sideshow himself.

CHAPTER 32

WHO CAST THE JEWEL

Otto De Morville was hardly his son, but his performance was worthy. Furrowing his brow, he tilted his head as if with great interest. "The abbey, hmm?"

"Oui, my lord. Bairnwood."

"And you are of the convent."

Honore glanced sidelong at Elias. Though he did not appear to listen, she guessed he tried over laughter, chatter, thudding goblets, and scraping knives. "Non, my lord. That was pretense."

His only show of surprise a blink, he said, "Surely you do not say you are a nun."

"I do not."

"Then?"

She leaned nearer, not for the first time noted the marked resemblance between father and son. "A servant, my lord."

The corners of his smile flexed. "As thought, the lady is also pretense."

"The lady is."

"And you have no right to wear your hair loose. You are a—"

"I am no harlot, nor have I ever wed. Though you find it difficult to believe a servant could be my age and yet possess virtue, I break no stricture in wearing my hair unbound."

"But you do in playing a noblewoman when that divine blood does not course you."

Divine, she mused. Though trying hard not to dislike the man, he made it easy. Gently, she cleared her throat. "That is open to debate, my lord. Though I cannot know for certain, it is possible I am noble at least one side of me." She moved her gaze to the trencher he had hardly touched as if fearful he shared it with one unworthy of placing her spoon near his. "Mayhap you ought to eat whilst you think on that."

He dipped into the stew that soaked the carved-out loaf of bread, stirred it, returned his attention to her. "You were born at the convent, your mother sent there to conceal her disgrace."

"Again, possible, whether she was of noble blood or my sire was—or both."

He nodded slowly. "Regardless, misbegotten."

"Or merely unwanted." She touched her lip. "I was born with a gap that had to be sewn closed. Imagine how frightening it must have been for those present at my birth. Thus, either the belief I could not survive or superstition made a foundling of me."

"I see," he said so solemnly she could almost believe he felt for her. He sat straighter. "What I do not see is your purpose. If you are not my son's lover, what?"

She felt the brush of Elias's shoulder against hers, then his breath stirring her hair. "As told, all will be explained later, Father."

"I would hear it now." Otto De Morville swept his gaze over the hall, said, "Privacy among the masses—oft better than privacy behind a closed door that conceals a listener on the other side."

Elias turned from the trencher and lady with whom he shared it, angled toward his father to make a wall of his body, and set a forearm on the table. "Over six months gone, a boy was stolen from Bairnwood Abbey—a foundling, one of many for whom Honore cares at the abbey."

His father made a wall of his own body, and though Honore had space aplenty, she felt as if squeezed between the two. "That is what took you from France?"

"Though I did not know he had been stolen, it was for Hart I went to England."

"Hart?"

"That is his name."

"How old?" Otto De Morville asked, and Honore knew from his tone he began to understand.

"Not yet eight."

"A foundling, you say. For what was he abandoned?"

Honore tensed, but Elias said, "His mother could not keep him."

For the best, she thought. No reason to further bias Otto De Morville. God willing, Hart would soon be free and Elias's father could be told of the mark of birth ahead of meeting the boy.

The older man took up his goblet, as he drank looked from Honore to his son, then asked, "The fate of this boy concerns you how?"

"As you must have guessed, he is my son. Your grandson."

Honore had hoped he would only put forth the possibility Hart was his. Could it be proved the boy was not, now there were two who would be angered by her deception.

"How can you be certain he is yours?"

"He is mine, Father."

Pray, let it be so, Honore sent heavenward.

Otto lowered his goblet. "So it was not enough to abandon your family to make England your stage. You had to sow children who could lay claim to us."

Elias drew a deep breath. "Only the one, and I loved his mother."

"A commoner?"

"That Lettice was."

His father glowered. "Yours or not, you need not take responsibility for him."

"I believe the Wulfriths would disagree." Some of Elias's anger visible beyond the mask he surely struggled to keep in place, he added, "Indeed, I am certain they would."

Clearly, his father did not like that, but he pressed, "If his own mother would not take responsibility for him, why should you?"

"Because I can. She could not."

A growl sounded from the older man. "Then find him and provide for him until he is of an age to make his own way. Whether you return him to the abbey or his mother—"

"She is dead, murdered by the one who stole Hart and fled to France."

The harsh lines in his sire's face eased but soon returned. "Then the abbey. Regardless, I would not have you bring him into my home."

"Be assured, I would not think to subject him to your hatred."

Feeling as if suffocated by tension on both sides of her, Honore hissed, "You are father and son. Pray, cease!"

She was not surprised Elias eased back, but that his sire did made her look sharply at him. And on his face she glimpsed disquiet.

His throat worked, then he said, "I still know not *your* purpose."

"Honore aids in retrieving my son," Elias said, "for a short time traveling as my wife—"

"Wife?" his father choked.

"Oui, to make it acceptable she accompany me without escort. However, as we neared Saint-Omer where I am better known, I thought it best to name her a distant cousin."

After a long silence, Otto said, "How close are you to finding the boy?"

"He is upon these lands. But be assured I shall do my best to recover him without Costain's knowledge. As it will be easier done aided by your men, how many accompanied you?"

"Three." It was said with grudging acquiescence. "Men-at-arms only, they are quartered in the barracks." When Elias inclined his head, Otto swung his regard to Honore. "It seems you are owed an apology—though only do you not seek to seduce my son the same as this Lettice."

Before her indignation could sound across the hall, Elias leaned so far in his shoulder pressed hers. "One more insult, and it may prove impossible not to humiliate our family—and lay ruin to whatever your reason for accepting Lord Costain's invitation."

Part consternation, part fear flashed in Otto's eyes. "Settle yourself, Elias. I but take measure of the situation that I may plan accordingly." He fit a smile that did not fit. "You have noticed Lady Vera is no longer a girl."

His words trampled Honore's heart that had no cause to place itself between father and son. She knew what he implied the same as she knew Elias was attracted to the young woman.

A good thing, she told herself. She had spent little time with the lady and her sister when shown to their chamber, but she liked her. Presenting as genuinely kind, a good young wife she would make Elias and, God willing, bear healthy children.

"Do we discuss this at all," Elias said, "we will not do so now."

His father raised his eyebrows. "Certes, we will discuss it, but it can wait." He looked to Honore. "Apologies. I am a disappointed man who, weary of waiting on grandsons, feels every year that passes without assurance the De Morville name shall pass to another generation. Can I be forgiven?"

Honore inclined her head, glanced at Elias as he turned back to his shared trencher.

Otto sighed. "I know. I am, have ever been, shall ever be a poor father. And husband. But it is too late to change."

Sensing the soft of the man beneath the hard, Honore said, "I do not believe that. Has not the Lord given you more years than many? You are...what? Three score?"

"Three score three."

"Nearly twice my age." She almost laughed at his look of disbelief. "I am aware I appear younger than thirty and two. A good thing, I am told and mostly I agree. Were my face beginning to wizen, I might gain more respect, hmm?"

He frowned. "I may be nearly twice your age, but you are more than twice that of Lady Vera."

And that mattered much, the young woman possessing seventeen more childbearing years.

Not wanting to think there, regardless if it was Lady Vera whom Elias wed or another, Honore said, "Even if the Lord does not grant you another score of years, surely there is time to better your relationships."

He appeared to consider it but said, "For what?"

Wishing she had not tried to fix what he would have remain broken, she retrieved her goblet. "Now it is I who must be forgiven. I tread where I ought not."

Determined to ignore the De Morvilles, she settled back and waited for meal's end when the troupe would be admitted to entertain late into the night, while outside the walls a sideshow was offered to the perverse.

Soon, Hart, she silently reached out to him. *You will be safe. We will weep over our parting. All you have suffered will be in the past. You will have the father you deserve. Soon.*

CHAPTER 33

SWEET PETALS STAY THE STEM

*B*est you return abovestairs."

Honore looked up at Elias as he escorted her from the dais. "Surely you do not believe Finwyn will be amongst those who entertain Lord Costain's guests?" she asked.

"Not to entertain, but he may move among the guests to search out those interested in a different sort of entertainment."

"Then neither of us can be seen."

"Thus, I shall observe from the gallery." He nodded at the balcony coursing one wall. Overlooking the hall, musicians engaged to supplement the music provided by the troupe were settling in with their instruments. "A good vantage from which to see and not be seen."

"I would like to watch with you."

Elias was tempted to agree since she would recognize the miscreant before he whose dealings with the man were fewer and under cover of night.

"Should he disguise himself as a performer," she pressed, "I know his stature and mannerisms well enough to recognize him sooner than you."

"I am thinking the same." He guided her past guests who gathered at the center of the hall while servants moved the dining chairs and benches to the perimeter to afford a better view.

Halting before the stairs, he said, "I shall follow shortly."

She slipped out of his hold and raised her skirt.

Though inclined to watch her ascend the steps, Elias distanced himself the sooner to shed lingering looks. The De Morvilles were of too much interest.

"Sir Elias!"

He donned a face, turned to the sisters. "Ladies."

"Did you enjoy the meal?" Lady Vera tilted her head, exposing her neck to the caress of torchlight.

"I did. I thank you and your mother for a glorious feast."

Her eyebrows rose above eyes that could not hope to match the blue nor depth of Honore's. "What was your favorite dish?"

How to answer when he knew he had eaten only because his belly did not ache? "Dear lady, that is like asking which of the Costain sisters is the loveliest—the light or the dark, the blue-eyed or the brown-eyed." He looked between them. "The one most accomplished at song or at dance."

Both laughed, pleasing to the ear but not as pleasing as another's laugh. Too, he liked another's smile better for its lack of perfection.

Lady Vera released a long, musical breath. "Food aside, there is one thing that might aid in choosing between my sister and me."

Telling himself he had only himself to blame, he said, "That is, my lady?"

She set her chin higher. "Which of us is more a woman than a girl?"

As there was no way to avoid offending one or both, she had him where she wanted him. But there was something to smile about, and he did, causing the triumphant turn of her lips to convulse.

"Lady Vera, you are a treasure worthy of being the only one in a man's keeping. I am sorry if my decision not to be that man offended, for I believe you will make a very good wife. But as I am certain I could not be as good and worthy a husband to you, it would be wrong to deny you the opportunity to find true happiness—and love."

Only when she settled into her heels did he realize she had been on her toes as if to better see his dismay. She clicked her tongue. "It is impossible to dislike you, Sir Elias."

"I cannot say I am sorry."

She laughed again, as did her watchful sister, then touched his arm. "Will you sit with us?"

He grinned. "And risk our fathers once more seeking to match us as *they* please?"

"You are right." She sent her gaze around the hall, narrowed it. "Methinks Sir Leofric a bit young—more a boy than a man—but I like him. He and his friend will sit with us, Gwen." She curtsied and drew her sister away.

Elias did not realize he was still smiling until the feeling of being watched drew his regard to the gallery. The musicians were visible on their seats near the railing, but not Honore. She stood in shadow to the left alongside a pillar, her presence and gaze entirely felt.

A stick thumped the floor, then Lord Costain's son boomed, "The performance is about to begin. Take your seats!"

Amid the rush to comply, Elias ascended to the gallery. Mostly ignored by those tuning their instruments, he strode behind them.

It was a mistake to share the dark with Honore he realized when struck by the longing to slide an arm around her and draw her back against him. But were they to work together and stay out of sight, it was necessary.

Peering across her shoulder, she said low, "Lady Vera is lovely and seems of a kindly disposition."

"She is."

"Methinks your father has chosen well."

"She is very young."

"That sounds a complaint. Most men—"

"I am not most men. When I wed, it is a wife I want, not a daughter I must raise to womanhood."

He felt her surprise. Though he meant what he said, he regretted sounding angry.

"Admirable," she murmured. "I did not mean to offend."

"You do not. What offends are men—especially ones old enough to be a father or grandfather—who steal a girl's youth, health, even her life to gain immortality by making sons on her. Men who think naught of disposing of daughters by wedding them to whoever proves most advantageous to their purses."

As the musicians began strumming, blowing, plucking, and drumming, she said, "Your father."

"One among many. When he believed me dead alongside my older brother, he ruined a girl who birthed only daughters ere she could give no more. Do I not soon provide a grandson, he will set her aside and ruin another."

"And yet you will not wed Lady Vera."

"Though now more a woman than a year past when I offended her family and angered my father by refusing to take to wife a fourteen-year-old, I will not wed one nearly half my age."

"But you seem taken with her."

"Calculated flirtation to make amends and ensure our welcome."

He heard her swallow. "Then whom will you wed so your sire does not ruin another girl?"

"I know not, but I have a year ere that must be done."

"A year?"

"To repair the rift with my sire, I gave my word that within two years I would wed a lady acceptable to both of us. One year remains."

After a long moment, she said, "You will make a good husband, Elias De Morville. And father."

The stick sounding again, its thump echoing around the walls and silencing the musicians, Honore turned forward.

Forcing his gaze past golden hair that tempted his fingers, Elias looked to the doors before which Sir Damien stood and felt excitement stir as if he were outside waiting to be let in, as if the tales he would tell swirled above his thoughts, the dance he would dance twitched his feet, the songs he would sing expanded his lungs.

When a hush of anticipation fell over all, Sir Damien stepped to the side and nodded at the porters.

The doors were swung wide, and against the night the performers were a feast of color, from painted faces to costumes, instruments, batons, balls, and exotic animals.

"The family of Costain are pleased to present Jake the Jack and his Troupe Fantastique!" Sir Damien announced.

The man at the fore, garbed in close-fitting chausses and tunic fashioned of blocks of red, black, and yellow material, and holding white batons, gave a sweeping bow. Then he leapt forward, tossed the batons high ahead of him, and twice sprang from hands to feet before recapturing the sticks.

As his audience roared and clapped, he dropped his head back and smiled out of a face colored white but for eyes and mouth rimmed in black. "Fantastique!" he shouted in an unnaturally deep voice. Then, running, tumbling, and dancing, the other performers entered the hall.

The first act, accompanied by the musicians in the gallery, was so breathtaking Elias could have lost himself in it if not for the reason he was here. He could not forget those exploited by a troupe likely led by Jake the Jack.

"I have never seen such," Honore whispered.

"Oui, they are very good."

She set a shoulder against a pillar. "A pity their hearts are black."

Once more struggling against pulling her into his arms, he said, "Hopefully, not all."

"Certes, Jake the Jack."

As he had concluded, and in that moment whatever he felt for Honore he felt more. No girl this. A woman unafraid to engage her mind ahead of her body.

Singing followed, causing other members of the troupe to take to the walls behind their audience. Most settled in, but some moved around the perimeter. It was these Elias observed and would have directed Honore to watch did she not point them out.

Next, a troubadour clothed in a tunic painted to look like chain mail and holding the reins of a great wolfhound fit with a saddle, transfixed all with the tale of ill-fated lovers Pyramus and Thisbe. So perfectly and passionately was it delivered Elias knew he could learn from the man were he able to give his undivided attention. He could not. And he was glad of it when he saw a male singer crouch behind a nobleman several seats removed from Otto.

"There," Elias said.

"I see him."

Over the next several minutes, with the troubadour's tale and accompanying song more annoyance than entertainment, they watched the exchange between nobleman and performer. It was so discreet it seemed no others noticed. Then the nobleman nodded, dipped into his purse, and as if merely clearing the hair from his brow, passed payment over his shoulder.

As the singer resumed his place against the wall, the thick-necked woman who had earlier bent herself out of shape approached the young knights seated with the Costain sisters. A quick end was put to that encounter by the one alongside Lady Vera. The knight backhanded the air and nearly struck the woman's face, causing her to retreat so quickly others would have noticed were they not enraptured by the tale.

Over the next half hour of dancing, juggling, and the display of exotic animals, more attempts were made to find an audience for Théâtre des Abominations and five more payments given.

Would Costain's guests collect on that for which they had paid at the intermission when drinks and viands were served, or at night's end? Likely intermission, and after the second half of the show, another batch of nobility would slip from the castle.

Minutes later it came to pass when the break was called and servants entered bearing platters and pitchers. Though it appeared all but two of the performers remained in the hall to make themselves available to admirers while easing their own thirst and hunger, six of the guests moved toward the great doors left wide open to cool the hall heated by a crackling fire and the press of bodies.

"I shall follow them and, if there is time, rouse my father's men," Elias said as he drew Honore across the back of the gallery. "You will return to your chamber."

"Can I not—?"

"Non. And pray, do not argue. I will not agree, and you will only delay my departure, giving them a chance to slip away."

"I will do as told," she acquiesced, and he left her on the landing and descended the stairs.

HONORE ENTERED the chamber she was to share with the young ladies and opened the shutters as Elias appeared in the bailey below. There was no sight of the guests who had departed ahead of him, and as he broke into a run, she prayed he would overtake them, be safe, and soon return with Hart and the others.

A quarter hour later, Jake the Jack departed the hall, and she feared if his destination was also Théâtre des Abominations, he would see Elias stole after his patrons. But with great leisure and turns, tosses, and catches of the batons, he crossed the bailey and settled in the shadow to the left of the inner gatehouse tower. The answer to what he did there was the noblewoman of middling years who joined him.

Honore could not see into the dark where torchlight barely stole, but she would remain at the window until Elias returned.

Leaning against the embrasure, she peered out across the castle to the dimly lit land. As the tents were erected back from the walls, she could see the tops of many and the glow of fires. Beyond them lay the wood, and possibly the sideshow.

"Lord," she whispered, "pray—"

Movement returned her gaze to the bailey, and she saw a knight pass beneath the raised portcullis.

She caught her breath. Not a knight. A squire. And not alone.

The head of the one whose arm he gripped was lowered, but though she could not see the face of the slight figure, all of her leapt.

She nearly called to Hart, but there were others in the bailey beyond the garrison patrolling the walls, and she dare not alert Jake the Jack. But a moment later he emerged as if she had called to her boy. Hands empty of batons, he stared after the two moving around the side as if to enter the donjon by way of the garden.

Had the man recognized Hart? Or did he merely suspect?

The woman who had joined him appeared and drew him back toward the inner wall. He shook off her hand, but as fear constricted Honore's heart, urging her to call out a warning, Jake the Jack returned to the shadows.

Honore ran.

With the guests in the hall resuming their seats for the second half of the performance, easily she moved past them and was waylaid only upon entering the kitchen corridor behind servants carrying platters of decimated viands.

"Honore!" Cynuit stepped in her path. "Is it not wondrous? I thought Sir Elias most entertaining but—"

"Later." She sidestepped.

"Something is wrong?"

No longer, she thought and called over her shoulder, "All is right. Enjoy the show."

All was not right, but nearly so. Thus, it was best the boy remain where he was safe.

Honore expected to find Theo and Hart in the heated kitchen, but amidst the servants setting aright the mess of many, they were not to be seen. Certain they could not have reached the hall, Honore guessed they were in the garden.

"Pardon!" she exclaimed when she bumped into a servant, nearly causing him to lose hold of an enormous tray upon which sat empty tankards and goblets.

His annoyance quickly replaced by a taut smile and deferential nod, she opened the door and stepped into a cool night all the more comfortable after the moist heat left behind. She closed the door, looked around.

Naught. Only vegetation softly lit by torches beyond the garden wall.

Thinking Theo and Hart must be hidden behind a tree or bush, Honore called, "Theo? It is Honore. Come out!"

A groan, not of a boy but a man.

She hastened down the path, heard the sound again, and corrected her course.

"Theo?" she said upon reaching the wooden gate and finding no one there. "Hart?"

Another groan, directly in front but not this side of the gate.

She fumbled with the latch and swung the gate open. In the shadow of the donjon, a familiar figure was on hands and knees. Alone.

Honore dropped down beside him. "Theo, where is Hart?"

He pushed back onto his heels, groped at the back of his head.

"I know not what struck me. I…had the boy." He shook his head, grunted. "Felt like a stick."

A baton. Jake the Jack had not returned to the shadows to continue his tryst. Recognizing Hart, he had retrieved his batons.

"He has taken Hart," she said. "You must help me get him back."

He lurched upright. "I have failed my lord."

"Theo—"

"Was bringing the boy to you. Let down my guard."

"Theo—"

"Should have stayed alert."

A slap landed, stinging her palm. Though there was not enough light to see the red of Theo's cheek, she saw the whites of wide-flung eyes. "Forgive me," she said, "but we have no time to waste."

"Of course!" He turned into the inner bailey. Were his legs not long and strong enough to compensate for the blow to his head that made it impossible for him to maintain a straight course, Honore would have led the way. As it was, hampered by skirts and a shorter stride, she was barely able to keep pace. And another thing slowed her as she ran past the glowering noblewoman whose tryst had been interrupted—pain in her heel that made her look behind.

Small, round objects were scattered across the hard-packed dirt, one of which made itself felt through her thin-soled slippers. Beads? She swept her gaze forward in time to avoid colliding with a man-at-arms who called after her, "What goes, my lady?"

The answer to that was Theo who had passed beneath the inner portcullis into the outer bailey where torches were more numerous, being set to light not only that place but the land before the castle.

The regard of those who patrolled the walls less weighty than when Honore had first entered here, likely a result of the festivities and the belief those who came and went were but performers, she ignored them. And picked out more beads—one here, two there, several kicked up by Theo's trampling before he stopped to question a man-at-arms alongside the outer portcullis. The latter nodded, gestured to the tents, and the squire hastened past.

As much as Honore longed to inspect the beads, she dared not lest Theo leave her farther behind.

When he halted just off the drawbridge, she overtook him. "What did the man-at-arms say?" she asked as he stared out across the camp.

"He confirmed one of the troupe, costumed with a heavily-painted face, left the castle minutes ago. The man claimed the boy with him was his son who had disobeyed and stolen into the donjon to watch the performance."

"Did he say which direction?"

"Just the tents."

She breathed deep. "He will take Hart from here. We must—"

There—more beads. She scooped them up, turned toward the castle to make better use of torchlight.

They were so simple they were almost crude, but smooth and familiar. Fairly certain they were her prayer beads, she recalled her loss of them to Finwyn who had sought to remove evidence the witch he intended to name her was God-fearing.

Meaning Jake the Jack was Finwyn, his face hidden by paint? Not possible, and yet no other explanation could she find. She who had assured Elias she could more quickly identify the miscreant had failed. But providing there were yet beads to be shed, they would lead to Hart.

"These." She thrust her hand toward the squire. "The prayer beads taken from me when Finwyn tried to drown me in the stream. He leaves a trail."

The squire frowned. "You think it was Arblette who struck me? I think you are wrong. I left him searching for Hart on foot—"

"It has to be him." She sighed. "Finwyn or not, the one who took Hart unwittingly marks his path."

"Then we follow the beads."

Their course remaining crooked and broken as they searched them out, once more he led the way.

CHAPTER 34

BRUISE NOT, BRUISE NOT

*T*héâtre des Abominations.

Had Elias not emerged from amongst the tents before the nobles went from sight, he might not have seen the covered wagon in near darkness sitting back from the encampment as it had not upon his arrival at Sevier. But as the patrons filed inside, light poured from the rear door, evidencing that except for the wagon's immense size, it was nondescript. On the outside. Inside was where the perverse satisfied their appetite for the less than nondescript, of which Hart numbered.

Hopefully, somewhere beyond the wagon Theo kept watch— all the more imperative since Elias had only one of Otto's men-at-arms, the other two so full up in their cups there had been no reason to rouse them.

Elias looked to the night sky across which a blanket of clouds moved, blocking much of the moon's light. It was of benefit, aiding in concealing him and the man-at-arms, but a watch had to be kept for breaks in the cover that could reveal them.

Returning his regard to the wagon, he considered further

obstacles besides having no other sword arms to command. At least two of the troupe were in the wagon, one likely the woman Theo had described, the other the performer who escorted the nobles there. Of immediate concern was the one who guarded the wagon's rear entrance.

Elias was of good height, but this man was unnaturally tall and broad. Much of his extra width was fat, as told by the way it moved when he paced, but it was supported by muscle that would easily heft the sword he wore.

Still, Elias was confident two trained at arms could overwhelm those set over the wagon, and more quickly were Theo near enough to make it three. But as much as Elias longed to attack now, he dared not lest the little ones were harmed in the attempt to free them.

Thus, patience. Once the nobles departed, there would be time to end what was an abomination only with regard to what the children suffered. If it proved impossible to hide from Costain what transpired, the Lord of Sevier would simply have to understand. And Otto.

Shortly, the wagon's door opened and the nobles exited, several shaking their heads, one exclaiming he would not believe it had he not seen it, another crossing herself as if she had looked upon the devil.

Elias did not like the thoughts and imaginings crowding his head and tightening his hands. They tempted him to act from a place of emotion rather than reason as the Wulfriths would have him do. Barring immediate danger to the children, he must await the best opportunity to free them.

As the nobles started across the meadow toward the tents, the man who had escorted them stepped from the wagon but remained on its landing, and coming behind was the woman. Red-headed and garbed in colorful scarves, she held a babe whose size and half-hearted cries revealed were it not yet walking it would soon.

Though Elias longed to signal the man-at-arms hunkering in the tall grass twenty feet distant, he held. And hoped when the woman turned back into the wagon he would glimpse his son.

In a graveled voice that revealed she was of a good age, she said something to the two men and pivoted. Scarves fluttering in the breeze, making it impossible to see what lay inside the wagon, she closed the door, once more making shadows of the men outside.

Good odds, Elias allowed, providing he and the man-at-arms incapacitated the two before the woman was alerted. Were she alone with the children, Elias ought to be able to kick in the door and overpower her before she harmed any. Hopefully, she would no longer be holding the babe.

The nobles having moved past Elias, he waited for them to disappear amid the tents, then signaled.

Staying low, the two advanced through the tall grass. And gained a dozen steps before movement past the man-at-arms and what sounded like grumbling returned both to their haunches.

The one approaching the wagon appeared to have a hunched back, but when he shouted, "Inès!" and the wagon door opened, the light spilling past the woman revealed it was Jake the Jack and he carried something over his shoulder. When that something began pounding on his back and naming him a devil, Elias knew it for a boy. Hart?

All of him straining to snatch his sword from its scabbard, he commanded himself to reason. The advantage of moments earlier was past. As they had waited out the nobles' retreat, they could wait out this man's.

But when Jake ascended the steps, dropped his burden to the landing, and dealt the boy a blow, Elias bellowed, drew sword and dagger, and ran. As did the man-at-arms.

The garishly costumed, brightly-painted performer wrenched up the boy and thrust him at Inès, then jumped to the ground. As he drew batons from beneath his belt, the enormous man placed himself to the left of Jake and pulled his sword, while the one who had escorted the nobles stepped to the right and drew a long knife.

The woman named Inès pushed the boy behind her but remained in the wagon's doorway as if to provide light by which to do battle.

"Honore!" a cry sounded from within.

Hart, Elias acknowledged with relief, then moved his mind to wielding sword and dagger.

"Theo!" The boy's voice again, and though the name jolted Elias, there was no time to ponder how it was possible it came off Hart's lips. Of greater import was his squire be near enough to answer the call. Though what was to come would draw the notice of the castle garrison, as remiss as they were in their duties that had allowed Elias and the man-at-arms to depart the castle without being questioned, it could be too late for them to give aid.

Seeing the three outside the wagon were ready for those converging on them, Elias shouted to the man-at-arms, "Take the one on the right," and set himself at the one on the left. Though he did not doubt Jake's batons could incapacitate—even kill—it was usually best to first eliminate blades most adept at bleeding a man and spilling innards.

Angling the Wulfrith dagger just above his head, Elias swept up his sword. When the big man lunged, Elias arced the blade of the latter high to counter his opponent's downward stroke. As sword met sword, he slashed the dagger downward. It was not yet known if his opponent possessed great facility with the sword, but the man was unprepared to deal with two blades that simultaneously parried and attacked. He roared when blood was taken from his shoulder.

Hearing the cries of frightened children, Elias adjusted his stance for the next meeting of blades and noted his opponent was, indeed, two hands taller. But the fat he carried slowed him.

A glance at Otto's man-at-arms revealed that though his sword had a much longer reach than the knife, his opponent defended himself well. As for Jake, he appeared prepared to defend himself, but seemed disinclined to aid his own men.

Poltroon, Elias silently named him. Though the fight would be more challenging three against two, it was preferable to Jake retreating to the wagon and using the children as defense.

Elias set himself at the big man again, and they traded several blows before the Wulfrith dagger once more spilled blood, a thrust to the man's chest going through fat and muscle and between ribs.

"Jake!" Inès called as Elias's opponent stumbled back and drew a hand from his chest to look upon crimson. "Aid Georges!"

"Do you require help, wee Georges?" Elias taunted. "A nursemaid, perhaps?"

The man's blade came down on Elias's just above his head, and in that moment of meeting, the Wulfrith dagger thrust again, piercing the abdomen.

Georges cried out and, as feared, Jake turned toward the wagon.

"Certes, you will get no aid from the boy who plays with sticks," Elias shouted. "See how the poltroon runs!"

That made Jake halt and look around.

Taking the opportunity to sooner ensure he did not make it inside the wagon, Elias knocked aside Georges's wavering blade, arced down and up again, and what his dagger left unfinished his sword did not.

As the big man dropped to his knees, Elias glanced at his father's man who had yet to put down his opponent. Whether he had more drink in him than thought or was derelict in keeping his sword skill honed, there would be changes when Otto's lands passed to his heir.

"Fight him!" Inès cried, though now Jake had no choice with Elias lunging at him.

"Get the wagon away!" the miscreant shouted, then whirled, swept up his batons, and crossed them before him.

Elias swung his sword with only as much force as was necessary to cut the nearest stick in two. When steel struck steel rather than wood, he knew he had violated the lesson to be prepared for the worst and later rejoice if it proved the best.

The impact for which he was not braced made him lurch backward, giving his opponent time and space to strike. Elias bent to the steel baton's punch to the gut, nearly went down when the second baton struck his upper arm that would have been his head had he not jerked up his shoulder.

Despite the pain reverberating down his dagger-wielding arm, he kept hold of the hilt and dropped back a stride. It was not enough to keep Jake from landing another blow, this one to Elias's outer thigh.

The pain was terrible, but not as much as Elias made it appear across the mask he slapped on. Lurching back, putting space between him and his opponent, he glanced at the man-at-arms. No help from that quarter, nor from Theo who, it seemed, had been unable to track the woman in the doorway. Or perhaps he had found her and now lay dead...

"Leave, Inès!" Jake commanded again. "I am near done with him."

"But the light!"

"Go!"

The door slammed. The only light that of the clouded moon and the glow cast by Sevier's torches and the camp fires, all became little more than shadow and would remain so until eyes once more adjusted to the dim.

Hence, again I go to the cellar, Elias told himself and consciously engaged all his senses as taught him by Everard in that darkness beneath Wulfen's hall.

Aching in too many places, he readied himself, but then a shout of pain sounded across the meadow.

WAS IT OF DEATH? And whose?

Unlike Theo who commanded Honore to stay put when they came around the tent beside which more beads were scattered, she could only stare at the scene across the meadow. The wagon and battling bodies in the light cast from its doorway were no longer visible, but the men had been there and still were as evidenced by the cry of one in pain.

"Not Elias," she gasped. "Pray, not him!"

Light again, but less intense where it shone from the front of the wagon and lasting only seconds. But it was enough to count three men—and the fourth that was Theo moving toward them.

Then the snap of a whip, the whinny of horses, and the bump of wheels moving over uneven ground.

"Hart!" Honore snatched up her skirts and ran. If Elias yet lived, he surely fought to remain so, and his squire would aid his lord before the children in the wagon. Thus, it fell to her.

"Please, Lord," she gasped between breaths needed to drive her body forward over unseen ground. Though her eyes were fairly accustomed to the dark, it was more the din of men battling and the rumbling wagon that guided her forward—and the cries of frightened children.

Her heart leapt when she heard a shouted command from one who sounded like Elias, but knowing she would be of more use to the children than a warrior, she veered away.

"Non, Honore!" That she heard clearly, and though she rejoiced it was Elias's voice, she did not slow.

Moments after skirting those who grunted and cursed amid the peal of blades, the clouds let the moon be. The light it cast provided enough to see the shape of the wagon picking up speed. And a man in close pursuit.

One of those Elias had fought? Or Theo, Elias having commanded him to the wagon? That possibility nearly caused her to give heart and lungs the respite they demanded. But she would not lose her boy again.

The figure well ahead drew alongside the wagon, and moments later he was at the front leaping onto the seat.

The wagon lurched, slowed, and Honore heard a woman scream.

Theo then, but still she ran. And loosed a scream of her own when the wagon careened opposite and tilted onto two wheels before slamming back to earth.

The cries of the children louder and pitched higher, Honore found more strength she had not known she possessed and reached her legs longer. Still, if not for Theo's efforts to slow the wagon, she could not have overtaken it.

She closed one hand around the rail alongside the steps, reached with the other, set her teeth against the pain of splinters sliding into her palms, and cried out when her shins slammed into the lower step.

As the wagon tilted again, she held on and swung to the side.

"I am here!" she called to the children.

When the wagon righted and slowed further, she got a foot on the step, then the other, but as she wrenched herself forward, she glimpsed a rider coming from the wood.

Ears filled with the children's cries and the woman's screams, Honore ascended to the landing. Keeping one hand on the railing, she reached for the door with the other, turned the handle, and pulled. It gave, but only at its middle and lower portions. It was fastened at the top where a child could not reach.

"I am here, Hart!" she called through the seam and yanked at the door. The ribbon of light widened, but the latch held.

"Help us, Honore!"

She wrenched again, heard the crack of wood, but she had not enough strength nor time. The rider came alongside, and as he leapt off his horse onto the landing, she recognized him.

CHAPTER 35

THAT WHICH IS SOUGHT

The big man was dead. The injured man-at-arms' opponent was dead. Jake the Jack bled out his last. And God willing, the one who fell upon Honore would soon meet his end.

Fearing the miscreant would take her with him into death, Elias cried out to the Lord as the woman wound around his heart flew off the landing with her attacker atop.

The two hit the ground and rolled apart. When one scrambled upright, moonlight confirmed his identity.

"Arblette!" Elias shouted as the man lunged to where Honore lay unmoving, but the miscreant did not alter his course.

Knowing he would reach her first, Elias halted and drew back the Wulfrith dagger. "Fly true!" he beseeched. A moment later, it knocked Arblette backward.

When Elias reached Honore, the man writhed on the ground ten feet distant, clutching at the dagger's hilt as he tried to drag the blade from his chest.

Dropping down beside Honore, Elias heard shouts, and a glance over his shoulder revealed soldiers running through the encampment. Costain's men. At last.

Gently, Elias raised Honore to sitting. "I am here. How badly are you hurt?"

Her eyes blinked open, and she choked, "The children."

"How badly, Honore?"

"Only my breath. The children—"

"The castle garrison are coming, and Theo has stopped the wagon." Elias had seen it lurch to a halt before he loosed the dagger and heard the last of Inès's screams. "I will go to them if you will give me your word you will stay here—not go anywhere near Arblette."

She looked to the man who lay dying. "I will stay."

He pressed his lips to her brow, then ran toward the wagon once more lit at the front. Whether Inès was alive or dead, Theo had gone inside. And still the children cried.

"Ere she was a whore, she was mine. Sweet and pure, and pretty."

Honore ceased breathing where she sat with knees gathered to her chest, eyes on the wagon whose door Elias had ruined. Though from where she had landed she could not see inside, the voices of Elias, Theo, and Hart heard above the distress of the little ones assured her she was not needed, tempted as she was to break the word given Elias.

"Mine," Finwyn gurgled past what she guessed was blood.

She did not want to look at him, it being enough to keep him in the corner of her eye, but she turned her head and seeing no movement about him, said, "You speak of Lettice?"

"The same—the angel who became a whore."

Honore glanced at the wagon, tried to make sense of the shadows moving amid lantern light slanting over the landing, down the steps, and across the grass. "*You* made her that," she said.

"Not I, though I profited from her ruin when it was complete." He tried to clear his throat. "After her troubadour left her with a babe in her belly."

Honore drew a sharp breath.

Finwyn made a sound that aspired to laughter. "Not my son. Not possible, though I wished it until she gave birth to that abomination."

Even as Honore winced over what he named Hart, hope clambered through her. Rising to her knees to better see Finwyn, she said, "Then Sir Elias *is* Hart's father."

"Sir Elias," he drawled, then coughed. "Mayhap. Mayhap not. As told, she was a whore, but I did not...make her one, though she said I did." That last was little more than a whisper.

It was hard to stay put with the tale unfolding and the din from the wagon making it difficult to hear him, but she dared not draw nearer.

"Why would she accuse you of such if you did not lie with her?"

"I made a babe on a friend of hers." More gurgling. "Thinking to force me to break my betrothal and wed her instead, the witch told Lettice of our tryst." He sucked air, rattled it out. "Though Lettice broke our betrothal, I refused to wed the trollop who betrayed me."

"But she carried your child."

"Mayhap, mayhap not. She was a sinner ere Lettice, and no matter how oft I look into that boy's face, never do I see mine. Still, when the lad was of an age to be useful, I took him from his aunt who had raised him following her sister's death."

Cynuit, Honore realized. "You are saying Lettice began selling her body because you were unfaithful?"

"Her mother was useless, a burden." He drew a wheezing breath. "Had she wed me, my grandsire would have provided for all, but instead of forgiveness, Lettice sold her body for extra coin."

"Out of desperation," Honore said. "She—"

"Nay," he snarled, "out of pride, spite, vengeance." He turned his head to the side and spat blood. "Then that troubadour came to Forkney and she thought their love would save her, but once fornication is in a woman's blood, no cure for it." He groaned low. "When she could no longer hide her pregnancy and lost her position at the castle, *I* saved her. I told my grandsire she carried my child and I wished to provide for her until the babe was born and she could find work. We kept her in coin enough that none starved, but then she birthed that devil-licked thing." Another attempt at laughter. "To dispose of an undesirable, she became further indebted. And there was much satisfaction in aiding her in prostituting herself."

"*You* are the vengeful one!"

"I am, and she is—was—to blame."

Refusing to argue, she said, "Why murder her?"

"Not intentional."

"You strung her up like a chicken for the pot!"

With what seemed sincerity, he said, "In that I found no satisfaction."

"You make no sense."

"Difficult when one is dying," he slurred. "Imagine my surprise when Lettice finished her night's work and was approached by a nobleman I recognized. Had he years past been a knight disguised as a troubadour? Or was he now a troubadour disguised as a knight?" He coughed. "The former, I guessed when it was not her services he sought but to learn if she had birthed his son. More proof was given by the size of the purse he gave her. After she departed, deciding to relieve him of more coin I told him his son lived and I could deliver the child."

"Thus, you summoned me."

"And you came, also like a chicken…to the pot."

Honore looked to the wagon. Still only shadows spilling out, but the children's cries were less anguished.

"But I did not mean to kill her," he said and sounded nearer.

Tensing for flight, she shot her gaze to him a moment ahead of the clouds once more covering the moon. Still, the light from the wagon told he had not moved.

"Of course you meant to kill her."

"I did not. She refused me the purse—money owed me—and ran for the door. I caught her, and she slapped and bit me." He arched his back, rolled his head side to side. "Lord, the pain!"

"What did you do to her?"

Just when she thought he would not answer, he said, "I flung her from me, and she hit a wall support...snapped her neck."

Honore swallowed to keep her supper down. "For which the witch you sought to make of me was to be blamed so suspicion would not fall on the one who sold her body."

"A good plan had you cooperated."

"Forever you will await an apology," she said and, hearing chain mail, looked across her shoulder at the half dozen garrison who neared.

Finwyn coughed up more blood, and she knew his *forever* could not be more than a few minutes.

"Honore!"

Hart's voice brought her head around, and she saw he had come onto the landing with Elias.

Lest he run to her and see the horror of Finwyn, she sprang upright.

"Remain here," Elias commanded. "I will bring her to you."

More aware of aches that evidenced it was not only loss of breath she had suffered, slowly she moved toward him as he leapt to the ground.

"Did you tell him?" Finwyn called.

She nearly halted for fear that though he professed he could not have fathered Hart, once more he would assert his claim and reveal what she had withheld.

Lord, she silently appealed, *if You are going to take Finwyn, do so now. Let me tell Elias of Finwyn and Lettice. Let me be the one to reveal the month of Hart's birth as already I should have done.*

But would she be here now, Hart and the other children delivered had she trusted Elias to keep his word to save Lettice's son? Though she tried to argue herself down to justify her lie, she knew Elias would have kept his vow. Still, she had not known it when first she withheld Finwyn's claim on Hart.

"Of course not," Finwyn taunted. "Had you told him, he would not—" He choked as if it were *his* neck in a noose.

Fear crawling up her at the realization death had drawn its carriage alongside him, she halted.

A moment later, Elias was at her side and bracing her arm. "I pray you are no worse than sore."

Seeing crimson on his tunic, abrasions on collarbone and throat, cuts from jaw to cheek and brow to hairline, she caught the scent of his exertion—and blood. "Only sore. You?"

"All will heal. Now come, there is a boy who misses you."

Why it should bother he named Hart that, she was too muddled to make sense of, but she would try. Later.

As if death had poured its passenger a bowl of silence, no further sound issued from the one who had taken a dagger to the chest. Answered prayer.

But the greatest answered prayer was the boy—*her* boy—who sprang off the landing into her arms.

Hugging him, she kissed the top of his head to which she did not have to bend as far as she had six months past.

"I knew you would come!" His tearful voice warmed her through the material of her gown. Then he began to cry and burble, "I am sorry, I am sorry. I will help more with the little ones. I promise."

She stroked his head, shushed him, called him Hart of her heart.

From a distance, Elias watched. As Honore and the boy no longer needed him, he had returned to Arblette to identify himself to Sevier's men and assure them the danger was past.

The explanation they had demanded he had given only as far as pointing them to the injured man-at-arms and saying an accounting would be provided their lord after his guests were settled for the night. Unwilling to offend Costain's friend and ally, they had gone to aid Otto's man who would surely apprise them of the reason he shared the ground with three dead performers.

Now, once more alone with Arblette, Elias turned the Wulfrith dagger into moonlight. It had done its work. The scourge of the one it had felled was no more.

As he wiped the blade on the hem of his tunic, he looked to the wagon and saw the boy catch up Honore's hand.

"Come see my little ones!" His voice was raw from the letting of emotions. "I took care of them as you would, kept them safe as you would, even gave them names as you would."

As he drew her to the steps, she looked around.

Knowing there was enough light for his expression to be seen, Elias smiled. And was ashamed by the false turn of his lips. All the children were safe, no good lives were lost, Thomas Becket had escaped France with none the wiser he was aided by a De Morville, and Honore would soon return to her work at Bairnwood. With Hart.

His mood further dampened. He had not wanted nor been prepared for the journey with Honore, even resented it lest it harm his family, and yet now he did not want nor was prepared for her return to England, especially if she took his heart with her.

As he watched the two step past Theo in the doorway and go from sight, he wrestled with disappointment he should not feel. Having convinced himself Hart was his, and now having witnessed the boy's courage, he wanted it more. But Hart was not his, as seen when the boy spun around and used his body to shield the child in the crate as Elias came through the doorway. Hart was another man's son, and Elias knew the one.

He returned his regard to the corpse whose blood he now wore, pondered Arblette's taunting of Honore, then set his shoulders and returned his dagger to its scabbard.

Life was about to resume its usual pace. Likely, a year from now it would be as unsatisfactory, perhaps more so when he delivered on his promise to Otto. Would he still be trying to forget the woman of honor who was as unattainable as Lettice? He feared so.

More curious. And most entertaining.

Neville chuckled.

"What is so humorous?" Desmond grumbled. "Still Becket's savior is out of reach."

So he was, though until his squire and that woman appeared, then the garrison and the one those watching from the wood had not known shared that place with them, it had seemed the knight was about to come into their hands.

Neville sighed. "Oui, but such a fun chase he leads, hmm?"

"Fun?" Raoul scorned. "I want a hot meal, fresh ale, and a pallet."

"Because you are soft, and for that the Lord punished you with common birth and rewarded me with noble." Neville raised his eyebrows. "Hence, I lead, you follow. I order, you obey."

That silenced him.

"How are we to get hold of De Morville?" Desmond asked.

"We bide our time." Ignoring the roiling of the two who sat their horses on either side of him, Neville smiled at the prospect of commanding more than these misfits. But were that day to come sooner rather than later, this biding must find its end before another delivered the archbishop to Duke Henry.

I come for you, Elias De Morville, he silently vowed as the one who would make him wealthy strode from the man he had put through with a Wulfrith dagger. It was good to know how excellent his aim. Not that he would fall to it. For that, men like Desmond and Raoul existed.

CHAPTER 36

COME DANCE THROUGH LIFE WITH HIM

*C*ostain was vexed by what was wrought outside his walls, and of greater offense he presented as bored when informed of the sideshow—until Elias revealed King Henry had expelled Troupe Fantastique from England. That revelation also cleared the disapproval from Otto's face. As both men owed allegiance to the duke, they would not wish to displease him. Too, there could be reward in claiming to have aided in ending Théâtre des Abominations.

Feeling every minute that neared the middling of night, Elias said, "If we are done, I would seek my rest."

Costain waved a hand. "Go. And pray, do not further disturb my household."

Elias dipped his head and closed the solar's door behind him. As he moved down the corridor toward the chamber he would share with Otto and two other visiting lords, he eased his shoulders.

All was well. Hart and the little ones had been discreetly conveyed to the chamber the Costain sisters ceded following the final act which saw the performers withdraw to their camp where they would learn of the deaths of four of its members, the loss of its sideshow, and the need to regroup.

It would be a blow to some, but likely a boon to the majority who had not benefited from Jake the Jack's perverse offering. Regardless, the troupe would depart Sevier on the morrow. As for Honore and the children, they would travel to Elias's home where arrangements would be made for their return to England once all were fit for the journey.

Elias did not realize he had paused outside the chamber given Honore and the children until he heard a sound of distress. He assured himself it was one of the little ones sleeping fitfully. And opened the door.

Kneeling on the hearth before a waning fire, Honore's head was bent and shoulders hunched.

He strode inside. "Honore?"

She looked around, put a finger to her lips, and nodded at the bed.

He considered the four cocooned in blankets—Hart on the left, the little ones on the right placed horizontally so they would not roll off.

Honore rose, and when she turned, he saw what was surely responsible for the distress that made him enter. In one hand she gripped a needle, the palm of the other evidencing short lines of blood.

"Close the door," she whispered.

He did as bid, crossed to her, and caught up her hand. Blessedly, her palm was only stuck through with splinters. "My brave Honore, why did you not tell me you were hurt?"

She tried to tug free. "It is a little thing."

Keeping hold of her, he lifted her other hand that clutched the needle. "All these hours you have suffered."

"They are only splinters, Elias."

"Dozens." He drew her to a chair, knelt at her feet, and took the needle from her.

"I can do it," she protested.

"I can do it better. Allow me."

Sensing her struggle, he looked up and saw how red her eyes and flushed her face. "You have been crying."

"Happiness and..."

"What?"

She shook her head. "It is over and the children are safe, and yet I keep seeing, fearing, feeling it all." She swallowed loudly. "The world is..."

"It can be dangerous outside your abbey walls, but it *is* over, Honore."

She nodded. "I know I am silly."

"You are not. Much has happened for which you were not prepared—as hardly was I, a warrior. There is nothing silly about your emotions, so do not begrudge yourself tears."

Eyes brightening further, she splayed her fingers. "I removed all from my left. The right is more difficult."

He moved that hand into firelight and began picking at the slivers. "How did you gain these?"

"The railing. I could hardly hold on when the wagon started to tip."

"My brave Honore."

"Elias?"

"Hmm?"

"Pray, cease naming me that."

Though he knew to what she referred and that she was right, he tried to ease the tension with humor. "Is it not your given name?"

"As well you know, you name me what I am not to you—what I can never be."

"Regardless, you are brave."

She went silent, after a time said, "I thank you for saving Hart and the little ones. You are a good man."

"As I strive to be, though often I fail."

"I doubt that."

"The possibility I could have made a child with Lettice proves otherwise."

"You kept your word to her—and me. And yet..."

He looked up, as ever marveled over her eyes.

She glanced at the bed. "Now is not the time to speak of such things."

She feared awakening the children, especially the boy. But Elias was fairly certain he knew what troubled her. She wished to know why he distanced himself from the son he had set out to rescue.

He returned to the splinters and when he drew the last free, said, "Have you any cloth with which to bandage your hands?"

Her smile was wry. "Much."

He stood, and she rose and crossed to the dressing table where lay a stack of linen strips provided for her menses.

After she washed her hands in the basin alongside which a hand mirror sat face down, he dried and bandaged them. "Better?"

"All will heal," she spoke the same he had earlier that evening.

Loath to leave her, he set a hand on her shoulder. "You and the children will accompany me to my home. When the little ones are fit enough to travel, arrangements will be made for your return to England."

Her smile was forced. "I thank you. For everything."

He knew he should not, but he slid his hand from her shoulder to her neck and tilted her face higher. "You are lovely."

Her gaze wavered. "No longer need you be so kind."

"It is not kindness that makes me speak such. I have known no other woman besides Lady Susanna as lovely on the outside as she is on the inside."

"That is enough," she hissed.

"I speak in truth." He picked up the hand mirror he guessed she had turned down, raised it between them. "Look."

She turned her face to the right. "Pray, cease!"

"Honore—"

"I know what I look like."

"You do not. If you did, never would you have worn the gorget as you do."

"I am not ashamed. I wear it not for my benefit but for those who fund much of the good work at Bairnwood."

"They are not here, Honore. It is just you and me. If you are not ashamed, as you have no cause to be, look."

"I was not ashamed before you," she gasped. "I vow I was not. I —" Horror flickered in her eyes as if she realized what she revealed.

"Honore, look."

She began to tremble, but though he hated he was responsible, she needed to see what he saw.

Moving the mirror aside, he leaned in and set his mouth on hers.

She stilled, and when she responded, she did so by speaking his name—with pleading born of sorrow rather than desire.

He raised his head. "I like your mouth just the way it is. Soft. Sweet. Pretty."

Her eyes moistened. "You make it difficult to leave you, and we both know I must."

He did, and he was selfish to offer something she could not take hold of anymore than he. "Oui, but ere we part, I would have you see the flower I see." Once more, he set the mirror in front of her.

Fear surfacing her eyes, she held her gaze to his above the silver rim.

"You have naught to fear," he said. "You have only to look."

It was his eyes Honore wanted to delve. In his she wished to remain. Though she had never looked long upon her reflection in a beaten silver platter or rippling water, she had a good idea of what she would see if she lowered her gaze.

Ashamed? That was too harsh a thing to feel for something over which she had no control and could not be blamed. But she was self-conscious as she had not been for years, so much she felt the tug on that side of her mouth more than ever she had felt it, and ten-fold greater when Elias looked upon the whole of her face, though he had given her no cause to believe him repulsed.

Then there was this longing to be as beautiful to him as she knew herself to be to God. Other than the young monk who never returned, she had wanted that with no other. All that had mattered was, absent the gorget, she move amongst her foundlings without frightening them. Elias wished her to believe the scar did not matter, and more and more she did, but was it truly of so little consequence that if he could be with her he would?

"Would you have me if you could?" She startled at hearing her whispered words, but he did not.

Sorrow dimmed his eyes, and he said, "I would. Now look and see the woman I would awake to every morn could I."

She believed him—at least, Elias who did not yet know what must be revealed. Would he forgive her when the tale of Finwyn and Lettice was told? If still he believed Hart his son, very possible, but surely he would look nearer upon the boy. What if he did not see himself in Hart's face as she did not? What if he saw Finwyn though she did not?

He had vowed to retrieve Lettice's son, so still he would be here. Still this night would have ended thus. Even so, it would not change that she had lied and he who thought well of her no longer had cause. Then what would he see when he looked at her?

That last made her lower her gaze down the silver surface. She nearly gasped over so perfect a reflection. There was no distortion, exactly what one would see peering into another's face. Or was there? She knew her eyes were very blue, but this blue?

"What is it?" Elias said.

"Are they really so blue?"

With a smile in his voice, he said, "Nearly. In daylight they are more brilliant, and the outer edges that now look black are purple."

Would the night also dim what she had yet to look upon, that whose distortion could not be blamed on the mirror? She curved her lips into a smile Elias said made her lovelier and moved her gaze down her nose. There was the ridge tugging the right bow higher than the left, but not as high as thought. Nor was it as pronounced as believed where it angled up toward a nostril. Of course, she *was* smiling.

By degree, she relaxed her mouth. The ridge became more visible, but Elias was right. It was not unsightly. Though it could not be overlooked, unlike that with which Hart and some of the little ones were born, her repaired lip rendered it acceptable.

She closed her eyes, opened them on Elias's. "I have looked. I have seen. And no more will I don the gorget."

She reached and, fingers brushing his, took the mirror and set it face up on the table.

The silence making it feel as if an embrace belonged in the space between them, she said, "You have met Hart's little ones?"

As if also feeling the intimacy to which they ought not succumb, Elias stepped back. "Briefly."

Then he was aware of their afflictions. "You know the names Hart gave them?"

"Only Alice. I heard him call her that."

She moved past Elias, and he followed. Halting on the side of the bed opposite Hart who slept facing them with a fist against his mouth, she said, "Alice you know." Lightly, she ran fingers through the soft red curls of the year-and-a-half-old billed as *Poseidon's Child* for her webbed fingers and toes.

She moved her hand to the head of the two-year-old boy whose brown hair also covered much of his face, arms, and legs, albeit not as thickly as that atop his head. "This is Jamie." He who had been called *Son of Boar*.

"And Rayne." She stroked the three-year-old girl's cheek that was nearly as white as her hair, the only real color about her the pink eyes that now moved behind her lids. Touted as born of angel and man, she had been called *The Nephilim*.

All these abominable names Hart, himself called *The Map*, had refused to use. He loved his little ones. If not for them, his resourcefulness would likely have allowed him to escape, but these three—and the joined twins who had passed—had needed him. Despite all he had endured, he was proud of being to them what she was to her foundlings.

He had helped settle them for the night, soothing them with song, prayer, and kisses on cheeks, noses, and brows. Regardless of who had sired Hart, a fine man he would make.

She shifted her gaze to him, saw he looked between Elias and her.

"We awakened you," she whispered. "Forgive us."

He frowned. "Are my little ones well?"

"They are. Alice breathes easier." It was the youngest Hart had been most concerned about since she had taken ill shortly after the joined twins passed.

He pushed up on an elbow. "You will help us get back to Bairnwood, Sir Elias?"

"Once all have recovered at my home where we journey on the morrow providing Alice is well enough to travel."

Hart smiled faintly, looked to Honore. "I forgot to ask if you saw the beads. Is that how you found me?"

She gasped. "*You* scattered them?"

"I did. When Fin came to France and I saw he had them, I feared he had hurt you. I stole them, and when Jake took me from Squire Theo, I dropped the beads until I ran out."

"How did you know I would find them?"

"I thought Squire Theo was Fin when he caught me in the

wood, and I fought him until I saw he was not. He told who he was and that you were at the castle with his lord." He glanced at Elias. "He said you had come across the channel to rescue us. After Jake struck down the squire, he warned if I cried out he would hurt Alice. I did not know you would find the beads, but when he put me over his shoulder, I took the necklace I had wound around my arm beneath my sleeve so Fin would not see it, chewed through the string, and said a prayer for each I dropped. And you came."

"As did Sir Elias," she said. "Much is owed him."

Hart narrowed his eyes at the knight. "Who are you?" he asked in the direct way she sometimes had to correct. Though she wanted to correct him now, she decided to let Elias determine whether to answer.

His hesitation bothered, just as when he had referred to Hart as a *boy*, rather than his son, as he guided her toward their reunion at the wagon. Too, she was disturbed by the weight of what she now realized was something between disappointment and apathy.

"But a friend," Elias said.

Then either he was no longer certain Hart was his or something made him certain he was not. Or wish he was not. Hart's face?

Though alert to how he and other foundlings were regarded on the rare occasion they encountered those outside their world, she had been unable to gauge Elias's initial reaction since she had been with Finwyn when Elias forced his way into the wagon. She looked to him now. His eyes remained on Hart, but naught in his face reflected fascination or revulsion.

Hart sighed. "I am glad you are Honore's friend. She has only us, you know."

Throat constricting further, she squeezed past it, "We shall speak more on the morrow. Now you must sleep."

He lowered to the pillow, set a hand on Alice's foot, and closed his eyes.

Avoiding Elias's gaze, Honore crossed to the door and opened it. "Good eve, Sir Elias."

He stepped into the corridor, and she closed herself in, extinguished the candles, and made her bed in the chair before which Elias had picked out every sliver that now felt as if embedded in her heart.

She pressed a hand to her chest, whispered, "A heart that is yours, Elias. Shall ever be yours."

CHAPTER 37

LOVE LOST NOW FOUND

Château des Trois Doigts
France

*A*ll but four.

Silly though it was, Honore felt the absence of beads over which she would never again slide her fingers. It seemed ungrateful to mourn the loss of so few when she should have been fortunate to recover only enough to assemble a bracelet. Instead, Hart and Cynuit had searched out enough to restring her necklace.

For the first hour of the ride, the prayer beads had soothed Alice as she pulled them over her webbed fingers and tapped them against her tiny teeth. Now she slept tucked between the saddle's pommel and Honore's abdomen. Though on occasion she became restless, coughing and rubbing her nose, she traveled well. Elias was to thank for that, having resisted his father's impatience over the sedate pace.

Once more, Otto De Morville grumbled they should have

made use of the covered wagon that would have allowed them to move more quickly, but Elias offered no further comment. At Sevier he had defended his decision to burn it in sight of the children, not only to symbolize the end of their bondage, but so it could never again be used for such foul means. And there had been the advantage of setting it afire during the troupe's departure—dire warning.

Honore peered past Theo whose arm was around the wide-eyed, thumb-sucking Jamie to Hart who straddled the back of Cynuit's saddle. As if awaiting her gaze, the boy smiled. It was not as genuine as she knew him capable of, but she had to believe that just as he was stronger for his ordeal, eventually he would recover sufficiently to reclaim a portion of his childhood.

She returned his smile and looked to Elias who rode ahead alongside his sire. With his back to her, she could not see the pale Rayne perched before him shrouded in cloak and hood at the insistence of Hart who said even blunted sunlight hurt her eyes and quickly burned her skin.

That these children are now safe and will be more so at Bairnwood is much for which to be grateful, Honore told herself. *So much my heart ought to be full.*

It was not, though it would have been had love of Elias not stretched it to so great a size that when they parted there would be a vast, empty space alongside love for her foundlings.

You are greedy, she chastised. *Be content with the love you have— more than many can hope for.*

Honore did not realize Elias had slowed until she neared and saw his father remained a length ahead.

He looked around. "Over the next rise you will have your first glimpse of my home, Château des Trois Doigts."

She drew alongside, guessed from the curl of Rayne's small body against his that she slept. "Three Fingers Castle," she said in English. "For what is it named that?"

He adjusted the little girl to ensure her seat, raised his left arm straight out in front of him, reins gripped in that hand, and swept his right hand to his jaw with three fingers splayed. He curled them inward, and with a low whistle released an imaginary string.

"The three-fingered draw of an archer," Honore said.

He smiled, once more settled an arm around Rayne. "As named by my great grandfather who built it on land awarded him by Duke William of Normandy one hundred years past."

"England's conqueror."

He inclined his head. "Hervé was misbegotten the same as William, of noble and common blood."

Above which few can rise, she reflected, *especially women.*

"It is said the two were as good friends as was possible with one such as William. But that is not what earned Hervé these lands. At the Battle of Hastings, William put to good use my ancestor's skill at archery and ability to command others of the bow. It raised Hervé to knighthood, gained him a worthy—albeit unwilling—bride, and made—"

"Unwilling?"

"That is another tale. Let me finish this one, hmm?" At her nod, he said, "And made of him a great landholder."

"Fascinating."

"And much to aspire to." He nudged his dagger's hilt with his elbow. "When like the prodigal son I returned to France, my father believed this a good start."

"Only a good start?" She glanced at the man ahead, wondered if he was privy to their conversation.

Elias shrugged. "He is exacting." He leaned toward her. "Ever he has demanded more of his sons than was demanded of him."

Otto De Morville's head came around. "Because *my* sire was hardly worthy of our name. I may not have had benefit of Wulfen training—and God knows how you gained it—but I make right what he made wrong."

"This I know," Elias said. "I but seek to explain our relationship."

"To one it does not concern." Otto moved his glower to her.

"In that you err, Father. I have a great care for Honore of Bairnwood, and much respect for all she has endured to aid me."

His father turned his head to peer over his other shoulder—at Hart, Honore guessed. When he looked back around, he asked, "Is he yours?"

After a slight hesitation, Elias said, "Certes, he is worthy of the name you highly esteem—as a man may prove worthier than I."

"Impossible," his sire bit, and Honore thought herself as surprised as he who surely had not meant to speak those words—and Elias whose head jerked.

The older man made a sound of disgust, pricked his destrier's sides, and spurred ahead.

"He loves you," Honore said as they watched Otto grow distant.

"He needs me," Elias countered. "And resents me for it. That is all."

"I think that is only what he wishes you to believe because he does not understand how he can care so much for his troubadour son."

"You are fanciful, Honore. You see love where there is not."

Were that true, she silently mused, *I would think you have more than a great care for me.*

"Where it is obvious," she said and eased her horse back from his.

CHÂTEAU DES Trois Doigts was impressive insomuch as could be a wooden castle slowly transitioning to stone, Elias reflected as he tried to see his home through Honore's eyes. Doubtless, when the fortress was first erected it had been worthy of Duke William's prize archer. It was yet worthy, so well built it had easily repelled those who sought to enter it uninvited over the last century, but it could be another decade before it rivaled other castles more quickly turned to stone.

I shall see it done in five years, Elias silently vowed, *not the ten Otto insisted upon.*

It was not mere hope. His father had passed that responsibility to his heir shortly after what seemed Elias's resurrection from the dead. More progress had been made these two years than in the decade before. The walls and towers of the outer bailey were entirely stone, those of the inner bailey nearing the three-quarter mark. Once the donjon's second line of defense was complete, section by section the timbers of the lord's living and working quarters would be replaced.

As Elias swung out of the saddle before the donjon, he silently affirmed, *Three years more, the latter two of which I will become a husband and, God willing, father.*

Having passed Rayne to one of the servants whom his father had shown great presence of mind to send outside to greet the party, Elias strode to Honore who was halfway out of the saddle. Gripping her waist, he lowered her.

She turned and smiled, another thing for which he was indebted to his sire. None of the women into whose care the little ones were given had shown surprise, curiosity, or dismay over those whose imperfections were obvious. Otto had surely warned them, though probably with an abundance of threat. However, in this instance Elias was grateful.

"Your home is impressive," Honore said.

He raised an eyebrow. "The donjon is in an unfinished state and some disrepair."

"It will be stone as well?"

"As quickly as time and funds allow."

"I would like to see that," she said unthinkingly, as evidenced by the lowering of her gaze.

As would I, Elias silently agreed.

"Sir Elias!" Hart appeared beside Honore. "May Cynuit and I go inside?"

"You may. I am sure my father has arranged for food and accommodations."

The boys bounded up the steps, followed by Theo.

"Your sire has been tolerant," Honore said.

Which she interpreted as love, Elias thought wryly, certain it was only grudging concession. He would not be surprised if Otto pushed Lady Vera on him again as payment for his tolerance. Of course, had there been a chance Costain would reconsider matching his daughter with Elias, after what had transpired on the night past he might no longer. Far better to pick from amongst others seeking her hand.

Elias offered Honore his arm. "Come meet my stepmother and sisters."

As their arrival was several hours ere supper, the great hall was far from its usual teeming self. No tables had been erected to accommodate the dozens who usually shared meals with their lord and lady. Excepting the little ones who had surely been delivered abovestairs to take their meals there, all were seated at the high table on either side of Otto—Theo, Cynuit, Hart, and the men-at-arms who had accompanied their lord to Sevier.

Seeing his stepmother sat at the hearth holding an embroidery frame in one hand, with the other pushing a needle through tautly-stretched cloth, Elias led Honore to her.

His father's young wife set aside her frame and stood. "I am glad you are returned, Elias."

"As am I." He inclined his head, introduced Honore.

"Well come," his stepmother said, then to Elias, "Your sisters have lain down for their afternoon rest. When they awaken, they will be pleased to see you."

"Doubtless, they will wish a tale."

Her smile had its usual weary edge, but she looked healthy. Time away from Otto was ever of benefit to one who had given her youth to a man old enough to be her grandfather. Certes, her daughters were her greatest happiness, possibly her next greatest was that her body could give no more. Thus, to ensure a convent did not separate her from her girls, Elias must provide the next male heir.

"After so long a ride, you must be pained with hunger and thirst." She gestured at the high table. "Pray, seat yourselves."

Honore thanked the lady, and Elias led her across the hall. There being only two chairs available, one alongside Otto, the other between Hart and a man-at-arms, Elias handed her into the latter and joined his father.

"I have word of that rascal, Becket," Otto said.

Though Elias did not peer down the table at Honore, he knew she had heard and also waited with held breath.

"A merry chase he leads Henry," his father said, "though never would I name it such in his hearing."

Elias picked a block of cheese from the platter between them, swallowed it down with ale.

"De Lucy found him," his sire continued, "confronted him at Saint Bertin's, and tried to persuade him to submit to Henry's will."

"Did he?"

Otto chuckled. "Refused, and quite the break that caused. De Lucy was Becket's vassal, you know. But no more."

"You think the archbishop will have to yield to Henry?"

"I think he must, but from what I hear tell of the man, I do not believe he will, especially if King Louis sides with him."

"What chance that?"

"Though Henry's men, Foliot and D'Aubigny, were well chosen to seek an audience with Louis, which I am sure will soon be granted if it has not already, the King of France is hardly inclined to accommodate the man who wed his cast-off wife without his permission."

Elias agreed. The union of Henry Plantagenet with France's

greatest heiress and former queen was a great sore unlikely to heal, especially since Eleanor of Aquitaine had given Henry what she had not given Louis—sons.

"Too, as Louis is exceedingly pious, he is more apt to side with a man of God than one who gives him good cause to name him the devil."

Though there was much to admire in Henry, Elias had no illusions about how ruthless their liege could be. His temper was legendary, his need to control men dangerous.

For the sake of the De Morvilles, Elias prayed England's king would never know of his role in Becket's escape. Unfortunately, that meant Elias could not reclaim the horses he had paid to send across the channel though done under a false name. His fine destrier, after which his father had asked this morn and been told there was no time to arrange for its crossing, would soon have a new master.

The conversation shifted to matters of the demesne, of greatest concern the delay of quarried stone to complete the inner wall. Elias assured his sire he would see to it and a half dozen other matters that interfered with the smooth working of Château des Trois Doigts.

An hour later, his stepmother escorted Honore to Elias's chamber that had been given her and the children for the duration of their stay.

The shorter the better, he told himself, and yet he conceded he would not mind were the shorter a lifetime.

CHAPTER 38

BY HONORE BOUND

Three days, Honore numbered as she stared at Elias where he stood before the chest containing his clothes. As he had been occupied with demesne business since their arrival and, a half hour past, Otto's wife and Hart had taken the children to the garden, there seemed no better time for confession.

"Can we speak, Elias?"

Chausses in one hand, tunic in the other, he turned. "If it is important. If it can wait, as it seems my sire cannot, better we speak later."

"It is important, but it can wait."

He inclined his head and crossed the chamber.

"This eve?" she called.

He paused in the doorway, chided himself for making much of Otto's wish for his son to accompany him to the nearest village. But something in Honore's tone told he would not like what she had to say.

The children were doing well, including Alice who breathed easier and no longer coughed. Likely, Honore wished to begin preparations for their departure, which meant Elias would have to reveal Hart was not his. Though he would make a place for Lettice's son if he wished a life beyond the abbey, which would be forced on Hart when he attained the age of ten, it was a decision the boy and Honore must make rather than a man who was not a father.

"This eve?" she said again.

"Much depends on the hour I return. But if not this eve, the morrow."

She nodded.

Elias meant to go straight to the stables where Otto awaited him, but the sound of children's voices and laughter as he came off the donjon steps drew him around the corner to the garden.

He peered over the gate. His little sisters rolled balls to Alice and Jamie who squealed and rolled them back. Rayne, ever well covered out-of-doors, was being bounced on the leg of a woman servant who shared the bench with Otto's wife who surprised at being so at ease with Hart's little ones.

Nearer, Cynuit and Hart knelt beneath a tree. The boys seemed fond of each other, a good thing if Hart decided to remain at Château des Trois Doigts since it would make it easier for him to part from Honore and those he called his *little ones.*

"It does look like a tooth," Hart said, examining something Cynuit held. "Do you think it is?"

"It has a curve to it like a fang," the older boy said. "But it could be a claw."

Hart took it, raised it to sunlight. And seeing Elias, jumped up. "Sir Knight, see what we found!"

Elias entered the garden. When the boy halted before him, once more his distinctive ears and nose drew notice ahead of the large mark of birth. But whereas when Elias had first looked on those features and been gripped by memories of the knight who beat him, now they held him loosely. Eventually, he would see only Hart.

"What think you?" The boy thrust nearer the tooth that might be a claw.

As Elias reached for it, his gaze drifted past and he looked near on the mark of birth. Though he did not know every curve and hollow of the island kingdom, it was not necessary to appreciate the wondrous rendering.

The lowering of Hart's hand moved Elias's gaze to his, and he saw wariness there. "Forgive me, Hart."

The boy jerked a shoulder. "Everyone looks. I just do not like when they touch or rub it to discover if it is only ink."

As he had surely endured in the wagon.

Elias lowered to his haunches, placing the boy slightly above him. "I am sorry for all you and your little ones suffered."

"I took good care of them, and when I am back at Bairnwood, I will help Honore with them so she does not have to work so hard."

Elias glanced at Cynuit who had returned to digging in the dirt. "Then given the opportunity to remain here with Cynuit in my service, training up into a man-at-arms—or of letters, if you prefer—still you would return to Bairnwood?"

He nodded, then frowned. "In two years, five months I will have to leave the abbey. Can I come to you then?"

The boy knew the end of his time at the abbey down to the month, perhaps even the day. Elias was about to assure him he would collect him himself—a chance to see Honore again—when realization struck. Had it knuckles, it might have knocked him back. Rather than the defect with which Honore had been born, the month of Hart's birth had to be the other thing she kept from Elias besides the identity of Thomas Becket.

Two years, five months until the boy was ten. It required little calculation to confirm what Elias already knew. Hart was of another, sown well before Lettice was found with that knight.

Elias had told himself she was faithless only the one time, but it was a lie. Another lie. Too many lies. Though this last one in which Honore claimed uncertainty over Hart's birth was not as dangerous as that of not revealing Elias aided his liege's enemy, it had been outright—

He backed up his thoughts. Non, a more dangerous lie it had been. It had set him on the path to Becket, and though it seemed the De Morvilles would escape retribution, it could ever be an axe above their necks ready to slip from the hands holding it— those of Becket and his brethren, the abbot of Clairmarais, even Honore who would surely do anything to protect her foundlings.

"Sir Elias?" the uncertain voice returned him to Hart. "Did you not mean it, that I can return here when I am ten?"

He wished he had not offered. Though he would not have to collect the boy himself, ever Hart's presence at Château des Trois Doigts would remind him of Honore.

"Sir Elias?"

"I meant it," he said gruffly.

The boy touched the mark of birth. "This may fade some the older I get. Though I would like to learn the sword, I could become a man of letters. Honore taught me to read."

Then he feared Elias would prefer to keep him hidden. Hating his inability to respond properly, Elias set a hand on the boy's shoulder. "I believe a hilt will better fit your hand than a quill."

Hart's lips curved. "When my work at Bairnwood is done, I will come back here."

"Two years, five months," Elias said and straightened.

Hart thrust forward that which had brought him to the gate. "What think you?"

That it was a light gray rock the elements had curved, thickening and blunting one end, thinning and pointing the other. But Elias also knew Hart had need of the wondrous imaginings of children of which Théâtre des Abominations had deprived him.

"Could be tooth or claw, but I guess the tooth of a very large beast, perhaps winged."

Wide-eyed, Hart closed his fingers around it. "A dragon's tooth," he pronounced and ran to Cynuit.

Leaving the boys to their chatter, the little ones to their laughter, Elias closed the gate behind him.

He had kept his father waiting. But what was another quarter hour?

~

"YOU LIED."

Honore had heard boots on the stairs but not expected they belonged to Elias who ought to be with his sire rather than accusing her of that of which she was guilty.

Hand on the door of the chamber she had closed behind her, having decided to join the children, she turned to where Elias strode the corridor.

"That is what I wished to speak to you about," she said when he halted before her. "The greater possibility Hart is not your son, though now it seems more likely he is—"

"He is not mine."

She swallowed. "You cannot be certain, but do you tell me when last you were intimate with—"

"That is of no consequence. I have just come from Hart who revealed the month of his birth which he had to have learned from you. However, ere he told what you withheld, I knew he was not mine. I knew it the moment I laid eyes on him. His eyes, nose, and ears are of the knight with whom I found Lettice, he who beat me, he whose armor I took, he who unwittingly revealed to the nobleman who bought him a drink that Lettice had birthed a child."

He had given her cause to fear he rejected Hart, so she ought not be surprised.

"Why, Honore? Why did you not speak in truth?"

She clasped her hands at her waist. "I feared you might not give aid in recovering Hart."

"Then you believe I am without honor—that I would not keep my promise to Lettice."

"I knew you not when you gave your word, though the more time I spent with you the more I believed you would keep it, especially as long as there was a good chance Hart was yours, but..."

"But?"

"Did I reveal the month of his birth, I felt I would also have to reveal another's claim upon him."

"You speak of the knight who beat me?"

"Non, Finwyn."

Elias took a step back.

"At the stream where he near drowned me, he said he had the right to dispose of Hart however he wished since he had fathered him. And when we found Lettice...what he did to her..." She shook her head. "I feared if anything could turn you from the promise made her, it was that so foul a being had fathered Hart."

Elias stared, then understanding shone from his eyes. "That is what he demanded of you last eve—if you had told me of his claim on the boy."

"He but taunted me, having minutes earlier disavowed the possibility Hart was his. And more he told." Honore paused over how much to reveal, then decided he ought to know all. "I am thinking you do not know that Lettice and Finwyn were betrothed ere your troupe came to Forkney."

His shoulders jerked. "I do not believe it."

"Last eve, he told that when he made a child—Cynuit—on her friend, Lettice broke their betrothal and began selling her favors to earn extra coin. He spoke of the troubadour come to Forkney, which is how he recognized you when you came looking for your son, and told that when Lettice's pregnancy caused her to lose her position at the castle, he and his grandsire provided for her and her family. Afterward…"

"Afterward?"

"Once Hart was given into my care, Finwyn aided Lettice in prostituting herself."

Anger deepened the lines of Elias's face. "Revenge on her that ended in murder."

"He said her death was not intentional, that they fought when she refused him the purse you gave her and he threw her against a wall, breaking her neck. Hoping to blame me for her death, he put her to the noose."

Elias was hardly recognizable, so dark and hard his face, so corded his neck she wondered if she should not have told all.

She touched his arm. "Even ere I knew all of it, I knew him unworthy of being Hart's father, so much I feared…"

"I would put the father's sins on the son." Elias held her gaze, and yet it was as if he looked at something beyond her. Did he question if he could have kept his word to Lettice?

He returned her to focus. "Without regard to endangering my family, you allowed me to believe I could have fathered a child I did not."

"I did not know it was impossible until you told it was the knight who beat you."

As if she had not spoken, he said, "The sooner to deliver us across the channel, you withheld from me the identity of Thomas Becket, allowing me to think I but aided a lowly, indefensible man of God attempting to flee persecution."

"I did, but—"

"At this moment, a man who is my liege's greatest enemy. If Henry learns I made it possible for the archbishop to slip through his fingers, all for which my ancestor fought at Hastings will be lost."

"You know I will never speak of it."

"Do I?"

"I will not!"

"Even to save Hart—or another foundling?"

She nearly denied it, but were a blade at a child's throat, she could not sacrifice an innocent to prevent the De Morvilles from forfeiting their lands.

Elias inclined his head. "Though I would not have a child die to save this demesne, such a choice would never even be imagined had you at least been honest about Becket. Still I would have crossed the channel for Hart, and though it might have taken longer to rescue him, I would have."

Chest aching, she lowered her chin. "What of Becket?" she asked. "Henry is vengeful. Had you not—"

"I have business to attend to, and you must begin preparing the children for the journey."

She reached to him as he pivoted, left her hand on the air as he strode toward the stairs. "I have ruined all," she whispered, then almost laughed. She hated that Elias thought so ill of her, but the outcome was the same. She and the children would leave France, and she would not see Elias again.

She closed herself in her chamber, dropped onto the bed, and pressed her face into a pillow.

CHAPTER 39

ONE WORD IS ALL IT TAKES

*O*tto De Morville had trespassed. Face florid, mouth tight, he snarled, "All to save a misbegotten boy not of your loins, see what you bring down on our house!"

Elias stared at his father who stood three steps below. Knowing he should not meet anger with anger, certain Otto had but happened on the exchange in thinking to collect his errant son and that he had a right to wrath over the danger to his lands, Elias resumed his descent and continued past his sire.

"Elias!"

"We will discuss it later, Father."

"We will discuss it now!"

"I have business in the village."

"Then we shall speak during the ride."

"I go alone." Elias continued to the hall and was grateful his father did not follow. He had much to account for regardless of what was overheard, but only after he could think in a straight line. He knew he wronged Honore at least as much as she wronged him, but she had deceived, had not trusted him just as

Lettice had not when he assured her he would provide for her family.

Elias's horse was saddled alongside his father's. It had not the strength nor reach of the destrier he could not reclaim, but it would suffice until he could secure another mount capable of more than merely transporting its rider—one who could partner with a man-turned-warrior when arms were called for.

Glad for the absence of weight and heat of chain mail, Elias declined accompaniment by the men-at-arms who were to have ridden with father and son—a decision that would once more make him question if he were worthy of a Wulfrith dagger.

THE KNOCK WAS INSISTENT, and it had the authority of Otto De Morville behind it. "I would speak with you, Honore of Bairnwood!"

She lifted her face from the pillow. Had Elias alerted his sire to the danger in which she had placed their family? She swung her feet to the floor and, wiping eyes and nose, crossed the chamber.

She opened the door. "My lord?"

He narrowed his gaze on her face. "I happened on your conversation with my son."

"Oh, I am sorry."

"Though I heard enough to know how serious the matter, you are going to tell me everything so I may find a way to plug up the hole you so kindly dug our family. Come, we will do this in the solar."

Shortly, sitting across the table from him, she told only what he needed to know. And yet from the way he looked at her, she thought he suspected the intimacy shared with his son and how deeply she felt for him.

"That is more than a hole," Otto rumbled. "That is a ravine even the surest arrow might not span."

"Forgive me, Lord De Morville. I did not mean to cause your family strife. I but wished to save a boy—"

"Whom you allowed my son to believe was his."

Though angry, it surprised he was not more so. "As you surely heard, I did think Elias could be Hart's sire despite Finwyn's claim." Hands clasped atop the table, she leaned forward. "Tell me what I can do to make it right."

"You can leave Château des Trois Doigts with all your children." He glanced at the window. "It is too late this day, but on the morrow."

She inclined her head. "Elias was to make arrangements—"

"*I* will ensure your return to the abbey. And you will do my son one kindness."

"Anything."

"Though he is angry now, I know he cares for you and would have a greater care had he not family to consider and promises to keep."

"He told you this?"

"Non, but I see what he does not believe I see, and that accursed troubadour's heart could ruin the De Morvilles if what you have wrought does not. As you must know, you are entirely unsuitable—your uncertain parentage and legitimacy, age, and the affliction you could pass to children born of your body. Though now Elias ought to have proof enough you are no fit for the De Morvilles, I would not have an impassable rift between my son and me should he forgive you and eschew his duty."

"I think there little chance of that."

"*Little* is too much where my family is concerned."

She nodded. "What kindness do you ask of me?"

"You shall remain in your chamber, neither showing yourself nor speaking with him. Come morn, I shall ensure he is away from the castle so you and the children depart without his knowledge."

Then she could not even wish him a good life. "I agree."

"And should he seek you after you are gone, you will stay inside your abbey and accept no missive from him."

"Methinks you overestimate your son's regard for me and underestimate his loyalty to you."

"Perhaps, but I will not lose him again. He—" His voice caught and alarm flashed across his face, but though he tried to cover his vulnerability with a stern face, it slipped before he could hide it behind the hand he gripped over his brow.

"You love him," Honore said. "This I know. I only hope you will tell him what you feel." She stood. "You have my word I will not see him again and he will not see me." At the door, she looked around and saw he remained behind his hand. "Elias offered Cynuit a position here. If your son is no longer inclined now he knows the boy is of Finwyn, would you send him to me so I may find him a good home?"

He lowered his hand. "Elias will keep his word. Cynuit may remain."

"But—"

"If I do not know my son as well as believed, I will send the boy to you."

"I thank you." She nearly added she thought it best Cynuit remain ignorant of his relation to his abuser, but she did not think either man would reveal it. Without further word, she closed the door.

Returning to her chamber, she began packing her few belongings and those of the children. Until Hart bounded inside to show her the rock he said Elias confirmed was a dragon's tooth, doubtless when the boy revealed his birth month, she remained dry-eyed. Then, so he would not see her tears, she sent him for ink and parchment.

But it was no frivolous errand. As much as possible, she would set aright the mess she had made of the De Morvilles.

CHAPTER 40

DO TRUST THE KNAVE

*T*rust. He might be forgiven for believing he had earned Lettice's, but Honore's was not his due. Though he hated her omissions and lies, she knew him too short a time to trust him.

It had taken the ride to the village to cool his ire and accept her wisdom. For years he had aspired to correct his flaws and become worthy of one day lording these lands, but she could not know that. All she had known for certain was had he not sinned with Lettice, there would have been no possibility he fathered her child. Hence, Honore would not have nearly lost her life at the stream, and Lettice would not have been killed over coin. No reason to trust him, and yet he had misdirected anger that threatened to undo him when he learned the date of Hart's birth that revealed Lettice had been unfaithful long ere he found her with the knight.

Though she had not claimed that was her only betrayal since the day Elias and she vowed they would not repeat the mistake of their one night together and would be with no other, he had persuaded himself of it, having seen the sweet of her soul and been certain only desperation would make her sell her body. That was surely how it began when her refusal to wed Arblette threatened her family's survival, but as concluded when she sought to send Elias away, likely for his sake more than hers it had become the quicker, easier way.

Broken by her first betrothed's betrayal and fearful of being broken by her next, she had not trusted Elias to provide though month after month he had given her the greater portion of his coin. Thus, Elias's anger at himself, Arblette, even Lettice, had spilled onto Honore who but protected the innocents whose trust *she* had earned. Were she to trust Elias as her foundlings trusted her, it would take time he could not give her without breaking his father's trust. But he could apologize and keep his word to see her safely returned to the life from which he had taken her.

A sennight—

Non, a fortnight and he would escort her and her charges to Bairnwood. "Where she does not belong," he said into the cool of day crawling toward night, which he had not expected to ride across. Blessedly, the dispute between the villagers was settled, both parties seemingly content with the concessions. At least in this Otto would be pleased—were he to spare it a passing thought beyond the danger in which Elias had placed their family.

He glanced over his shoulder at the receding village, noted lights being lit against the dark, and as he swept his gaze forward again, caught movement ahead.

Two riders. He did not know them at this distance, but their mounts were swift and sleek. And they came at him from the left.

Brigands? Urging his mount to greater speed, Elias veered to the right and assessed his defenses—sword and dagger, no armor or warhorse.

The demesne having long been at peace, he sensed this was something beyond happenstance, something that had lain in wait. The troupe? Or Henry's men seeking the one who aided Becket?

The former, he prayed but did not believe it, certain none of the troupe possessed such fine horses.

They were gaining on him, but he was well acquainted with the wood he might have to delve to leave them behind. Moments later, he accepted he must enter the trees, but as he neared, another appeared to the right. And there was enough light on that triumphant face to see it was Neville Sorrel who sought to scissor Elias between himself and his men, all of whom had drawn swords.

Elias turned his mount sharply, and as he spurred toward the tree line drew his own sword. He had allowed anger to transform a warrior into prey, but he would not further betray his training by making it easier for the miscreant to take him to ground—and prove Durand Marshal right. Ere the baron had been his friend, he had scorned Elias's award of a Wulfrith dagger, believing it was out of gratitude Everard jeopardized his family's reputation. It had caused Elias to train harder and as often at Wulfen as he was in England. But if he fell to Neville, despite being outnumbered three to one, Marshal would be proven right since victory in battle was not all to do with the swing of a sword and thrust of a dagger.

The first line of defense was to be prepared, the next to be vigilant, and neither had he been since departing Château des Trois Doigts. He yet ached from blows sustained at Sevier, was without armor, absent an escort, and mounted on a horse without training in battle.

"Will I never learn?" he growled, then recalled what Everard had said when he set upon Elias two squires soon to earn their spurs.

When possible, first pull the teeth.

That he must do again, this time against three. He had not seen any of these men fight, but Neville must be the teeth, having received knighthood training with Count Philip of Flanders who suffered no men of the sword not truly of the sword. Extinguish this threat and more quickly the others were snuffed out.

Elias went to the darkening wood, heard Neville curse as he followed, set a course amongst the densest trees and foliage that would soonest take them from sight of his pursuer's men. God willing, their search to make sense of the direction from which sword song sounded would delay them in aiding their lord, providing Elias time to best Neville before the knave became two and three.

The beat of hooves behind sounding more distant, Elias glanced around. Neville had dropped back, surely not due to his destrier being unable to keep pace. Because he sensed a trap in a wood better known to prey than predator? Because his men were no longer in sight?

Regardless, Elias's mount was faltering, its strength and stamina unable to match a warhorse's. If its rider did not act now, soon he would face three.

Elias reined around, giving rise to a cloud of dust, loam, and decaying leaves from which he emerged with a jab of spurs, a bellow of challenge, and a setting of sword.

Amid the coming of night and the wood's long low shadows, he glimpsed Neville's wide-eyed surprise and the shift toward uncertainty.

Lest he turn back to gather his men to his side, Elias shouted, "Run, craven coxcomb! Back to your wet nurse! Back!"

The knight bared his teeth, and as his destrier responded to a vicious jab of spurs, drew back his sword.

Steel struck steel, blade slid down blade, and as Elias's met chain mail, Neville's opened the shoulder of his opponent's mantle and tunic and sliced flesh.

Only scored, Elias assured himself, though with his pulse thrumming and the need for survival numbing him, it could prove worse.

He brought his horse around, and with his blood coloring Neville's blade, the two charged again.

Elias moved as if to deliver a backward stroke, and at the last moment ducked, arced his blade down, up, and slammed it against the inside of his opponent's sword. The blow nearly knocked Neville out of the saddle, and Elias's next swing delivered to the man's back dropped the miscreant over his horse's neck.

No blood gained, none expected, the mail once more protecting its wearer. But when Elias came around, he saw the knight leaned heavily to the side as he struggled to control his destrier.

Knowing his men would soon appear, Elias rode after him to ensure he pulled all the teeth. As he came alongside the hunched knight and raised his sword to bring its hilt down on the man's helmeted head, Neville jerked aside and tried to swing his sword. With little effort, Elias delivered the blow and Neville tumbled to the ground.

Victory, but would it be enough to return Elias to Château des Trois Doigts now the men-at-arms had appeared? Only if they paused to aid their lord where he landed between two great oaks.

Instead, they came straight for Elias, one on either side.

Certain they would keep pace with each other, providing no opportunity to be eliminated one at a time, and it would be of great detriment to leave his back vulnerable to them, Elias brought his horse around and charged to the left of the men. But as he readied his sword to meet that of the one veering toward him, a crack resounded around the wood, his mount lurched, and Elias launched himself out of the saddle lest he be pinned beneath his horse. Moments later, the animal thrashed ten feet away, its leg broken.

"Merciful Lord," Elias appealed as he tightened his grip on his sword and turned to rise before Neville's men were upon him.

He made it to sitting before a wave of darkness rose from the backs of his eyes. He had landed hard.

"A pity our lord—God rest his soul—believed you worth more alive than dead," said the smaller of the men who looked down on Elias from atop his horse. "But methinks he was right in that King Henry will pay better to watch you swing for aiding the good archbishop."

Fighting back the black that would see him stripped of arms and bound over the back of a horse, Elias gained his feet and looked between the men. "Though I do not believe the two of you capable of killing me, the only way you will deliver me across the channel is as a corpse." Setting his teeth against the ache and wet of his shoulder, Elias pulled the Wulfrith dagger from its scabbard. "Come. One at a time if you are not afeared of an injured knight, together if you are as craven as your lord."

Anger lit their faces, but the bigger one laughed. "Better a live craven man than a fool dead one." He considered the Wulfrith dagger. "Though Raoul prefers you alive, being a greedy knave, dead is good with me."

Elias had only the warning of a look passed between the two before they attacked. With his sword he parried the blade of the big man, with his dagger slashed the back of the hand with which Raoul gripped his hilt. He ducked the big man's next swing, thrust with the dagger and stabbed a thick thigh from which chain mail had fallen back.

As the man roared, Elias pivoted and knocked aside Raoul's sword that would have made a fine beginning of separating head from neck. Another thrust of the dagger at a soft belly bent Raoul forward, and Elias had only a glimpse of crimson spilling onto the horse's coat before he returned to the big man.

As he slammed aside the blade aimed at his chest with such force he relieved his attacker of his weapon, he felt a burn across his upper back. Raoul had no wish to die alone. Lest the man's next blow prove mortal, Elias arced his blade around. When his blade came off the other's, he swung again and unseated Raoul. But before Elias could return his attention to the big man, that one's great weight landed on his back. As it carried him to the ground, he felt a sharp pain in his side as if he had torn a muscle.

He landed face down but, blessedly, remained in possession of sword and dagger, the former stretched above his head, the latter pinned beneath his chest.

Elias swept his sword arm back, blindly reaching his blade toward the one atop him, shouted when the man gripped his wrist and slammed it to the ground where he held it as he rose and straddled his prey. Then he began driving a fist into Elias's ribs.

Grunting with each blow, Elias strained to free his sword arm and raise his chest enough to free the Wulfrith dagger. The fist struck him in the jaw, and once more he fought the currents seeking to drag him into unconsciousness.

Be worthy, Elias De Morville! he called to the warrior standing on the other side of the troubadour who, twice beaten, twice humiliated, twice unable to defend himself let alone others, had vowed never again to be without recourse.

He did not realize his hold on his sword hilt had loosened until he felt the man's fingers prying at them.

Kicking his way back to the surface, Elias emerged from dark water into the wood's deepening shadows, tightened his sword hand, strained the muscles of arms, shoulders, and back, and shoved upward.

The big man fell to the side and took Elias with him. The night sky coming into view, once more Elias felt pain beneath his ribs, but there was no time to dwell on it. Though his sword remained useless whilst his opponent gripped his hand, the Wulfrith dagger was freed.

He swept it across his chest, down, and inward. It slid between his opponent's ribs, causing the man to release his hold. As Elias rolled off, a bloodied blade came toward him. He stopped it with a slam of his forearm, dropped to the ground, and rolled several times more to distance himself.

He longed to remain there to recover his breath, strength, and presence of mind over which the dark once more moved, but he dare not rest until the danger was past.

Once more feeling the pain of something torn, he pushed upright, gripped his side, and looked from Raoul who stared at the heavens to the man's comrade whose eyes rolled as blood ran from his mouth.

Moving his regard to the Wulfrith dagger's jeweled hilt embedded in the man's side, Elias returned his sword to its scabbard and tried to stride forward but could manage only small, faltering steps. He bent and, when he pulled his dagger free, became aware of warm moisture on the palm pressed to his side.

It was covered in blood. Reminded of the crimson-coated blade he had knocked aside, he searched out the dagger loosely held by the big man. When the miscreant had launched himself onto Elias's back he had stuck it in his opponent, retrieving it only after Elias dealt him a similar injury.

"Dear Lord," Elias rasped. "I cannot die here."

Then stanch the blood and get yourself astride, the warrior commanded.

Elias backed against a tree and slashed strips from the lower portion of his tunic. One piece he folded into a thick square and pressed to the gash, the other two he wound tightly around his waist.

After dispatching his horse to end its suffering, with great effort he mounted the big man's horse and secured himself to the saddle.

His first thought was to ride to the nearby village, but two things set him toward the castle. As the village healer dealt mostly in herbs, the physician had to be summoned when one of her charges suffered dire injury. Thus, Elias could more quickly deliver himself into the man's care. Then there was the missing person of Neville Sorrel who was not where he had fallen. The sooner Otto was alerted to the man's incursion on his lands, the greater the chance he could be captured.

"Lord, keep me conscious," Elias prayed as he guided his mount out of the trees, then he ground his teeth against the greater pain to come and spurred forward.

VOICES. Shouts. The clatter of hooves.

Honore rose from the chair in which she had dozed and hastened to the shuttered window. She winced over the whine of hinges lest it awaken the children and peered down into the torchlit bailey.

Three riders were before the steps. As she settled her gaze on the one in the middle slumped over his mount's neck, the other two dismounted and called for the physician. It was a robed Otto who first appeared on the steps, descending two at a time.

"Elias," Honore gasped. She need not see the face of the man the soldiers struggled to remove from his saddle to know here was the one she loved.

"He bound himself to it," a soldier called to the other, and light flashed across the blade severing the rope.

Then Elias was pulled from the saddle into his sire's arms.

"Elias!" Otto shouted as his son's pale face turned up toward Honore. But his eyes were closed, what remained of his torn tunic stained with blood.

Honore knew she should remain in her chamber as she had agreed, but she could not.

She snatched up the robe Otto's wife had loaned her, as she shoved her arms into its sleeves swept her eyes over the children on the bed. Grateful their sleep was not disturbed, she slipped from the chamber and belted the robe as she ran bare-footed to the stairs. When she flung herself into the hall, she saw Otto had lain his son on the high table and the physician who had tended Alice bent over him.

"Clean cloths, boiled water," the man called as he cut through Elias's tunic and two servants ran to the kitchen.

"Lord De Morville," Honore gasped as she ascended the dais.

His head came around, and though this eyes met hers, she felt as if he looked through her. "When he did not come back, I sent men to search for him." His eyes brightened, mouth convulsed. "Too late. Now I shall lose my son. This time forever."

She looked to Elias. Was he already lost to them? He was pale and bloodied, and though his chest rose and fell, one had to look close to catch the movement.

Stepping to the table's edge, she closed a hand over his. "Elias?"

His fingers jerked beneath hers.

She looked to the physician, watched him carefully peel away the bandage from a side wound. It was not as unsightly as feared —a straight cut no wider than her thumb.

The man's eyes met hers. "Let us pray the blade hit nothing vital."

Lowering her lids, silently she beseeched the Lord to save His beloved Elias.

"Neville." The strangled breath of that name opened her eyes. The meaning of it straightened her back. The narrow of the eyes before hers made her gasp.

Before she could think what to say, Otto moved her aside and bent near his son. "That is who did this to you?"

"Neville Sorrel," Elias said low. "He knows the aid I gave Becket...sought to deliver me to Duke Henry. I injured him, killed his men." He coughed. "He escaped. Must stop him."

"Know you the direction he went?"

No answer, and when Otto drew back, Honore saw Elias's lids had lowered.

His father looked around, but no longer did he look through Honore. "You did this to my son."

"My lord," the physician said, "best you deal with this Neville now. There is naught you can do here. It is in God's hands upon mine."

Otto drew a breath that raised his shoulders, then gripped Honore's arm. "Return to your chamber," he said as he drew her off the dais.

With a backward glance at Elias, she moved out of the man's hold, crossed the hall, and ascended the stairs.

A half hour later, she watched from her window as a dozen knights and men-at-arms departed the castle in search of Neville. Shortly, Otto came to her, confirmed arrangements for her departure with the children on the morn, and once more secured her promise to stay out of Elias's life—if he yet possessed one.

Providing he was not lost to his family, Honore was content that never again would she set eyes on one who had suffered much in pursuit of a son not his.

When the wagon that would convey her and the children to the coast rumbled over the drawbridge at dawn, all she knew of Elias was he had survived the night and the physician believed he had a greater chance of living than dying. *If* infection did not set in.

CHAPTER 41

HIS LIFE TO SAVE

*H*onore."

Otto lifted his head from the mattress, as he blinked away sleep wondered if he imagined the voice of one he could not yet accept was lost to him—he who had gone into a deep sleep four days past from which the physician told he was unlikely to awaken.

As much as was possible for eyes growing old, Otto brought his son to focus. A glimmer between narrowed lids evidencing he had heard right, he leaned near. "Son!"

"Honore," Elias repeated.

Otto had been glad to see the woman who caused so much misery depart, but in this moment he wished her here to give his son what might be the only thing that could prove the physician wrong.

Elias swallowed loudly. "Where?"

"Here," Otto lied, knowing that had a channel crossing been possible she was now on English soil. "With the children." That last was not false, he salved his conscience. "When she returns to the donjon, I will bring her to you."

His son's lids lowered so suddenly, it was as if they were weighted.

Otto rose from his chair and lowered to the mattress edge. "Son?"

Elias drew a shaky breath, grimaced on an exhale that ended on her name. "Honore."

"If you wish to see her again, stay here with me."

Barely, Elias raised his lids. "Unsuitable," he slurred. "Oui, but I...cannot leave it as I did."

"You will see her soon."

"Your...word."

Another lie, but anything to keep him from slipping away. "My word you have." Otto reached to the cup from which he and others who kept watch dribbled wine onto Elias's tongue. "To regain your strength and be present when she arrives, you must drink and eat."

"After...sleep."

"Non." Otto raised his son's head, set the cup against his lips, and eased a stream into his mouth. It slid out the side. "Drink!" Otto grated, then with pleading said, "If not for me, Honore. She cannot come until you are well enough to receive her."

Though fatigue and pain shone brightest from Elias's eyes, Otto glimpsed suspicion there.

"The physician's orders, Son."

Elias parted his lips to receive the wine. It was slow going, but he swallowed half before drawing his head back.

Otto set the cup on the table and eased him onto his pillow. "Honore."

"I will send word." Otto stood, and as he strode to the door glanced over his shoulder for no other reason than to see his son awake and allow that sight to replenish the vessel of hope.

He opened the door, nearly ordered the passing chambermaid to summon the physician who had gone to the outer bailey to tend the smithy's apprentice. Determined to keep up the pretense Honore was near, Otto strode the corridor and caught the woman's arm as she started down the steps.

Surprise jostling the linens she conveyed to the laundress, Otto scooped them from her and dropped them on the floor.

"Milord?"

"With all haste, send for the physician," Otto said low. "Tell him my son has awakened."

She bobbed her head, hiked up her skirt, and descended the steps.

When Otto returned to the chamber and saw Elias's lids had lowered, he feared his heart would snap. It was no measured stride that carried him to the bed, no composed face upon which his son opened his eyes, no mere easing of the shoulders as relief emptied Otto's lungs.

"Neville?" Elias rasped.

Otto reached to the cup. "Drink first."

As Elias complied, Otto pondered whether falsity would better aid in his son's recovery. Reveal Neville had escaped capture and likely made his way to the King of England? Or tell the miscreant had been captured and slain? Whereas one tale could give Elias another reason to live beyond Honore so he might avenge himself on his attacker, the other could give him ease, allowing mind and body the rest needed to heal.

Otto nearly went the way of revenge, but that was more the way of sire than son. It could further wound Elias whose pursuit of the boy had endangered the De Morvilles, especially as it could be weeks—even months—ere he rose from bed.

Elias strained his head back, compressed his lips.

Otto set aside the cup. "Rest easy, all three of your attackers are dead. Our family is safe."

He was certain he had chosen well when his son's tension eased. "Forgive me for the ill...upon our house."

"It is done." Otto touched his forehead to his son's, an affection that surprised him. He straightened, knew from Elias's frown the gesture also surprised him.

Otto cleared his throat. "Now all that remains is for you to heal and resume your place as my heir."

"Your heir," Elias murmured.

That had been the wrong thing to say, a reminder of his duty to his family though that woman's name had first come off his lips.

"I have sent for the physician. As soon as he confirms you are fit to receive visitors, you can speak with Honore."

"I would speak with her first. I must...make it right."

"So you shall." Otto listened for the physician who must be apprised of the need to keep the hope of Honore alive. When Elias was strong enough, he would be told she was gone. And accept it as being for the best.

Elias closed his eyes.

"Son?" Twice more Otto called his name, but no response, nor when the physician appeared and subjected Elias to all manner of examination.

The man straightened. "I believe you, my lord, but though infection has not set in..." He shook his head. "Be thankful the Lord granted you this time with him."

Otto dropped into the chair and hung his head. "I cannot lose him," he groaned and admitted to himself what he could admit to no other. It was more the loss of his boy that distressed him than the loss of his last male heir.

"My lord, you need your rest. I will sit with him."

Otto longed to reject the physician's offer, but since lifting Elias's near lifeless body from the saddle he had slept in one and two hour snatches. He pushed upright. "I thank you, but ere I give him into your care, I must speak with you. Come into the corridor."

When the physician returned to his patient minutes later, Otto lingered outside the chamber to pour prayer unto God.

A hand touched his arm, and he snapped his head up, gentling his expression when he saw it was the young woman whose body Elias accused him of ruining. And so he had, though she made no such charge.

He touched her cheek. "Wife."

Her smile was slight. "Come to bed. I will hold you."

He ought to be offended by words that reduced him to the helplessness of a child, but her eyes were kind, and he longed to be held as he had not been since the passing of the mother of his sons.

He nodded and followed her to the solar.

She held him, and as sleep drew him to its bosom, she said, "They love, Otto. Does Elias live, let him choose the one with whom he spends his life."

Silly woman.

"The same as once you were blessed," she reminded him that though his own father had opposed his son's marriage to a widow aged twenty and five, narrow of hips, and frail, he had relented.

But in this Otto could not. Though Honore appeared to be of good childbearing build, she was even less a young woman, likely half common, and misbegotten. It was asking too much.

As he moved toward sleep, he returned to begging the Lord for what *He* might deem asking too much.

Bairnwood Abbey
England

IT WAS good to be home, and yet all of her was not here. A large piece had been left outside these walls. One she could never retrieve. One that would die with Elias.

Cease, she told herself. *You are not here to bemoan what can never be but to pray for what can be.*

Thrusting aside selfish Honore, she returned to prayer for Elias's healing. Though certainly not alone in beseeching the Lord to raise him from depths that sought to push dirt over him, perhaps her voice alongside those of his sire and others would add enough volume for God to spare a moment to ensure Elias's recovery.

Forehead pressed to the chill floor so long the stone tiles were warm by the time the bells called the sisters to service, Honore pushed back onto her heels. She lingered as she ought not with those outside soon to be inside, then raised her gaze to the altar with its carved figure of Jesus on the cross.

"Heal him," she whispered and reached to the gorget. Fingers encountering bare throat, she nearly smiled. Each time she departed the dormitory, one nun or another asked after the covering's absence, but none had shone disapproval on her when she told she would no longer wear it. And the one who had reminded her to conceal her lower face the day Finwyn summoned Honore to the wood had said she was glad.

Still, Honore had no desire to displease Lady Yolande who would threaten to pull her donations if she saw Honore did not keep her imperfection concealed. Thus, as continued to be habit, Honore exited the chapel by way of its side entrance.

Her timing was poor. As she stepped onto the path that led to the dormitory, the lady of three score appeared. This day she had decided to attend a service she often eschewed. There would have been time for Honore to turn her back to the one walking amidst nuns, but it so reeked of shame she continued forward and did not avert her gaze when the lady's pounced on her.

Honore smiled as Elias had advised, but though the expression made the scar less noticeable, it seemed to offend more.

Lady Yolande altered her course and stepped in front of Honore. "For what do you go about uncovered?" She peered down her long, thin nose as some sisters continued past while others halted.

"The same as you, my lady." She glanced at the lightly clouded sky. "Though it is hardly warm this early in the day, the breeze is not much more than a plaything."

"As well you know, it has *naught* to do with warmth."

Honore clasped her hands at her waist. "I do know it. Thus, no longer do I wear the gorget."

"If you think to move amongst those who generously provide for your undesirables, you shall wear it."

There the threat, but Honore determined that if God did think her beautiful as the abbess had long assured her, surely He would provide.

"I will not, my lady. Good day to you." As she stepped around the woman, she looked to the nuns who had paused and recognized them as those who had been novices on the day Cynuit had last come to the abbey. Among their youthful ranks was the older one from whose girdle hung prayer beads similar to Honore's.

"Hedge-born devil's spawn," Lady Yolande snarled and Honore felt a constriction around her throat almost as tight as when Finwyn nearly drowned her. Then she was yanked back by the neck of her short mantle and released. Her feet fell out from under her, rear end landed hard, back met the ground.

As she blinked at the sky, the lady stepped alongside. "No one disrespects me, especially your kind who know only how to take what you have not earned and, rather than show gratitude, demand more. Always more."

Honore had no time to form a response opposite that toward which outrage sprang her to sitting. And she was grateful. Far better a noblewoman set herself at another than she who would have enough to answer for when she stood before the abbess.

It was the oldest of those new to the order who shoved Lady Yolande so hard the woman barely kept her feet beneath her. "Ungodly!" cried the nun, hands at her sides folding into fists. "You are the nails that staked our Lord to the cross—the piercing points, cruel shafts, hard heads, ugly rust beneath blessed blood. You ought to be as ashamed as I am horrified one so unholy makes her home among the holy."

Open-mouthed, Lady Yolande stared.

"Sister Sebille!"

Realizing her own jaw had lowered, Honore raised it as she turned her head toward the one whose aged voice brimmed with authority.

Skirts snapping, veil flapping, the abbess strode forward with the speed of a much younger woman. As she passed the group of nuns from which Sister Sebille had separated herself, her eyes shifted to the one who had foregone the gorget—she who jumped up and deferentially nodded.

Honore would bear the blame for this, but better her than the new sister who could not know the strength of the enemy she made of Lady Yolande.

"Abbess Abigail," Honore appealed, "this is my doing."

"This I know." The woman halted. "You could not bend a little, Honore?"

Biting back the response that a *little* was not what the lady demanded, Honore said, "Forgive me, I could not. I am done wearing the gorget as it is not meant to be worn." Honore looked to the one who had become her champion, was surprised the lady appeared far from contrite. Indeed, she looked as if she assembled more insults behind her lips—until her gaze moved to Honore. Then her face softened.

As Honore gave a smile of gratitude, she was struck by the woman's name the abbess had called out and realized here was the one Wilma and Jeannette told had aided with the foundlings in

Honore's absence, she who had not shown herself since Honore's return with Hart and three more foundlings.

"Sister Sebille but defended me," Honore addressed the abbess.

"She laid hands on me," Lady Yolande shrilled. "And the vile things she said—that I am ungodly...unholy." She snatched the waist of her gown, jerked it as if it had been put askew. "You are remiss in training up women of God, Abbess. Be assured the bishop will hear of this."

Honore stepped toward the lady. "She is not to blame."

"Honore!" Abbess Abigail rebuked. "Take yourself to my apartment. And you as well, Sister Sebille. There is much wrong to set aright."

"Indeed there is," Lady Yolande spat.

"Go, Honore and Sebille!" Those words resounded with such portent, Honore was further alarmed. Penance was not new to her, though it was years since her transgressions warranted more than greater time spent in prayer. But of utmost concern was what might befall Sister Sebille from whom more restraint was expected.

Stiff in her step, the nun crossed to Honore. "Let us walk together."

Neither spoke until they entered the abbess's apartment, then the nun said, "She is a mean soul, has she a soul at all. Ungodly. Unholy. Truth!"

Honore turned at the center of the room. "I cannot disagree, and I am grateful for your kindness in defending me, but it would have been better had you not. Now you will do penance and Lady Yolande will make misery of you."

The woman halted before Honore. "My only regret is displeasing the abbess, but even if I must spend a sennight on my knees it will be worth it."

"You are courageous, Sister Sebille."

Something shifted in the woman's eyes. "I learned courage at the knee of one whose love became a blight when she discovered I was not who her husband gave me to be. But that courage I mostly concealed, as I have determined I will not do at Bairnwood."

Deciding the tale behind the woman's riddled words mattered not, Honore said, "I have wished to seek you out since I returned two days past."

"For?"

"Your work with the foundlings. Wilma and Jeannette tell you were of great aid and the little ones are fond of you."

The woman looked down, but not before Honore saw tears in her eyes. "Years ago, I hoped to have children of my own. As with so many things, that hope died by another's hand." She looked up. "And by mine because I hid my courage. In that we are the same, both of us of thirty and two ere we came out from behind our coverings."

Honore took a step back, surprised not only this woman knew her age, but their years numbered the same. Sister Sebille's life must have been hard. "How do you know my age, Sister?"

The woman lifted the prayer beads attached to her girdle, stepped forward and touched those around Honore's neck. "I do not need the abbess to confirm that once these two strands were one—that in truth *I* am Honore of no surname, *you* are Sebille Soames. *I* am misbegotten, *you* are legitimate."

Certain the woman was mad, Honore made her next step of retreat more deliberate.

Sister Sebille held up a hand. "I have thought through this meeting a hundred times, but it could have been done better. Forgive me."

Calm, Honore counseled. *Her mind may not be right, but she is of no danger. Only a woman who has attached herself to you.* Because of the one whose love became a blight? It mattered not. Sister Sebille had been good to the children and surely meant no harm. Still, Abbess Abigail would have to be informed.

Honore forced a smile. "You surprise, is all."

"And frighten. I do not mean to, and I assure you I am sane. When the abbess comes, we shall confront her together, and then you need not fear me at all. She will confirm what you are to me and I am to you."

"Confirm?"

"I am your half sister."

CHAPTER 42

BRAVE MAIDEN HE AWAKES

Château des Trois Doigts
France

*H*onore."

Once more, Elias's voice inserted itself in Otto's prayers, but it did not sound hoarse or fevered. It was so calm and softly spoken, it was as if she were here and he but acknowledged how pleased he was to see her.

Otto lifted his brow from atop his son's hand. Elias's eyes were closed, face unlined and lacking the flush of fever that had set upon him shortly after the physician gave the Lord of Château des Trois Doigts less hope of seeing his son hale again. Was he passing out of this world?

"Non," Otto groaned and thrust upright. He gripped Elias's coarsely-bearded face between his hands, and as he had done time and again since his wife bid him, said, "Come back to us, and with my blessing you will wed the one you love."

Elias's lids rose slightly. "Methinks I have..." He swallowed hard. "...gone to heaven. But what do you here?"

"You are very much alive, Elias." Otto retrieved the cup and put it to his son's lips. Unlike the last time Elias had consciously taken drink, he gulped down the contents.

Otto set a hand on his son's brow. It was not cool, but neither did it burn.

"I would see Honore."

Otto hated he lied again, but he would have nothing trouble his son. "As she is so concerned for you she does not eat or sleep well, I sent her and the children with my lady wife to Château Faire for a few days of rest."

Elias's lids narrowed. Did he see the falsity on his sire's face, hear it in his voice? Or did he know the woman too well to believe she would leave him as he lay dying?

"Where is she, Father?"

As Otto searched for an answer that would satisfy without alarming, his son began to struggle onto his elbows.

"Your stitches, Elias—"

"Where is she?"

"Soon she will be here."

He dropped onto the pillow, said, "She is gone."

Otto nearly denied it, but there was too much certainty in his son's voice.

"Did she go of her own will? Or did you send her away?"

Otto eased back onto the chair. "It being mutually agreed she depart as planned, I provided her and the children an escort all the way to Bairnwood. If a channel crossing was possible, she is home."

Elias released a long breath, closed his eyes.

Otto did not wish him to return to sleep, but as the physician told rest was the best curative, he let his son be.

A quarter hour later, Elias awoke again.

Otto squeezed his arm. "Once you are recovered, I will send for Honore."

"Why?"

"I gave my word."

"Your word?"

Did he not recall his sire's vow that if he pulled himself up out of death he would have the woman he loved? Certes, he had heard nearly every time it was spoken, having eased and several times smiled. If he did not recall—

Non. The word given he would keep. "Time and again I assured you that if you returned to us you could have Honore for your own."

Surprise lit Elias's eyes, then anger. "I will not take her to mistress, nor would she so ruin herself."

"I speak of marriage, Son. If she will have you as I believe she wishes, you will have her as I believe you wish."

Still his expression remained far from pleased.

"No lie, Elias. When you are recovered, I will bring her back across the narrow sea. You will wed and, I pray, give me grandchildren as quickly as possible. She is, after all, no girl."

"As I would not have her be."

"Most evident." Otto turned to another matter. "I have decided to pass the demesne to you ere my death so I might witness how much more worthy is my heir."

It seemed Elias might smile. "I require no more incentive beyond Honore to rise from this bed."

"Still, you will be lord, Elias."

"It sounds as though…you have a great care for me."

"More than ever I can say."

One of Elias's eyebrows rose, though nowhere near the height to which it surely aspired. "Even now you cannot say it?"

Did it need to be said when it was well enough shown? Otto silently scorned, then acquiesced. "Ever I have loved you, Son. Ever I shall."

The tears moistening the eyes of a warrior with the heart of a troubadour made Otto uncomfortable, and more so when the sting and blurring of his own eyes told they shone as bright.

"I love you, Father." It was not the first time Elias had gifted his sire those words, but the mutual profession gave them greater depth.

"Now tell," Elias said, "why must you bring Honore to me when it is more fitting I go to her?"

The righting of another lie. "You recall I told Neville was dead, our family safe?"

Elias tensed.

"It may not be a lie, but I fear he lives." Otto blew a breath up his face. "My men were unable to overtake him. Though I pray he does not go to Duke Henry empty-handed, I think it likely. Thus, to sooner relate your version of events that caused you to aid Becket, I sent ahead a missive detailing what transpired."

Anger again. "You forced it from Honore?"

"I did not. She told me all, and ere departing gave me the missive and instructed me to do with it as I thought best. That I did."

After a long silence, Elias said, "You say it was mutually agreed she leave, and yet I struggle to believe she would do so until certain of my recovery."

"She blamed herself for what befell you and feared you would not forgive her. And I blamed her and did not wish you to forgive her. For that, I gained her word she would stay out of your life." As his son tried to rise again, he closed a hand over his shoulder. "I will send word to her abbess and—"

"I shall go myself. She needs to hear from me I do not hold her responsible, that all the ill was worth the lives of those children, that I would have her to wife, that you will embrace her as Lady of Château des Trois Doigts." Elias collapsed onto the pillow, shuddered breath out on the words, "I will bring her home."

"But if Henry—"

"He can as easily punish me here in Normandy as in England. That I will also deal with when I am out of this accursed bed."

"Will the Wulfriths stand your side?"

"I will not endanger their relationship with Henry. Once I am assured Honore is safe from her king's wrath, I will go to her." He closed his eyes. "Now I must sleep."

Shortly, he breathed deep, and for the next hour Otto counted every rise and fall of his chest. When the physician confirmed the worst was past, Otto dropped to his knees and continued the longest conversation he had ever had with God.

Much gratitude.

Much praise.

Much beseeching that even if Elias and Honore gave him no grandchildren, he would be the father so worthy a son deserved.

CHAPTER 43

THY LOVE DOTH SLAY

Bairnwood Abbey
England

"I feared you knew, Sebille. How long?"

The nun lifted her prayer beads, met the abbess's gaze. "I did not know for certain, but I suspected when I was nine and you gave me these."

Honore looked between the two women, tried to understand how those words could be the first to exit their mouths when the abbess entered.

"When the woman my father fooled into believing she was my mother came for me after his disappearance and took me from here, I was so afraid to go with her, I looked back and saw a girl near my age wearing beads the same as these, also a short strand. I would have thought naught of it, but her lower face was covered and made me think of the infant my father told I had replaced— she who was said to have died at the abbey from a defect that made it impossible for her to nurse."

Sister Sebille looked to Honore. "A month ere your birth, I was born of our father's sin with a noblewoman not his wife. When your mother rejected you for your defect, our father brought you here to die where my mother had birthed me and left me to be raised. Though I would not know it for years, he gave me your name and took his misbegotten month-old daughter to his wife with tale he had prayed for the healing of the defect and God worked a miracle—"

"Enough!" Honore cried. "This is absurd."

"You are Sebille Soames," the nun continued, "and the name that has long hung around your neck was first mine—Honore of no surname."

Honore snapped her gaze to the abbess. "It cannot be."

"She speaks true." The old woman sighed. "Your sister has guessed all I was to hold close. She was given your name and became much loved by your mother for the miracle of her healing. But when the Lady of Lexeter discovered that for nine years her husband had fooled her, she threatened your sister's life. Thus your father returned her to us."

The room was turning around Honore. Or was *she* turning?

"Come, sit." The woman who thought herself Honore took Honore's arm and guided her to a chair. "I know the deceit is unimaginable, but it is so. And I added to it by taking revenge on your mother for what she—"

"What of your father?" Honore asked.

"*Our* father died shortly after returning me here. Then his wife came to reclaim the daughter she knew I was not. I did not tell her he had revealed to me the truth of my birth and yours. Instead, I set my mind and heart to making her love me again." She drew a shaky breath. "But no matter how hard I tried, she hated me, making of me little more than a servant and denying me every chance at happiness. It was years ere I accepted what could not be changed, and then I was so embittered I became vengeful, pretending to scrape and bow while behind her back I worked ill to turn her son from her."

"Son?" Honore snatched at another sibling she was to believe she had.

"Your brother, my half brother whom I love very much. His name is Lothaire, and he will be pleased to know you, as will his wife."

Honore pressed fingers into her temples. "Does my mother know I survived?"

Sebille shook her head. "She passed recently, unaware the one she rejected lived."

Honore wished she could feel more than a twinge of regret. Had her father not refused, likely her mother would have had her afflicted daughter set out. She looked to the abbess who had come to stand over Sebille's shoulder. "Did my sire know I lived?"

"He did."

"Did he love me?"

"I believe so. When I sent word the infant expected to die was receptive to taking milk through a reed, it was he who engaged the physician to close up your lip. The procedure nearly killed you, but when you healed, you thrived. Once a year your father visited to observe you from a distance. He was proud of you and provided substantial funds so one day you could take vows if you wished."

Feeling the beads beneath her fingers, Honore looked to the strand that was now four beads shorter than that of the woman kneeling before her. "Why did you give us these, Abbess?"

"The hope of providing you the comfort of prayer. And sentiment. You were sisters, and though you were not to know it, I wished to bind you to each other even if only by a string of beads made into two. Now they are reunited, I pray it a good thing."

"It is," Sebille said. "I have someone else to love." She looked nearer upon Honore. "Do you think you might come to care for one who shares half your blood?"

It was said with such longing Honore ached for the woman whose lovely childhood had been worse than lost. "I am all astir," she said. "This is much to take in, but I like you, and I am in your debt for defending me to Lady Yolande, for which you will suffer."

"She will not," the abbess said and lowered into the chair near Honore's. "I have informed her of my decision, which I pray the bishop will support. Henceforth, the bulk of Bairnwood's funds are to be dedicated to the care of foundlings."

Sebille's gasp nearly matched the volume of Honore's.

The abbess inclined her head. "The lady will be leaving us. By week's end, the foundling door will be completed and word sent out across the barony and those surrounding it that parents unable to care for their children may leave them with us, assured they will be well cared for and placed in good homes when possible. As for the boys who are not placed by the time they attain their tenth year, I believe funds can be raised to construct outside our walls a dormitory, small chapel, and workshop where they can learn a trade." She moved her gaze to Honore. "The blessings begun with you shall multiply."

Of a sudden feeling very fragile, as if a mere breath would birth hundreds of cracks, Honore could only stare. But when the need for air became so painful she had to fill her lungs, she clapped hands to her face and sobbed into them.

Arms came around her. She told herself this was enough, that into the space of her heart where Elias dwelt she could settle more foundlings, consigning the man she loved to a corner so distant she might forget him there.

"Methinks these are not entirely happy tears," the abbess said.

Honore lifted her moist face. "I am very happy."

"I am aware, and yet the sorrow with which you returned to Bairnwood continues to burden you."

Sebille drew back. "What troubles you?"

Though tempted to hold close her ache, Honore said, "It is hard to believe that in so short a time I could love the man who retrieved Hart, but much I feel for him." She looked to the abbess who had been told of Elias's belief Lettice's son was his and what had transpired in the quest to rescue the boy, though not of the aid given Thomas Becket.

There was alarm in the old woman's eyes, and Honore shook her head. "Fear not. Just as I greatly value my chastity, he is honorable despite a mistake made in his youth."

"I do not question that."

"Then?"

"Now it is known you are noble both sides and legitimate, if he feels for you as you feel for him, he might come for you were he told. And more than ever you are needed here."

"Worry not, Abbess. I have no intention of claiming the Soames name. And even if I did, it would be of no use. I have endangered Sir Elias's family, am responsible for his injuries, and…" She trailed off, sent up another prayer for his recovery. "…I gave his father my word I will have no further contact with him. Bairnwood shall remain my home."

"But what if he does come for you?" Sebille asked.

"I do not believe he will, but should he, I will not see him." Honore looked to the abbess. "I will keep my word to his father, and Sir Elias will wed one of better childbearing years to ensure the De Morville name continues."

"I am glad you choose this life," the abbess said. "You yet have so much to give the Lord." She turned her gaze upon Sebille. "What think you of serving the Lord other than by way of prayers for the dead, Sister?"

"If you speak of working with foundlings, I would like that."

"Then providing Honore agrees, it is settled."

Honore considered this found sister whom Wilma and Jeannette liked well, nodded. "It is settled."

CHAPTER 44

TURNS DARK TO DAY

Marlborough Castle
England

$\mathcal{E}$lias had been prepared to stand alone before King Henry, but when he came seeking an audience at Marlborough Castle, Sir Durand and Lady Beata appeared. He had felt a fool for not seeing their advance, but their warm greeting put him at ease —as much as was possible for one whose actions could bring a swifter end to the De Morville name than lack of a male heir.

"You have no say in this." Durand leaned toward Elias. "I know not how much I can sway Henry, but I will stand your side."

Elias shook his head. "This is my mess. I would not have you bear the cost of defending me."

Beata also sat forward. Dark braid catching between her shoulder and her husband's, she said, "It is what friends do, Elias. Certes, were there time to summon Everard Wulfrith, he would also be here."

As Otto had wished, but Elias had refused to send an appeal to Everard, not only because the man was soon to be a father again— and as told by Beata had been so blessed a sennight past—but because Elias was determined to do this himself. And yet, as if the Lord agreed with Otto that support be given by friends, the day of Elias's arrival at court coincided with the departure of Durand and Beata who had been summoned by Queen Eleanor that she might look upon the two she had matched—they who would ever be grateful for her meddling.

"What of your children?" Elias said, knowing the two were eager to return to their infant twins, a healthy boy and girl.

"One more day will do no harm," Beata said.

"We know you can do this on your own," her husband prompted. "We but wish to ease the passage if possible—and a rough one it may prove, as fitful as Henry is over Becket."

Pride nearly caused Elias to more forcefully protest their aid, but the hope of keeping Honore from her sovereign's wrath made him accede. "I thank you, my friends. I shall be glad to have you at my side, though I ask you speak naught unless Henry has me dragged before the executioner."

They agreed, though he did not quite believe them, then Durand eyed the slants of sunlight streaking the great hall. "We are to meet Queen Eleanor in the garden to receive her blessing for our safe travels. I am sure she will be pleased to see you again, might even be compelled to speak with her husband on your behalf."

Too much to hope for, Elias thought. But her reaction, she who likely knew of Honore's missive that Otto had sent ahead and whatever tale Sir Neville had carried, could better prepare Elias for his meeting with Henry.

Elias stood and grimaced at the ache in his side that reminded him he was not fully healed. He followed the hand-holding couple outside beneath a cloudless sky that made these last days of autumn seem nearer their middle. Quite the blessing, travel from Château des Trois Doigts having been chill and weepy, and more so during the channel crossing. Now if the Lord would extend that blessing, calming the storm that could rise in England's king...

"There are her ladies." Beata nodded at women chatting before an arbor. "Eleanor will be near."

The ladies greeted Durand and Beata, puzzled over Elias, then said the queen waited on them.

The three stepped past, and there on a bench sat Eleanor, face turned up to the sun.

"Your Majesty," Durand called.

Without looking around, she said, "Come, come."

"We bring our friend, Your Majesty, one we are certain you will welcome."

"Oh?" Still she did not look their way.

"Sir Elias De Morville," Elias announced himself.

She turned her head, and her eyes widened. "Otto's pup!"

As she had called him when, following his knighting by Everard, she informed him of his brother's death that would make him heir if he reconciled with his sire.

The three halted before her, bowed.

"Why, this is most fortuitous, Sir Elias."

"Your Majesty?"

"That we should deliver unto our husband the vassal with whom he heartily wishes to speak."

Elias tensed further.

"Such courage to deliver yourself to England—all things Becket considered. We cannot speak for our husband, but it inclines us to believe what that little nun wrote."

"Nun? You speak of Honore of Bairnwood?"

"That is her name. She is not of the sisterhood?"

"She is not, Your Majesty, though she is responsible for the abbey's work with foundlings."

342

"Only a servant, then. Well, that casts this business in a different light." She clasped her hands at her waist, studied his face. "Do you love her?"

He took a step back, felt Beata's hand on his arm.

"Ah, Sir Elias, it may prove more difficult to return you to our husband's good graces than thought." She flicked a hand at a nearby bench and, when they were seated, continued, "We ought to make quick work of this lest, for once, Henry does not keep us waiting."

"He is to meet you here?" Elias asked.

"He is. Now give answer, Sir Elias."

Though he preferred to feign ignorance, he said, "I love her."

Amidst Beata's gasp of surprise, the queen said, "Since we are guessing she is common, what do you intend? Make her your mistress?"

Elias held her gaze. "My wife, if she will have me."

She made a face. "We could arrange a far more suitable match, one that would increase holdings you will not have when your father disavows you for wedding so far beneath his wishes."

Struggling against revealing how greatly she offended, he said, "When I returned to my family, I vowed to do my duty, Your Majesty—to wed a woman of whom my sire approves. Do I wed Honore, that vow I will not break."

"What say you?"

"My father has granted I may wed where I will, no matter the woman's class or how many years she has."

"It is not possible you speak of Otto De Morville."

"I do."

"Then he either grows exceedingly soft in old age, else loses his wits."

"Regardless, he will accept Honore of Bairnwood as the mother of his grandchildren."

Eleanor held up a hand. "How many years has she?"

"Thirty and two, Your Majesty."

She gave a curt laugh. "Does your father know this?"

"He knows she is four years beyond me, and though he prefers I marry a girl the same as he, on this he yields."

She quieted, and he guessed she was thinking of the greater gap between Henry and herself, Eleanor having been born more than ten years before her husband. "Well, as long as you begin making babes straightaway, you should be able to assure Otto's name passes to another generation."

"As soon as I have made my peace with your lord husband, I will bring Honore to Château des Trois Doigts."

"Elias," Durand said low and tilted his head to the right. He had sooner sensed they no longer numbered four.

A glance at Eleanor revealed her momentary confusion over Durand's warning. Then she smiled and said, "We are pleased by your loyalty to the Duke of Normandy, Sir Elias. But of course it is for our lord husband to determine how true your allegiance." She leaned forward. "Neville Sorrel may think to play him for a fool in the hope of stealing De Morville lands, but as we know well, the greatest of England's kings is no puppet." She sat back, once more turned her face to the sun. "He should be here soon."

And so he was, though not immediately. Doubtless, he would have none think him disposed toward eavesdropping. Better he was believed omniscient.

"Marshal," the king said as he strode from amongst the trees at their backs, "you and your lady wife leave us this day?"

All three rose, turned, bowed to the man whose hair shone more red in sunlight.

The faltering of Henry's bow-legged stride almost believable, he motioned them to straighten. "Elias De Morville," he growled, "we thought we would have to command you to court to account for your traitorous actions."

"Methinks, Lord Husband," his queen said, "you will be gladdened by what the friend of Everard Wulfrith has to tell."

Elias saw irritation flicker across Henry's tanned, freckled face, felt his own rise. He ought to be grateful for Eleanor's reminder that Elias was backed by a member of the family on whom the king relied to strengthen England's defenses, but this was between Elias and Henry.

"Your Majesty," Elias said when the king halted between the benches, "I have come to account for the events that found me in the company of your archbishop."

"No longer our archbishop," Henry crossed his arms over a chest that strained the seams of a tunic so unremarkable one might question if the one who wore it was, indeed, a king. "Our queen, Lord Marshal, Lady Beata," he acknowledged each, "methinks this knight capable of speaking in his own defense. Leave us."

Ere they departed, Beata once more squeezed Elias's arm. Providing he was not clapped in irons, her husband and she would be waiting for him at the end of his audience with Henry.

The king strode to the place his wife had occupied, lowered, jerked his chin at the other bench. Once Elias reseated himself, Henry said, "We are in receipt of the missive written by Honore of Bairnwood and sent by your sire. Is it true what she wrote?"

"As I was severely injured in an encounter with Sir Neville and his men, I know only what my sire told of the missive. What I know for certain is that the woman is of good character, so much I am sure she accepts more responsibility for—"

"Good character? She admits to deceiving you. Did she?"

Elias inclined his head. "To save a boy who—"

"Théâtre des Abominations," Henry interrupted again. "The same we ejected from England and you put end to, we understand."

"Without regret, Your Majesty. Truly, it was an abomination."

"Neville reports he saw you and others in the company of that..." A sharp breath pinched Henry's nostrils. "He saw you in the company of Becket on the road to Clairmarais."

"That is so."

"Even then you did not know it was Becket you aided?"

"I did know, Your Majesty, it being revealed during the channel crossing."

"Then you have no excuse for your betrayal."

"What was done was done, Your Majesty."

"You could have delivered Becket to us."

"I could have, but my greatest concern, selfish though it may seem, was overtaking those who might further harm the children of whom they made objects. Too, you will not like this, but if any might understand, it is you who is said to have loved Becket as a brother. I cannot know all that has gone between you, but I think him a good man, and rather than walk the easier path of taking advantage of your friendship, he chooses a path toward which he believes God points him. And you."

"Us?" Henry's ruddy cheeks reddened further.

Knowing the waters here were too deep to be negotiated carelessly, Elias said, "I do not think you would have made him Archbishop of Canterbury did you not believe him able to discern the voice of God, Your Majesty."

"He is divisive, adept at making one believe him sincere and loyal. Never did he have a care for us—only what we could do for him. And see what we did, raising him high above his station? He fooled me!"

Elias caught Henry's shift from referring to himself en masse to standing alone in being fooled. "I pray not, Your Majesty, that it is merely a misunderstanding between godly men who will soon reconcile."

"Never!" The word was ejected with such force saliva fell just short of Elias, then the king said again, "He fooled me."

"I do not believe that, Your Majesty."

"You do not *wish* to believe it. But if he can fool a king, how hard for him to fool you?"

The waters were not as deep as thought, Elias mused. This was the place he had hoped to lead Henry, and here they were. The only sense that could be made of how quickly they reached it was that England's passionate, temperamental king was emotionally stung by the loss of his friend and ally.

"I still cannot believe he fooled me, Your Majesty, but if so, I pray for your forgiveness."

Henry groaned, smacked the heel of his palm against his brow. "Thomas!" he rasped and stilled. When he lifted his head, his eyes were more veined. "Neville told De Lucy recognized the ring worn around the neck of Honore of Bairnwood as being the same we gave Thomas years ago. Why would he give it to her unless never did he value our friendship?"

"A wedding ring made it appear she traveled with her husband that she not suffer the reputation of a woman without proper escort. It being the smallest of rings any of us wore, the archbishop sacrificed it."

"But it was seen upon her at Saint-Omer after you parted from Thomas. You say she forgot to return it?"

He was not saying that, but not wishing to lie, Elias shrugged.

Henry nodded. "Surely he is missing it now."

Then he was not truly certain Becket had fooled him?

"We should never have made him archbishop. Still he would be our chancellor, still he would be as a brother to us." Henry shook his head, after a long moment, said, "Do you truly believe reconciliation possible?"

Elias wanted to, but so far over the edge was their friendship pushed that, regardless of who was in the right, each man had given the other cause to distrust.

"I do not know, Your Majesty, but I pray for reconciliation."

Henry dropped his head back. Like his wife, he sank into the sun's warmth. After a time, he said, "What do we do with you, Sir Elias whose sire I esteem?"

"Forgive the fool, I pray." Intentionally, Elias equated himself with the fool Henry believed Becket made of the King of England.

Henry lowered his chin, raised his eyebrows. "What of Sir Neville?"

"I would be pleased to meet him at swords, Your Majesty."

A bark of laughter sounded. "Of that we are certain. We understand he nearly sundered your life."

"Not he, Your Majesty. One of two men he set upon me, both of whom forfeited their lives to me."

Henry moved his gaze down Elias. "You are fully recovered?"

Then he might allow the two to cross blades? Though the physician advised Elias do no more than engage in sword practice for the next several weeks and with less force than usual, Elias would welcome the challenge. "Well enough, Your Majesty."

"Perhaps," Henry mused, then said, "Neville did seek to do us a service by delivering one who might reveal Becket's whereabouts."

"In that I am of no benefit, Your Majesty. Becket and I parted at Clairmarais so I might continue my search for the boy. I know not where he can be found."

The king's mouth tightened. "Too late now. The ever pious King Louis has granted him asylum and financial aid and written to the pope on his behalf. Thus, less and less it seems the Church will order Becket to return to England to answer to his king."

"Still you could seek reconciliation."

He grunted. "You ought know Sir Neville wishes your father's lands—your inheritance."

"That does not surprise, but I ask you to reconsider. If punishment is due, I am resolved to it, even if the price is my life. Pray, do not punish my sire who has never given you cause to question his loyalty."

Henry considered him, swept up a hand. "Rise, Sir Elias."

As he did so, the king's eyes moved to the Wulfrith dagger. "You are fortunate our ire has cooled these weeks since Neville came bearing news of your betrayal, fortunate you came of your own will and humbled yourself, fortunate we hold Honore of Bairnwood more responsible for Becket's escape."

"Your Majesty, she but sought to more quickly—"

"This we know, and we are grateful to both of you for putting an end to a great offense to God. You need not worry we shall retaliate against her or Bairnwood."

"I thank you, Your Majesty."

"As we were saying, you are most fortunate, Sir Elias." Henry stood. "Though now we have less regard for friendship than ever we did, you seem wise in your choice of friends."

Everard and Durand. Though Elias wished he did not require their influence, he was grateful for it with one such as Henry Plantagenet.

"Another thing," the king said.

"Your Majesty?"

"We do not like nor trust Neville Sorrel."

Elias waited, certain he would elaborate were he not pressed.

"Where others failed, he seduced the fairest, most loyal of Queen Eleanor's ladies."

Was Henry among those who failed? As all knew, he had appetites beyond his wife.

"Now *that* is a fool," Henry said.

Fairly certain the question was answered, Elias said, "Indeed, Your Majesty."

"We shall tell him you are cleared of wrongdoing and order him to return to his family in France with the advice he keep his distance from our most loyal vassal, Otto De Morville. And you, Sir Elias, will be more cautious in future as to your traveling companions so you not further disappoint us and your father."

"I thank you, Your Majesty."

"Easily reversed, we assure you. As for the fine horses delivered to Boulogne over which a watch has been kept to discover who aided Thomas, we shall order them released to you."

Elias had not even hoped there. Containing a smile, he said, "I thank you."

"One more thing, De Morville."

349

"Your Majesty?"

"Get thee wed—and soon. It is time you gave your sire heirs."

"Be assured, Your Majesty, I shall."

Henry backhanded the air. "Your leave is granted."

Elias bowed and went in search of Durand and Beata.

CHAPTER 45

HERE BEGINS OUR TALE

Bairnwood Abbey
England

The answer is the same, Sir Elias. She will not see you."

The same, though this time delivered by the abbess three hours after the first refusal, surely the sooner to see Elias depart, which he had said he would not do until he spoke with Honore.

As it would soon be dark, he considered the parchment in his pouch he wished to place in Honore's hand, that which had made all his days abed tolerable.

"Godspeed your journey, Sir Elias."

"Abbess!" He stepped nearer the portcullis between them, heard her sigh as she came back around.

"Much gratitude is due you for aiding in rescuing Hart and the little ones," she said, "but it does not extend to forcing Honore to open a door she wishes to remain closed."

"If I could speak with her but a few minutes—"

"You will not, Sir Elias."

He opened his pouch. "Then will you give her something?"

She eyed the rolled and bound parchment he passed through the bars. "What is this?"

"Ink made into letters made into words made into song."

She raised an eyebrow. "You take the long way around an answer, Sir Elias."

He smiled. "My sire says the same."

Her lined face grew more so. "Honore is my charge, has been since she came to us as an infant not expected to live. She is as near a daughter as I have. Thus, I can be forgiven for being protective of a grown woman, can I not?"

He inclined his head.

"Do you give this into my keeping, you do so knowing I will deliver it to her only if I determine its contents are not of detriment."

Elias nearly withdrew it. What he had written was for Honore alone. But if the abbess's trespass more quickly delivered the woman he loved…

He inclined his head. "So be it."

Her age-spotted hand turned around it. "If she does not come to you ere dark is upon day, ride on and leave her to her work here, Sir Elias."

That he would not agree to. Blessedly, she did not ask it of him. When she went from sight, he strode to where Theo stood with the horses.

"You think she will come out, my lord?"

"If not, I shall find a way in."

∽

DARK UPON DAY. No Honore.

Had the abbess determined his words were of detriment? Or had Honore dismissed them?

A few more minutes, Elias assured himself. *She will come.*

And there, movement on the other side of the portcullis—a robed figure, as were nearly all those glimpsed beyond the bars. He strode forward and nearly cursed as the great inner doors were closed against night.

Very well, he *would* ride on—to the nearest inn. On the morrow, he would return.

As he started toward Theo, he heard a metallic scrape and looked to where a small iron door was set chest-high in the wall. Though the light of a candle held by the one who beckoned revealed it was not Honore who opened the door, he altered his course.

Shortly, a sweep of his gaze over what lay inside confirmed this was the foundling door he had overheard Honore tell Hart was being installed so the services of one such as Arblette were no longer required.

Directly below the opening before which stood a woman who looked to be two score aged was an elevated cradle, fastened to its rim a bell to alert those of the abbey a child had been left in their care, and opposite a wall of bars in which an iron door was set. A jail cell of sorts, doubtless kept locked to ensure the foundling door was not used by any of ill intent. Though few men could get their shoulders through the opening, some of slight build could manage it, as well as many a woman and child.

Elias returned his regard to the woman. "I am hoping you have word of Honore."

"I am Sister Sebille. You are the same Sir Elias who is Lady Beata's friend?"

Elias frowned. Unable to recall if there had been occasion to mention Beata to Honore, he said, "I am."

"Then you know my brother."

"Do I?"

"Baron Soames."

It was good it was several years since Beata's father, hoping to force her to wed Baron Soames, had tainted Elias's drink to foil his watch over the lady. It had left Elias heaving and humiliated. Blessedly, Durand had overtaken the wedding party, and it was he who gained a worthy, fitting wife. Elias knew Beata's father was to blame for turning Elias's insides out, but Soames had been party to that deception. Though the baron had made restitution and gained Abel Wulfrith's grudging respect while training at Wulfen, Elias himself had no cause to think well of the man.

"I believe your brother has as little liking for me as I have for him, Sister Sebille."

She scowled. "Then you do not know Lothaire."

Elias was tempted to respond that it suited him, but it was wrong to offend one who surely loved her brother. "You are right. But tell, Sister Sebille, what has he to do with Honore?"

"As the abbess surely told, Honore declines to grant you an audience."

He nodded. "Did the abbess give her the parchment I entrusted to her?"

"She did. Though I was sent away ere Honore read it, that she did not come to you surely means she disregards your words."

Did she speak true? Or was this the abbess's means of ridding herself of him? "I do not know that I believe you."

"No lie, Sir Elias, as evidenced by my proposal you leave Bairnwood—"

"Not until I have spoken with Honore."

"To that I aspire, Sir Elias, but methinks there a better way."

"Which is?"

"It will come as no surprise to the abbess should my brother visit me. He can get you inside these walls and in front of Honore."

That Lothaire Soames would be granted access to Bairnwood was no reach since his sister dwelt here, but how to get to Honore?

"When I am summoned by my brother's arrival, I will ensure

Honore accompanies me. Providing you are discreet, keeping your head down, perhaps playing the part of Lothaire's squire, you ought to escape the abbess's notice. And once Honore is introduced to my brother, we will leave the two of you to converse in private."

Suspicion crawled all over Elias. "Why would a woman I know not whose brother dislikes me, do me this kindness?"

As she stared at him, he heard a soft click reminiscent of Honore. He glanced at the arm the woman crooked against her waist, saw she rubbed at beads secured to her girdle.

"I care for Honore," she said. "If possible, I would see her blessed with the love of a good man as was denied me. You do love her, do you not?"

"I do, as told in the parchment."

"Then a more direct course is required, and I believe my brother will provide it."

"What makes you think he will give aid?"

"You wrong Lothaire in believing him more worthy of dislike than friendship, Sir Elias."

He could not imagine progressing to friendship with the man, but he would not offend.

"Too, when you tell him of our meeting and my insistence he bring you to Bairnwood, that should suffice. He loves me nearly as much as I love him."

Still Elias doubted it would be easy to gain his help.

"Take these." She bent her head, a moment later extended a strand of beads. "Give them to him as proof you and I have spoken."

By the light of dusk, Elias examined them. "'Round her neck Honore wears the same," he said. "Do all within your walls?"

"They do not."

"Then?"

As if she heard something, she peered over her shoulder, then started to close the iron door. "The sooner you seek my brother, the sooner you will see Honore." That last barely made it between door and frame, then he faced iron.

He looked to the sky, altered his plan. It would be after middle night he reached Heath Castle where he had passed last eve after meeting Durand and Beata's babes, but all the nearer he would be to Wulfen Castle. There Durand had told Soames trained with Abel, Soames having paused en route to gift blankets his wife made for the twins.

Elias nodded. This time on the morrow he would be at Wulfen where he had left Elias Cant to reclaim Elias De Morville. God—and Lothaire Soames—willing, when next he was at Bairnwood he would bring out the woman he wished to make his wife.

~

"WHAT DID IT SAY?"

Honore turned from the hearth where the abbess had left her an hour past, looked to the woman in the doorway who was more to her than a sister in Christ. And somewhere beyond Bairnwood was their brother as revealed weeks past. Though Sebille wished to send for him so he could be told he had another sister, Honore had beseeched her to wait.

With all she had gained—Hart, his little ones, and the first babe to enter Bairnwood by way of the foundling door—she was not ready to face further gain, not whilst she yet deeply felt the loss of one she had not truly lost since he had never been hers.

Blessedly, Elias was not lost to all, being alive and well enough to travel to England. To see him one last time she had nearly gone out to him. But to do so would have risked her resolve to keep her word to his father.

"I understand if you do not wish to tell me," Sebille said.

Even if Honore wanted to reveal what Elias had written, she could not, the words lost to her when she set the two bound parchments atop lazy flames here in the outermost room of the abbess's apartments.

For the best, the abbess had said, *unless you have decided your place is not here continuing the work you began in giving children hope they had not before you.*

Honore had felt manipulated, all of her straining to know the words written by the man who risked much in crossing the channel should the king learn of the aid given Thomas.

Returning her regard to Sebille, she asked, "Is he gone?"

"He is."

For the best, she reaffirmed. Elias might have forgiven her and want what she wanted, but twice she had given his father her word. Though noble and legitimate, at thirty and two and having betrayed the King of England, she was wrong for Elias, his family, people, and lands. Her place was where she could better the lives of those otherwise abandoned to the wood.

"You saw him depart?" Honore asked.

"I did."

She breathed deep. "I hope that is the end of it."

"Truly, you would not have him return?"

"My place is here as ever it has been."

"But were he to offer marriage—"

"I would refuse, Sebille. It would serve neither of us. He has his duty to his family, and I have mine to Bairnwood."

The woman's brow lined. "You do not trust Wilma and Jeannette—and now me—to care for the children?"

And Hart, Honore mused. Though the restlessness that had reaped discord between him and her before his abduction had hardly abated following his ordeal, he better controlled it and took pride in helping with the foundlings. As of yet, he made relatively few complaints, did not shirk his responsibilities, and had not stolen away from the abbey.

"I do trust you," Honore said, "but even the abbess agrees my work must continue, and now the foundling door is working, more help is needed, especially since Lady Yolande departed with her coin."

"But—"

"All is as it should be." Honore drew the veil up off her shoulders and over her hair. "Now I must put the children to bed." As she crossed the room, she felt Sebille's gaze and guessed she sought evidence Honore possessed the rolled parchment. She would find none.

CHAPTER 46

OF RAVELING

Wulfen Castle
England

*D*urand Marshal was merciful, aware not only was Elias unequal to the task of quarterstaffs due to injuries not yet fully healed, but his mind was elsewhere—namely on Lothaire Soames who had departed the enclosure with Abel Wulfrith where the two had practiced at swords. Now the warriors observed the contest between Elias and Durand. *If* what had come to a quick end could be called that.

Having arrived at Wulfen with Durand last eve, shortly after all bedded down, there had been no opportunity to speak with Soames. Nor this morn when, awakening late as usual since sustaining injuries that nearly killed him, Elias descended to the empty hall.

He had satisfied his hunger in the kitchen then gone in search of the one Sister Sebille believed could gain him admittance to Bairnwood. Finding Soames battling with Abel in the midst of young men determined to prove worthy of a Wulfrith dagger, Elias had approached Durand who made good use of his visit by training squires. Though reluctant to practice with Elias, he had yielded.

As evidenced by how often Durand did not deliver a blow easily landed, he did not believe Elias well enough healed. Still, it had felt good to beat against another's weapon and feel blood pound through his veins.

Now having lost his quarterstaff, the butt of Durand's against his chest, Elias splayed his arms.

"Well met, Durand!" Abel called. "As for you, Sir Elias, we shall have to get a good quantity of drink in you to learn what so distracts."

On the night past, Elias had not revealed to the Lord of Wulfen he had come to ask a boon of Soames. Still, Abel surely knew it was more than distraction that rendered the troubadour knight a far from worthy opponent.

Durand tossed aside his quarterstaff, and he and Elias strode to the two men.

"You read me near as well as your brother, Everard," Elias said. "But drink is not required to loosen my tongue." He looked to Soames. "What distracts is the reason I asked Durand to accompany me to Wulfen."

"Ah, I thought something afoot," Abel said. "But if it can wait a while longer, first I would have the two of you bear witness to the award of a Wulfrith dagger." He nodded at Soames.

Then the man was worthy. "It can wait," Elias said.

"You agree to bear witness?"

"I would be honored," Durand said without hesitation.

"Elias?" Abel raised his eyebrows.

"I trust your judgment."

"As well you should." The Lord of Wulfen turned away. "Once we are shed of this filth and stink, we shall meet in the solar."

Two hours later, following the ceremonial award of the

dagger, Elias informed Soames he was at Wulfen to speak with him. The man's surprise—and suspicion—palpable, he had suggested they converse outside, but Elias assured him there was no need, that Durand knew and Abel ought to.

Thus, seated around the great table where they would take supper later, Elias told the tale of the boy who was not his son, the flight of Thomas Becket, and the woman he hoped to make his wife.

Soames agreed to his sister's plan—with the proviso it wait. He was a month gone from his expectant wife. Due to return to her on the morrow, he would not disappoint her. Thus, three days hence he would meet Elias and give aid in breaching Honore's walls.

THE TALE of Théâtre des Abominations, renamed Théâtre d'Innocents, found a rapt audience in the young men gathered before the hearth. And provided Durand further insight into what had befallen his friend.

Elias had sensed his deepening disquiet throughout the performance that, despite the absence of Becket, required little embellishment to put a lean in bodies and gapes upon many a mouth. Thus, as those training toward knighthood prepared to bed down, Elias was not surprised when his friend dropped into the chair across from him.

"You have something to say." It was no question Elias put to him.

Durand stretched his legs out before him. "I am sure I need not remind you once I questioned your worthiness, believing Everard's award of a Wulfrith dagger done more out of gratitude than merit."

"You need not."

"No longer do I question it, Elias. Indeed, I have not since ere

Beata and I wed. But from the disparaging of the hero of your tale
—albeit cloaked in jest—and that you did not own to him being
Wulfen-trained, still you question it."

Elias leaned back. "There was very little exaggeration to my
tale. Though in the end I prevailed, it was surely by God's grace.
Were I truly worthy of the dagger this day awarded to Baron
Soames, I would have better prepared and protected myself—
more, those in my charge."

Durand gave a short laugh. "You think being Wulfen-trained
makes one incapable of error? Invincible?" He raised an eyebrow.
"Certes, I am far from that, and I trained here from childhood.
Even those who bear the name Wulfrith sometimes fail
themselves and others."

That Elias knew, and yet—

"Of the scars you see upon Garr, Everard, and Abel," his friend
continued, "several were life-threatening. Then there are those
unseen."

Of which Elias was not unaware, many the Wulfrith tale
shared with him.

"Surely more than any other place, Wulfen brings out the best
in one who aspires to defend family, home, and country. Thus, do
you look without prejudice to the man in your tale, you will see
there the heart of a troubadour that has made ample room for the
warrior to defend all entrusted to him. Not flawlessly, but
exceedingly well." Durand sat forward. "Better said, worthy."

Persuasive. Because Elias wished him to be? Because he longed
for assurance he would not disappoint his family and people?
Because one unworthy had no right to seek Honore's hand in
marriage?

Durand dropped back in his chair, grumbled, "Perhaps not in
all ways worthy."

The frustration rumpling his face made Elias laugh. And it felt
good. "Tell, how am I unworthy?"

"In the grave disservice you do Everard by questioning his

judgment as once I did. Now, just as I do not question Abel's judgment in awarding Soames a dagger, you ought not question he who raised you above many a knight. God's grace, I agree, but grace given a warrior."

Though part of Elias resisted casting backward, as best he could he looked without prejudice upon the man in his tale—there the troubadour with whom he believed himself most familiar, there the warrior ever he questioned. Beginning with learning he might have fathered a child, the latter was most often present throughout a journey in which his knightly skills had been tested as never before. Errors aplenty, but those he had defended lived, and against odds he yet breathed.

Everard's training given a troubadour knight. God's grace given a warrior...

Elias breathed deeply, nodded. "I believe you have set me aright, Durand. Do I have occasion to tell again the tale of Théâtre d'Innocents, I will not disparage my hero." He smiled. "Well, perhaps a little poking and plucking. There *is* fun to be had with his failings. And forget not the lessons."

"Certes, you will have occasion, Elias." Durand stood, and as he turned toward the stairs, put across his shoulder, "As you should, my friend."

CHAPTER 47

AND TRAVELING

Bairnwood Abbey
England

She had thought herself prepared, Sebille having told she sent word to her brother days past. Though she assured Honore she had not revealed the reason for the summons, the man who awaited his sister in the largest of Bairnwood's guest rooms did not look questioningly at the second woman who entered and halted in his shadow. It was almost as if he expected her.

Sebille closed the door, crossed the room, and embraced her brother.

He returned the affection, causing Honore to hope one day he would be fond enough of her to grant a brotherly embrace.

"I am pleased to see you," Sebille said when he released her.

"As I am to see you, *Sister* Sebille." He reached to the purse on his belt, opened it, and removed a strand of beads. "I am certain you have missed these."

"So I have."

Honore frowned. To keep from thinking on Elias's words forever lost to her, she had so immersed herself in her work she had not noted Sebille's beads were missing. For what had she sent them to her brother?

The woman turned back. "This is Honore, Lothaire."

He inclined his head, causing the sparse light come through the one window whose shutters had been set back to sweep blond hair caught close at the nape.

Of a similar shade to her own, Honore noted. And the face Elias had her look upon in the mirror bore a strong, albeit feminine, resemblance to this man's.

"I am pleased to meet you, Honore, though there is another—"

"Hold," Sebille said as he started to turn. "I am grateful you so quickly answered my summons, but ere we speak of the reason, there is something you must know."

He raised an eyebrow.

Sebille drew her sister forward and met resistance. "Come," she entreated. "I vow he does not bite."

Reluctantly, Honore yielded and halted before the man whose height well exceeded hers and Sebille's.

She knew when the eyes roving her face noted her scarred lip and saw there a question that seemed more disbelief than curiosity.

"Oui," Sebille said, "she lived. And as I was given her name when our father exchanged us, she was given mine."

He drew a sharp breath, and his eyes lowered to the beads around Honore's neck.

"You see it," Sebille said. "All these years she had the other half of that which the abbess gifted me ere your mother came to return me to Lexeter." At his silence, she prompted. "Have you naught to say?"

He swallowed. "It is...difficult to believe I have two sisters."

A sound—or was it a stirring of air?—moved Honore's gaze to

the right of Baron Soames. The far corner alongside the bed was painted with shadows in various shades of dark. Was it a tall chair there?

Gently, Sebille squeezed Honore's arm. "It is only recently revealed and verified by the abbess, but methinks Honore does not yet believe she is no longer alone in the world—that she has a sister and brother, that I am the misbegotten one and she is noble both sides."

Not a chair, Honore determined. A presence, as of one capable of breath.

Sebille gripped her arm tighter as if to keep Honore from venturing where her gaze had gone. "Near a miracle, is it not, Lothaire?"

"It is." Out of the corner of her eye seeing him reach to her, Honore returned her regard to him, startled when his hand cupped her jaw. "Did our father know you lived, Honore?"

"He knew," Sebille answered for her. "It was he who sent the physician to repair her lip, he who provided funds should she wish to take vows."

"But you did not," he said.

Honore started to shake her head, but he did not ask for confirmation. True, her gown was a different color from Sebille's, but the style was the same and the hair veils identical, and oft she was mistaken for a sister by visitors not of the Church. Was she wrong in believing though he had not known she was his sister he had knowledge of Honore of Bairnwood before his arrival?

Eyes once more drawn to the corner, Honore said, "My work is with foundlings."

"So it is."

Again, no questioning. *Do I only imagine Elias here?* she wondered. *Or has this sister who believes a future for us possible aided him in entering Bairnwood?*

She moistened her lips. "Who is here with you, Baron Soames?"

He dropped his hand from her. "One whose presence was meant to be revealed sooner."

The shadows shifted and Elias stepped into the light. Whole, no evidence of death crouching near as when last she had seen him.

Though she rejoiced at further proof the Lord had answered her prayers, it hurt terribly to be so near him again.

He halted alongside her found brother, said, "You gave me no choice, Honore."

His voice tempted her into arms she sensed would open to her. And make what was hard to let loose almost impossible.

"You should not have come," she said and looked to Sebille. "You had no right."

Her sister's eyes moistened. "I could not stand you forsaking love the same as I."

"I do not forsake love. My place is at Bairnwood with those I do love."

"Are you saying you do not love me?" Elias asked.

She raised her chin higher. "I am not without feelings for you, but they do not compare to what I feel for others." It was true, though not as she would have him believe. "I am very glad you are recovered from the injuries for which I am responsible, but now I would have you go with all haste lest you fall into King Henry's hands."

He took a step nearer, and she had to fight the impulse to retreat born of fear the opposite impulse would see her in his arms. "Ere I journeyed to Bairnwood," he said, "I was with King Henry at Marlborough. Your missive sent ahead by my sire and the audience Henry granted has seen all set aright." His mouth curved slightly. "We made our peace. The De Morville lands are safe."

Such relief swept her she nearly sought a hand hold. "I am pleased. It is said our king is much aggrieved by his break with the archbishop."

367

"He is." Elias looked to the other two. "I would speak with Honore alone."

She had nearly forgotten them. "There is naught else we must discuss, Sir Elias. Methinks it best you return to France forthwith."

"Did the abbess give you my missive?"

She tensed. "She did."

He looked disappointed, as if hoping its absence explained her rejection. "And?"

She raised her eyebrows, gave back, "And?"

"Knowing how much I feel for you, that is all you can say?"

She did not know how much he felt for her—at least by way of the missive. That he was here told he felt enough he would not keep his word to his father and would be ruined if she did not keep *her* word. Then when Otto De Morville passed, his people and lands would suffer for lack of one worthy to rule.

"That is all," she said.

A muscle in his jaw convulsed. "Read it again."

Could one read ashes, she might. "I need not."

He took another step toward her. "Read it again, Honore."

"Impossible. I burned it."

His eyes widened.

"It was of no use to me," she rushed on. "A great service you rendered Hart and the little ones, and I am grateful, but that is where we end. Now if you will not go, I must." She looked to her brother and, ignoring his weighted brow said, "Let us speak later."

"I meant every word," Elias said as she turned away.

The ache in his voice made her falter, but the need for breath kept one foot moving in front of the other—down the corridor and stairs, into the courtyard where still there was not enough air to breathe deep.

"Honore?"

She gasped, looked to the right at the abbess whose habit was covered by a woolen mantle now autumn had lost its battle to hold back winter. Honore's bones were not so old she had taken the time to don her own covering when Sebille received word of her brother's arrival, but now she wished she had. Of course, the chill coursing her had little to do with the cold.

"What is wrong, Child?" The abbess halted before Honore.

"I am but tired."

The woman's brow bunched. "As hard as you work, I am not surprised, but you look as if you might cry." She glanced past Honore. "Were you in the guest house?"

"Oui, Sebille's brother has come. I have made his acquaintance."

"Was he unkind?"

"He was not. Indeed, I will be glad to know him better when I am rested."

"Then go and lie down a while."

"The children—"

"I will aid Jeannette."

The two walked side by side, but as they neared the dormitory, Honore said, "First, I would go to the chapel."

"I think that a good thing."

Honore turned aside. Had she looked around ere entering the chapel, she would have seen the abbess turn back the way they had come.

SHE HAD SO little regard for his feelings, she had set his words afire. The only sense Elias could make of it was he did not know her as believed. Just as he had not truly known Lettice.

"Fool," he muttered. Exiting the guest house where he had left Soames with one of what had become two sisters, he stepped into the path of the elderly woman to whom he had entrusted the missive of which ashes had been made.

"Sir Elias!" She clapped a hand to her chest as if to hold her heart inside.

He should have taken more care with his departure. Doubtless, she would guess it was by way of Soames he had stolen into the abbey. "Abbess."

Slowly, she lowered her hand, then sighed heavily. "I have been selfish."

"Selfish?"

"You have seen Honore, have you not? And she has seen you?"

He inclined his head. "She rejected me the same as when she would not come out."

"Not the same, Sir Elias. And it is my doing."

"Yours? *She* burned my missive."

The corners of her mouth convulsed. "The Song of Honore. So very beautiful."

Then as warned, she had read his words before sharing them with Honore. "A pity she did not think it beautiful."

"How could she? I—"

"She does not feel for me as I feel for her. That she could not make more clear."

She set a gloved hand on his arm. "She knows not how true your feelings because she did not read of them."

"What?"

"As told, I have been selfish, holding to her because I did not think I could bear for her to slip away."

"Pray, make sense, Abbess."

"After reading your words in private, I bound up the sheets. When I gave them to her, I reminded her of her duty to the foundlings and told her no good could come of pretty words from a man she could not have. Thus, I advised her to burn the parchment rather than read words that could burn themselves into her heart and pain her to her end days."

Struggling to contain his anger, Elias said, "A man she could not have? You read my words. They revealed my sire gave me leave to wed as I choose, and that I choose her."

"Selfish and sinful, as time and again I have repented since the Lord refuses to lighten my heart no matter I assure Him I did it for those He loves that Honore might save them from the dark of the world."

The relief pouring into Elias was so great it doused much of his anger. He *did* know Honore. She was but unaware the impossible was possible.

"I am sorry, Sir Elias. Regardless of what she may have said, I am certain she feels much for you. And when you have remedied what I wrought, I believe she will answer as you wish."

He drew a long breath. "You are forgiven. Now pray, point me to her."

She looked across her shoulder. "The chapel, doubtless trying to pray away her heartache."

"I may go to her?"

"I ought not allow it, but at this hour she is likely alone."

He caught up her hand, kissed her wool-covered knuckles. "I thank you."

Her aged face, framed by veil and gorget, lightened. "I can think of none more deserving of the love of a good man. Make her your own, Sir Elias."

He pivoted and could not control strides aspiring to the reach of a run. He nearly wrenched open the chapel door, but in this he exercised control. He eased it open and, as he slipped inside, swept his eyes over the interior. The only movement was that of flickering light and shadows cast by altar candles. No evidence anyone was within. Had Honore departed?

As he strode the aisle, glancing pew to pew lest he miss her where she bent forward, he heard a soft sound as of a door closing. Might she have heard his entrance and hastened from sight?

He halted, considered whence the sound issued. Would it be

sacrilegious to enter the opposite side of the booth in which confessions were received and sins absolved with only a screen separating one from their confessor?

Though Elias counseled himself to wait for her to come out, the possibility it was not Honore and she might now be further distancing herself made him go where he ought not.

CHAPTER 48

DEAR LORD, PRAY BLESS US WELL

ootsteps. No whisper of slippered feet. The creak of leather.

Honore stiffened shoulders that had begun to convulse before she heard the chapel door open. She had not minded the interruption of prayers so fumbled even the Lord might have difficulty putting together pieces scattered all around, for it was not truly prayer that caused her to seek the chapel. It was privacy in which to cry, certain if she could do so whilst her emotions were so near throat, lips, and eyes she might empty them.

One long ugly cry, she had told herself, *then nevermore.* But it was as if the one who came within sought her. The abbess? Beneath her mantle had she worn winter boots? Possible, but these footsteps seemed to carry the weight and stride of a man. Moments later, they halted outside the confessional.

Not Elias, she told herself. Her words had too deeply wounded. Were he not astride, soon he would be. Had Sebille sent their brother?

The door by which a priest entered the other side of the

confessional opened, and through the screen with its fingertip-sized holes she saw the backlit figure of a man of familiar height and admirable breadth.

Though the light was not overly intrusive and the screen provided cover, it was impossible to go entirely unseen. Still, she retreated to the bench's far corner.

"Honore."

She pressed herself more deeply against the confessional's walls.

Leaving the door open, Elias lowered to the bench on the other side. "The abbess sent me."

Breath rushed from her.

"I come armed with her explanation of why my missive was put to flame, her apology, and her blessing."

He could not speak true. But how else could he have so soon found her?

"Honore?"

She unstuck her tongue from her palate but could not think how to use it.

"Very well, listen. And recall when last we were in a chapel."

Her first kiss. A longing for life beyond these abbey walls.

"That was not the only time I thought of you in rhyme and song," he said, "but it was then I began to want more than the Honore made of ink and words and parchment. And wish I did not, believing you were out of reach."

She could not get her hand to her mouth quickly enough to muffle a sob.

He leaned near the screen. "Come out that you may see me and I may see you."

She shook her head.

"Then give me your hand."

"What?" she whispered and saw him press his left hand to the screen.

"Give unto me, Honore."

She hesitated, but as if of its own will her hand reached and set itself against the screen. When her fingertips encountered the warmth of his on the other side of the holes, she caught her breath.

"Do you wish to know the words I wrote which the abbess persuaded you to set aflame?"

"I do not want to hurt more than already I do."

"They were not meant to hurt but give hope—better than hope."

Was it possible? Non, never would his father accept her. The matters of legitimacy and nobility were resolved, but still she was of an age unlikely to provide many, if any, heirs, and then there was the possibility her affliction could be passed to children she bore.

She shook her head. "The words are gone, Elias. And methinks it for the best."

"They are not gone, and were they it would not be for the best."

"They are ash."

A huff of laughter. "This troubadour spent too much time composing them not to know them by heart. Now listen, and I will speak what I inked whilst moving as little as possible to sooner chase you across the narrow sea."

Another sob escaped.

"Are you listening?"

She nodded.

"Pray, come closer."

She pried herself out of the corner, scooted to the bench's edge, and set her brow on the screen.

"Close your eyes."

"Why?"

"I want you to see our camp in the wood, see me across the fire as I saw you, feel my hands in yours as I felt yours in mine. Dance with me again."

She closed her eyes, and not for the first time remembered. "We are dancing."

When his breath moved the hair on her brow she knew his face was also near. "Here is Song of Honore."

Not just words—a song. For her.

His heat against her fingertips she also felt against her brow when he pressed his forehead to the screen.

"By honor bound, to seek the found," he began, "here begins a tale, of raveling and traveling beyond the moonlit veil."

Honore was transported from the dance before the fire to the night she answered Finwyn's summons. And from out of the trees had come Elias in search of Hart.

"The arrow flies, the dagger plies, beware the mists of dream. A swing of rope, the snap of hope, the broken unredeemed."

The sorrow that slowed and deepened his voice made her throat tighten as she also recalled Lettice in the cottage.

After a long silence she knew had naught to do with performance, he righted himself with a deep breath. "Look not behind, thou will not find, plucked petals without bruise. Moments in time, loss feeding rhyme, see what the Lord now strews."

Hope and wonder infused those last words coming off his tongue with greater speed, as if amid the foul he found something lovely.

"So fair is she, humble beauty, the heart she doth provoke. Her eyes, her eyes, her lips deny what truth the blue hath spoke."

At the realization she was the something lovely found, she gasped, "Elias!"

Pressing fingertips and brow more firmly to hers, he said, "Pray do not hide, be by his side, and breathe the air he breathes. And let him kiss what he shall miss, if heart he seeks to sheathe."

Such beautiful words she had put to flame. Though naught could come of them, a fool she was. They *did* burn themselves into her heart, but more than pain her to her end days as the abbess warned, surely they would sustain her knowing this man felt enough for her it could be named love. And had she not destroyed the parchment, his words would have been with her forever, even if she grew so old she forgot them. When the ill of the world drew near, closer she could have clasped them.

"Do not weep, Honore," Elias rasped, and she startled at the realization she *did* cry, and he had interrupted his tale to console her. "This ends well, I vow."

Swallowing convulsively, she nodded against his brow.

"Forgive the fool who cast the jewel, sweet petals stay the stem. Bruise not, bruise not, that which is sought, come dance through life with him."

Once more she found herself in the camp, savoring the sight and feel of Elias.

"Love lost now found, by Honore bound, one word is all it takes. Do trust the knave, his life to save, brave maiden he awakes."

Struggling to contain further tears, she whispered, "Could I, I would dance through life with you."

Once more leaving off his tale, he said, "One word. That is all it takes."

He was wrong, for just as he had given his father his word, so had she—twice. If Elias could not keep his, she must keep hers or she would be responsible for the rift between father and son.

When she did not speak what he wished, he said with what seemed chagrin, "Dramatic me. I ought not have started with Song of Honore, but let us finish." Then once more he gave volume to his voice. "Thy love doth slay, turns dark to day, here begins our tale. Of raveling and traveling. Dear Lord, pray bless us well."

So much certainty amid finality. And more so when he said, "And there ends the first part of Song of Honore so the second may commence wherein smitten Sir Elias and fair *Lady* Honore wed."

The title might be her due, but she would not claim it lest it expose her brother and sister to speculation over a secret best held close. Too, of what use when her life was with her foundlings?

"My sire told he required you have no contact with me," Elias said, "in person or by way of missive."

She had not expected Otto De Morville to reveal that. Lifting her brow and hand from the screen, missing the warmth of his, she sat back and looked into his glittering eyes. "He did. And after the injuries you sustained and that I am no match for the heir of Château des Trois Doigts, I cannot begrudge him."

"You *are* my match, Honore. My only match."

"Elias—"

"As told, I ought not have started with Song of Honore." He cleared his throat. "You know the missive I entrusted to the abbess was of two parchments?"

"That I saw."

"And now you know how the second read. What you do not know is what was told in the first."

"Elias, though I am much moved you would break with your sire to be with me, and I do wish to be with you, we have promises to keep. Thus, I cannot be part of your tale."

"Honore—" he began, then growled, "This is absurd." He stood, and when he turned away, her heartache surged. Just as when her deception had been uncovered at Château des Trois Doigts, this encounter also ended with anger. No touch of hands, no sweet words, no fond farewell, no look behind.

She lowered her chin, whispered, "I love you. That truth the blue hath spoke."

The door was flung open, and she snapped up her chin as Elias dropped to a knee on the threshold. "This is too important for there to be anything between us. Give me your hand." At her hesitation, he said, "Pray, trust me."

Slowly, she raised her right.

"Your left."

She gave it to him and trembled when he took it in his own, slid a thumb across her knuckles, and straightened her fingers.

"If you wish to dance through life with me, once the banns are read, here this shall be evermore." Onto her finger he slid a band of silver in which was set a sapphire. "Though my sire will not rejoice as much as I, he shall be glad his son and heir has someone to love through the ages."

She looked up. "You truly believe he will accept me now it is known I am legitimate and full noble?"

"Already he accepts you. As written on the first parchment, he has given me leave to wed where I will, fully aware it is you I shall take to wife."

She blinked. "But why would he allow it?"

"His young wife is wiser—and more persuasive—than thought, he is more fond of this knave than believed, and he likes you more than he will say." He smiled, raised his eyebrows. "One word. That is all it takes, brave maiden."

"Elias," she choked and came off the bench and landed against his chest.

He wrapped his arms around her. "Not the word I was looking for, but it will do."

For minutes neither spoke, then Honore dropped her head back. "I wish I had not burned the parchments."

"For what do you need the written word when you shall have them spoken to you any time you wish?"

"You are right, but... When you and I are done with our raveling and traveling in this world, such beauty ought not be lost —especially to our children does the Lord so bless us."

"Then I shall write them for you again."

She smiled. "I love thee, Elias De Morville."

"So the blue hath spoke, but I like it better come off your lips." He lowered his head, breathed into her, "I love thee, my humble beauty."

EPILOGUE

Château des Trois Doigts, France
Summer 1171

*F*our 'round her skirts, four very fine." Elias made quick strides of the distance separating him from his wife and children seated on a blanket at the river's edge. "Kiss the lady, taste her wine." He winked, briefly set his mouth on the smiling one turned up to his. "Boy and girl, two of each. Kiss their brows"—he did so, scooped up the youngest—"and now beseech."

"Papa!" crowed he who had recently taken his first steps, every tiny tooth visible beyond most remarkable lips.

Elias grinned. "Otto!"

The one named after the man who had passed five months after holding his fourth grandchild, squealed and stuck sticky fingers in his father's mouth.

Elias nibbled them, pulled them out, and frowned over tips stained as pink as the boy's lips. "Raspberries?"

"Strawberries," Honore said and rose from amidst their other three—Elias named after his sire, Abigail named after the departed abbess, and Sebille named after her aunt. "We picked them, set aside half for Cook, and gorged on the rest." Honore patted her midriff. No bulge, neither of a meal too heavy nor another babe.

Of that last, Elias was not disappointed. Four children in rapid succession his beloved had gifted him, her body seemingly eager to make up for lost time. Blessedly, all but Otto the younger had been relatively easy births. As healthy as the others but considerably larger, he had so damaged Honore's womb Elias had come close to losing her. After great care and much prayer alongside Otto the elder who had long ceased to name her his daughter-in-law, preferring to call her his daughter, Honore had healed. And Elias had returned to their bed where they made love without risk of losing wife and mother to further birthings.

"Now then, back to my beseeching." Elias clasped hands with Honore, looked to their children. "I must needs speak with your mother," he said, then called to those downstream, "Cynuit! Hart!"

The young men whose training at arms had added bulk to bodies aged seventeen and fourteen, thrust the ends of their fishing poles into moist ground and came running.

Elias was proud of them. Cynuit was as fierce of sword as he was compassionate. Hart, who had remained at Bairnwood until the age of ten to aid Sebille and Jeannette in continuing Honore's work with foundlings, was increasingly competent with weapons —especially the bow—and less self-conscious about the mark on his face. Fine young men.

Honore leaned near, asked low, "Is something amiss? We expected you two hours past."

"Naught amiss, fair wife. Only tidings aplenty."

After giving their children into the care of the young men, Elias led Honore along the river. "The first of the tidings is from my stepmother." She who, following the death of her husband, would not be dissuaded from moving with his sisters to Château Faire to give Elias and Honore more space for their family. "She would like to visit a sennight hence and wished to confirm we shall be present. I sent word that as it is weeks ere we depart for England, she is most welcome."

"It has been months! I will be glad to see her and the girls."

"As shall I, though I sense she has purpose beyond a family visit—that of securing a betrothal for my eldest sister."

"Sir Damien of the Costains?"

As his wife knew, the sire of the widowed knight had suggested a match. "Still I think the fifteen-year difference in their ages too great. But if my sister and stepmother are both receptive, I will consider it. Regardless, I will not be rushed in deciding something as important as one's happiness."

Keeping pace with him, Honore leaned up and kissed his jaw. "Have I told you lately how happy *I* am?"

He halted, glanced behind to ensure they were distant enough from those engaged in a game of chase, then pulled her into his arms. "You have." He kissed her. "Have I told you?"

"Every day."

"Ah, thy love doth slay!"

She laughed, lowered to the bank, and patted the grass. "Tell me the rest."

He settled beside her. "It seems we must add another destination to our travels." Those which included the wedding of Baron Wulfrith's daughter, which it was expected the entire family would attend—including its newest members—and a visit to Bairnwood where Honore would be reunited with her sister, Abbess Sebille, and her brother, Lothaire, who had become a friend to Elias nearly as dear as Everard and Durand.

"Then we will be longer in England than planned?" she asked.

"Not England. We are to begin our journey a few days early to join Duke Henry at Argentan ere we cross the channel."

She frowned. "For what?"

He angled his body toward hers and touched her chest. "Thomas."

She caught her breath, drew from her bodice the prayer beads onto which she had long ago threaded the archbishop's ring. "I thought all resolved."

"It is. Our meeting with Henry is more a request than a demand." He lifted the ring, rotated it so each gem caught light. "If you are agreeable, England's king would like this returned to him."

Honore's heart ached as it did each time she thought on what had transpired last December. Not even a full month returned to England following years of exile, Thomas had been murdered in the cathedral at Canterbury. Vehemently, Henry denied ordering his death. He claimed the four knights who struck down the archbishop—including one Hugh De Morville, not related to Elias —had acted of their own accord after their sovereign raged over Thomas's continued divisiveness.

Hoping Henry had not given the order, Honore asked, "Does he say why he wishes Thomas's ring?"

"In memory of their younger days when they were as brothers." He raised his eyebrows. "It is for you to decide."

She considered that which was of little value to a king who had dozens—perhaps hundreds—ten times as fine. Were this ring truly esteemed, surely its value was measured more by sentiment than the materials out of which it was fashioned. And that was further supported that only now Henry wished it returned.

She peered across the land that could have been lost to the De Morvilles. Though Henry was no stranger to ruthlessness, he had pardoned Elias and not opposed his marriage to the one responsible for leading his vassal astray. And when Otto the elder informed his liege he wished to raise a modest abbey dedicated to the care of foundlings so Honore could continue her work on the continent, Henry had provided a portion of the funds. That abbey having been completed two years past, already it had blessed dozens of children and their parents. Henry was a muddle of a man, but amid the bad was good.

Honore nodded. "It is his."

"Regardless of whether I am foolish in believing his request sincere," her husband said, "I think it for the best."

She lowered the ring. "What other tidings?"

"Also from Henry. He wishes a gift for Eleanor."

"You are to provide one?"

"I am—Song of Honore."

That performed for the queen when Elias and she were summoned to Eleanor's court in Poitiers whilst Honore was five months pregnant with Otto the younger. The queen and her daughter, Marie, had asked the troubadour knight for a song of love. And been charmed by the one he performed.

"Then we must also journey to Poitiers, Husband?"

"Blessedly not. Henry but wishes by my own hand I put to parchment your song. He will deliver it."

As had been promised Honore, she had her own copy. Elias had inked the words, each verse on a separate piece of vellum, commissioned a monk to illuminate the pages with colorful borders and illustrations, and bound all between leather covers. It was the first of seven songs composed for her—one for each year they loved—and though soon her books would number eight, ever Song of Honore would be her favorite. There had begun their tale, one that now included four children.

Though she wished to believe the gift of Elias's prose to Eleanor would be given and received as a token of love, as Henry and his wife had grown so distant they lived entirely separate and his infidelities had become less discreet, Honore feared not.

"What is it?" Elias asked.

"I am hoping Henry's gift to Eleanor will move them to reconciliation. But I wonder if it is too late."

He sighed. "It does seem if the rift is not yet as wide as that which tore between Henry and Thomas, it may soon be."

"And then?"

"Who can say, but methinks Henry would do well to keep close sons who are increasingly worthy of their father's reputation.

Thus, he might have warning well in advance of the threat they could prove with the force of their mother behind them."

"Does that happen, Henry and Eleanor's tale—the one of their hearts—will surely be at an end."

Elias tipped up his wife's face. "As never shall ours be."

She laid a hand on his jaw, stared long into his eyes as he stared into hers, then teased, "Dare I trust the knave?"

"You dare, for ever you shall be the best part of my tale, Honore whom I love."

SONG OF HONORE

By honor bound
To seek the found
Here begins a tale
Of raveling
And traveling
Beyond the moonlit veil

The arrow flies
The dagger plies
Beware the mists of dream
A swing of rope
The snap of hope
The broken unredeemed

Look not behind
Thou will not find
Plucked petals without bruise
Moments in time
Loss feeding rhyme
See what the Lord now strews

So fair is she
Humble beauty
The heart she doth provoke
Her eyes, her eyes
Her lips deny
What truth the blue hath spoke

Pray do not hide
Be by his side
And breathe the air he breathes
And let him kiss
What he shall miss
If heart he seeks to sheathe

Forgive the fool
Who cast the jewel
Sweet petals stay the stem
Bruise not, bruise not
That which is sought
Come dance through life with him

Love lost now found
By Honore bound
One word is all it takes
Do trust the knave
His life to save
Brave maiden he awakes

Thy love doth slay
Turns dark to day
Here begins our tale
Of raveling
And traveling

Dear Lord, pray bless us well

~

Sir Elias De Morville
To his beloved Honore
The year of our Lord
Eleven Sixty Four

~

Dear Reader,

There being only so many hours in a day and far more books in one's to-be-read pile, I'm honored you chose to spend time with Sir Elias and Honore. If you enjoyed their love story, I would appreciate a review of THE RAVELING *at your online retailer—just a sentence or two, more if you feel chatty.*

For a peek at the new AGE OF CONQUEST *series, unveiling the origins of the Wulfriths, an excerpt is included here and will soon be available on my website: www.TamaraLeigh.com. Now to finish that tale for its Winter 2018/2019 release.*

Pen. Paper. Inspiration. Imagination. ~ Tamara

~

For new releases and special promotions, subscribe to Tamara Leigh's mailing list: www.TamaraLeigh.com

AUTHOR'S NOTE

Thomas Becket, how you intrigue!

In Sir Elias and Honore's tale, the Archbishop of Canterbury was to be so secondary a character he warranted but a mention here and there, a sighting, perhaps a brief encounter. But greedy Thomas—or was it this author?—wanted more. And how exhilarating it was to make his quarrel with King Henry II and self-imposed exile a pivotal part of *The Raveling*.

During my research, often I found myself sympathizing with this "turbulent priest" over what led to his break with Henry. Thus, though I tried to avoid taking sides since—confession time—I was not present, I became rather fond of Thomas Becket. And it surely shows.

In reconstructing the archbishop's flight from England and disastrous return after years of exile, I drew from many resources, but my favorite are: *Thomas Becket* by John Guy and *The Lives of Thomas Becket: Selected sources translated and annotated* by Michael Staunton. If your curiosity is piqued, get your hands on these.

As ever, thank you, dear reader, for joining me on my romantically-minded medieval journey ~ Tamara

AGE OF CONQUEST EXCERPT

MERCILESS: BOOK ONE

THE WULFRITHS. IT ALL BEGAN WITH A WOMAN.

From Tamara Leigh, a new series set in the 11th century during the Norman Conquest of England, unveiling the origins of the Wulfrith family of the AGE OF FAITH series. Releasing Winter 2018/2019

CHAPTER ONE

Sussex, England
15 October, 1066

The battle was done. England was on its knees. And in the space between horrendous loss and brazen victory, a new day breathed light across the dark. But no beautiful thing was it, that splayed wide to the eyes more terrible than the half moon had revealed and the ripening scent forewarned.

The bloodlust that had gripped thousands on the day past yet treading the veins of Cyr D'Argent, he felt it further displaced by revulsion and dread as he moved his gaze over the gray, mist-strewn battlefield.

Among the crimson-stained bodies of numerous Saxons and numbered Normans, he glimpsed blue. But was it the shade that eluded him throughout his night-long quest to recover the last of his kin?

Might his eldest brother and uncle yet breathe amid the slaughter? Might they be found the same as the third D'Argent brother whom Cyr had culled from gutted Saxons at middle night —though cruelly wounded, yet in possession of breath?

It did not seem possible a dozen hours after the death of England's king had decisively ended the battle, so decisively that few would argue the crown was destined for Duke William of Normandy. Still, Cyr would continue his search until he had done all in his power to account for the fate of those he held dear.

As he traversed a blood-soaked battlefield so liberally cast with bodies no straight path was possible, he questioned if his youngest brother and cousin remained among those searching for kin and friends. If not, it was only because they succeeded where Cyr failed. Regardless, hopefully both would keep their swords to hand. Of greater concern than the daring Saxon women and elderly men retrieving their fallen were the profane of his own divesting the dead and dying of their valuables.

"Lord, let us not search in vain," Cyr prayed. "Let my brother and uncle be hale and whole, merely seeking us as we seek them." Possible only if they had gone a different direction since Cyr looked near upon all who had crossed his moonlit path.

Another stride carrying him to a heap of bodies that boasted as many Normans as Saxons, he drew a deep breath and rolled aside two of the enemy to uncover the warrior garbed in blue. The face was too bloodied to make out the features, but the man's build was slight compared to a D'Argent. The only relief in the stranger's death was the possibility Cyr's kin yet lived.

He straightened, and as he turned from the sloping meadow toward the next visible blue, what sounded a curse rent the air and ended on a wail.

Farther up the slope, an aged Saxon woman whose white hair sprang all around face and shoulders wrenched on the arms of a warrior she dragged backward. Was it a dead man she sought to remove? Or did her loved one yet live?

Struck by the possibility his own sword was responsible for her struggle and heartache, Cyr was pierced by regret he did not wish to feel. It was the work of the Church he had done. Or was it?

Before the question could infect a conscience holding its breath, he thrust it aside and started to sidestep one of his own—a chevalier with whom he had crossed the channel. Younger than Cyr by several years, his eyes had lit over talk of the reward he would gain in fighting for William and the hope it was sizable enough to allow him to wed the woman awaiting his return home. She would wait forever, a Saxon battle-axe having severed links of his hauberk and breastbone to still the heart beneath.

Cyr swept his gaze over the bodies of long-haired, bearded enemies. Struggling against a resurgence of bloodlust that demanded justice for the young Norman, forcefully he reminded himself it was for kin he searched through night into dawn, not to wreak vengeance on the dead and dying.

Purpose recovered, he raised his head and considered the bordering wood of Andredeswald where what remained of the Saxon army had fled on the afternoon past. Had his brother or uncle been among the Normans who gave chase into the trees?

Only had they turned berserker, as sometimes happened to the most sensible and disciplined. Indeed, the battle madness beyond courage had pried away Cyr's control when two chevaliers fell on either side of him. Surrounded by axe-wielding Saxons, he had yielded to the fury lest he join his fellow Normans in death.

Finding little comfort in recall of his superior skill and reflexes, he veered toward the wood where the ranks of dead began to thin. At the base of a hill to the right sat a young Saxon woman.

The soft mournful strains of her song stirring the mist surrounding her, she bent over one whose head she cradled. Regardless of whether or not her kin still lived, she bared her heart to loss. And her body to violation if the Normans picking over the fallen determined to plunder her as well. Until the duke granted the Saxons permission to retrieve their dead, they risked much in venturing onto the battlefield.

Concern for the woman distracting him from his purpose, he lengthened his stride to more quickly move past her.

To the left, a half dozen Saxons sprawled atop Normans, beyond them one of his own crushed beneath a bloodied and bloated warhorse. Ahead, impaled on a single arrow, enemy embraced enemy. But no recognizable blue.

As he neared the Saxon woman, more clearly he heard her song. Being ill-versed in the English language, her words held little meaning, but its lament made him ache such that were it not for what he glimpsed beyond her, he would have veered away.

The mist hung heavier there, the bodies deeper. Thus, he could not be certain it was the blue he sought amid the browns and russets of the Saxons, but something told him there he would find his kin.

Feeling blood course neck and wrists, hearing its throb between his ears, he moved toward the fallen with his sword going before him.

Of a sudden, the woman's song ceased.

Cyr rarely faltered, but he was jolted when she raised her head and her sparkling gaze fell on one responsible for the death of scores of her people. Like a candle beset by draft, a myriad of emotions crossed her face, including alarm when her regard moved to the blade he had cleaned on his tunic's hem.

Once more regret dug into him, but it eased when he was past her and fairly certain his search yielded terrible fruit.

He sheathed his sword, and with strength he had thought nearly drained, cast aside Saxons who had met their end atop a Norman chevalier. The latter clothed in a blue tunic rent and blood-stained in a half dozen places, Hugh D'Argent's close-cropped head lolled with the removal of the last enemy whose long hair his enormous hand gripped. There in the place between neck and shoulder was a cut that had severed the great vein, confirming the eyes staring east toward home would never again look upon France.

A shout broke from Cyr, and he dropped to his knees. He could not have expressed in words exactly what he felt for his uncle who had been coarse, hard, and demanding, but what moved through him dragged behind it pain that would go deeper only had the blue clothed his eldest sibling. He had cared much for the man who trained him and his brothers in the ways of the warrior. Now Hugh was lost to all, most tragically his son who would add another scar to the visible ones bestowed on the day past.

Eyes burning, Cyr gripped a hand over his face. An arm one of two younger brothers had lost to a battle-axe. A handsome face his cousin had lost to a sword. A life his uncle had lost to a dagger. And the eldest D'Argent brother who should not have been amongst Duke William's warriors? Whose fate would he share?

"Accursed Saxons!" Sweeping his blade from its scabbard, he thrust to his feet.

Bloodlust pouring through him, his mind and body moved him to swing and slice and thrust, but somehow he wrenched back from a precipice of no benefit to any. Better he pursue those who had fled to the wood. However, as he stepped over a Saxon he had thrown off Hugh, he stilled over how slight the figure. And the face...

He stared at one who could be no more than ten and two, then looked to the others he had tossed aside. Boys. All of them. Boys who had given their lives to bring down the mighty Norman. Boys intent on defending what was now no longer theirs to defend. Boys who would never grow to men. Boys soon to return to dust.

Another lay farther out. Smaller than the ones who had toppled Hugh, he sprawled on his belly, arms outstretched as if to crawl home and into his mother's arms. And the fifth boy was the one over whom the Saxon woman bent.

Her brother? Likely, for she appeared too young to have given life to one of that age.

Guilt gaining a foothold, he reminded himself of the papal blessing bestowed on Duke William for the invasion of England, as evidenced by the banner carried into battle. More than for the crown promised and denied William, more than for the land and riches to be awarded to his followers, the Normans had taken up arms against the heathen Saxons for the reformation of England's Church. Regardless of who had died on the day past, first and foremost they had done it for the greater good. Had they not?

Trying to calm the roiling that was no fit for a warrior, he breathed deep, filling mouth, nose, and throat with the scent and taste of death never before so potent. He expelled the loathsome air, but it was all there was to be had. Breath moving through him like a wind, chest rising and falling like a storm-beset ocean, he sent his gaze up his blade to its point.

Were we not justified? he silently questioned. *Was I not?*

Images of the day past rushed at him—the flight of arrows, slash and thrust of blades, shouts and cries from savagely contorted mouths, blood and more blood. And laid over it all, the faces of ones who could barely be named young men.

Distantly separated from his uncle and eldest brother, Cyr's sword arm could not have taken any of the boys' lives, but considering how thoughtlessly he slew the enemy, ensuring those come against him did not rise again, it was very possible had he been alongside his uncle, he would not have noticed their attackers were children. Like Hugh, he would have put them through.

"Boys," he rasped and dropped his head back. The bones of his neck popping and crackling, ache coursing shoulders and spine all the way down to his heels, he slammed his eyes closed. But more vividly memories played against the backs of his lids, and with ground teeth he gave over to them.

CHAPTER TWO

Aelfled of the Saxons stared at the warrior in horrified anticipation of his desecration of the dead, and when it did not come wondered if here was God's answer to the prayer flung heavenward when the Norman pig drew his sword. Whatever stayed his hand, his survey of the savagery had landed on her and the boy before moving to the blade that had surely let much blood. The blood of her people...

Were she not pulled taut between the Lord whose comfort she sought and hatred over what had been done the Saxons, the barbarian might have made her tremble with fear. Instead, what spasmed through her was anger so reckless and unholy she dare not look longer upon the warrior—just as she dare not allow him to see that from which she had turned back quaking fingers.

She tugged up her skirt's hem. Hoping she would not cut herself, she slid the beautiful instrument of death into the top of her hose, glanced at the warrior to ensure he had not seen, and returned her attention to the boy dragged from beneath the blue-clad Norman.

Lids flickering, chest rattling, he would not reach his eleventh winter. In her arms he would die rather than the arms of his mother who had lost her husband a fortnight past when he joined King Harold in defeating the Norwegian invaders at Stamford Bridge. Thus, it was for Aelfled to carry tidings to Lady Hawisa that another was stolen from her, this time by the Norman invaders.

She looked around, wondered if any of those moving among the dead carpeting this portion of the battlefield was her lady. During the ride to Senlac on a horse shared by both women, time and again Hawisa had risen above weeping and cursing to cry out to the Lord to keep her son safe. Were she not near, it was because she had moved her search farther out. Never would she depart until given proof of her son's presence or absence, be he alive or dead.

Soon dead, Aelfled once more pushed acceptance down her tight throat to her aching heart. Loathing herself for believing the word of one who, struggling to suppress tears over his sire's death, had spouted vengeance against any who sought to conquer England, she reeled in her searching gaze and paused on the boy's companions where they had landed when the Norman tossed them off. Village boys, all of an age similar to the one she held, all christening themselves men by taking up arms against the invaders. To their mothers, Aelfled must also carry news of loss beyond husbands, fathers, and brothers.

"Merciful Lord," Aelfled whispered, then caught back a sob as anger once more moved her head to toe. Merciful? Where was His mercy when Saxons sought to defend their homeland? Where was His mercy when boys abandoned childhood to wield arms? Where was His mercy in allowing Normans to cut down Saxons like wheat to be harvested? Where was His mercy—?

Appalled at the realization her faith was bending so far it might break its backbone, she gasped, "Pray, forgive me, Lord. 'Tis not for me to question You. But I do not understand."

"Aelf," breathed the one whose head her hand rested upon.

Blinking away tears, she bent closer, causing her throat to spasm over the odor of spilled blood. During her search for her lady's son, the sight and scent of death had twice caused her to wretch, but though her belly had been emptied of foodstuffs, there was bile aplenty eager to make the climb.

"I was trying…to be a man, Aelf."

For that he brought sword and dagger to the battlefield, while the village boys carried any implement they could bring to hand. The sword and dagger of her lady's son were gone, but that had not stopped him. Though she could not be certain the weapon beneath her skirts belonged to the fallen Norman, it seemed likely, and as evidenced by its bloodied blade, it could have dealt the killing blow.

The boy whimpered. "Aelf?"

"Wulf?"

"I tried."

She attempted to smile encouragingly, but it was as if something learned was forgotten. "You more than tried," she choked. "You succeeded, and I am proud of your defense of England as I know your father would be and your mother shall be." Such lies, but perhaps they would ease the pain of his passing.

"Then you forgive me for…not keeping my word?"

They were both liars, but the damage done could not be undone. "Naught to forgive, Love."

His eyes widened, and the corners of his dry, cracked lips barely creased as if neither could he remember how to smile. "Love. Truly, Aelf?"

That she did not mean in the way he meant it, but what was one more lie? "Ever and ever, here on earth and in heaven, dearest."

"Love," he breathed, then passed from this world comforted by the belief the one he had vowed to wed when Aelfled entered his mother's service years past—she who was now ten and eight to his nearly eleven—loved him as a woman loved a man to whom she wished to be bound.

She touched her lips to his forehead, and as her tears fell on his slackening face, prayed, "Lord, receive this boy. Hold him close. Let him know Your peace and beauty. Give his mother—"

"Mon Dieu!"

She snapped up her chin, swept her gaze to the warrior who interrupted her audience with God as if he, arrayed in Saxon blood, were more entitled to call upon the Almighty.

Where he had dropped to a knee alongside his fellow Norman, he beseeched in a voice so accented it took longer than usual for her to render Norman French into English, "Forgive me my sins."

Her breath caught. Never in her hearing had such humble words sounded so sacrilegious. Without considering what she did, she eased Wulf to the ground, staggered upright on cramped legs, and drew her meat dagger from its sheath on her girdle.

The warrior gave no indication he heard her advance, and soon she was at a back made more vulnerable for being divested of chain mail. As she raised her dagger high, she looked upon hair cropped short the same as most Normans. And stilled at the sight of so much silver amid dark. She had thought her enemy no more than twenty and five, yet he was silvered like men twice his age—though not as much as the one before whom he knelt.

She gave her head a shake, determinedly lowered her gaze to his back. But no nearer did she come to committing that most heinous sin, her conscience forcing her to retreat a step and lower the blade.

"Pray, Lord," the Norman spoke again, "forgive me."

Dark emotions tempered by horror over what she had been moved to do, Aelfled said in his language, "Do you truly believe He gives ear to a savage, a murderer, a slayer of children?"

When he neither startled nor looked around, his still and silence made her question if this were real, but such sights and scents were not to be imagined. She was here. He was here. And her lady's son and thousands of others were dead.

He continued to ignore her as if confident she could not—or would not—harm him. And so she waited, for what she did not know, and it was she who startled when he straightened. As he came around, revealing a face that confirmed he was below thirty years of age, she raised the dagger to the level of her chest.

Though she had seen he was marked by her slain people from brow to toe, she was unprepared to be so near evidence of his bloodlust and had to swallow to keep bile from her mouth—and breathe deep to match her gaze to his, the color of which could not be known absent the spill of light across the battlefield. Not that it mattered. To her, ever his eyes would be black.

They slid to her dagger, the tip of which was a stride and thrust from his abdomen—were he of a mind to remain unmoving while she did to him what he had done to her people.

Returning his gaze to hers, he said with little emotion, "Offensive or defensive?"

Ashamed his words caused her lids to flutter, she bit, "Were I a man, offensive."

He inclined his head. "Were you, you would not have been allowed near my back—would be gasping your last."

That she could dispute only were her size and physique equal to his. Standing nearly a foot taller, shoulders as vast as any warrior, he had to be twice her weight.

"How do you know my language?" he asked.

The question surprised, though it should not. Few Saxons spoke Norman French, and even fewer among the lower class of freemen to which she belonged. But there was no cause to reveal she served in the household of one whose Norman husband's family had dwelt in England since the reign of Edward, the recently departed king who was fond of Normans owing to his exile amongst them previous to being seated upon the English throne—the same throne Harold had next ascended and from which Duke William had toppled him on the day past.

As Cyr waited on an answer not likely to be given, once more he considered the dagger whose sole purpose the Saxon would have him believe was defense. Even if only for a moment, it had come close to being used offensively against one who shed his hauberk on the night past to more quickly search among the dead.

He had sensed she came to him to put the blade between his ribs, but in the grip of prayer—more, something so foreign he could only guess it was that great slayer of souls known as apathy —he had done naught to prevent her from adding his death to his uncle's.

Returning his regard to her face, he realized he had fallen far short of one of the most important skills possessed by a man of the sword, that of being observant. Until that moment, he could not have well enough recalled her features to describe one whose pooled dark eyes, delicate nose, and full mouth were framed by blond tresses whose soft undulations evidenced they had recently lost their braids.

She might not be called beautiful, but she was comely enough to become the pick of the plunder once the less honorable Normans came looking for sport. Though her French might be nearly without fault, it would be of little use to one who numbered among the conquered, especially were she of the lower ranks as her simple gown suggested.

He started to warn her away, but in a husky voice almost sensual in its strains, though the rough of it was likely beget of tears, she said, "You have not answered me."

Casting backward for what she had asked, he recalled words spoken while he beseeched the Lord's forgiveness. Did he truly believe the prayers of a savage, a murderer, a slayer of children would be heeded?

Offended as he had not been earlier, he fought down ire. There was much for which he required forgiveness, but he was none of what she named him. He was a soldier the same as her men with whom he had clashed. And she who had witnessed a humbling to which he had only subjected himself in his youth mocked him for it.

"My prayers are between God and me," he growled. "His forgiveness I seek, not yours, *Saxon.*"

She set a hand on a thin psalter suspended from her girdle, its leather cover stained at its upper edge. "What of the forgiveness of a mother soon to learn one most precious to her is lost? What of she who shall mourn her slaughtered child unto death?" The woman jerked her chin at the boy whose blood had likely stained the psalter, then with more contempt than he had managed, added, *"Norman."*

Cyr was not steel against imaginings of such loss he knew must be greater than that felt for a brother gone too soon. Had the eldest D'Argent son not survived the battle, never would their mother recover.

The Saxon lowered her chin, slid the dagger in its sheath, and stilled. It was the psalter that gave her pause, and as he watched her slowly draw her hand away, he knew she had been unaware of the blood upon it.

A sound of distress escaping her, she pivoted and started back toward the boy.

It was then Cyr became aware of gathering voices and looked down the hill across the meadow. The Normans who had slept off the day's battle were rousing.

"You should leave!" he called.

She halted alongside the boy, peered over her shoulder. *"I am not the one who trespasses."*

He shifted his jaw, allowed, "You are not, but those who have little care for who has the greater right to be here will care even less when the unfolding day allows them to look near upon their dead."

Her brow furrowed, and he knew she questioned his concern.

Then she laughed, a sound that might have soothed a beast were it not so barbed.

"You are not safe here," he snapped.

She narrowed her eyes at him, swept them over the body-heaped meadow. "This I know, just as I know none of England is safe whilst beasts like you trample it."

"You are a woman alone."

Her hands curled into fists. "What care you?"

What *did* he care? She was no concern of his—unlike Hugh whom he ought to be delivering to his son. Still, he said, "Leave!"

"When I am done." She lowered, whispered something to the boy who had surely heard his last, then slid her arms beneath him and drew him against her chest. What followed was so great a struggle she would not get far even if she managed to regain her feet. The boy was young but of a build befitting one destined to defend his people.

Cursing himself, Cyr strode forward and caught her around the waist. As he pulled her upright, the boy rolled out of her arms onto his side.

She swung around. "Loose me, *nithing!*"

He did not know the meaning of the word, but having heard it shouted by her people during battle, it was something to which one did not aspire. Staring into eyes the rose of dawn confirmed were so dark as to be nearly black, he demanded, "What do you?"

She strained to free herself, but she would go nowhere without his leave. Chest rising and falling against his, she said, "I would take him to the wood that he be returned to his mother as whole as he remains—that his body not suffer desecration."

That to which grief over Hugh had nearly moved Cyr. As if he had committed the ungodly act, the weight of guilt grew heavier. And urged him to atone. Though he longed to leave the woman to her fate, he set her back and scooped up the boy.

"Non!" She snatched the child's arm.

"I mean you no ill, Woman. I would but see you sooner gone

that I may deliver my uncle from this carnage and resume the search for my brother. Now loose the boy and lead the way."

Lips parted as if to protest further, she searched his face for a lie she would find only were it imagined. Then her shoulders lowered. "I thank..." As though rejecting the expression of gratitude, she gave her head a shake and turned.

The wood was near, and though she did not venture far into the deeply-shadowed place where what remained of the Saxon army had fled and some might yet lurk, he engaged all of his senses lest he find himself set upon.

At an oak so ancient a dozen men could conceal themselves behind it, the young woman halted and turned her head in every direction.

"What is it?" he asked as he came alongside.

"Our horse. It is gone."

Cyr tensed further. "*Our* horse? You did not come alone?"

He more felt than saw the gaze she settled on him and the wariness there. "Non, the boy's mother and I rode together."

"Then she has taken your mount and departed."

She shook her head. "She would not leave without her son. Another took it." She looked past him toward the battlefield, and he guessed she intended to return there to search for one soon to grieve the death of a child.

Though Cyr wanted to command this Saxon to make haste to those of her own who would aid in delivering the boy home, it would be futile. If she heeded him at all, the moment he resumed his own search she would do as she wished.

So be it, little fool, he silently conceded, *it is not on me but you.* He would complete this act of atonement, give one further warning, then attend to his own kin.

"This seems a good place," he said.

She stepped around the backside of the tree, and he followed her several strides distant from the roots. As he settled the boy on

405

the ground, she unfastened the girdle hung with psalter and dagger and unsheathed the latter.

Immediately Cyr's hand itched for his own dagger opposite the sword on his belt, but the intent of hers proved neither offensive nor defensive.

She dropped to her knees, planted the blade's tip in the ground, with great sweeps of the arms cleared the thin layer of leaves, then retrieved the dagger and began assaulting the earth.

"Surely you do not think to bury him?" he barked.

A shudder moving her bowed shoulders, she turned her face up to his. "But a depression covered over with leaves to conceal him should your kind come to the wood." She swallowed loudly. "They will, will they not?"

Some would, whether to search out fellow Normans felled by Saxons during their retreat or plunder. "They will."

As she resumed digging, Cyr unsheathed his dagger and paused to consider the intricately fashioned pommel, hilt, cross-guard, and blade. The rising sun scantily penetrating the canopy did not light the latter's silvered length, though only because he had not wiped it clean the same as his sword.

He stared at the stained steel and saw again those who had fallen to it when it had been necessary to wield two blades to preserve his life and the lives of other Normans. The shedding of blood was inherent in being a knight and certainly not unknown to him previous to the day past, and yet in that moment it seemed almost repugnant, and more so when he looked to the one at his feet.

For the first time he noted that, unlike the others pulled from atop Hugh, this boy was arrayed in finery not of the common. A chain was visible above the neck of his tunic, garments were fashioned of rich cloth, boots cut of good leather, belt buckle shone silver, and the empty scabbards at his hip were faced with polished horn.

"Who is he?" Cyr asked.

The woman stabbed the earth again but did not pry the dagger free. Wisps of perspiration-darkened hair clinging to her brow, she tilted her face up. "A child."

He gnashed his teeth, said between them, "Is he of noble blood?"

"He is—rather, was." She nodded as if to force the clarification on herself. "Just as he was of your blood."

It took Cyr no moment to understand, but he could not think how to respond.

The corners of her mouth rising in an expression too sorrowful to be a smile, she said, "Oui, on his sire's side."

Then he was born of a union between Norman and Saxon, the former likely drawn from one of the families who had long resided in England. If his father had sided with King Harold as seemed likely, he would forfeit all when Duke William ascended the throne—had he not already on the battlefield the same as his son.

"Who were you to him?" he asked.

"Were," she breathed, then in a huskier voice, said, "Maid to his mother and, on occasion, his keeper." A small sob escaped her. "As fell to me on the day past."

Did she count herself responsible for his death?

"If only we had not come south. Had we remained in Wulfenshire as my lady..." She squeezed her lids closed, shook her head.

"Wulfenshire?" he turned the name over. Though during the fortnight since the duke's army arrived on the shore of Sussex he had become familiar with the names of places within a day's ride of their encampments, here was one he had not heard. Wondering if it was near Yorkshire where England's usurping king had defeated Norwegian invaders days before the Norman landing and for safety's sake her lady had brought her son south, he asked, "How far north?"

The woman's eyes flew open, and there was alarm in their

depths as of one surprised to find she was not alone. Then came resentment, and she dropped her chin and reached to her dagger.

Cyr did not understand why he wished to know how the boy had come to be here, but what he did understand was it was not for him to question.

Huffing and grunting, the woman returned to driving her dagger into the land to which she had been born. Again. And again.

Cyr knew he ought to leave her, but he muttered, "God's mercy!" and pulled her upright. As she drew breath to protest, he said, "Do you stand aside, the sooner we shall both be done here."

"I do not need—"

"Stand aside!" He pushed her toward the boy, then it was her enemy on his knees. With one hand he plunged his blade into the ground, with the other scooped out displaced loam and rocks. Though reviled at making a tiller of soil one of two weapons that had elevated him above many a chevalier, there was satisfaction in the thrusts and twists that cleaned the blood from the blade as the wounded earth yielded up the depth sought.

One foot, Cyr told himself, *then I shall leave her to whatever fate she chooses.*

So intent was he on a task unbecoming a man of the sword, once more he committed the deadly error of exposing his back to the enemy—not the woman but any number of her men lurking in the trees. However, not until he heard rustling leaves, skittering rocks, and labored breathing did he heed the voice urging him to attend to his surroundings.

Thrusting upright, he swept his dagger around. But as he closed a hand over his sword hilt, he recognized the one come unto him. The cause for the woman's great draws of breath was the boy she carried, he who had tried to crawl back to his mother, he who had aided four others in severing Hugh's life.

And whose young lives your uncle severed, his rarely examined conscience reminded. *Mere boys.*

Murderous boys, he silently countered, but with so little conviction it yet served, rousing anger better suited to the nephew of a dead man. "What do you?" he demanded.

Near the boy Cyr had conveyed to the wood, she eased her burden to the ground, sat back on her heels, gripped her knees, and raised a face tracked with tears. "He also has a mother, as do the other three."

Darkness once more rising through him, Cyr looked to the depression in which he stood. Did she expect him to enlarge it to accommodate all who had spilled Hugh's life? Hugh who had yet to know such consideration? Hugh whose body might even now suffer plundering?

"It must be widened," she said.

He thrust his dagger into its scabbard, growled, "Not by my hand."

She pushed upright. "Then by mine."

"So be it." If she had no regard for herself, why should he?

As he started past her, she said, "It would be a lie for me to thank you."

He did not believe that. Not only had she drawn back from expressing appreciation earlier, but he sensed her declaration was an attempt to convince herself they were enemies. Still, it was good to be reminded they stood on opposite sides of the great fire set on the day past. Just as Normans would rebel against any who sought to yoke them, so would Saxons. Indeed, were the fire well enough fueled, it could rage for years across this island kingdom.

"Just as it would be a lie for me to welcome false gratitude," he said and, assuring himself he would think no more on her, strode toward the battlefield.

"Norman!"

He cursed, turned.

Hitching her skirts clear of her slippers, she hastened forward and held out the psalter.

Cyr spared it no glance, instead looked nearer on a face the rising sun confirmed was as lovely as thought—so much he was tempted to brush aside blond tresses to view all of it. And she surely saw the temptation, wariness softening the hard light in her eyes and causing her to retreat a step.

Still, she extended the psalter. "Take it."

He flicked his gaze over it, lingered over the blood. Was this spite? An attempt to bait him? Punish him?

"For what?" he asked.

"Prayer and guidance, of which methinks you are in greater need than I."

The warrior wanted to reject that, but the man who felt twisted and bent out of a shape so familiar as to be comfortable could not.

"It is in my language," she said.

He frowned. "I know less of the written than the spoken, so of what use?"

She tilted her head, causing a tress to shift and expose more of her slender neck. "Do you and yours not learn the language of the conquered, how will you govern your new subjects?" She raised her eyebrows. "Or is that not your duke's intent? Does he—do you —mean to kill us all?"

Baited, indeed. And yet he snapped at her hook. "It is not our intent!"

She thrust the psalter nearer. "I dare not ask for your word on that, but if you speak true, here is a good place to start—a means of enlightening your kind on how to rule those from whom you have stolen lives, hearts, even souls. And of course, let us not forget land."

He could not. Though he wished to believe he and his younger brothers had accepted the invitation to join Duke William's forces more for the Church than the possibility of becoming landed nobles the same as their father's heir, it was a lie.

Perhaps that was what made him yield though the woman

greatly offended—and further offended when their fingers brushed as he accepted the psalter.

She snatched her arm to her side and, setting her chin high, said, "Methinks you will not mind the stain, *Norman.*"

As if he rejoiced in the blood of her dead. As if he had not shown her mercy and compassion. As if he had not sought to protect her.

Anger his only comfort and defense, he flung the psalter at her feet. "Take that and be gone."

She lowered her gaze, stared at her offering until raucous laughter sounded from the battlefield.

And so it began. "They come," Cyr warned.

She shifted wide eyes to his, and he was glad for the abundance of fear if it meant she would leave this place. "So they do," she said softly and turned away.

He stared after her as she moved toward the fallen youths. Though it was past time he left her, he longed for reassurance. "You will depart?" he called.

For answer, she stepped into the depression and began plying her dagger. Were it only to accommodate the second boy, he would leave her to it, but if she intended to collect the other three...

As he strode forward, he glanced at the psalter fallen open to a page of precise text on one side and a simply-rendered cross on the other.

Halting before her, he demanded, "Will you take yourself from here after these two are covered over?"

"I will not."

He dropped to his haunches, but she continued to drive her blade into the ground. "For the love of God—if not yourself—leave the other boys!"

"Non."

Then it is on her, he told himself. But when she stabbed her blade into the ground again, he closed a hand over her fist gripping the hilt. "Unlike your lady's son, the others possess nothing worthy of plunder."

Her head whipped up. "Still they could suffer desecration, and if their bodies are moved they may not be found again." She swallowed loudly. "They must go home. They absolutely must. Now"—she jerked free—"collect your dead and leave me to mine."

As she resumed her assault upon the earth, Cyr straightened. Assuring himself he had done all he could to save her and vowing he would forget her, he strode opposite.

ALSO BY TAMARA LEIGH

CLEAN READ HISTORICAL ROMANCE

THE FEUD: A Medieval Romance Series
Baron Of Godsmere: Book One
Baron Of Emberly: Book Two
Baron of Blackwood: Book Three

LADY: A Medieval Romance Series
Lady At Arms: Book One
Lady Of Eve: Book Two

BEYOND TIME: A Medieval Time Travel Romance Series
Dreamspell: Book One
Lady Ever After: Book Two

STAND-ALONE Medieval Romance Novels
Lady Of Fire
Lady Of Conquest
Lady Undaunted
Lady Betrayed

INSPIRATIONAL HISTORICAL ROMANCE

AGE OF FAITH: A Medieval Romance Series

The Unveiling: Book One

The Yielding: Book Two

The Redeeming: Book Three

The Kindling: Book Four

The Longing: Book Five

The Vexing: Book Six

The Awakening: Book Seven

The Raveling: Book Eight

AGE OF CONQUEST: A Medieval Romance Series

Merciless: Book One (Winter 2018/2019)

INSPIRATIONAL CONTEMPORARY ROMANCE

HEAD OVER HEELS: Stand-Alone Romance Collection

Stealing Adda

Perfecting Kate

Splitting Harriet

Faking Grace

SOUTHERN DISCOMFORT: A Contemporary Romance Series

Leaving Carolina: Book One

Nowhere, Carolina: Book Two

Restless in Carolina: Book Three

OUT-OF-PRINT GENERAL MARKET REWRITES

Warrior Bride 1994: Bantam Books (Lady At Arms)

Virgin Bride 1994: Bantam Books (Lady Of Eve)

Pagan Bride 1995: Bantam Books (Lady Of Fire)

Saxon Bride 1995: Bantam Books (Lady Of Conquest)

Misbegotten 1996: HarperCollins (Lady Undaunted)

Unforgotten 1997: HarperCollins (Lady Ever After)

Blackheart 2001: Dorchester Leisure (Lady Betrayed)

Virgin Bride is the sequel to *Warrior Bride; Pagan Pride* and *Saxon Bride* are stand-alone novels

For new releases and special promotions, subscribe to Tamara Leigh's mailing list: www.TamaraLeigh.com

ABOUT THE AUTHOR

Tamara Leigh signed a 4-book contract with Bantam Books in 1993, her debut medieval romance was nominated for a RITA award, and successive books with Bantam, HarperCollins, and Dorchester earned awards and places on national bestseller lists.

In 2006, the first of Tamara's inspirational contemporary romances was published, followed by six more with Multnomah and RandomHouse. Perfecting Kate was optioned for a movie, Splitting Harriet won an ACFW Book of the Year award, and Faking Grace was nominated for a RITA award.

In 2012, Tamara returned to the historical romance genre with the release of Dreamspell and the bestselling Age of Faith and The Feud series. Among her #1 bestsellers are her general market romances rewritten as clean and inspirational reads, including Lady at Arms, Lady Of Eve, and Lady Of Conquest. In winter 2018/2019, watch for the new Age of Conquest series unveiling the origins of the Wulfrith family. Psst!—It all began with a woman.

Tamara lives near Nashville with her husband, a German Shepherd who has never met a squeaky toy she can't destroy, and a feisty Morkie who keeps her company during long writing stints.

Connect with Tamara at her website www.tamaraleigh.com, Facebook, Twitter and tamaraleightenn@gmail.com.

For new releases and special promotions, subscribe to Tamara Leigh's mailing list: www.tamaraleigh.com

Made in the USA
Middletown, DE
21 November 2018